Beyond the Fence Line

Holly Capella

In Loving Memory of

Carl & Myrtle Morris
"Nannie & Pop-pop"

ACKNOWLEDGMENTS

Copella Books: First Paperback Edition 2025
Cover Artist: Daniela Owergoor
Dani-owergoor.deviantart.com
Horse Photographer: Tommy Dunleavy
Printed by KDP, an Amazon.com Company

PUBLISHER'S NOTE

Chapter 1

Major's Thunder Basin Ranch was the name boldly wood-burned into the thick, horizontal lodgepole pine beam, tall above the ranch gate. The iconic, diagonal brand MTB was burned on both sides of the ranch name. Sturdy lodgepole pine vertical beams held the double, split rail fence gate in place. Alongside the vertical beams on either side, stacked fieldstone was mortared together, giving the entrance a sturdy, rugged appearance. Built in 1858, as indicated by the year etched on the stone, the ranch had been around for many generations. Of course, the original homestead was built deeper on the property and later abandoned for the newer home. An older car that had seen better days, puttered beneath the tall sign, entering the property. Beyond the gates was a long, tree-lined dirt driveway that resembled a tunnel of trees. Four-rail wooden fencing could be seen beyond the trees on either side, containing massive, green pastures.

The older car drove cautiously down the lengthy driveway that seemed to extend forever. Upon finally entering the clearing, just a little after sunrise, the grand, two-story ranch house and equally large barn came into view. The forty-by-eighty-eight-foot Great Plains, ten-stall horse barn with run-out stalls and ten-foot lean-tos on both sides, had a post-and-beam timber frame with stonework around the base. Because the second-story hay loft was half the size of the main level, the barn had an A-frame appearance. Beyond the barn, the grand house, painted bright white with black trim and shutters, was now fully visible in all its gloriousness. Four large white pillars extended from the porch beyond the second floor balcony to the roof of the second floor. The original structure, built in 1882, was two stories high, while the additions on either side were each one story high. The driveway continued to the right, with a large parking area just off the kitchen entrance, located furthest from the barn, where the older car finally came to a stop.

Five-year-old Mazie Crane sat quietly in the large rocking chair that dwarfed her, enjoying the motion it made as she bounced her legs, creating air pockets in her yellow, flowered dress. She hummed softly to herself, proud of her new yellow dress. Mazie was a cute little girl with dark brown, shoulder-length hair and big brown eyes with excessively dark eyelashes. Mostly quiet and perhaps a bit on the shy side, Mazie stared across the ranch at the not-so-distant barn. Mazie was mesmerized by the eight beautiful horses saddled in western tack tied to the two lodgepole pine hitching posts. There were four bay horses, two chestnuts, one gray, and one black horse, all patiently waiting for their riders to take them on some amazing adventure, or so Mazie thought. Although she was hungry after their long car ride in the early morning hours, Mazie wouldn't complain. Her mother promised they would get breakfast after they arrived and got settled, so they would be eating soon enough. Right now, her mother was talking with a very pretty woman, who seemed so friendly and kind, in Mazie's opinion.

Mazie's mother, Liddy Crane, was an attractive woman in her mid-twenties, with shoulder-length, dirty-blond hair and hazel eyes. She stood about five-foot-six with a somewhat athletic build, which came from working long hours on a labor-intensive job to support her daughter. Liddy became a single mother after her husband died last year. She dressed in worn, moderately dated clothes and sensible shoes, since they were almost all she could afford. Liddy didn't typically wear makeup, primarily due to not having the time to apply it, let alone buy much of it. Today, she wore a little eyeliner and neutral-colored lipstick, as she was visiting her old friend and had a couple of days off work. Liddy's friend and the lady of the house was Dee Major. Dee was a beautiful, dainty, petite woman, standing only about five-foot-three, with shoulder-length, medium auburn hair and dazzling blue eyes. She was about thirty years old, being only a couple of years older than Mazie's mother.

Just about everyone would agree that Dee was the nicest, friendliest, and most positive person they'd ever met. Even with how unkind life seemed to have treated her, she still had a warm, genuine smile for everyone. Mazie's mother sat on the double, handcrafted rocking swing alongside Dee while they talked. Some of what they said was loud enough for Mazie to hear, while other parts of their conversation were barely a whisper, obviously not meant for her ears.

"I really appreciate you doing this for me, Liddy," Dee announced while beaming with delight. "It means the world to me. Not many people would move halfway across the state to help out an old friend. My brothers-in-law are wonderful, don't get me wrong, but when it comes to keeping a house and raising a little boy--" She shook her head almost shamefully. "They're pretty damned clueless. Sometimes, it's like having three little boys."

"I hear that," Liddy remarked with a tiny, humored chuckle. She then turned serious. "I know your MS can be trying some days. I just hope I can relieve some of your burden."

"I feel a little guilty for bringing you in like this," Dee replied somewhat timidly. "I know what you went through with your husband last year wasn't easy."

"In sickness and in health," Liddy reminded her. "I was glad I could be there for him until the end." She tensed slightly, then managed a tiny smile. "I want to be here for you, Dee. The longer you can stay at home, the better off you'll be."

Dee smiled weakly and nodded. "I couldn't agree more." She hesitated, then choked on her emotions. "The doctors said the cancer has spread, and my MS will only get worse. I suspect when I go down, it'll only be a matter of a few months before the suffering is over."

Liddy held her breath and tried to keep her emotions in check for the sake of her little girl sitting on the rocking chair not far from them.

"A friend, uh, is bringing the rest of our things in his truck," Liddy announced, choking on her sorrow. "Mazie and I are supposed to meet them in town for lunch. Afterwards, they'll follow me back here with their truck and help unload our things."

"I'll ask Dalton and Colt to stick around after lunch and help," Dee offered.

"No, that won't be necessary," Liddy replied, then shifted uncomfortably. "There's not really that much. Just boxes of clothing and a few personal items. If it hadn't been for my grandparents' old library table, I could have fit most of it in my car."

Dee appeared sympathetic and patted Liddy's arm. "I know you've had a rough year, Liddy," she announced softly. "But you're going to love the in-law suite. It has two large bedrooms, its own bathroom, a kitchenette, and the most beautiful, rustic living room with plenty of natural light. All fully furnished. Dalton and Colt even put down new carpeting in the bedrooms for you. You'll have all the privacy you want, and, of course, you'll have free run of the rest of the house as well."

"That's kind of you, Dee, but you didn't have to go to all that trouble for us," Liddy informed her. "I'm here to help you."

"I want you to think of this as your home, Liddy," Dee insisted. "Dalton and Colt promised you'd feel completely welcome and appreciated."

The porch door opened, interrupting the tender moment, and one of Dee's two brothers-in-law appeared on the porch. Dalton Major was a tall, sturdily built man, standing roughly six-foot-four, with a full head of short, dark hair and medium-length sideburns. The man in his mid-twenties was clean-shaven but always seemed to have a hint of a five o'clock shadow. He was classically handsome, unmistakably cowboy. Despite his stern appearance, his smile was somehow warm and told a different story. He hesitated when he saw Liddy with Dee on the porch swing.

"Liddy," Dalton announced and smiled a little more warmly as their eyes met. "It's nice to see you again. It's been a long time."

"Over eleven years," Liddy reminded him. "At Dee's wedding here at the ranch."

"Wow, yeah," Dalton replied, unable to wipe the grin from his face. "We were fifteen or sixteen back then."

"Yes, I remember," Liddy replied with a soft laugh. "Seems like a lifetime ago."

"Not that long ago," Dalton assured her. "I remember it well. My first slow dance."

"My first time seeing a hay loft," Liddy added while raising her brows.

Dalton grinned, seeming slightly embarrassed and at a loss for words. Dee eyed the exchange a moment, then gently cleared her throat and managed a tiny smile.

"Dalton, would you take little Mazie out to the barn and introduce her to Brandt and some of the horses?" Dee asked, then raised her brows. "Maybe show her around a little before you fellas take off to tend to the cattle? Liddy and I have a few things to discuss before I get them some breakfast and show them their new home."

Dalton nodded knowingly and then approached Mazie. "Hello, Mazie," he announced while smiling warmly. "I'm Uncle Dalton. Would you like to see the horses?"

Mazie smiled, eagerly nodded, and accepted Dalton's large hand that was now extended to her.

Chapter 2

*D*alton led Mazie into the newly built barn that had five stalls on either side with barred, rolling doors. There was a huge tack room to the left, as well as a wash stall and a small office to the right of the entrance. The broad, concrete aisle between the stalls was tidy and neatly swept. Ten-year-old Brandt Major was brushing off a large, eighteen-year-old bay pony tied to one of many rings bolted into the walls. Brandt was a sturdy young boy, having worked the ranch for many years already despite his age. His slightly longer, dark hair was a little unkempt, possibly from always wearing cowboy hats while 'working' outside. He was a cute boy with an innocent look, though his uncles would tend to disagree. Despite his age and size, he looked like a miniature cowboy from his black Stetson hat to his brown western boots. Mazie couldn't take her eyes off the pony and the boy brushing it. She didn't get to see many ponies, and she'd *never* seen a boy quite like Brandt. Dalton and Mazie approached and paused near the little cowboy. Mazie stared at the slightly larger pony, awe-struck by its beauty.

"Brandt," Dalton announced to the busily working boy. "This is Mazie. Her mother's going to be helping your mother out around the house. They're going to be living with us for a while."

Brandt eyed the little girl, groaned, and resumed brushing the pony. Mazie was too busy staring at the pony to notice the boy's disinterest.

"Can I pet your pony?" Mazie asked.

"No," Brandt scoffed without looking at her. "He's my pony, and I'm not sharing him."

"Brandt," Dalton scolded. "You're being rude to a guest, and we don't talk like that to ladies."

"She's not a lady," Brandt informed his uncle. "She's a little girl, and if she's living here, the guest rule doesn't apply."

"How about the 'I'm gonna whoop your ass' rule?" Dalton snapped. "Think that rule applies?"

"What's going on out here?" another man demanded in a gruff, commanding tone, as he stepped out from the small office, easily frightening Mazie.

The other man, Colt Major, stood an imposing six-foot-one with a lean, athletic build, common among wranglers. His hazel eyes seemed to be the only thing not intimidating about the man. The rough-looking cowboy in his late twenties had short, light brown hair and some facial stubble, but not enough to constitute a beard. Uncle Colt folded his arms across his broad chest as he stood in the barn aisle and glared at his nephew. Mazie clung to Dalton's hand, remaining fearful of the intimidating man.

"Are you mouthing off again, boy?" Colt demanded, showing less tact than Dalton had.

The gruffness of his voice and the harshness of his words further frightened the little girl, who attempted to hide behind Dalton's leg. Brandt looked at his Uncle Colt, immediately turning defensive.

"You're not my father," Brandt launched in anger. "My mom's not sick, and we don't need girls hanging around the barn!"

Brandt untied the pony, swung onto it bareback, and raced down the aisle from the barn and toward the field. Mazie watched the scene unfold, frightened yet awestruck at how effortlessly the boy rode the pony.

"Someone's getting his backside tanned tonight," Colt muttered.

Tears immediately streaked down Mazie's face. "I didn't mean to get him into trouble," she sobbed. "I don't need to pet the pony."

Mazie pulled her hand free from Dalton's hand and bolted from the barn, running the entire distance back to the house porch, practically diving onto her mother's lap. Having seen the boy race across the field toward the woods on his pony, it was easy for Dee to assume what must have transpired in the barn. Dee reached over and gently stroked Mazie's hair.

"You have to forgive Brandt, Mazie," Dee gently announced. "He lost his daddy two years ago, and he's worried about me."

"The mean man in the barn said he was going to tan his hide," Mazie softly sobbed. "I didn't mean to get him in trouble."

"If I promise Uncle Colt won't 'tan his hide', will that make you happy?" Dee asked, somehow knowing which man was 'the mean man'.

Mazie looked up, wiped the tears from her face, and then nodded.

Dee smiled and laughed. "Okay, I promise no one will be tanning anyone's hide."

11

*L*ater that afternoon, shortly before Colt and Dalton would be returning for lunch, Dee stood at the kitchen counter grilling cheese sandwiches to go with the pot of canned tomato soup. Although it wasn't the ideal lunch for hardworking wranglers, everyone seemed to like it, and it was the best Dee could manage these days. The relatively modern, bright kitchen was a combination of tan and cranberry colors, featuring several counters, as well as a large island counter. There were dozens of cabinets, a large pantry, and a big kitchen table near a spacious bay window. Lighted fans lined the cathedral ceiling, keeping the room cool on warmer days. Brandt hurried into the kitchen through the back mudroom entrance while wearing a huge grin on his face.

"Mom," he announced excitedly. "Uncle Dalton is giving me one of the big horses to ride. He says I'm ready for a real horse."

"That's wonderful, Brandt," she replied while glancing at him over her shoulder. "You're growing up so fast. Pretty soon, you'll be driving Uncle Colt's pickup truck."

"That would be so cool," he announced and jumped into one of the chairs at the table.

As Dee turned with the sandwiches on a platter and set them on the table, her legs suddenly gave out beneath her, and she nearly collapsed to the floor. She caught onto the table and just about fell to her knees.

"Mom!" Brandt cried out and ran for her.

She clutched his hand and the table edge while trying to pull herself to her feet. Brandt pulled out a nearby chair and helped her into it.

"You're supposed to use Grandpa's old cane," he reminded her in a somewhat scolding tone. "If you want to get better, you need to use the cane."

Dee smiled despite knowing that there was no 'getting better' anymore. "Yes, I suppose I forgot," she replied, then caught her breath and patted the chair alongside her. "Brandt, please have a seat. We need to talk."

Brandt appeared tense and slowly moved onto the vacant seat. "What is it, Mom?"

"Our family will be going through some pretty big changes in the upcoming months," she gently informed him. "Liddy, my longtime friend, and her daughter are moving in with us this afternoon. They're returning after lunch with their things. Liddy is going to help me around the house, and I need all the help she can offer."

"Yes, Mom," Brandt replied almost timidly. "I want you to rest more."

Dee smiled and nodded. "You're a good boy, Brandt," she whispered.

"Tell Uncle Colt that," he muttered.

"You need to cut your Uncle Colt some slack," Dee insisted. "The two of you buck heads because you're too much alike."

"I'm nothing like Uncle Colt."

Dee snorted a laugh. "Sure, you're not," she remarked, then gave him a serious stare. "When Liddy and Mazie get here, I want you to be nice to them. They're coming because I need them. As a personal favor to me."

"Can't you find someone without a little girl?" Brandt asked. "Girls are so annoying. She's going to follow me around, snoop in my room, and babble on and on about nothing." His eyes then narrowed as he stared at his mother. "Have you ever heard little girls scream? It's like a banshee war cry."

Dee placed her hand on Brandt's hand. "Mazie's father died last year," she informed him. "She's been through a lot. Do you remember how broken up you were when your father died?"

Brandt frowned and sadly looked down. "Yes, ma'am," he replied.

"She's going to be scared living in a new place filled with strangers," Dee informed him. "Everything is changing for her. We need to make her feel welcome." She gently squeezed his hand. "I need you to look out for Mazie as if she were your own little sister. She needs you to look after her."

"If I look after her, will that make you feel better?" he asked.

"Yes, it would be a great burden off my mind," his mother replied.

"I'll look after her, but I don't want her following me around or hugging me," he announced.

"You don't have to hug her," Dee insisted. "But I can't promise she won't follow you around. If she does follow you, it's only because she looks up to you, and that's a wonderful compliment."

"Now you're just making stuff up," Brandt muttered.

Uncle Dalton held Mazie's hand as they walked into the barn later that afternoon, where Brandt had just finished saddling his large bay pony. Mazie seemed apprehensive about approaching the explosive boy after their earlier interaction.

"It's okay, Mazie," Dalton informed her. "Brandt has something he'd like to say to you." Dalton eyed Brandt and raised a commanding brow. "Brandt--?"

Brandt drew a deep breath and seemed to swallow his pride as he looked at the timid little girl. "I'm sorry for my behavior this morning when you asked to pet my pony," he informed her. "A gentleman doesn't act like that toward a lady."

"It's okay," Mazie replied, seeming relieved, and now smiled. "I'm not a lady. My mommy says I'm a tomboy." She then indicated the pants she wore. "See--no more dresses."

"I suppose that's a start," Brandt remarked, then forced a smile and indicated his pony. "This is Gizmo." He untied the reins from the ring on the wall. "Uncle Dalton said you're going to be staying with us, so I suppose I'll have to teach you how to rope and ride." He drew a deep breath and extended the reins to her. "You're going to need your own horse so you can have Gizmo."

Mazie stared at him with surprise and cautiously took the reins. "You're giving me your pony?"

Dalton smiled, proud of the little boy, and had to look away to keep him from seeing it.

Brandt made a face and waved her off. "I've outgrown him, and he's more your size anyway," he informed her. "Uncle Colt said I'm ready for a big horse now."

Mazie cried out with enthusiasm and threw her arms around Brandt's waist, clinging to him as if she'd never let go. Brandt jumped with surprise and held his hands in the air while glaring at his uncle. Dalton laughed while shaking his head.

"In about six years, you're going to be begging girls to hug you," Dalton informed him.

"Get it off me," Brandt muttered to his uncle.

Chapter 3

*L*ess than a year later. Well-dressed men and women, mostly wearing black, stood on the front porch paying their respects to Dalton and Colt. Despite the heavy traffic of guests within the house, Brandt sat quietly in one of the rocking chairs furthest from the door and stared off into the horizon. His expression was void of all emotion. Everyone passing eyed him sympathetically, but each knew to let him grieve in his own way. Liddy stepped onto the porch from the house with Mazie in tow, shadowing her mother and looking sad. Liddy offered a tiny, polite smile to those on the porch.

"Please, help yourselves to the buffet in the dining room," she informed them.

The guests headed inside as if on command, while Dalton and Colt remained on the porch with their glasses of whiskey.

"You did a great job, Liddy," Dalton informed her while offering a tiny smile.

"Dee would approve," Colt added.

Mazie saw Brandt sitting quietly on the other side of the porch. She released her mother, approached the boy, and stared at his expressionless face. He didn't look at her, and neither spoke. Mazie climbed onto the rocking chair with him, squeezed in beside him, and clung to his arm while resting her head on his shoulder. Colt and Dalton watched the unfolding scene. Brandt didn't protest or comment. Instead, he placed his arm around her and held her. Colt and Dalton smiled, somewhat relieved, then looked back at Liddy.

"We wanted to talk to you, Liddy," Dalton announced while fidgeting slightly. "As the boy's legal guardians, Colt and I want you to stay on here at the ranch."

"We're, uh, in no way prepared to raise a little boy," Colt added somewhat uncomfortably. "The boy needs a mother, and he's really taken to you these past nine months."

"And Mazie's good for him too," Dalton assured her. "Would you consider staying?"

"We just want what's best for the boy," Colt announced.

"And us," Dalton added, seeming tense. "Between the two of us, we couldn't keep a house to save our lives."

"Of course, I'll stay," Liddy replied, adding a warm smile. "Dee was my best friend growing up, and I want what's best for her son. He has two excellent father figures, but he also needs a motherly figure."

"We appreciate that, Liddy," Dalton replied, then tensed while casting a quick look at Brandt with Mazie. "We're really worried about him. He hasn't grieved over his mother's death yet."

"Everyone grieves in their own time and in their own way," Liddy reminded them. "Give him time."

Mazie woke after midnight that night to a small commotion within their in-law suite in the west wing.

Mazie's frilly, neutral-colored bedroom featured tan carpeting and bold, floral-print wallpaper. The definitely feminine and frilly tan canopy bed had light tan curtains bunched at each of the four posts. There was a white wicker desk and chair, along with a tan dresser and a matching armoire. Proudly displayed in the corner of the room was a newly-built, three-story, handmade dollhouse. Each floor, with at least two rooms on each, was fourteen inches tall and big enough to accommodate Mazie's twelve-inch dolls. Mazie crawled out of bed, rubbing her tired eyes, and padded into the living area. The living room was rustic, featuring hardwood flooring, stone walls, and exposed ceiling beams. The large windows were floor-to-ceiling and let in plenty of light during the day. There was a massive fireplace made of the same stone as the walls, with a lodgepole pine beam serving as the mantel. The old leather sofa, chair, and loveseat were placed in the middle of the room, near the fireplace, adding to the room's coziness. With the large, colorful throw rug in the middle, the room had a lot of visual warmth.

The lights were on in the living room, but her mother wasn't there. Liddy's bedroom door was open only a crack, and the commotion appeared to be coming from there. Mazie cautiously approached her mother's room and pushed the door open. Liddy's bedroom was also decorated with a feminine flair, but with an adult in mind. The walls were a bold mauve color, with black-and-red trim that matched the curtains. In contrast, the carpet was a blueish gray. The queen-sized bed had a black wrought iron headboard and footboard. She, too, had an armoire, but the rest of her furniture was clearly antique. The tall dresser, mirrored dresser, and end tables were Burl & Walnut Victorian Renaissance with marble tops. Mazie scanned the room and saw Brandt sitting on the bed with her mother, clinging to her and sobbing.

"Mommy," Mazie asked with concern. "Is Brandt okay?"

Liddy continued to cuddle and comfort the boy. "He's fine, Mazie," she gently replied while stroking his hair. "He's just missing his mother. He's going to stay with me tonight. Go back to bed. Everything is okay."

"Can I sleep with you, too?" Mazie asked softly.

Liddy smiled sympathetically and motioned Mazie to the bed. She hurried to them, crawled onto the bed, and clung to Brandt while he sobbed in her mother's arms.

*T*he following morning, Liddy stood in the bedroom doorway with her mug of coffee. Dalton appeared in the open suite doorway and lightly tapped on the frame.

"Sorry to bother you, Liddy," Dalton announced. "But Brandt wasn't in his room--"

Liddy smiled and motioned him closer. Dalton approached and looked into the bedroom through the open doorway. Brandt and Mazie slept peacefully on Liddy's bed in each other's arms.

"Is that the most adorable thing you've ever seen?" Liddy asked.

Dalton snorted a tiny laugh and affectionately caressed her shoulder. "I don't know what we'd do without you, Liddy."

Chapter 4

*O*ne year later. The sun wasn't even up yet when seven-year-old Mazie rushed out of the house and onto the porch, looking toward the barn with its light on.

"Brandt?" she called out, but there was no response.

Mazie ran off the porch to the barn, entering only a moment later. She looked around and saw Brandt among the eight saddled wranglers' horses. Twelve-year-old Brandt was on his way to being a hearty teenage boy. His dark hair was still a little unkempt from wearing his cowboy hat outside all day. He seemed to grow taller and taller every day and was probably already the same height as his mother had been. Although still lean and now a bit lanky, he would eventually grow much taller and fill out like his uncles. Brandt was saddling his own black gelding, which had four white socks and a bold white blaze down its face. Mazie approached him with a slightly puzzled look.

"You're gonna miss breakfast," she informed him.

"I don't have time," he announced. "I have to get the horses ready for today."

"Are we going out riding?" she asked, then hurried for her pony in its stall.

"No, we aren't going riding," Brandt informed her.

She ignored his response and led Gizmo from his stall. "You're saddling your horse," Mazie announced. "That means we're riding. Can we ride to the old cabin?" She was practically giddy. "That place is so creepy!"

Brandt groaned and turned toward her. "I'm working the cattle today," he informed her. "It's time I pulled my weight around here. I'm not a child anymore."

Mazie brushed Gizmo and barely glanced at the boy. "Do we get to rope them?" she asked enthusiastically.

"There is no 'we'," Brandt informed her somewhat sternly. "You're not going."

She stopped brushing her pony and looked at Brandt with surprise. "Why not?"

"Because you're a little girl," he informed her. "Girls don't work the cattle."

She became offended. "Do too!"

"Uh, no," he announced and raised his brows. "They don't. Go inside and play with your dolls. This is men's work."

"I don't play with dolls," she huffed.

"Sure you don't," Brandt scoffed while tightening his horse's girth. "We'll just pretend GI Joe and He-Man weren't having a tea party with Ken and Barbie."

"GI Joe happens to like tea," Mazie insisted. "He also likes Barbie. They're getting married this weekend."

Brandt cast a look at Mazie, who now carried her smaller saddle across the aisle to her pony. "GI Joe is *not* marrying Barbie," he snapped back. "That's my GI Joe. Don't involve him in your little girl fantasies."

Mazie placed the saddle on her pony's back with some effort. "You're so mean," she scoffed. "There's no way I'm marrying you now."

"Good," Brandt snapped back. "I don't want to be part of your fantasies either. And stop saddling Gizmo! You're not going along!"

"Am too."

"Girls are so annoying," Brandt muttered, then put the bridle on his horse.

Colt entered the barn and paused in the doorway. "Hey," he announced boldly. "Why aren't the two of you at the breakfast table?"

"I wanted to get a head start on saddling the horses for this morning," Brandt announced proudly while looking back at his uncle. "Almost done."

Colt approached and checked the rigging on the saddles. "You did a fine job," he announced, then eyed Brandt's saddled horse. "Why did you saddle your horse?"

"I'm going with you," Brandt informed him cheerfully. "School ended yesterday, and you said I could work the cattle this summer."

"I said you could help," Colt reminded him. "You're not going out with us for the entire day."

Brandt stared at his uncle, surprised and disappointed. "I'm old enough," he reminded him. "You said I could."

"No, I didn't," Colt remarked firmly. "I said you could help. You're not ready to spend the entire day working cattle."

"That's not fair!"

"Neither is you not cleaning your room like I asked you to," Colt snapped back. "You want more responsibility, but you don't do what you're told."

"Why do I have to clean my room?" Brandt demanded. "Liddy cleans my room."

"Liddy isn't your personal maid," Colt informed him. "I asked her not to clean your room anymore. Now unsaddle that horse, go inside, eat your breakfast, and start working on your house chores." His look was stern. "We'll discuss adding some cattle responsibilities *after* you show you're responsible enough to handle your house chores."

"House chores are for girls," Brandt informed his uncle. "I want to do man chores."

Colt groaned and rubbed his eyes. "Where did I go wrong?" he muttered, then looked at Brandt. "Not only are you not working the cattle at all today, but I want you to clean up after breakfast. You're going to help Liddy with all the cleaning around the house until you learn to appreciate everything she does around here." He again indicated the horse. "Now, unsaddle that horse and get your ass inside. There's a stack of dirty dishes with your name on them."

As Colt turned and left the barn, the thundering sound of steel horseshoes striking concrete was heard. When he looked back, Brandt raced across the field toward the woods on his horse. Colt sneered and shook his head in anger.

"I'm going to whoop his ass so hard his great grandkids will say ouch," Colt muttered.

"Brandt," Mazie called out and raced past Colt on her saddled pony with just its halter and lead rope. "Wait for me!"

Colt stared after the little girl riding bareback as she galloped off into the still dark morning. "Mazie!" he cried out. "Come back here!"

Mazie raced her pony after Brandt's much faster horse across the large field toward the woods. "Brandt, wait up!" she cried out. "You're going too fast!"

Brandt looked back at the girl chasing after him. "Go away!" he yelled back. "Stop following me!"

As his horse entered the path within the dark woods, he slowed to a trot but didn't stop. Mazie suddenly cried out from somewhere behind him. Brandt stopped his horse at the scream and spun around on the path. Mazie lay on the ground just inside the woods as the wildly jumping pony spun, its saddle turned sideways on its back, and ran across the clearing to the farm.

"Mazie!"

Brandt rode back to her, leapt from the horse's back, and ran for the motionless girl.

"Mazie," he cried out and fell to his knees alongside her. "Mazie!"

Mazie slowly lifted her head and started crying while clutching her arm. "It hurts!"

Brandt gently touched her arm, and she again screamed. "It's okay, Mazie," he gently announced while removing his bandanna. "You're going to be okay." He placed his bandanna around her arm and neck to create a sling, then helped her to her feet.

Mazie cried out and clutched her leg. "It hurts!" she again screamed and nearly fell back down.

Brandt clung to her, keeping her from falling. "I've got you, Mazie," he announced while tears streaked his face. "It's okay. I've got you."

He swooped her up into his arms and carried her to his patiently waiting horse. With some effort, Brandt hoisted her up to the saddle of the taller horse.

"Grab the horn with your good arm," he instructed.

She sobbed while doing as he told her. As she clung to the saddle horn, he boosted her up the rest of the way. She swung her good leg over the saddle while still crying from the pain. Brandt then patted her leg.

"Okay, just hang on," he gently announced. "I'll get you back to the farm."

Mazie sniffed, stifling her sobs, and clung to the saddle horn while Brandt led the horse back to the clearing. As he walked the horse along the field, Colt was already on his horse, galloping toward them. Dalton could be seen near the barn, mounting his horse as well. As Colt got closer, Brandt broke down sobbing.

"I didn't know she'd fall off," Brandt informed his uncle. "I didn't know she'd get hurt."

"Actions have consequences, Brandt," Colt scolded him while jumping from his horse. "I'll deal with you later."

Colt attempted to assess Mazie's injuries without moving her.

Brandt wiped his tears and sniffed. "She may have broken her arm and sprained her ankle," he informed his uncle.

Colt touched Mazie's face while looking into her eyes, where she sat on Brandt's horse. "Are you okay, darling?" he asked in a soft voice.

Mazie sniffed and wiped her tears. "It wasn't Brandt's fault," she replied. "Gizmo got scared in the woods. He didn't mean to toss me."

"You're going to be okay," Colt informed her with a warm smile. "We'll take you to the doctor and get you all fixed up."

"Don't be mad at Brandt," Mazie just about pleaded. "It wasn't his fault. I rode after him. It's my fault."

Colt groaned and shook his head. "You need to stop defending him," he informed her. "It just gives him an excuse to keep messing up."

"But I love him," Mazie replied. "I don't want you to punish him."

"I love him too," Colt informed her. "That's why I need to punish him."

§

*B*randt sat impatiently on the porch later that morning with his Uncle Colt. Both came to life when they saw Dalton's truck in the driveway approaching the house. Both stood and waited for the vehicle to stop. Dalton and Liddy got out of the truck and then helped Mazie out. Her arm was in a hot pink cast, and her ankle was wrapped in a pink ACE wrap. Brandt ran off the porch to them and hugged Mazie. She eagerly returned the embrace and then smiled excitedly.

"Look," she announced, holding up her arm in the cast. "They gave me a cool pink cast!"

"Yeah, that's pretty awesome," Brandt replied, then helped her to the porch, supporting her while she limped with each step.

"See that squiggle? The doctor signed my cast," she announced. "Will you sign my cast, Brandt?"

"Yeah, of course," he replied.

Liddy and Dalton exchanged looks and shook their heads. After nearly facing death a couple of hours ago, all Mazie cared about was Brandt's attention.

"I have a surprise for you," Brandt informed the little girl.

"A surprise?" she gasped excitedly. "What is it?"

"You'll see."

Brandt helped Mazie through the house, across her mother's apartment, and into her bedroom. There was a large vase filled with wild flowers on her little table in the center of the room. Mazie looked around her vacuumed floor, neatly made bed, and freshly dusted furniture. She then looked back at Brandt.

"Did you clean my room?" she asked with surprise.

"Yes," he replied, then took her to the dollhouse in the corner. "And, I thought you'd like to know--" He opened the doll house to reveal GI Joe in a tuxedo and Barbie in a wedding dress. "GI Joe asked Barbie to marry him, and she said yes."

Mazie cried out excitedly and looked at Brandt. "They're getting married this weekend?"

"Yep," Brandt replied. "And we're going to bake them a cake and everything."

Mazie cried out excitedly and hugged Brandt. "Thank you, Brandt!" she announced. "I love you!"

Brandt returned the embrace. "I love you too."

Mazie excitedly sat on the floor in front of the dollhouse. "Will you have a tea party with us?" she asked.

Brandt managed a smile and nodded. "Sure," he replied, then moved onto the floor with some discomfort.

Mazie gave him a strange look. "Did Uncle Colt whoop you?"

Brandt maintained his smile. "It's okay, really," he informed her. "A man owns his mistakes."

Chapter 5

Eight-year-old Mazie watched as thirteen-year-old Brandt started up the large farm tractor just outside the equipment barn. The newer tractor roared to life, causing Mazie to jump. She eyed him skeptically, although he didn't notice.

"I don't think you're supposed to use that without Uncle Colt or Uncle Dalton around," Mazie reminded him.

Brandt finally looked down at Mazie on the ground below, appearing almost arrogant. "I drive the tractor all the time," he insisted. "Besides, I just need it for ten minutes to pull the side-by-side out of the ditch."

"I don't think you were supposed to use that without permission either," Mazie remarked.

"Which is why I need to 'borrow' the tractor," Brandt informed her. "To get the side-by-side out of the ditch so Uncle Colt doesn't find out I 'borrowed' it."

Mazie cocked her head, not understanding his logic. "Wouldn't it be easier just to follow the rules?" she finally asked.

Brandt looked back at her, grinned, and raised his brows. "Where's the fun in that?" he teased.

Mazie groaned and rolled her eyes. "Boys are so stupid," she muttered.

"At least we're not afraid of spiders," Brandt countered with an air of arrogance.

Before Mazie could respond, Brandt drove the tractor across the farm. Mazie folded her arms across her chest and huffed while watching him drive away.

"Could have at least offered me a ride," Mazie muttered, then ran after him.

Mazie followed the tractor to the tree line more than one hundred yards from the equipment barn, where an older side-by-side was stranded practically on its side in the decent-sized ditch. Mazie stayed out of his way and watched as he skillfully turned the tractor around and backed it up in line with the back bumper of the side-by-side. She couldn't deny she was impressed with the way he handled the massive tractor. The back wheel of the tractor suddenly slid into the ditch, surprising Brandt. Mazie gasped, then covered her eyes while shaking her head. She was no longer impressed. Brandt assessed the situation and then attempted to extract the tractor from the ditch. The wheel in the ditch spun, digging it deeper into the soft ground. On his next attempt, the entire tractor leaned heavily, now fully stuck. Brandt shut down the tractor, then spun on the seat and stared at the situation behind him. He frowned and shook his head.

"I think we're going to need to borrow the pickup truck," he remarked.

"Uncle Colt will be back soon," Mazie casually reminded him. "We should wait for him. You're in enough trouble already."

"That's why we need to fix our mistakes on our own," Brandt informed her, then frowned. "I don't want another whooping."

"Then why do you always do things that get you whooped?" Mazie asked.

Brandt turned defensive and groaned. "How am I supposed to know?" he demanded. "Uncle Colt says it's my mouth that gets me in trouble, but he always takes it out on my backside." Brandt remained sitting on the crooked tractor while lost in thought. "I just need to figure out how to get the truck keys off the pegboard in the kitchen without Liddy seeing me."

Mazie was momentarily lost in thought before eyeing Brandt on his leaning tractor. She appeared somewhat curious and almost afraid to ask.

"Does it hurt a lot?" she asked.

"Does what hurt?" Brandt asked, glancing back at her.

"Getting your backside tanned," she replied.

"It hurts enough," Brandt replied, then snorted a laugh. "Not that you have to worry about that."

"That's because I behave," Mazie reminded him.

"No, that's not what I mean," Brandt groaned. "Girls don't get whooped."

"They don't?" Mazie asked, surprised.

"No, silly," he announced, then shook his head. "Don't you know anything? Real men don't hit women. It's a rule that's etched in stone somewhere."

Uncle Colt's truck flew along the field and came to a skidding stop not far from them. Mazie jumped with surprise while Brandt just groaned and let his head fall against the steering wheel.

"What the hell is going on here?" Colt demanded in his gruffest 'I'm gonna whoop your ass' voice.

"The side-by-side slid into the ditch," Brandt explained. "I was trying to get it out."

"And how did the side-by-side get into the ditch?' Colt demanded in an arrogant tone. "You're not supposed to be driving that or the tractor without permission and supervision."

"I know, but--" Brandt began, but was interrupted.

"I did it," Mazie announced, surprising Brandt.

Colt stared at Mazie, stunned by the confession, while Brandt climbed off the tractor, unable to take his eyes off her. Colt turned toward Mazie, stood straight, towering over her, and folded his arms across his chest, wearing his best intimidating look.

"*You* took the side-by-side out?" Colt asked, although not convinced, then indicated Brandt. "Did Brandt ask you to lie for him?"

Mazie couldn't deny she was suddenly intimidated while staring up at her Uncle Colt. It was possibly the first time she thought he was scary since their initial meeting. She was so frightened, she couldn't even respond. She just shook her head. Colt looked from Mazie to Brandt with skepticism, then back at Mazie.

"If that's the truth," Colt informed her. "Then you'll be the one getting a whooping." He cocked his head while staring at the little girl. "Is that the truth, Mazie?"

Mazie stared at Uncle Colt a moment with a horrified look on her face. She'd never been whooped and never witnessed a whooping. Mazie couldn't deny that the thought was even more terrifying than the perceived whooping. She held her breath and stood her ground.

"That's the truth, Uncle Colt," she informed him. "I did it. Not Brandt."

Colt hesitated a moment, almost stunned, as if expecting a different response. He finally drew a deep breath, then released it.

"Okay then," he replied.

"Come on, Uncle Colt," Brandt announced somewhat boldly. "She's obviously lying. I mean, let's be real." He pointed back at the two vehicles in the ditch. "This has me written all over it. I did this. If anything, she tried to stop me."

Colt tried hard to hide his smile and nodded, then pointed to the house. "Go find your mother," he announced to Mazie. "We'll discuss why we don't lie later."

Mazie looked from Colt to Brandt, frowned, and then shamefully headed back to the house. Once she was far enough away, Colt looked back at Brandt and indicated the tractor and the side-by-side.

"You know you're in a lot of trouble, boy," Colt informed him.

Brandt lowered his head and nodded. "Yes, sir."

Colt placed his hand firmly on Brandt's shoulder, causing him to meet his uncle's gaze. Colt's grin seemed oddly out of place.

"Today, you learned a valuable lesson," Colt informed him. "So I'm going to overlook this mess of yours."

Brandt stared at his uncle, confused. "What lesson?" he asked.

"You owned up to your mistakes and didn't let Mazie take your punishment for you," Colt replied. "Protecting your family is your number one priority."

"So Mazie isn't in trouble for lying?" Brandt asked. "She was protecting family, too."

Colt chuckled warmly and pulled Brandt to his side. "That's right, son," he announced. "You're finally getting it. I think you're actually growing up."

"Then why am I so confused?" Brandt asked, still stunned that he wasn't getting whooped.

"Because life is confusing," Colt replied. "And it's going to get a lot more confusing before it finally starts making sense." He released Brandt and indicated the mess in the ditch. "Come on. Let's get this sorted out."

Chapter 6

Nine-year-old Mazie helped her mother set platters of breakfast items on the kitchen table while Dalton filled two thermoses with coffee at the main counter. Mazie had grown a lot in the last two years. Although her hair remained long, she often wore it in a ponytail so she'd fit in with Brandt. The days of dresses were gone entirely, as she had a new lifestyle to maintain, and she didn't want to give Brandt any reasons to exclude her from games and farm chores. These days, she didn't even own a dress anymore. Her mother had lost the battle getting her to wear them ever again. Liddy and Dalton both turned at the same time and nearly collided. Dalton laughed while holding onto the thermos.

"Sorry," Dalton announced cheerfully. "You had right of way."

"I should have looked where I was going," she responded with a laugh.

"Oh, I should tell you," Dalton remarked. "I'm heading back early today. I need to run to town this afternoon for a tractor part, so I'll grab lunch in town."

"I could have lunch ready early for you," Liddy informed him, giving him a sideways glance. "What time will you be returning home?"

"Around ten," he remarked casually. "It'll be too early for lunch. I'm fine with grabbing something in town."

"Can I go to town with Uncle Dalton?" Mazie asked while setting a platter of bacon on the table.

"Sorry, darling," Dalton announced to Mazie. "I'm going to be gone most of the afternoon, and you'd only be bored."

Mazie frowned at being struck down.

"Besides," her mother remarked while eyeing her. "You're cleaning tack in the barn all morning. You promised Uncle Dalton. You don't clean tack, you don't get money for that computer game you wanted."

"I can do that after lunch," Mazie insisted.

Liddy shook her head. "Nope," she announced. "After lunch, you and I are picking berries, and then we're making muffins."

Mazie rolled her eyes and groaned. "Baking," she muttered. "Stop trying to domesticate me, Mom."

Liddy and Dalton exchanged looks and mouthed. "Domesticate?" Both tried to keep from laughing at Mazie's big-girl vocabulary.

There was a commotion from within the mudroom beyond the kitchen, catching everyone's attention. Colt entered in his stocking feet with fourteen-year-old Brandt only a step behind him, still wearing his cowboy boots. Brandt was already as tall as Liddy and still had plenty of growing to do. His dark hair was still unkempt from wearing cowboy hats most of the day, and he seemed to have an allergic reaction to getting haircuts recently, balking at the idea whenever it was brought up. Given his rapid growth spurts, Brandt was now extremely lanky despite eating his weight in food.

"Why not?" Brandt demanded. "I have the money."

"Because I said not," Colt informed him, then glared at his nephew's feet. "Take off those damned boots, boy. You mess the kitchen floor, and you're cleaning it."

Brandt groaned in frustration and returned to the mud room to remove his cowboy boots. He then entered in his stocking feet.

Liddy eyed his dirty socks and shook her head. "No wonder you hardly have any whites in the wash," she remarked. "How many days do you intend to wear those socks?"

"I don't know," Brandt replied while flopping in his seat at the table. "Next time I shower, I suppose."

"When's the last time you showered?" Dalton demanded while eyeing his nephew.

Brandt grabbed a piece of toast and took a bite out of it. "I don't know," he scoffed. "A few days ago. I wasn't keeping track."

"Show some manners, boy," Colt snapped and eyed the toast in his hand. "Not everyone is seated, and we haven't said grace."

Brandt moaned and tossed the piece of toast onto his plate. "I don't know who you're trying to impress, Uncle Colt," he remarked. "You're not too worried about manners out in the back forty. You and Bill, standing by your respective trees, having pissing contests."

"You said a bad word," Mazie teased Brandt.

"That's different," Colt informed him.

"Trying to see who can literally piss farther," Brandt remarked and cocked his head. "When it comes to manners, I win."

"What is wrong with you, boy?" Colt demanded. "Talking that way in front of ladies?"

"Can guys piss standing up?" Mazie then asked Brandt.

Colt groaned and rolled his eyes at Mazie's newly acquired 'word of the day'.

Brandt turned and looked Mazie directly in the eyes. "Yes, guys piss standing up," he informed her. "Watch television once in a while. You might learn something."

"Stop teaching Mazie bad words," Dalton huffed and joined them at the table.

"I'm not teaching them to her," Brandt announced defensively, then pointed at her. "She's literally under my feet twenty-four-seven!"

"Not with the way your feet smell," Mazie informed him.

Colt laughed and high-fived Mazie. She giggled and slapped her hand to his.

"My feet don't stink," Brandt insisted.

"If you never shower, they do," Colt remarked.

"I don't need to shower," Brandt informed him. "I swim in the pond every day. Taking a shower would be repetitious."

"What's repetitious?" Mazie asked the boy sitting alongside her.

"Seriously," Brandt announced while glaring at her. "Watch some television."

Once Liddy was seated, Dalton led them in grace. After he was finished, everyone except Brandt helped themselves to the home-style breakfast. Brandt looked across the table at his Uncle Dalton.

"I want to buy a dirt bike, Uncle Dalton," Brandt announced. "I have the money, but Uncle Colt is giving me a hard time."

"A dirt bike?" Liddy gasped and then looked at Dalton with horror.

Mazie attempted to pass the bowl of scrambled eggs to Brandt, but he wasn't paying attention to her. She groaned and placed a helping onto his plate, then passed the bowl to Colt on the other side of her.

"We're not bringing this up at the breakfast table," Colt insisted.

"You're just afraid Uncle Dalton will take my side," Brandt remarked.

"You only want some dirt bike to impress those older boys you think are your friends," Colt announced. "You're going to get yourself killed trying to impress those bigger kids."

"Sure, there are other boys at school who have dirt bikes, but I'm certainly not trying to impress them," Brandt scoffed.

Mazie attempted to pass Brandt the home fries, but he didn't even look at her. She groaned and placed a helping of home fries on his plate as well.

"Those things are dangerous," Liddy remarked.

"So are horses in the wrong hands," Brandt informed her, then indicated Mazie as she placed bacon on his plate. "Case in point."

"Hey," Mazie cried out and set the plate of bacon down. "I'm a good rider."

"You ride a pony," Brandt informed her. "And you fell off him ten times already."

Mazie sneered at Brandt and removed the bacon from his plate. "No bacon for you."

"We'll discuss this later," Dalton informed Brandt. "It's not breakfast table conversation."

"You think he should be allowed to have one, don't you?" Colt just about demanded of his brother.

"Actually, I do," Dalton replied, then shrugged. "He's responsible enough to ride one."

"Are you sure that's a good idea?" Liddy asked Dalton.

Brandt shot an irritated look at Liddy across the table. "You don't get a vote on this," he informed her. "You're not my mother."

Colt and Dalton suddenly erupted into irritated groans and hostile words. Liddy took the comment pretty hard and looked down at her plate.

"That was uncalled for," Dalton snapped back at Brandt. "Apologize to Liddy, or instead of a discussion on dirt bikes, we'll be discussing how long to ground you."

Brandt drew a deep breath, then looked at Liddy, who appeared broken and defeated. "I'm sorry, Liddy," he gently announced. "I didn't mean any disrespect."

Liddy forced a smile and nodded. "Thank you," she replied.

"Good," Colt announced and looked around the table. "We're wasting daylight. We'll discuss this on the ride out to the cattle. Eat your breakfast before it gets cold."

Brandt was about to reach for one of the platters when he saw his plate was already filled for him. He glanced at Mazie, who happily ate her breakfast without a care in the world. Brandt swiped the strip of bacon from her plate. When she glared at him, he bit into it while mocking her. Mazie sneered at him, but then quickly changed her tune.

"Can I borrow your new computer game?" Mazie asked Brandt.

"No," Brandt snapped back. "And stay out of my room."

"I wasn't in your room," she insisted.

"You were, too," he remarked. "You're *always* in my room."

"Your room is dirty, and it smells bad," she replied. "I wouldn't go in there."

"Oh?" he demanded. "Then why am I always finding your long hair all over my pillow?"

"That was one time," she insisted. "And if you changed your sheets once in a while--"

"Stay out of my room!"

"Thank God there's only two of them," Colt muttered.

Chapter 7

*L*ater that morning, a little before ten o'clock, Mazie quietly opened the front door after nearly two hours of cleaning tack. She looked around the hallway, obviously up to something. Although Mazie didn't hear her, she was certain her mother was in the kitchen or perhaps the laundry room. Mazie quietly shut the door and then crept up the main stairs. She hurried along the second floor hallway and paused before Brandt's bedroom door. A store-bought sign clearly read, "Keep Out!" Mazie opened the bedroom door, slipped inside, and shut the door behind her. Brandt's bedroom was clearly a boy's room. It had hardwood flooring with a large area rug covering it, and the wallpaper was off-white with small light-blue designs. The king-sized bed featured a black wrought iron headboard and footboard, complemented by a solid blue bedspread. All the decorations, from the longhorn steer horns to deer antlers, were masculine in nature. Although supposedly clean, the room was still somewhat messy, as usual.

Mazie removed her boots and grabbed the laptop from the nightstand. She hesitated only a moment to look at the framed photo of Brandt on his pony between his mother and father on their horses that was taken in front of the massive gate. Brandt's father was sitting atop a beautiful, flashy black and white Overo paint gelding. Apparently, that horse died shortly after his father's death. Anytime Mazie saw a picture of that horse, she couldn't help but stop and stare at it. Mazie then jumped onto Brandt's sloppily made bed with his laptop, placed a pair of headphones over her ears, opened the computer, and found the game she liked. She leaned back against the pillow and headboard and attempted to play the game. She was defeated almost instantly, groaning in disgust. Mazie heard something outside, alerting her to potential trouble. She tossed the laptop and headphones aside, jumped off the bed, and hurried to the window. Mazie saw Dalton ride up to the house and dismount, which was odd, since he usually dismounted at the barn. As he tied the horse to the rarely used hitching post by the front porch, Mazie was actually relieved he hadn't gone into the barn. He may have noticed she wasn't in the tack room cleaning saddles.

When Dalton entered the house, she assumed she was safe. Mazie returned to the bed, repositioned the headphones, and again resumed her game. She only played for a minute or two when she was again killed in gory, graphic detail. Mazie made a face and thumped back against the pillow, hearing something crinkle. She removed the headphones, set the laptop aside, and reached under the pillow. When she pulled a magazine out and saw the mostly naked woman on the cover, Mazie made a face, then hesitated, suddenly curious. She opened the magazine, saw pictures of nude women inside, and gasped in horror, shutting the magazine. As she was about to return the magazine beneath the pillow, the bedroom door opened. Brandt stood in the doorway and saw Mazie on his bed with the dirty magazine in her hand.

"What are you doing in my room?" Brandt cried out, then turned angry while storming across the room and snatching the magazine from her. "I told you to stay out of my room!"

"Why do you have that?" Mazie asked, referring to the magazine.

"None of your business!" he shouted in anger and yanked her off his bed. "You're a damned pain in my ass! Now get out!"

Mazie just about fell to the floor from the jerking action and spun to face him with surprise. She'd never seen him looking that angry before.

"And never come in here again, you stupid little girl!" Brandt shouted.

Mazie could barely control her emotions at his cruel words. She grabbed her boots and ran from his room, hurrying down the hall. Mazie nearly collided with her mother as she suddenly appeared from one of the upstairs bedrooms.

"Mazie?" Liddy called after her daughter. "Mazie, what happened?"

Mazie didn't stop or even acknowledge her mother's question. A second later, Brandt bolted into the hallway, saw Mazie heading for the front stairs, and hurried after her.

"What's going on?" Liddy demanded. "Why were you yelling at her?"

Brandt hesitated when he saw Liddy and appeared moderately suspicious before peering into his Uncle Dalton's bedroom through the partially open door. When the door slowly shut from the inside, Brandt gave Liddy a strange look. Liddy appeared slightly tense as she ran her fingers through her slightly mussed hair, then met his gaze and straightened, her look turning stern. Brandt stared at her a moment in silent question, shook his head, and ran for the stairs.

$\mathcal{M}$azie sat in the corner of Gizmo's stall while holding her knees to her chest and sobbed softly while the pony stood over her, keeping watch. When she heard the stall door roll open, Mazie lifted her head.

Brandt frowned and shook his head. "You should know better than to run off like that," he informed her. "If they can't find you, I get in trouble."

"Leave me alone," she muttered and rested her cheek on her knees, avoiding looking at him.

Brandt entered the stall, closing the door behind him, and approached her. "Come on," he announced. "Let's go back inside."

"I'm not going anywhere with you," she insisted without looking at him.

Brandt groaned and sat alongside her on the stall floor, covered in a thick coating of wood shavings. He rested his head against the stall wall behind him.

"I'm sorry I yelled at you," he announced in a soft, sincere tone.

"You called me a stupid little girl," she whispered. "You hate me."

"I don't hate you," Brandt replied with a groan. "I'm getting older, Mazie. I need my privacy."

"Why?" she asked and glanced at him. "What does that even mean?"

"You wouldn't understand," he replied with a defeated sigh while raking his fingers through his hair. "When you get older, you'll understand."

"Boys are the stupid ones," she informed him. "They don't make any sense."

"Well, you're not entirely wrong," Brandt replied, then finally looked at her. "See, when boys--" He hesitated. "Girls, too. When we get older, we need time alone to, well, figure things out."

"What things?"

"Well, when boys start taking an interest in girls, it gets, well, confusing," he replied. "And we need time, private time, to sort things out so they're less confusing."

"You're not making much sense," she remarked.

"Exactly," he announced while studying her. "If you ever want me to make sense again, you need to respect my privacy so I have time to reflect and figure things out." He held his breath a moment. "I know I've been *moody* lately, and I sometimes say things that hurt you, but I don't really mean them. When you get older, what I'm telling you will all make sense. I just can't explain it in a way that you'll understand." Brandt sighed while looking into her eyes. "I just need you to trust me. You need to be patient with me, and know that when I say hurtful things, I don't really mean them."

Mazie stared at him for a long, confused moment. "I trust you, Brandt," she replied. "I don't understand any of it, but I trust you."

"Am I forgiven?" he asked, adding a tiny smile.

Mazie laughed, then clung to his arm and rested her head on his shoulder. "Yeah, you're forgiven."

"Good," he replied while swiftly standing, then extended his hand to her and pulled her to her feet. "I don't need Liddy giving me the third degree about tormenting you again."

"I do have one question," she announced as they left the pony's stall.

"What's that?" he asked while latching the door behind them.

"Why do you have that magazine with naked women in it?" she asked.

Brandt groaned and avoided looking at her. "It's a boy thing, and you'll never understand," he replied. "Don't make me try to explain it."

"Okay."

"Well, that was easy," Brandt muttered, then glanced at her as they walked through the barn. "And I'd consider it a personal favor if you didn't mention the magazine to Liddy, Uncle Colt, or Uncle Dalton either."

"Will you get in trouble?"

"Probably."

"I won't say anything," she replied, then sighed. "I think there's something wrong with you, but I won't say anything."

Chapter 8

*B*efore sunrise the following morning, Brandt wearily left the house, purposely shutting the screen door behind him, forcing Mazie to stop on the other side. She groaned loudly, opened the door, and ran after him, happily jumping around like a playful puppy on his heels. It was the same torturous game of twenty questions every morning since the beginning of summer vacation.

Mazie's enthusiastic, "Can I tend the herd today?"

A listless, "No."

"Can I ride out as far as the old homestead with you?"

"No."

"What about the woods' edge?"

"No."

"Why are you so grumpy?"

"Tired."

"Why are you always so tired?"

"Not enough sleep."

"Why don't you get more sleep?"

"Because a certain nine-year-old girl, high on sugar, doesn't leave me alone," he scoffed, then turned to face her just outside the barn. "Can you tone down your enthusiasm at least until after breakfast? I can't deal with all your energy until after I've had my coffee."

"When did you start drinking coffee?"

"When I started waking up so damned tired," he groaned, frustrated.

"I hope you figure things out soon," Mazie informed him. "You used to be fun in the morning."

They entered the barn to the sounds of horses happily snickering for their morning grain. Brandt didn't seem to have any enthusiasm for the horses this particular morning either. Mazie ran ahead of Brandt to the grain bin and scooped grain into the large wheeled bucket while Brandt leaned against the wall just outside the feed room and appeared as if he'd fall asleep. When Mazie wheeled the bucket from the feed room to the first stall, Brandt listlessly followed and scooped grain into each horse's feed bucket. He gave a small scoop to Gizmo, who didn't really need grain, but always gave him a 'taste' to keep him happy. As Brandt wheeled the bucket past Gizmo's stall, Mazie looked into the stall above the bars when the pony didn't react to food in his feed bucket.

"Gizmo?" Mazie called into the stall.

There was no response. Since Mazie was too short to see much above the stall wall between the bars, she headed for the stall door and rolled it open. Gizmo lay on his side in the severely disheveled bedding, covered in sweat, and groaning loudly with each labored breath.

"Brandt," Mazie called out. "What's wrong with Gizmo?"

Brandt approached the open stall door and looked inside. "Giz?"

When the pony didn't react or even lift his head, Brandt grabbed the pony's halter and ran into the stall. He slipped the halter over the pony's head and pulled on him.

"Come on, Giz," Brandt announced, sounding slightly panicked. "Get up."

Gizmo again groaned but made no effort to get up. Brandt looked back at Mazie.

"Get Colt and Dalton," he cried out.

"Is he okay--?"

"Now, Mazie!"

A few minutes later, Mazie ran to Gizmo's stall behind Uncle Dalton. Brandt was still attempting to get the pony on its feet. Dalton immediately groaned and shook his head. Colt approached and handed his brother a stethoscope. The pony didn't even react when Dalton kneeled alongside it and listened to its belly, checking several places for gut sounds. Dalton frowned, looked at Brandt eye-level across from him, and shook his head.

"It's either impaction or colic," Dalton informed him.

"There's Banamine in the feed room," Brandt reminded him.

Colt stood alongside Mazie in the stall doorway with his hands on her shoulders, keeping her out of the way.

"Brandt," Dalton announced just loud enough for him to hear. "Look around. He's been rolling for hours. At best, he's twisted, but he's probably already ruptured. Either way, it's too late."

Brandt stared into Dalton's eyes for a long moment, then looked across the stall at Mazie standing in the stall doorway. When she saw the look in Brandt's eyes, her expression dropped.

"He's going to be okay, right?" Mazie asked before she started to tremble. Horror swept over her. "Brandt, he's going to be okay, isn't he?"

Brandt closed his eyes, released the lead rope, and sat against the stall wall without responding. Mazie suddenly cried out and ran into the stall, collapsing next to the pony's head. She frantically tugged on his halter, attempting to pull him to his feet.

"Get up, Gizmo!" she cried out while tears streaked her face. "Come on, Gizmo, get up!"

Brandt now held his head in his hands, unable to handle Mazie's emotional pleas with the dying pony.

"Brandt," Dalton gently announced from across the groaning pony. "Take Mazie into the house."

"No," Mazie screamed, refusing to release the pony's halter.

While sobbing uncontrollably, Mazie looked across the stall and saw Colt's saddened expression while he fiddled with his revolver. Her tear-filled eyes widened in horror at the sight of the gun.

"No," she again screamed and clung to the pony's head, shielding it with her body. "Don't let him do it, Brandt! He's going to kill my pony!"

Colt hesitated, turned away, and rubbed his eyes, burdened by what he had to do and how it was already affecting Mazie.

"Brandt," Dalton gently but firmly announced. "Take Mazie inside."

Mazie sobbed over the pony while clinging to its head and gently stroking its face. Brandt finally lowered his hands and lifted his head, looking directly at Colt.

"You're not shooting Gizmo," Brandt announced in a firm tone. "We're going to get the vet and let him make that call."

"Brandt--" Dalton remarked while attempting to convey the situation without actual words. "We know what he's going to say."

"I don't care," Brandt retorted. "If either of you puts that pony down, Mazie's never going to forgive you."

"He's suffering," Dalton gently reminded him.

"The vet can be out here in fifteen minutes," Brandt insisted. "Another fifteen minutes isn't going to matter at this point. Give Mazie those fifteen minutes." He raised his brows. "My father gave me that pony. I think I should have the final say. If money's the issue--"

"No, of course that's not the issue," Dalton replied, then drew a deep breath before looking at Colt.

"It's probably the wrong call," Colt remarked, then shook his head. "But I don't want to be known for the rest of my life as the uncle who killed Mazie's pony." He groaned softly. "I'll get the vet out here right away."

As Colt walked away, Dalton fell onto his backside and leaned against the opposite stall wall. Brandt slid closer to Mazie and the pony's head and gently caressed Gizmo's face alongside her. She sniffed as she attempted to wipe away her tears.

"He's going to be okay, isn't he, Brandt?" Mazie asked softly.

"No, Mazie," Brandt gently replied. "But you'll be able to say your goodbyes."

Chapter 9

Mazie walked through the field that led to the woods just after dark and approached Brandt, where he sat in the grass overlooking Gizmo's fresh burial site, his face buried in his bent knees. She sat snuggly against him, wrapped her arms around his arm, and rested her head close to his shoulder. Brandt lifted his head without looking at her and secretly attempted to wipe away his tears.

"You shouldn't be out here," Brandt muttered, not looking at her. "It's dark. Liddy's going to worry about you."

"She's more worried about you," Mazie replied while nuzzling his arm.

"I'm fine," Brandt muttered, lacking conviction. "It was just a stupid pony."

"Gizmo was not a stupid pony," Mazie responded sadly, then drew a deep, shaken breath. "You said you don't mean it when you say hurtful things."

Brandt groaned softly and wiped the tears from his eyes, attempting to keep her from seeing. "You're right," he replied. "I didn't mean it. It's just--" He hesitated and drew a deep breath. "Men aren't supposed to show emotions, and they're not supposed to cry."

"That's a stupid rule," Mazie remarked. "Who made that up?"

"I don't know," Brandt replied with a soft groan. "It's just the way it is, I suppose. People see it as weakness."

"I wouldn't think you're weak if you wanted to cry," Mazie announced while clinging to his arm as she stared at the fresh grave. "You stood up to Uncle Dalton and Uncle Colt. You wouldn't let them kill Gizmo. You're the bravest man I know."

Brandt sniffed, wiped away his tears again, and smiled. "As long as you think so, that's all that matters," he replied, then placed his arm around her shoulder and pulled her against him.

Mazie clung to Brandt, burying her head into his chest, and fought her own tears.

"I miss him already, Brandt."

"Me too," Brandt replied softly into the top of her head. "Will you promise me something, Mazie?"

"Umm hmm," she replied.

"Don't tell anyone that I cried over a pony," Brandt muttered into the top of her head.

"I won't," she replied, then hesitated. "Uncle Colt and Uncle Dalton cried over Gizmo."

Brandt pulled back just far enough to meet her gaze while raising his brows.

"They did?"

She nodded, then returned her head to his chest, finding comfort against him. "See. Men do cry."

*O*ne week later, Dalton's pickup truck pulled up to the barn, pulling the smaller, two-horse stock trailer. Mazie excitedly ran from the house while Colt and Liddy followed with less enthusiasm.

"I can't believe Dalton let him get a dirt bike," Liddy scoffed and shook her head. "I'm so disappointed in that man."

"I'm still trying to figure out how I was outvoted," Colt muttered.

All three approached the truck as Dalton and Brandt got out, looking a little too pleased with themselves.

"Look at that," Liddy scoffed to Colt. "*Two* teenage boys."

Colt snickered softly and patted Liddy's shoulder. "You're raising one girl and three boys," he informed her. "You should probably ask for a raise."

Mazie ran up to Brandt and Dalton, bouncing around with too much enthusiasm.

"Will you take me for a ride?" she asked excitedly.

"Absolutely," Brandt announced cheerfully.

"Absolutely not," Liddy cried out and immediately received a stern look from Mazie.

All five headed to the back of the horse trailer to unload Brandt's new dirt bike. Dalton and Brandt exchanged knowing smiles.

"There was a slight change of plans," Dalton informed them. "We saw something better."

"With a little more horsepower," Brandt added.

Both laughed at some inside joke.

Colt held his head and groaned. "I've got a bad feeling about this," he muttered.

Once Dalton opened the back door, Brandt disappeared inside the trailer and emerged leading a ten-year-old, flashy black and white paint gelding. Mazie, Colt, and Liddy stared at the horse with some confusion.

"It's a horse," Colt remarked while cocking his head. "What happened to the dirt bike?"

"He's gorgeous," Mazie gasped as her eyes lit up. She immediately approached the horse and coddled it before looking at Brandt. "He looks just like the one your father rode in those pictures in the tack room. The coolest horse in the world."

"Yeah, I knew you'd take one look at him and fall in love," Brandt remarked to Mazie, then smiled and handed her the lead rope. "I bought him for you. He's yours."

Mazie stared at Brandt, surprised and possibly shocked. "What?"

"I don't really need a dirt bike," Brandt replied, then shrugged. "Just spook the cattle anyway. You, on the other hand, need a horse."

Mazie uncertainly accepted the lead rope without taking her eyes off Brandt. "You really bought him for me?" she gasped.

Liddy placed her hand over her mouth and looked away, attempting not to cry.

"Uncle Dalton and I agreed," Brandt informed her. "You need a grown-up horse now." He shrugged. "And I know how much you loved my father's horse in the picture. It was only right."

Mazie fought her tears and threw her arms around Brandt's waist. She held onto him and tried to keep from crying.

"Thank you, Brandt!"

He rolled his eyes with a defeated groan, then placed his arms around her. "Always with the hugging," he muttered, then managed to wiggle free from her hold. "There is one contingency on this gift horse."

Mazie eyed him somewhat suspiciously.

"You'll need to learn how to rope off a horse," Brandt insisted. "You can't be any kind of wrangler if you don't know how to rope properly."

"Will you teach me?" she eagerly asked, her eyes lighting up.

Brandt chuckled softly. "Of course I will," he replied.

Chapter 10

Ten-year-old Mazie sat on the porch with her colored pencils and a spiral notebook on her bent knees. She appeared to be happily doodling when her mother stepped onto the porch. Liddy watched the contented girl engrossed in her 'work' and couldn't help but smile. They'd been at the ranch for five glorious years, and Mazie seemed to be living her best life. Liddy slipped back into the current moment.

"The boys will be coming back for lunch soon," Liddy informed the pre-teen girl, who didn't bother looking up. "Would you like to help me in the kitchen?"

It always sounded like a question, but Mazie knew it wasn't really. It was more of a polite command.

"Two minutes, Mom," she replied without missing a pencil stroke.

Liddy stared a moment longer, now curious. "What are you working on?" she asked. "School's been out a couple of weeks now."

Mazie grinned but still didn't look up from her notebook. "I'm writing a story," she insisted.

"A story?" Liddy asked, somewhat surprised, then smiled proudly. "What kind of story?"

"It's a story about a boy and his pony," Mazie replied.

"Really?" Liddy remarked and withheld her chuckle. "Any boy I know?"

"No, Mom," she replied and finally looked at her mother, cocking her head. "It's fiction."

Liddy was taken aback, then almost laughed. "Well, maybe you'll let me read it when it's finished," she announced.

Mazie returned to her notebook. "Maybe," she casually replied.

Liddy couldn't resist chuckling, then shook her head while turning for the door. "Five minutes," she announced. "Then you need to wash your hands and help me in the kitchen."

"Yep."

Liddy remained humored as she entered the house, once again leaving Mazie to her book about a boy and his pony. The sound of galloping hoof beats caught Mazie's attention. When she looked up, she saw fifteen-year-old Brandt galloping back to the barn. Mazie excitedly shut her notebook and sprang to her feet as Brandt jumped off his horse. He no sooner tied the horse when Uncle Colt galloped across the field and abruptly stopped by the barn near Brandt. Mazie slowly sank back in her rocking chair, wanting to wait out whatever spat the teenager was having with his cantankerous uncle. Colt did a flying dismount before the horse had even stopped. Mazie stared in awe. She loved how the guys did that and wanted to learn that little trick herself. She frowned when Colt aggressively approached Brandt. Obviously, Brandt did something stupid again. It was mostly his mouth that got him into trouble, and Brandt had been talking back to Colt a little too often lately. Mazie didn't pretend to understand Brandt's cranky moods, but everyone seemed to think it would pass.

"I didn't do anything," Brandt yelled back at Colt. "Stop accusing me of things."

"I keep finding cigarette butts around the barn," Colt launched back. "Never mind that it's extremely dangerous to smoke in the barn, but I won't have you smoking at all. You're fifteen, for Christ's sake!"

"I'm not smoking," Brandt shouted back defensively. "Where would I even get cigarettes?"

"From those hooligan friends of yours," Colt scoffed. "Mischief and mayhem."

"I'm *not* smoking!"

"Fine," Colt snarled. "As soon as we're finished cooling our horses, we'll go up to your room together and have a look."

Brandt sneered and loosened the girth on his saddle. Mazie darted from her rocking chair and quickly slipped into the house. She immediately bolted up the stairs, making as little sound as possible, and paused before the bedroom door with the "Keep Out" sign. Beneath the sign, handwritten, were the words, "This means you, Mazie!" Mazie opened the door without a second of hesitation. Upon entering the room, it was obvious that Brandt had been slipping on his overall room-cleaning duties. He didn't even put forth a half-assed attempt at making his bed that morning, and there were dirty clothes strewn about the floor. She couldn't deny that it grossed her out just a little. Mazie hurried across the room to Brandt's bedside table, opened the nightstand drawer, and removed the pack of cigarettes along with the lighter. She was about to leave the room when she hesitated and went back to the bed. She slipped her hand between the mattress and box spring and removed three girly magazines.

Mazie took the items and headed for the door, then stopped again. She took a moment to gather the scattered, dirty clothes from the floor and stuff them into the nearby hamper. Boys were so messy! She again hesitated, then ran back and quickly made the bed. Although sloppily made, it was better than it had been. Mazie then left the room and hurried to the kitchen stairs. As she reached the back stairs, she heard her uncle and Brandt coming up the front stairs.

*L*ater that evening, Mazie sat on her bed, resting against the headboard, and again wrote in her notebook with a colored pencil. Since it was summertime, there wasn't a mandatory bedtime, but Mazie wanted to spend a little 'alone time' working on her 'masterpiece'. Within her bedroom, she could hear her mother and two uncles on the back patio, having a drink before bedtime. Being all three were on the back patio, Mazie was slightly surprised when she heard a faint tapping on her door. She looked up, now curious.

"Come in," she announced.

The door barely opened when Brandt slipped in and shut it behind him. He leaned his back against the closed door and eyed her where she sat up in bed.

"Oh, it's you," she remarked, then returned to her notebook. "I thought you'd be out with your friends, Mischief and Mayhem."

"Funny," Brandt scoffed, then raised his brows. "I know it was you. Where's my stuff?"

"Stuff?" she asked, finally looking up. "What stuff?"

"You know what stuff," he demanded.

She nodded to the nightstand drawer closest to him. Brandt approached the small nightstand and opened the top drawer. He removed his cigarettes, lighter, and girly magazines.

"I really wish you'd stay out of my room," Brandt muttered.

"If I had, you'd be grounded," she reminded him.

Brandt placed the cigarettes and lighter in his pants pocket, then subconsciously rolled up the three magazines in his hand while fidgeting.

"Probably," he muttered while looking down, and frowned. "Thanks for having my back."

Mazie looked up and stared at him, slightly surprised. "That must've hurt," she remarked.

Brandt snorted a laugh and managed a tiny smile. "A little," he replied, then held up the rolled magazines. "You saved me a little embarrassment, although it's probably more embarrassing that you know about them."

"Just confirms that you're weird," she informed him, then hesitated and cocked her head. "It doesn't make you cool, you know."

"What's that?" Brandt asked.

"Smoking," she replied.

Brandt frowned and subconsciously patted his pants pocket with the outline of the cigarette pack. "Yeah, I know," he replied. "I actually can't stand it."

Mazie stared at him, completely confused. "Then why are you doing it? To upset Uncle Colt?"

"No, definitely not," Brandt groaned, then shrugged. "All my friends smoke."

"Again, not cool," she reminded him.

Brandt collapsed onto the edge of her bed while looking down at the bedspread. "You don't understand what it's like," he informed her. "Half my friends moved away, and the other half don't go to the same school anymore since they redrew the township line. I'm having a tough time fitting in, and it's only going to be worse next year when I go to high school."

Mazie studied Brandt's defeated look for a moment in silence. "Is that why you're so moody lately?"

"Maybe," Brandt muttered. "I don't know. I always fit in before. All my school friends were ranchers. We were all raised the same. I thought everything was perfect." He hesitated. "Now, I feel like I'm the outcast. I never worried about going to school smelling like horses or cattle before, but I'm self-conscious about it every day. The other boys act like there's something wrong with me." His head remained down. "My grades suck, and I don't have time for school anyway. I should be here working the ranch, where I'm needed." He finally lifted his head and met her gaze. "I think I'm going to drop out when I turn sixteen."

"No, Brandt," Mazie announced and slid across the bed closer to him. "You don't want to do that."

Brandt shrugged. "It doesn't matter if I graduate," he informed her. "I know what I'm doing with my life. I'm going to be a wrangler like Uncle Colt and Uncle Dalton. I don't need a diploma for that. Why go through the hassle?" He managed a tiny, defeated smile. "I'm not smart like you, Mazie."

"I want to be a wrangler too," she insisted. "I want to work the cattle with you, but Mom says graduating is important." Mazie then hesitated. "You're not stupid, Brandt. When I call you that, I don't really mean it." She placed her hand on his shoulder. "You're the smartest boy I know."

Brandt looked back at her while tilting his head. "I'm not smart," he informed her. "You're wicked smart. You could probably go to college and everything."

"You could, if you wanted to," she informed him.

"There'd be no point," Brandt insisted.

"For me, either," Mazie reminded him. She then groaned and sat on the edge of the bed with him. "Face facts, Brandt. Even if Uncle Colt said you could drop out, there's no way Uncle Dalton will allow it. If you just did a little work, you'd pass without any problems."

"I'm not good at studying," he reminded her.

"So, I'll teach you," she announced. "I wasn't any good at riding and roping, but you taught me. It's my turn to teach you something."

"Well, your roping still sucks," Brandt reminded her, then grinned slyly to see if he got a reaction.

Mazie rolled her eyes.

"But, if you want to waste your time trying to help me," he remarked. "I suppose it would be ungrateful and not very gentlemanly of me to give up without at least giving it a shot."

"We'll get started tomorrow," she announced.

"School doesn't start until September," Brandt reminded her.

"Wouldn't hurt to get a head start," Mazie replied. "We can review different subjects while doing chores together. I'll make some flashcards on your weaker subjects."

Brandt groaned. "I'm already dreading this."

Chapter 11

*T*hirteen years later. Mazie was now twenty-three years old and a beautiful, grown-up woman. She rarely wore her hair in ponytails anymore, except when she was exercising, and the days of wearing sports bras and dressing like a tomboy were behind her. She left those behind, along with the ranch. Now, she often wore a little eyeliner and more neutral shades of lipstick. She'd also traded her cowgirl boots in for high heels, which usually hurt her feet, but they looked good when she wore skirts and dresses. After her morning jog, Mazie sat on the marble bench in the apartment complex garden, filled with mostly green, leafy plants and a few colorful perennials. Mazie held her knees to her chest while lost in her own thoughts as she watched the sunrise. It was going to be another beautiful day, and yet she sat in the garden feeling uninspired. Her watch suddenly beeped, returning her to reality and reminding her that she needed to get moving or risk being late.

Mazie stood and headed across the courtyard within the city apartment complex, returning to her apartment on the sixth floor. After a quick shower, Mazie changed into her black business-casual pantsuit and black high heels, then caught a taxi to work. She checked her watch several times as she crossed the office building lobby and just barely made the elevator. Once she reached the fourteenth floor, Mazie paused before the third suite door. On the frosted glass was the company name, Davenport Productions. She drew a deep breath, preparing herself for another day, and entered the suite, greeting the receptionist on the way to her office. Mazie's office was ultra-modern with large windows along the entire side wall, marble flooring, and textured tile walls. Frameless bookshelves occupied the wall behind her minimalist wooden desk with drawers. There was no warmth, charm, or personality to the office, but it was functional and projected success. Mazie barely got a cup of tea made when there was a knock on her open office door. She turned and saw her boss, Davenport, the owner and president of Davenport Productions.

Mazie's boss was a gruff-looking man in his late thirties to early forties. His skin was weathered, possibly from basking in the bright LA sun for a few too many years, and his short dark hair was receding, although not enough to be considered bald. He was five-foot-ten and built moderately lean, being neither athletic nor muscular from the pampered life with which he'd grown accustomed. Complimenting his outward appearance, he had a deplorable personality to match. Although caring little for anyone other than himself, he was a great ass kisser when it came to his movie stars. Mazie, on the other hand, was always on the short end of his not-so-charming personality. Despite the way he treated her, she heard from numerous sources that she was one of the few people he actually liked. Davenport entered her office in a whirlwind of enthusiasm and cast himself into the chair in front of her desk.

"We found it, Mazie," Davenport announced proudly while pulling up something on his portable tablet. "It's perfect!"

Mazie sat on the edge of her desk and accepted the tablet from him. Before even reading the article, her eyes instantly gravitated to the scenic picture. Mazie's heart nearly sank when she saw the gates to Major's Thunder Basin Ranch. The majestic picture was so familiar, it was almost haunting. Mazie felt her entire body tense, and she immediately looked at her boss. He stared at her, somewhat surprised.

"You're not going to read the article?" he asked.

"Are you sure this is the place?" Mazie asked, almost unable to get the words out.

"Well, I need you to go out there and scout it out first, but it's exactly what we've been looking for," he informed her before turning suspicious. "Is something wrong? You don't like it?"

"It's just, well," she began, then held her breath a moment before blurting out the ugly truth. "I know the guy who, uh, runs the place."

"That's in our favor."

"Well, we sort of had a falling out five years ago," Mazie informed him.

Her boss shifted in his chair and gave her the look he always used right before telling her she had no choice but to do what he wanted.

"Our options are limited, Mazie," Davenport reminded her. "I can send someone else out there to broker a deal with him, but I know how these cattle rancher types can be. They don't like strangers. We hired you four years ago because even the worst of the worst were willing to deal with you. You've got that 'girl-next-door' appeal." He studied her a moment longer. "Now, are you telling me you won't even attempt to broker this deal for us? The company that pays you handsomely for your best efforts?"

"I'm not saying I won't," Mazie insisted. "It's just that his feelings toward me might kill the deal before it's even brought up. He may not even want to talk to me."

"Did you dump him at the altar?"

"No, of course not," Mazie interjected, then fidgeted. "Our relationship wasn't like that. We were more like, well, brother and sister."

"If you didn't leave him at the altar, I don't see any reason why you can't broker this deal," Davenport insisted. "And, despite what you seem to be inferring, I'm willing to bet money that he'd be willing to talk to you, but it's you who doesn't want to talk to him."

Mazie couldn't respond to his comment, which told him everything he needed to know. Her boss leaned forward and studied her.

"It's your job, Mazie," Davenport announced. "Either you go out and do your job or be replaced by someone who will." He leaned back in his chair. "What are your thoughts now?"

Mazie knew damned well he'd carry through with his threat, and she needed her job. She'd never find anything else in the entire city that paid as well as her current position. It's why she tolerated her boss.

"Okay," Mazie replied with a defeated sigh. "I'll talk to him by the end of the week."

Her boss smiled and leaned back in his chair. "That's what I like to hear."

$\mathcal{M}$azie sat at her desk all afternoon, staring at her phone while tapping her pen repeatedly on the leather desk blotter. She was still gathering her courage to make the phone call. She had an ingenious plan, if only she could muster the nerve to make the phone call. She'd call her mother, arrange for her to come to the city, and have her mother pitch the deal to Brandt. After all, she lived in the same house with him for the last eighteen years and saw him multiple times a day. Surely she could find five minutes to talk to him about the studio's offer. If it was so easy, why couldn't Mazie force herself to pick up the phone? There was a tapping on her closed office door, nearly startling her. She took a moment to contain her racing heart and attempted to relax.

"Come in," she announced.

The door opened, and her friend from the office building entered, looking a little too cheerful for Mazie's mood. Andi was an attractive woman in her late twenties with long, nearly black, wavy hair. She was a short, petite woman, standing only a little over five feet tall, dressed in an exceptionally fashionable manner.

"Hey, Mazie," Andi announced while crossing the room and flopping into the closest chair. "I thought you went out. I tried calling a couple of times this afternoon, but you didn't answer."

"I've been working on a proposal," Mazie remarked, then frowned. "It's a real pain in the ass."

"Anything I can help with?"

"You can dial my mother's phone number and make sure I don't hang up the phone before she answers," Mazie informed her.

"Your mother?" Andi asked with surprise. "I thought the two of you got along."

"We do, it's just--" She hesitated and considered her words carefully. "Davenport is putting me in a bad situation with, well, Brandt, and I don't want to deal with it."

"Oh, Brandt," Andi announced. "Your rancher friend from childhood."

"Yeah, that's the one." Mazie roused her best smile. "What brings you slumming down to the fourteenth floor? Tired of the view from the twentieth floor?"

"Hardly," Andi replied, then laughed. "I just wanted to let you know that I passed your manuscript along to my literary agent friend."

"I appreciate you doing that," Mazie replied, feeling slightly rejuvenated. "I've had that thing sitting around collecting dust for a few years now, and I could really use some suggestions on how to finish it." She cringed. "Maybe I should have reread it before you let him look at it. I can't even remember the last time I touched it. It's probably filled with typos."

"He's just doing it as a favor," Andi reminded her. "He's not going to care if there are typos. He knows it's an incomplete rough draft, and he's more than happy to help you out."

"As long as he has low expectations," Mazie informed her. "It's not as if it's a thriller or anything. Pretty boring stuff. I'd just like to say I've finally finished writing an actual book."

"I know what you mean," Andi replied. "I was thrilled when I finally finished my first needlepoint pillow. Took nearly ten years, but I did it."

"Oh?" Mazie remarked while smiling. "I'd love to see that sometime."

"Yeah, so would I," Andi announced. "The puppy tore it up two days later."

The phone rang, startling Mazie. She looked at the caller ID and just about gasped.

"It's my mother," Mazie whispered.

"And that's my cue," Andi announced and stood. "Talk to your mother, you big baby."

Mazie frowned as her friend left her office, shutting the door behind her for some privacy. Mazie took a deep breath and then picked up the phone.

"Mom, hi," Mazie announced into the phone. "I was, uh, just thinking about you."

"I hadn't heard from you in almost a week," Liddy replied from the other end. "I figured I'd better call and check on you. See when you're planning on coming home for a visit."

"I doubt that's happening," Mazie informed her, then smiled. "But I'd love to bring you out here. The boss's private jet can even pick you up if you don't mind an early morning flight."

"Mazie," Liddy groaned lowly. "I've come out to see you a dozen times already. Just once, I'd like you to come home for a visit. Everyone misses you. They want to see you."

Mazie shifted uncomfortably and struggled for something to say. "I can't, Mom," she finally replied. "I just, well, I just can't."

There was an unusual silence.

"Why can't you tell me what happened?" Liddy lightly demanded. "I've been more than patient, Mazie."

"We just can't get along, Mom," Mazie insisted. "I don't want to fight with him."

"Tell me what you fought about," Liddy pressed. "I'll find a way to smooth things over between you."

"Have you tried asking him?" Mazie finally asked.

"He keeps insisting there's nothing wrong between you," Liddy replied. "That man is more stubborn than you are."

"Look, Mom," Mazie announced. "I need you to do me a favor. It'll take you two minutes."

There was another pause.

"No, Mazie," Liddy scoffed, standing firm for once. "If you want me to do you any favors, you need to come out here and see me. We don't have to meet at the ranch, but you have to come out here. I want you to come home even if it's only to the diner."

Mazie groaned lowly. "Fine," she replied. "I'll take the company jet out tomorrow morning. I should be able to meet you at the diner for breakfast. Nine o'clock?"

"I'll agree to that," Liddy replied. "But I'll pick you up at the private airfield instead."

"That's fine," Mazie replied. "My flight should be there around eight or eight-thirty."

"See you tomorrow morning."

Mazie hung up the phone, sank back in her chair, and groaned loudly.

Chapter 12

avenport's nineteen-million-dollar, nine-passenger Cessna Citation private luxury jet stopped not far from the small private terminal lounge. Once the steps were lowered, Mazie departed the plane. She wore a simple yet expensive sleeveless black dress, a short black jacket over it, and two-inch black heels. Mazie stopped halfway down the few steps when she saw the brand-new, silver pickup truck. Mazie internally groaned at the sight of Colt and Dalton leaning against the front end of the vehicle with boyish grins on their faces. At almost forty-seven years old, Colt hadn't changed much. He maintained the same athletic build from his younger years, but with a few extra pounds, and his light brown hair was now buzzed close to his head. Despite some changes, he retained his facial stubble to maintain his gritty look. Dalton, who was now in his mid-forties, also hadn't changed much over the years. He maintained his imposing physical appearance, though no longer as lean as in his youth. His hair, although still thick, was kept a little shorter with a few gray strands peppered throughout, but he was still a ruggedly handsome man.

Mazie smiled and approached them, carrying only her leather messenger bag. Both men greeted her halfway, overjoyed to see her.

"Who's that beautiful city girl?" Dalton cried out and hugged her, almost refusing to let her go.

As soon as Dalton released her, Colt joined in. "Look at you, all dressed up," Colt announced and gave her the same, bone-breaking embrace.

Between the two of them, they must have asked her a dozen questions in the few yards it took to reach the truck. She was immediately scooted into the middle of the front bench seat, positioned between the two men. Despite her initial surprise at seeing the two men instead of her mother at the airfield, she couldn't deny that it was good to see them again after five years.

"Where's your bag?" Colt asked as he drove the truck away from the airfield. "Did we forget to grab it?"

"I don't need a bag," she informed them. "I'm only visiting for the day."

"That's not what Liddy said," Dalton informed her. "She said you were staying the entire weekend."

"I think she was mistaken," Mazie remarked. "If I don't leave by six o'clock tonight, I won't have the jet until Monday morning."

"Monday morning works," Colt announced.

"I'm leaving tonight," she insisted. "My boss is expecting me tomorrow morning to review our current projects."

"What kind of jerk boss makes you work on Saturday?" Colt demanded.

Dalton gently cleared his throat. "We make the guys work Saturdays," he reminded him.

"Completely different situation," Colt insisted. "Working on a cattle ranch is like working in a hospital. You need all shifts covered."

"If my 'jerk boss' works Saturday, I work Saturday," she informed them. "That's the way it is." Mazie then asked the question she needed to ask. "Where's my mom? She said she was picking me up at the airfield."

"I believe she was changing the sheets on your bed and freshening your room," Dalton replied. "She'll be at the diner by nine."

"That's good," Mazie replied. "I was hoping you weren't planning on taking me to the ranch because that wasn't part of the plan."

Dalton and Colt glanced at each other past Mazie and frowned.

"Oh, so we're going to the diner first?" Dalton asked, now curious.

"I'm starting to think no one let us in on the actual plan," Colt remarked.

"And this is why I didn't want to come home," Mazie informed them. "Out of fear that I'd be abducted and forced into an intervention."

"I'm pretty sure I heard nothing about an intervention," Colt insisted. "And the abduction was only mentioned in jest. At least, I'm pretty sure it was just in jest." He then looked past her at Dalton. "Abducting her *was* in jest, right?"

"With Liddy, there's really no telling," Dalton casually replied.

Mazie eyed both men sitting on either side of her like centuries on duty. "You guys still aren't funny," she informed them, to which they both laughed.

§

*C*olt and Dalton dropped Mazie off at the small country diner, where her mother was already waiting outside to greet her. Forty-five-year-old Liddy was still as attractive as she was when she first arrived at the ranch all those years ago. Her dirty blonde hair was now a little longer, and she seemed to take extra care fixing it. Now that she had the time and money, she wore eyeliner and lipstick most days. She maintained her athletic build, mainly due to the time she spent exercising, now that she didn't need to work as hard as she had before working at the ranch. Life had been far kinder to her in the past two decades than in her early twenties. She traded in her worn, moderately dated clothes and sensible shoes for more stylish outfits and more expensive, sensible shoes. Liddy happily hugged Mazie in front of the diner, not caring at all if they blocked the entrance.

"It's been so long since I've held my baby," Liddy announced for the entire town to hear.

It was endearing and embarrassing at the same time. They received a few stray looks from several locals, but none commented. Liddy then ushered Mazie inside, where they found a booth near the back of the relatively crowded diner in a less-traveled area for more privacy. After the standard Q&A session and the waitress taking their breakfast order, Mazie decided to dive right into her reason for showing up with little advance warning. She wasn't sure she could deal with finding out why her two uncles thought she was staying the entire weekend. That would have to wait until later.

"Mom, about that favor," Mazie finally managed to blurt out her thoughts.

"Oh, yes, I'm sorry," Liddy announced and gave Mazie her full attention along with a smile that almost made Mazie suspicious. "What was it you wanted to ask?"

"My boss wants to film a couple of scenes at the ranch," Mazie informed her. "Because he lost the last location to a surprise flood, he's willing to pay a sizable chunk of change for the privilege, and it's only for a relatively short period of time. Two weeks tops with minimal crew. It's a fantastic deal and great exposure for the ranch."

Liddy held up her hand, stopping Mazie from completing her sales pitch. "Why are you telling me all this as if you're trying to sell me on it?" she asked. "Is that the favor you wanted from me? You want me to pitch the idea to Brandt?"

Mazie shifted uncomfortably in her seat. "That was the general idea," she muttered while frowning.

"No, absolutely not," Liddy announced, firm. "The fact that the two of you don't talk and haven't talked in five years is where I draw the line. You need a favor from Brandt? You talk to Brandt. Talk to each other like adults and get over this disagreement between you two. I'm not getting drawn into it unless it's to resolve the problem between you."

"Mom, you don't understand," Mazie tried to explain without really explaining.

"So make me understand," Liddy replied almost commandingly. "Unless he did something violent or criminal, you can work it out."

Mazie looked down at the table while maintaining her frown. She didn't know how to respond. Meeting with Brandt face-to-face was right up there with walking on broken glass. She didn't know how she'd do it, even if it wouldn't actually kill her.

Liddy leaned back in her seat and stared at Mazie for a long moment before speaking. "I'm sorry for raising my voice," she announced. "But things had to be said." Her mother straightened proudly. "This is what's going to happen. We're having Brandt's twenty-ninth birthday party tomorrow, and you are requested to attend. And when I say request, I mean required."

"You've been hanging out with Uncle Colt too long," Mazie muttered, then ran her fingers through her hair while sitting forward. "I don't think that's a good idea."

"I don't know what's going on between the two of you, but it's his birthday," Liddy reminded her. "I know he misses you, and he'd want you there."

"Too many things were said, Mom," Mazie remarked. "Things I don't want to talk about. It's just--it's better if we didn't rehash it."

"Fine, don't talk to him," Liddy scoffed. "But you're coming for Brandt's birthday BBQ tomorrow, and that's final. He's been like a son to me and a brother to you, so call your boss, tell him you're taking off tomorrow, and be at that party."

Mazie groaned, then removed her cell phone from her pocket and pressed a button while holding the phone to her ear.

"Hey, Ross," she announced into her cell phone. "It's me. Could you drop off my bag in the private terminal before you fly out tonight? It, uh, looks like I'll be staying until Monday." Mazie listened to the man on the other end. "No, that's not necessary. I'll pick it up on my way to the motel."

"Motel?" Liddy demanded, then raised her brows, silently scolding her daughter. "You have a perfectly good room at the ranch."

Mazie sank in her seat, somehow feeling like a teenager again and in trouble for something. "If it's really no trouble," she announced to the pilot on the phone, "I'll text you the address of the ranch."

Liddy smiled almost smugly and sipped her tea like an aristocrat. Her mother had clearly won that round. Mazie disconnected her call, sent the promised text to the pilot, and finally looked at her mother.

"Do they still have rental cars at the local garage?" Mazie asked.

"You don't need a rental car," Liddy insisted. "Your Jeep is at the farm and is in perfect working condition. I sometimes use it on the weekends."

Mazie wasn't sure when her mother turned into a clone of her Uncle Colt, but she was doing a good job at impersonating him. Mazie sank back in her seat. It was going to be a long weekend.

Chapter 13

As Liddy and Mazie were leaving the diner after breakfast, Mazie felt an overwhelming sense of dread. Being taken back to the ranch somehow felt like the Green Mile. A slow walk to her execution with her mother leading the march. The thought of seeing Brandt after five years was enough to evoke a range of emotions, all too complex to comprehend.

"Oh, my God!" a woman screeched. "Mazie!"

Mazie looked up and saw her old childhood friend, Melissa. Her friend had transformed into a beautiful young woman. Possibly even considered glamorous. Melissa was a tick under five-foot-four with sparkling hazel eyes and a bright, unforgettable smile. Although considered heavyset throughout high school, she was now just slightly robust, with curves in all the right places. The simple country girl had become more of a fashion statement, wearing modern and alluring clothes that definitely cost more than she could afford when they were younger. The last time she saw Melissa was right before her friend left for college. Mazie was aware that Melissa had gotten a job in their hometown that paid enough to afford a lifestyle she had never had growing up. Melissa was finally living her dream. Mazie's smile returned as the two women shared a warm embrace, before Melissa pulled back and looked Mazie over in the dress and high heels, with genuine surprise.

"Wow, you clean up nicely," Melissa remarked. "Are you wearing makeup?" Her eyes widened as she gasped and pointed at her feet. "And high heels?"

Mazie looked at her shoes and laughed. "Yeah, unfortunately," she replied. "Where I work, I'm at the low end of high maintenance. Security at the office building probably wouldn't even let me in if I took it down even one notch."

"Well, you're gorgeous," Melissa insisted. "Too fancy for this one-horse town."

"Me?" Mazie announced. "Look at you! You look like you belong in LA!"

"I'd be lying if I said I didn't do a little shopping on Rodeo Drive," Melissa announced with a giggle. "Where do you work?"

"I work for Davenport Productions in Los Angeles."

Melissa's expression suddenly dropped. "Not the film company," she gasped.

"Yeah, that's the one," Mazie replied.

"Wow," Melissa gasped and grabbed Mazie's arm. "We definitely have to catch up, but not without Cameron. She'd never forgive us."

Mazie eyed her mother, patiently waiting not far from her sporty four-wheel-drive car. "My, uh, ride is ready to leave," she remarked. "Unless you wanted to--"

"Absolutely," Melissa cried out, then waved to Liddy. "It's okay, Mrs. Crane. I'll give her a ride home in a couple of hours."

Liddy nodded and returned the acknowledging wave before getting into her car.

"She's not happy," Mazie muttered while secretly hiding her grin. "She's hoping Brandt and I will bury the hatchet this weekend."

"Are you still not talking to him?" Melissa asked, somewhat surprised.

"It's not that I'm not speaking to him," Mazie explained. "It's more like 'actively avoiding'."

"Don't catch me up just yet," Melissa insisted. "We're heading to the bank to grab Cameron for lunch. She'll want to hear all the juicy details, too."

It was only a short walk through the quaint little town, past the small park to the bank. Melissa and Cameron often met for lunch during their breaks and ate in the park. Mazie was glad it wasn't a 'walking' lunch since she wouldn't get far in her heels. The local bank was old-school both inside and outside. It was a two-story, block-stone building with stunning architecture, featuring rounded stained-glass windows and faux pillars in the front. Just inside, beyond the tacky carpeting, was a long, multiple-teller desk with old-fashioned bars on each window, possibly straight out of the 1800s. Most of the old wooden walls were now painted white to brighten the interior. Melissa hid Mazie behind her as they approached Cameron at her teller window.

Cameron was still the same beautiful, fresh-faced girl that Mazie remembered. She stood about five-foot-five with sandy blonde hair that hung down to her shoulders, blue eyes, and a beautiful smile. She still flaunted her perfect body, but in a more graceful manner than when she was younger. It was apparent that Cameron had matured the most out of all of them.

"Hey, Cam," Melissa announced. "I brought you a surprise."

Cameron looked up and smiled. "Oh?"

Melissa stepped aside to reveal Mazie. Cameron's eyes widened, and she suddenly screamed loud enough to startle the entire bank. Cameron put up her closed sign, then ran around the back of the other tellers and bolted through a security door. She excitedly hugged Mazie, then pulled back and studied her.

"Wow!" Cameron cried out. "You look--" She shook her head. "There are no words."

A well-dressed man in a suit appeared from the security door and approached Cameron.

"What is going on out here?" the man just about demanded. "People think we're being robbed."

"Sorry, Blake," Cameron announced, unable to contain her grin. "This is my friend, Mazie. I haven't seen her in five years. It was quite the surprise."

Blake was a somewhat attractive man in his early thirties, with short, sandy-brown hair. He was built lean to athletic, standing about six-foot. Given the small-town atmosphere, his suit seemed particularly expensive, though Mazie worked with many producer types who wore far more expensive suits.

Cameron proudly introduced her friend to her boss. "Mazie, this is my boss, Blake."

Mazie stared at the unfamiliar yet somehow familiar man, taking a moment before finally recognizing him from her past.

Chapter 14

*F*lashback. Eleven-year-old Mazie had blossomed into a beautiful pre-teen young lady. Although she still wore her longer hair in a ponytail, she maintained her outwardly tomboyish appearance, often wearing oversized flannel shirts and her cowgirl boots. Her mother hated the flannel shirts, particularly because they were excessively baggy, and Mazie had refused to tuck them in. She was going through a frumpy, pre-puberty stage. Where most girls seemed to lean toward wearing dresses and experimenting with makeup, Mazie just wanted her baggy flannel shirts. And privacy. Plenty of privacy. Her body was in a state of transition, and she wasn't happy about it. Mazie didn't want to be reminded that she was different than Brandt, and she certainly didn't want him to realize it either. She attempted to sink into obscurity while cleaning her saddle, pretending she didn't hear the ongoing feud that started earlier that day. Sixteen-year-old Brandt squared off against his Uncle Colt, who somehow didn't seem nearly as intimidating now that Brandt was older.

Brandt was already almost six-foot-tall with plenty of growing left. He wasn't nearly as lanky as he had been just a couple of years ago, now finally starting to fill in. Despite all the changes he'd been going through, his dark hair remained slightly longer and still unkempt from wearing cowboy hats most of the day.

"I'm sixteen, Uncle Colt," Brandt insisted with his arms folded across his now broad chest. "I don't see why I can't go."

"And the boys you want to hang out with are college kids," Colt reminded him. "You're not hanging out with a bunch of older kids at the pond. There's going to be drinking and lewd behavior."

"They're my friends," Brandt informed him. "I won't be drinking. Everyone who's anyone will be there for the pond and the bonfire. If I don't go, they're going to think less of me."

"Well, then they're obviously not your friends, now are they?" he demanded.

"You're not being fair," Brandt insisted.

"You're right," Colt replied. "Because life isn't fair. Deal with it, boy. You're not going, and that's final."

Rather than continue the argument, Brandt frowned, accepted the loss, and walked away. Colt drew a deep breath and leaned on his horse's rump while shaking his head. He caught Mazie's glance and suddenly realized she'd been there for the whole tantrum. Mazie sighed and shook her head.

"Where did we go wrong with that boy?" Mazie remarked and then resumed cleaning her saddle.

Colt hid his smile and had to turn away to keep from laughing.

*T*hat afternoon, Mazie sat straight and perched on her chair across the kitchen table from Brandt, who sat slouched while chewing the sides of his fingernails.

"Why don't I remember that question the last time we went through this?" Brandt just about demanded.

"Because you were too busy chewing your fingernails instead of paying attention," Mazie huffed and returned to the booklet. "You may turn right on red if you: A. Stop first and check for pedestrians. B. Are facing a red arrow. C. Are in the left lane. D. Slow down first."

"D. Slow down first," Brandt replied.

"A. Stop first," she informed him, then groaned with disgust while attempting to scratch her back with her colored pencil. "We've gone over this so many times, I could pass this test."

"Mind your manners, shrimp," Brandt scoffed. "Or else, once I get my car, your little butt can keep taking the bus to school."

"What kind of car are you going to get?" Mazie asked, now curious as she resorted to scratching her back on the chair. "Something cool?"

"None, if Uncle Colt and Uncle Dalton don't raise my allowance," Brandt muttered, then sighed with defeat. "I'll probably get a beater truck."

"What's a beater truck?" she asked while again attempting to scratch her back with the pencil.

"An old truck held together with baling twine, Bondo, and duct tape," Brandt scoffed.

"Sounds attractive," Mazie muttered while making a face.

"Yeah, that's what all the girls will say too," Brandt groaned.

Mazie scratched her back again with the pencil and suddenly yelped while lurching forward. Brandt groaned and sat up straight.

"Didn't you learn your lesson about scratching with pencils when you had the cast on your arm?" Brandt demanded.

Mazie suddenly jumped up from her chair and attempted to grab the pencil seemingly stuck through her shirt. Brandt leapt from his chair and approached her.

"What did you do?" Brandt cried out. "Jab yourself with it?"

"I don't know," she cried out while frantically attempting to reach it, now in actual pain.

"Stop moving," Brandt insisted, grabbing her arm and forcing her to remain still.

He plucked the pencil from her back and then checked her shirt for blood. Brandt suddenly hesitated and felt her back.

"What is that?" Brandt asked.

Mazie attempted to pull away from him, but wasn't strong enough. "Nothing," she cried out. "Leave me alone."

Brandt ignored her and lifted her shirt in the back. When he saw a thick layer of duct tape across her back, he stared in horror. The entire area surrounding the tape was red and inflamed.

"What the hell--?" Brandt gasped. "What happened?"

"Leave it alone!"

"Liddy!"

*L*ater that afternoon. Mazie sat up in bed, holding her knees to her chest with her face buried in her legs as she softly sobbed. Liddy was leaving the room as Brandt approached with a concerned look on his face.

"Is she okay?" Brandt asked.

"Just some minor abrasions and irritation," Liddy replied. "Nothing a little ointment won't cure. She'll be fine in a day or two."

"What happened?" Brandt whispered. "Why was she wrapped in duct tape?"

"Some kids from her school were teasing her," Liddy informed him. "But she's pretty embarrassed, so that's all I'm going to say."

"Can I see her?" Brandt asked.

Liddy nodded, then left the room. Brandt approached the bed and sat on the edge facing her.

"Hey, are you okay?" Brandt asked.

Mazie sniffed but didn't respond.

"Did the other kids do this to you?" Brandt asked. "Who were they?"

"I did it to myself," she whispered between sniffs.

"Why, Mazie?"

There was a strange moment of silence as she considered whether she wanted to confess or not.

"The other kids make fun of me," Mazie whispered with a trembling voice. "I don't like them. None of the other girls have them."

"I wouldn't like those kids either," Brandt insisted.

"Not the kids," she sobbed. "*Them*. None of the other girls have *them*. And they're only getting *bigger*."

Brandt suddenly tensed and stared at her, finally understanding what she was saying. "You used duct tape as a binder?" he asked, stunned. "To conceal--?"

"It was stupid," Mazie whispered. "It worked, but I couldn't get it off." She sniffed and lifted her head while harshly wiping her tears from her face. "I don't know what to do."

"There's nothing to do," Brandt insisted. "You'll be a little tender and itchy for a day or two, but the irritation will go away."

"Not that," Mazie huffed. "How do I get rid of them? I can't be a wrangler with boobs."

Brandt shifted uncomfortably but kept his attention on her. "You don't get 'rid' of them," he informed her. "And who said you can't be a wrangler if you have boobs?"

"You did," she replied.

"I never said that," he suddenly protested.

"You don't want to hang out with girls," she reminded him. "You said so when we first met. As long as I'm one of the boys, you'll let me hang around."

Brandt nearly fell off the bed, unable to process what she was saying. "Jesus, don't let Uncle Colt hear that, he'll skip right past whooping and go straight to castration." He moved further up the bed, putting himself closer to her. "Mazie, I was a stupid little boy back then. I said stupid stuff. Half the crap I say now is still stupid. I'm the last person you should listen to." He drew a deep breath, met her tear-streaked gaze, and gently wiped away her tears. "You are who you are, Mazie. It doesn't matter how you look or dress, we're family, and I'll accept you the way you are. Don't ever hide who you are from me. In this house, we can be ourselves. The kids who bully and shame us don't matter. Not even a little."

Mazie sniffed while staring at Brandt, then managed a tiny giggle. "You sound like Uncle Colt."

"Yeah, pretty sad, huh?" Brandt remarked, then leaned forward and kissed her on the top of the head. "No more stupid stuff from you. You're smarter than that."

Chapter 15

*I*t was nearly ten o'clock that evening, and everyone had turned in. Mazie woke to the sound of horses snickering. She crawled out of bed and looked outside her bedroom window, which lined up with the distant barn. She saw Brandt sneaking into the barn. Mazie considered it only a moment, then changed and hurried from the house. Mazie approached the dimly lit barn and entered. It was odd that he had only turned on the tack room light rather than the main barn lights. Brandt was nearly finished saddling his horse when he saw her and jumped.

"Jesus, Mazie," he moaned. "You scared me. What are you doing up?"

"I saw you sneaking out here," she replied.

"I wasn't sneaking."

She raised a skeptical brow. "You didn't turn the barn light on," Mazie remarked. "You saddled your horse in the dark. That's sneaking."

Brandt groaned at her logic. "Fine, I was sneaking out," he informed her. "Uncle Colt said I couldn't hang out at Old

Mill Pond with my friends, which is completely stupid and unfair."

Mazie folded her arms across her chest and raised her brow. "I've heard about your friends," she informed him. "They're all pretty stupid."

"Yeah, funny," he scoffed. "Don't you dare tattle on me."

"I won't," she muttered before her eyes suddenly lit up. "Can I come?"

"No," he replied firmly. "Guys only. No girls allowed."

"You know," she announced, matter-of-factly. "You're still mean."

"Good," he scoffed and mounted his horse inside the barn. "Go to bed, and keep this to yourself. I'll be back before anyone knows I'm gone."

She frowned and waved him off. "Yeah, whatever," Mazie muttered. "Have fun."

Mazie watched Brandt ride across the pasture and head into the woods. She considered it only a moment, then smiled and headed for her horse's stall.

*B*randt sat around the massive bonfire with his older friends, both guys and girls. Old Mill Pond was aptly named because of the old, well-preserved grist mill. The old mill was a beautiful, two-and-a-half-story stone building with a large, mostly intact wheel still attached to one side. The grist mill seemingly rose from the depths of the large pond. Beyond the pond was a large, grassy area where the teenagers had set up their bonfire. Nearly a dozen cars were parked on the secluded, overgrown lane, which wasn't visible from the road, making Old Mill Pond the perfect teenager hangout. Oddly enough, teenagers had been coming to the local hangout for many generations, yet the police never raided the underage drinking parties. It was an unspoken rule, letting kids be kids. The teenagers played loud music, drank beer, and had a good time around the bonfire and skinny-dipping in the pond. Several boys watched two drunken women dance around the bonfire in their lacy bras and underwear. There were plenty of snickers and lewd comments.

Mazie tied her black and white horse, Katona, alongside Brandt's black horse and made her way closer to the fire. One of the boys checked her out as he passed and handed her a bottle of beer. She eyed the bottle with a strange look, then continued to case the scene. At least one couple was making out in the pond, and possibly engaging in more intimate activities. Two other couples were seen making out not far from the bonfire, and strange moans were heard from somewhere out of sight. As Mazie got closer to the bonfire, she received several looks from the guys.

"Careful, boys," one of the guys announced and nodded at Mazie several yards away. "We have some jailbait joining our party."

All the guys instinctively looked for the aforementioned young one, also catching Brandt's attention. When Brandt saw Mazie, he spit out his beer.

"I'll be right back," Brandt announced and made a beeline for Mazie.

Brandt snatched the beer bottle from her hand and tossed it aside, then caught her arm, pulling her several feet away before spinning to face her.

"What are you doing here?" he demanded.

Mazie looked at the drunken women now dancing topless. "I thought you said it was boys only?" she remarked, then indicated the older girls. "Those girls don't have any tops on."

Brandt spun her around and blocked her view of the naked women. "I told you not to come here," he scoffed.

"No, you told me not to follow you," she insisted. "I didn't follow you. I know where Old Mill Pond is without following you."

"Mazie, I'm going to kill you," he snarled and pulled her back toward the horses. "You need to go home. You can't be here."

"Why not?" she demanded. "You're here."

A drunken college boy walked past and eyed them, then snickered at Brandt. "That's a no-no, Brandt," he announced. "Way too young."

Brandt tensed and waited for the guy to pass before looking back at Mazie. "You need to leave, now," he insisted. "This is no place for a little girl."

"Stop calling me a little girl," she scoffed and pulled her arm from his hand. "I hate when you call me that. I'm practically a teenager."

College-aged Blake approached them and casually leaned on Brandt's shoulder while eyeing Mazie. "Who's your friend, Brandt?" he asked while grinning. "Introduce me."

"She's not my friend," Brandt insisted. "She's my, uh--" He became frustrated and shook his head. "Never mind. She was just leaving."

"I don't want to go," Mazie insisted. "I don't even know any of the people here. I want to meet your friends."

Two high school senior boys approached Mazie, grinning. "What's going on, Brandt?" the first older teen asked. "Who's the girl?"

"Kind of young but cute," the second guy remarked.

"She's eleven, and she's off limits," Brandt informed him.

"Eleven?" the older teen asked, then laughed. "Our first real virgin. Get the girl a beer!"

The second guy laughed while moving in on them. "Get her a juice box," he teased.

There was a round of laughter at Mazie's expense, not that she entirely understood what they were even talking about. She didn't drink juice boxes.

Brandt stepped in front of Mazie and glared at the three older teenage boys. "She's just a kid," he announced. "Show some respect."

"Nothing but respect, Brandt," Blake announced while laughing. "We brought easy fucks, but you brought us an honest-to-goodness virgin to corrupt."

Mazie eyed the drunken man with a slightly bewildered and concerned look. Before she even knew what had happened, Brandt punched his friend in the mouth with a fast, hard hit. Blake immediately dropped to the ground and writhed around while clutching his bleeding mouth.

"Don't *ever* disrespect Mazie," Brandt snarled in anger, then glared at the other older boys, prepared to take them on, if necessary.

Mazie looked from the older teen on the ground to Brandt's tightly clenched fist with scraped and bleeding knuckles. She couldn't deny she was almost stunned at what she'd just witnessed. She'd never seen Brandt behave that way before, and it was a little frightening. The three older teens must have seen what Mazie saw and slowly backed away from Brandt.

"You need to leave, Brandt," one of the guys announced.

"Way ahead of you," Brandt snarled back without even twitching.

The older teens helped Blake to his feet and backed away from Brandt. Once the guys were closer to the bonfire, Brandt loosened his fists, grabbed Mazie's arm, and yanked her behind him toward the horses.

"What's happening?" she cried out.

"We need to get out of here before one of them grows a pair and looks for payback," he announced.

"Payback?" she asked.

Brandt untied their horses and effortlessly tossed her onto her horse. The raw power behind him was a bit alarming. As Brandt mounted his horse, Mazie looked across the field and saw several older boys approaching them. Brandt untied the remaining horses from his position on his horse, then yelled at the horses, scaring them away. He then spun his horse and chased Mazie across the field. The older boys could be heard shouting and screaming profanities at him. Mazie rode alongside Brandt at a gallop until they reached the woods, where they slowed and took the trail at a fast walk.

"What happened back there?" Mazie asked, now slightly panicked by how quickly things had escalated.

"A bunch of pissed off, drunken Neanderthals," Brandt informed her.

"Yeah, I got that," she remarked. "But why did you hit the guy? That only pissed them off."

"They were drunken college boys, Mazie," he replied. "Drunk and not thinking straight. If I hadn't made an example of the first one, they may have outnumbered me to get to you."

"Why would they care about me?" she asked with surprise. "They don't even know me. I certainly didn't piss them off."

Brandt groaned and vigorously ran his fingers through his hair. "They wanted to have sex with you, Mazie," he finally blurted out.

"Ewe!" she cried out. "That wasn't happening."

Brandt released a deep sigh. "They may not have asked nicely," he replied.

"But you said they were your friends," she insisted, now confused. "Why would your friends even think something gross like that?"

"I guess they weren't my friends," he informed her, then shook his head. "I hate when Uncle Colt is right."

They rode a moment in silence.

She finally looked at him. "Why are some guys like that?" Mazie asked.

"Not enough ass whooping growing up," he muttered.

"Well, I guess we don't need to worry about you then," she remarked.

When Brandt cast a sideways look at her, Mazie flashed a smile at him. He hid his smile and chuckled softly.

"I really hate you, you know that?" Brandt remarked.

"Yeah, I know," she replied. "I love you too."

δ

*P*resent day. Mazie stared at Blake after remembering their only meeting as he politely smiled with his hand extended to her, like he wasn't some perverted bastard twelve years ago at Old Mill Pond. Extreme loathing suddenly swept through her. Mazie wanted to deck him, but she sucked up her anger. Through gritted teeth, Mazie managed a smile that probably made her look like a serial killer and shook his hand.

"Yes, Blake," she announced as politely as she could manage. "We met briefly once at Old Mill Pond."

Blake was surprised to hear her reference to Old Mill Pond and roused a slick smile. "Really?" he remarked. "I can't believe I don't remember meeting you. I guess you changed a lot."

"Yeah, actually, I did," Mazie replied as a sinister smirk crossed her face. "I was only eleven years old at the time."

Horror instantly swept over Blake as he suddenly remembered her, possibly reliving the entire incident at the pond with vivid clarity. His crude sexual innuendos toward an underage, eleven-year-old girl, if found out, wouldn't settle well with anyone in town, especially since he held a respectable and prominent position with the bank. While turning several shades of red, Blake might have been reevaluating some of his life choices.

"My friend popped you in the mouth," Mazie informed him, then smirked and cocked her head. "Those were the days, huh?"

Melissa and Cameron shifted their looks from Blake to Mazie as their smiles instantly faded. Cameron let out a horrified gasp while Melissa showed less tact.

"He was *that* boy?" Melissa cried out while pointing at Cameron's boss, as if identifying him in a police line-up.

Blake immediately shifted uncomfortably and excused himself before rushing back through the security door, vanishing from sight.

Chapter 16

*W*hile catching up with her friends on a park bench, Mazie enjoyed the sunshine and the fresh air. Being back in the small town was a significant leap from her home in Los Angeles, where she had lived for the last five years. Of course, the park in town had nothing on the serenity and wide open spaces of the ranch. Mazie felt goosebumps of anticipation about setting foot back on the ranch after all these years. She couldn't deny she missed her old home, but returning was going to be a complicated mess with its own anxiety.

"Are you really staying the entire weekend?" Cameron asked, bringing Mazie back from her thoughts.

"Between my mother and my boss, I seem to have little choice," Mazie informed her. "My boss, I get. He doesn't care about my thoughts and feelings, but my mother is a bit of a disappointment."

"Your mother always seemed pretty perfect to me," Melissa remarked. "I mean, my mom's a little flighty."

"And my mom sometimes forgets I exist," Cameron muttered.

"Well, unfortunately, my mother only cares that Brandt and I put our differences aside," Mazie informed them. "She's making me approach him with my boss's proposal when she could easily ask him for me. She wants us to talk face-to-face, as if that will fix everything between us that's broken."

"So this proposal from your boss's production company," Melissa began. "If Brandt agrees, what would they be filming at the ranch?"

"A lot of scenery," Mazie replied. "And a few outdoor scenes requiring close-ups that they don't want to do in an indoor studio set. Scenes that require actual horses rather than animatronic ones. Things like that."

"Any famous actors or actresses paying a visit to our little town?" Cameron asked, immediately catching Melissa's attention.

"Will there be any?" Melissa practically gasped, as if the thought finally occurred to her.

"Probably a couple of days with the main actors," Mazie replied. "But mostly stunt people, film crew, and fillers."

"Fillers?" Cameron asked.

"Extras," Mazie replied. "A lot of times, they find extras at the filming location."

"You mean, people from here?" Melissa asked, her eyes lighting up.

"I can see you guys are getting ahead of yourselves," Mazie informed them, turning stern. "Brandt hasn't said yes yet, and I have my doubts he'll agree to it. He's always been rather private about the ranch, and he has little use for city people, which means he'll absolutely hate the Hollywood types."

"I promise, we won't get our hopes up over this potential movie," Melissa announced, then grinned almost deviously. "Just tell us who's playing the lead in the movie, and we'll back off."

Mazie held her breath, then groaned softly. "Malcolm Wexler and Sandra King."

Cameron and Melissa stared at her a moment with their eyes wide and were about to explode at the news when Mazie held up her finger, silencing them.

"That's between us," Mazie threatened.

Both women nearly bubbled over, barely able to keep from crying out. They almost bounced out of their seats, but kept from opening their mouths.

"I'll talk to Brandt," Melissa announced, almost too quickly. "If it gets Malcolm Wexler here, I'll even give Brandt a pedicure and a bikini wax."

"I'm not sure I'd go that far," Cameron remarked while making a face. "But I'd be willing to wash and wax the entire herd, if it'd help."

"I appreciate the offers," Mazie remarked. "And if that's one of his stipulations, I'll get back to you. For now, I just need to find him a birthday card for tomorrow. I'll worry about the rest when the time comes."

"We'll find a card at the general store," Melissa announced, bubbling over. "We can go after Cameron returns to work, before I drive you out to the ranch." She then grinned and laughed. "I'll tell you all about Peter on the drive home."

"Peter?" Mazie asked, genuinely surprised. "What about him?"

"I heard he's coming back home to visit for a couple of weeks," Melissa announced.

"Supposedly, he's pretty successful in Los Angeles," Cameron added.

When it was time for Cameron to go back to work, they tossed their trash in the bin and headed back to the main drag. Cameron said her goodbyes and hurried into the bank, making it with a few minutes to spare. Melissa and Mazie then continued through town, heading toward the general store. The old general store resembled an older, refurbished two-story Colonial house. There were tall floor-to-ceiling windows in the front beyond a covered porch on the main level and smaller windows beyond a balcony on the second floor. There were rocking chairs and small tables with chairs for patrons to sit and enjoy the warmer days. Most of the time, the chairs were occupied by older men waiting for their wives. As they approached the store, Melissa's grin faded, and she slapped Mazie on the arm.

"Look who it is," Melissa muttered with noted disgust in her tone.

Mazie looked up the sidewalk a few yards and saw a young woman she hadn't seen since high school graduation. Mazie's sneer matched Melissa's.

"Tina," both scoffed under their breath.

Tina hadn't changed much over the years. She was still beautiful and slender, but her dark hair was now a little shorter. Not surprisingly, her taste in clothes seemed more expensive. She dressed like a fashion model and found a new flair for applying makeup that looked more natural than when she was a young teen. Not surprisingly, she had been the first girl in school to wear makeup. Unfortunately, beyond that beautiful exterior lurked an ugly, evil woman, and Mazie somehow doubted she had changed over the last few years. She couldn't simply forget this woman who once tormented her daily from the eighth grade straight through their senior year. Although Tina didn't see them, Mazie stared at the woman and recalled their last intentional interaction, which had been almost ten years ago, when she was just a young teenager.

*F*lashback. Thirteen-year-old Mazie followed her mother around the kitchen while she prepared breakfast.

Mazie was growing into a beautiful young teenager. She still wore her longer hair in a ponytail and maintained her outwardly tomboy appearance, but she had finally ditched her baggy flannel shirts now that she had discovered the joys of sports bras. The tighter, the better was her motto. At least the other kids didn't notice her as much, and only a select few teased her about her appearance these days. In fact, with her hair in ponytails and her tomboy outfits, most of the kids didn't pay much attention to her at all, which was fine by her. Most importantly, Brandt didn't treat her any differently, which is what she wanted most.

"It's just a bonfire at Old Mill Pond," Mazie insisted. "All my friends are going."

"After dark without adult supervision?" her mother remarked, then shook her head. "No, absolutely not."

"I'm sure Tina's brother will be there," she insisted. "He's eighteen."

Liddy paused and glanced at her daughter. "So there's going to be older boys there," she announced. "That's what I'm hearing."

Mazie groaned and collapsed against the counter. "Mom, you're killing me!"

"And you're killing me," Liddy informed her, then indicated her hair. "I found another gray hair. We all know who gave that to me."

"Yeah, Brandt," Mazie replied. "Like the other ten. One for each year you had to put up with him."

"Don't talk about Brandt like that," Liddy scolded.

Eighteen-year-old Brandt entered the kitchen from the mud room. He now stood well over six foot with a solid, athletic build and amazingly broad shoulders. His dark hair was slightly longer but well-maintained, particularly when he wore his cowboy hat whenever he was outside. His face was clean-shaven with only ever a hint of a five o'clock shadow. Brandt was looking more and more like a man with every passing day.

"What did I do this time?" Brandt just about demanded and gave Mazie's ponytail a swish as he passed.

"Stop that," she snarled at him.

Brandt chuckled at her expense, then started setting the breakfast table.

"Did you wash your hands?" Liddy asked Brandt with a commanding glare.

"Yeah, sure," he replied, then shrugged.

Liddy continued to glare at him until he groaned. "It's horse dirt," he insisted. "The clean kind." Liddy kept a firm glare until he again groaned. "Fine."

Brandt moved between Liddy and Mazie at the sink and pushed Mazie aside with his arm. She stumbled away from him, then turned and tried pushing him. She couldn't even move him. Brandt washed his hands and didn't even bother looking at her.

"Gonna have to try harder than that, shrimp," he remarked, humored by her effort.

Mazie pinched his exposed lower arm. Brandt cried out, then immediately spun, placing her in a mild chokehold, and gave her noogies with his wet hand.

"Stop it, stop it!" she cried out while fighting his arm. "Your hands are all wet and smelly!"

Liddy groaned and rolled her eyes.

Dalton entered the kitchen from the mud room, saw them, and shook his head. "Will you two give it a rest?" he moaned.

"He started it!"

"Yeah, right," Brandt huffed. "You've been a menace ever since you got out of your training bra."

Colt entered the kitchen from the mud room and glared at them. Brandt and Mazie became still and stared back at Colt. Without a word from Colt, Brandt released Mazie, and both minded their own business.

"Order restored," Liddy announced.

"Why is it that dead-eye stare never works for me?" Dalton demanded.

Colt poured himself a cup of coffee and eyed his brother. "Because you never whooped either of their asses," he announced. "The stare means nothing if you don't have something to back it up with."

Once they all sat down at the table for breakfast, Brandt, who was always seated alongside Mazie, purposely man-spread, taking up all of his space and most of hers. During grace, Mazie stomped on his foot. Brandt gasped in pain and finally moved out of her space. They again received looks from all three.

"How old are you, boy?" Colt demanded.

Brandt grinned slyly. "Eighteen last month."

"But you're still in school, right?" Colt asked, although it sounded more like a statement.

"Well, yeah, it's my senior year," he replied, then eyed his uncle somewhat quizzically. "Why?"

"I'm thinking I'm still within my rights to whoop your ass," Colt replied. "Stop picking on Mazie."

"I'm rethinking leaving them alone together this evening," Liddy muttered.

Brandt glanced at Liddy across the table from them and smiled. "No can do, Liddy," he announced proudly. "I have a date tonight."

"You can cancel your date," Dalton informed him. "You know the three of us are going to that engagement party tonight. You remember? The one you couldn't go to because you agreed to stay home with Mazie, who wouldn't go because she refused to wear a dress."

"She's thirteen," Brandt insisted while indicating Mazie. "The girl is a holy terror in her own right. She's perfectly capable of staying home by herself."

Mazie nearly jumped out of her seat but remained calm. "I can stay home by myself," she insisted. "I'm old enough. And I'm certainly more mature than *him*."

Brandt shrugged. "She's not wrong."

"Please let me stay home by myself," Mazie begged her mother.

Liddy cast a sideways look at Mazie. "No, and that's final."

"And you're staying home with her," Colt informed Brandt.

"I can't cancel my date," Brandt insisted, clearly annoyed. "Plans were made. Money was spent."

"Oh, it's that kind of date," Mazie muttered.

Brandt sneered at Mazie while placing his arm on the back of her chair. His fingers clutched her sports bra in the back, indicating he would snap it, as he leaned closer to her.

"You're being rude," he scoffed lowly.

"And you better rethink your next move *very* carefully," she snarled back. "I know where you sleep."

Brandt groaned, loosened his fingers, and looked around the table. "Couldn't she sleep over at a friend's house?"

"I could go for that," Mazie announced hopefully.

"Yeah, I don't think so," Liddy muttered. "No friends and no party."

Colt then looked at Brandt. "And no date."

"I'm eighteen with my own truck," Brandt announced while looking at both uncles. "Exactly when do I become free of all this?"

"I don't know," Colt announced while shaking his head. "But it's not going to be tonight."

"Fine," Brandt scoffed, then glared at Mazie. "I'm torching Barbie's dream house tonight."

Chapter 17

Mazie lay sprawled on the sofa in the family room, the remote control in her hand, and lazily surfed from channel to channel. The main house's family room featured two elegant sofas facing each other over a large, antique coffee table, with a huge stone fireplace serving as the room's focal point. The television was located on the far wall, within a large bookcase, and had a door that could be shut to hide it when there was company, although there was rarely any since Dee's death. Mazie wore a permanent frown on her face, still sulking about the party, while watching nothing in particular. Brandt suddenly rolled across the back of the sofa, landed behind her, and easily rolled her off the seat and onto the floor with a thud. She cried out, then sprang to her feet, the remote control still clutched in her hand.

"I hate when you do that!"

Brandt snatched the remote control from her and casually rested on the sofa in the same position she had been just moments earlier.

"I'm older and have more seniority," he replied with little care. "Low man on the totem pole shuts her pie hole."

"Fine," Mazie snapped, then flopped on top of him, crushing him below the belt.

Brandt groaned and pushed her off him, instantly clutching his groin while attempting to recover. "Not nice," he gasped.

Mazie was quite pleased with herself and then took the spot on the sofa near his feet. Brandt placed his feet on her lap and waved his toes under her nose.

"Stop it," she snarled.

He scratched her chin with his sock-covered toe. "Make me."

Without hesitation, she grabbed his foot and tickled it. Brandt cried out and pulled his feet away from her.

"Miserable little sea urchin," he muttered while sitting up. "I'm missing out on the biggest date of my life to keep you alive. The least you can do is give me a good reason not to stuff you in Barbie's dream house."

She snatched the remote control from him and changed the channel. "Sorry you're not getting laid tonight," she scoffed.

Brandt shot a look at her. "Since when do you talk like that?" he demanded. "And what makes you think--?"

"You left the box of condoms on your nightstand," she informed him.

"Stay out of my room!" he launched back, now seeming somewhat flustered.

Mazie cast a look at him and raised her brows. "Oh, my God," she announced with surprise. "Did I actually embarrass you?"

"We're not having this conversation," he snapped back while snatching the remote control from her. He changed the channel back to what he was watching. "At least not until you're old enough to vote."

Mazie stared at the television for a long moment, then cast a sideways glance at him. "Did you cancel already?" she asked almost timidly.

"No, I got her parents' voicemail," he muttered. "I'm waiting for her to call me back."

Mazie straightened and turned to face him. "You know I can look after myself," she informed him while keeping her voice down so the adults in the house wouldn't hear. "There's no reason why you can't leave after they go. They'll be gone until midnight, you know."

Brandt eyed her, contemplating it, but didn't turn. "If they find out--"

"They won't," she insisted and moved closer to him on the sofa so they could speak confidentially. "There's no reason we should both be miserable tonight. I can take care of myself. I'll be fine."

"Are you going to do anything stupid?" he asked, now glaring at her through squinting eyes.

"No, of course not."

He turned toward her and leaned closer. "If I go out, you can't leave the house," Brandt insisted. "I mean it. Not even out to the barn. No riding and no friends over. If you get so much as a papercut, I'm a dead man."

"Just leave me your laptop, and I'll play games all night," she informed him.

"Deal," he replied, then pointed a warning finger at her. "Don't burn the house down making popcorn either."

"I promise, I won't."

*T*he older compact car pulled up to Old Mill Pond and parked in the grass alongside several other older cars, all belonging to teenagers. Mazie and her friend, Tina, got out of the back while Tina's brother, Tanner, got out of the driver's side. Tina was one of the more popular girls in Junior High and had been Mazie's friend since grade school. She was a beautiful, slender girl with long, silky, dark hair that fell past her shoulders. Tina started wearing makeup over the last two years, as did most of the girls in school, which seemed weird since it just made them look older. Even so, Mazie liked hanging out with Tina. She had a different kind of energy that made Mazie more comfortable being a girl, even defending Mazie when other girls picked on her in earlier years. Everyone liked Tina, especially the boys. Tina's brother, Tanner, was a high school senior who played just about every sport. He was a tall, well-built teenager with short light brown hair and some facial stubble that he referred to as a beard, even though it didn't really look like one.

There were at least two dozen kids, ranging in age from early teens to late teens, sitting on blankets around the bonfire and swimming in the pond, even though the water must have been frigid, since it was only sixty-five degrees that time of night. Most were drinking from plastic cups while loud music played from a portable stereo. Mazie looked around with some surprise at the amount of activity and many faces she'd never seen before. Apparently, some kids came from other schools. Mazie and Tina were instantly handed drinks in large plastic cups by random passing boys. Tina was already excited at the party atmosphere, while Mazie was slightly apprehensive now that she was here, particularly that she'd lied to Brandt. When several boys began paying attention to Tina, she seemed to forget that Mazie was even there, leaving her sitting on a blanket, watching the bonfire by herself. She had hoped her other friends, Melissa and Cameron, would be there, but Tina had earlier admitted she hadn't even invited them.

Mazie sipped her drink and watched as giggling, topless girls ran from boys. When the boys caught the girls, they tossed them into the cold pond. Mazie was suddenly uncomfortable and looked around, hoping to see Tina's brother. Maybe Tanner would take her home. When she didn't see Tina's older brother anywhere, Mazie decided it had only been half an hour. Perhaps the party would get better if she just gave it a chance. Unfortunately, there didn't seem to be anyone to really talk to. The girls were all giddy as they flirted with the boys, who seemed to surround them in packs, while the rest were boys hanging out together, talking and laughing loudly. It reminded her of the ranch hands later in the evening at their bonfires. Of course, the ranch hands were typically drunk. Certainly, that wasn't the case here. Everyone was under the legal drinking age. Mazie tried to relax and took another sip of her drink.

Chapter 18

*B*randt entered the house with little enthusiasm and a defeated look. He paused by the hall table, leaned on it a moment, and then looked at his reflection in the mirror. Brandt stared at himself and frowned, disgusted with himself. He finally straightened and looked down the hall.

"Mazie," he called out.

When there was no response, he headed into the kitchen and then entered the staff wing.

"Mazie," Brandt again called as he approached Liddy's in-law suite. "Mazie?"

He tapped on the door, then immediately entered the suite. Brandt approached Mazie's bedroom and peered inside.

"Mazie?"

When he didn't see her, Brandt cursed softly and headed for the nearby phone. He snatched it from its base and punched in a phone number. Brandt waited only a moment before it was answered.

"Hey, it's Brandt," he announced to one of his friends on the other end. There was a pause. "That's not important right now. Are there any parties going on tonight?" He listened to the response, his irritation growing. "Do you know if any of Mazie's friends were going?" When he heard the response, Brandt frowned in disgust. "Thanks. I'll talk to you later."

Brandt disconnected the call and ran from the suite.

$\mathcal{M}$azie held her head while stumbling past the pond dock. Everything seemed almost hazy, and she felt unusually unsteady. Something didn't seem right, but she didn't know what it was. Mazie saw her friend not far from the pond, talking with two older boys. Tina was excessively giddy as the boys took turns trying to hold her and even kiss her. Despite Mazie feeling that their 'attention' was inappropriate, for some odd reason, Tina seemed to be enjoying it.

"How about we go skinny dipping?" one of the boys suggested to Tina.

Mazie approached them and clutched her friend's arm. "I don't feel right," she informed Tina. "Can your brother take us home?"

"It's a party, Mazie," Tina replied, sounding almost annoyed. "Chill, okay? Have another drink."

"Was there alcohol in those drinks?" Mazie suddenly asked her friend, who only seemed interested in talking to the boys.

"Of course there is," one of the boys announced and then laughed. "Getting you drunk was the only way you were going to loosen up."

"What?" Mazie gasped, then looked at her friend. "Did you know they spiked the drinks?"

"Come on, Mazie," Tina moaned while adding an irritated eye roll. "You need to lighten up. Of course, we were planning on getting drunk. Have another drink. Maybe you'll actually fit in."

As if on command, another boy approached and handed Mazie a plastic cup. "Your drink," he announced cheerfully while appearing happily buzzed.

Mazie again looked back at her friend as she attempted to keep her balance. "Where's your brother?" she now demanded. "I want to go home."

Tina groaned and shook her head. "Not for another few hours," she scoffed, turning angry. "It's early. Just go sit down somewhere if you're going to be a total buzz kill." She rolled her eyes. "Jesus, if I knew you were going to be like this, I would have brought Melissa instead. She might be a heifer, but at least she knows how to have fun."

"Melissa is our friend," Mazie retorted defensively. "Don't talk about her like that."

"She's *your* friend," Tina scoffed. "You could be popular if you half-tried, but not if you keep hanging around girls like Melissa and Cameron."

"Fine," Mazie snarled and cast her drink aside. "I'll walk home."

"I'll walk you home," the boy beside her announced while adding a sly grin.

The boy then placed his arm around her waist, pulling her closer to him. Mazie attempted to push him away, but somehow seemed to lack strength. That's when she felt herself internally panic. She didn't remember the last time she'd felt this weak and helpless. An older pickup truck suddenly flew up to the scene around the bonfire and skidded to a stop, tearing up ground and grass and catching everyone's attention. The drunks laughed, thinking it was funny. Although she was having trouble focusing, Mazie was almost positive it was Brandt's truck. The driver's side door flew open, and Brandt jumped out.

"Mazie!" he called out in a loud, gruff voice, oddly sounding like Uncle Colt. Brandt looked around with a rare look of anger on his face. "Mazie!"

"Brandt!" she cried out and attempted to pull away from the boy with his arm anchored around her waist.

When Mazie nearly fell from attempting to pull away, the boy caught her and laughed while holding her against him.

"You should sit down before you fall down," he announced and continued to laugh. "There's a nice, quiet spot over this way."

"Brandt!" Mazie now screamed.

Brandt saw her struggling against the boy holding her in his arms and hesitated only a moment to reach inside the truck. He emerged with his old baseball bat and made a beeline for Mazie and the boy. Several guys and girls quickly moved out of the path of the raging bull in Ariat cowboy boots. When the boy saw Brandt coming directly for him, he jumped back, accidentally knocking Mazie to the ground. Brandt took an aggressive batting stance and glared at the boy.

"Get the fuck away from her, or I'll rearrange your face," Brandt snarled in a tone that easily frightened the boy as well as Mazie.

The boy took off across the field, fearing for his life from the irate man. Brandt looked around while approaching Mazie, standing over her where she remained on the ground.

"Party's over!" Brandt shouted in a voice that echoed her Uncle Colt and startled nearly every kid.

The drunken kids stared, momentarily surprised, and then laughed at him. Mazie never saw Brandt looking as fierce as he did tonight, except maybe two seconds before he punched his friend in the mouth a couple of years ago.

"The police will be here in ten minutes," Brandt snarled while grabbing Mazie's hand and pulling her to her feet.

The action was so quick, she nearly fell back down again. The world also seemed to be spinning faster now, and she was having a hard time focusing. Brandt swiftly plucked Mazie off her feet and into his arms.

"Clock's ticking!"

Brandt carried Mazie to his pickup truck, deposited her on the passenger side seat, and slammed the door. He then rounded the front to the driver's side as Mazie's so-called friend stumbled toward his truck.

"Can I get a ride home?" Tina asked him, now concerned about the threat of the police. "I can't find my brother."

"Fuck you," Mazie snarled past Brandt from the passenger seat.

Brandt eyed the drunken girl in his truck, then gave Tina a shrug. "She's the boss," he replied, then jumped into the truck and slammed the door. "Don't worry. I'm sure the police will give you a ride home."

Brandt's truck kicked up dirt while spinning around in a wild circle, burned out in the grass, and then sped across the field to the dirt road.

Chapter 19

Mazie clung to the toilet in her mother's in-law suite and heaved several times. The country-style bathroom had an old claw-foot bathtub between a large standing cabinet and a single-sink vanity, with bright white tiled flooring. Brandt crouched alongside Mazie and attempted to tie her hair up into a ponytail between heaves. Each time she heaved, he grimaced and tried to look away, possibly feeling nauseous himself.

"I feel like shit," she moaned while gasping for air as she fell onto her backside before the toilet. "Why is the room spinning?"

"You're drunk," he informed her.

Brandt wet a washrag and wiped vomit residue from her lips and chin. She stared at him almost helplessly as he cared for her in her vulnerable condition.

"I'm so sorry, Brandt," she whispered, now almost down to tears. "I didn't know there was alcohol in the drinks. I trusted Tina. She knew they were putting vodka in my drink, and she let them. I think she even encouraged them to do it."

"Well, Tina is a shitty friend," Brandt informed her. "But, in all fairness, you're pretty shitty too. I thought I could trust you, but you lied to me."

"I know, and I'm sorry," she whispered. "I just wanted to go to the party. Tina hangs out with the cool kids, and I just wanted them to like me."

"Those kids weren't your friends, and I suggest you look somewhere else for new ones," he informed her.

She stared at him for a long moment. "I don't know what would have happened if you hadn't shown when you did," she whispered while holding back her tears. "I was so scared."

Brandt sighed and gently helped her to her feet. She clung to him for support as he walked her from the bathroom.

"I'll always look out for you, Mazie," he informed her as they headed across the apartment for her bedroom. "But you have to be honest with me."

"You wouldn't have let me go if I told you the truth," she replied.

"Probably not," he agreed. "But if I had, I would have stuck around and kept an eye on things. I'm not Uncle Colt, Mazie. I don't want to put you in a bubble, but I also don't want to see you hurt either."

Brandt helped her into bed and removed her shoes. She leaned against the headboard and softly sobbed.

"I was so scared."

Brandt moved onto the bed, sat alongside her, and pulled her into his arms. She clung to him and softly cried on his shoulder.

"You're okay, Mazie," he whispered while holding her. "I'll always look out for you."

"Are you going to tell Mom about tonight?" she asked, almost timidly, while clinging to him.

"No, of course not," Brandt replied into the top of her head. "I'll get into just as much trouble as you. Maybe more."

"What if Mom figures it out?" she asked, her concern evident.

"Just stay in bed tonight and tomorrow," he replied. "Tell your mother you're having 'girl problems'."

"Think she'll buy it?"

"Definitely," he replied. "And the best part? Uncle Colt and Uncle Dalton won't ask a single question."

"How do you know all this stuff?"

"There are plenty of girls at school," he informed her. "Trust me. Nothing makes a guy turn tail faster than a tale of periods and cramps."

Mazie managed a tiny laugh. "Boys are so weird."

azie spent a better portion of Saturday in bed. Some of it was from nausea, but most of it was nerves. She even had dinner in their in-law suite off the main kitchen. By the time Sunday morning arrived, she felt as good as she ever had and was ready for brunch with the family. While her mother worked on brunch, Mazie and Brandt set the table, giving them time to talk without Liddy overhearing.

"I guess you're feeling better," Brandt remarked.

"Much better," Mazie replied with a soft groan. "I never want another repeat of that. I hate being sick."

"Considering the assholes you call friends, you're lucky being sick was the worst that happened," Brandt informed her. "That boy had less than honorable intentions, you know."

"I know," Mazie muttered, then groaned. "I think he wanted to kiss me." She immediately made a face. "I barely knew him, and I certainly didn't like him."

"You would have been lucky if kissing you was all he had on his mind," Brandt muttered, then hesitated and looked at her. "What happened the other night scared me, Mazie, and I don't want to worry about your safety all the time, especially since I'll be working the cattle full-time after I graduate high school. I taught you how to ride, rope, and drive a tractor. Now, it's time you learned how to defend yourself. You need to learn how to throw a punch and shoot a rifle."

Mazie's eyes widened in near horror as she shifted her gaze from her mother's turned back, then moved closer to him.

"Don't say things like that in front of the 'M.O.M'," she announced, spelling out mom. "She'd tan both our hides if she hears that."

"That's why I'm going to teach you away from the ranch," he informed her. "We'll ride out to the old homestead. That's where Uncle Colt first taught me to shoot a rifle, and I was only ten. It's way past time you learned."

Mazie shifted looks at her mother, who didn't seem to hear any of their conversation. "Will you teach me to drive the pickup truck, too?"

Brandt eyed her a moment and seemed to consider the request. "Okay, but we'll have to do that a few of the afternoons when I pick you up at school," he informed her. "We'll practice on the dirt road by the old homestead."

Mazie was pleased with the response. When she caught her mother eyeing them almost suspiciously, Mazie moved away from Brandt and resumed setting the table. During their Sunday brunch, Colt and Dalton fussed over Mazie, expressing concern for her well-being but asking few questions. Brandt had been right. Giving her mother 'girl problems' as the reason seemed to keep the guys from asking too many questions. Since Sunday was their day off, everyone was in a good mood and ready to relax the entire day. Dalton then cleared his throat while eyeing Colt. As if on cue, Colt looked at Brandt.

"Your Uncle Dalton and I want to have a talk with you in the study after breakfast," Colt announced.

Brandt looked at his Uncle Colt with surprise and some concern. "About what?" he asked. "What did I do now?"

Mazie immediately tensed. She was sure they somehow figured it out, and they were both going to be grounded for the rest of their lives.

"You didn't do anything," Dalton insisted. "We just need to talk."

Brandt groaned and now picked at his food. "That can't be good."

Both men laughed.

"Got a guilty conscience about something?" Colt joked while grinning.

"No," Brandt announced while holding his head up proudly. "I'm practically a saint."

Liddy hid her smile while Colt and Dalton laughed aloud.

§

*A*fter breakfast, while the guys were in the study talking with Brandt, Mazie suddenly felt a surge of nervous energy and paced the living room not far from the study. She couldn't stop thinking that they somehow figured out what happened on Friday night. She worried that Brandt was in some sort of trouble for leaving her alone, and she was in trouble for sneaking off to the party. Brandt made quite a commotion at the bonfire, and some of the kids may have told on him. If he got into trouble, it was all her fault, and she was sure whatever punishment he received should be on her as well. When she heard the study door open, she peeked into the hallway. As Brandt entered the hallway, he looked almost stunned. Colt patted him on the shoulder as he passed. When Dalton did the same, Mazie became alarmed. They were going to whoop him to death, she just knew it! Once both uncles had left the house, Mazie hurried into the hallway and approached Brandt.

"What happened?" she gasped, her concern evident. "Are you in trouble?"

He seemed unable to look at her for a moment and slowly shook his head, possibly still in shock. "No, not at all," he muttered.

"What happened?" Mazie again demanded.

Brandt looked at her with the same strange look. "They said when I graduate high school, the ranch will be turned over to me."

"Turned over?" Mazie asked, somewhat confused. "What does that mean?"

Brandt came back to life, then looked at her and smiled. "It's mine," he informed her, shaking his head in disbelief. "The house, the land, the business. It's all mine."

"I thought Uncle Colt and Uncle Dalton owned the ranch," Mazie remarked.

"So did I," he replied, almost unable to comprehend what he had been told. "Being the oldest son, my father was given first opportunity to keep the ranch. Apparently, he had to buy out Uncle Colt and Uncle Dalton if he wanted to keep it. So he bought them out. When my father died, my mother had lifetime rights, but the ranch was left in a trust for me until I turned twenty-one." He hesitated and again shook his head. "Unless my uncles believed I was responsible enough to handle it at eighteen." Brandt suddenly laughed. "They both think I'm responsible enough. Can you believe that?"

"Actually, no," she remarked, then gave him a strange look. "So that makes you Uncle Colt's boss?"

Brandt eyed her, then grinned and chuckled. "Yeah, I suppose it does."

"Things are about to get interesting around here," Mazie muttered, then eyed him suspiciously. "Are you going to fire him?"

"What?" he asked with surprise. "No, of course not."

"I just thought with the way he treated you--"

"He was tough on me because he knew I had to be responsible, if I was going to run the ranch someday," Brandt informed her, then looked around. "I think I finally get it."

Mazie again eyed him. "Wait a minute," she announced. "Uncle Dalton pays me to muck stalls and tack the horses. Does that now mean *you're* my boss?"

Brandt smiled and laughed. "Yes, it does," he teased her. "*You* work for *me*."

Mazie frowned and sneered her distaste. "Ewe," she muttered.

Brandt grabbed her around the neck from behind and put her into a mild chokehold while laughing and giving her noogies.

"So you'd better be nice to me," he informed her. "If you want to be the first girl wrangler on my ranch."

Mazie squirmed out of his arm and spun to face him. "You mean it?"

"Well, I'm not officially in charge until after I graduate high school," he informed her. "But I don't see why you can't be a wrangler starting this summer." He then scolded her with a look. "You're still going to muck stalls and tack up the horses."

"Yeah, I don't mind," she announced excitedly, then hugged him briefly before pulling away. "I'm going to tell Mom." Mazie then took off for the kitchen.

Chapter 20

Mazie returned to the present day and stared at her *former* friend, who was standing near the general store. She barely said two words to Tina since that night at Old Mill Pond, but they still went to the same school together for another five years after that. Five years of Tina relentlessly tormenting her almost daily for being a poor farm girl with a servant for a mother. Pointing at her and making comments about her smelling like horses and cattle, even though she didn't, since she showered and washed her hair every morning before school. Despite all the torment, Mazie survived relatively unscathed, because people like Tina and her newly found stuck-up friends didn't matter, as Brandt liked to say. She had family and other friends who did matter. Tina glanced in their direction, seemingly looking through them, not even seeing them, which was for the best. Mazie didn't think she could deal with Tina right now anyway. Melissa met Mazie's gaze and sneered her distaste for the woman.

"That little bitch made school life a living hell for both of us," Melissa scoffed. "Believe it or not, she hasn't changed at all since high school."

Melissa indicated the store, and both continued toward the entrance. For as miserable as certain girls in school made life for Mazie and her friends, Brandt didn't have it any better. In many ways, what he went through was far worse. Girls were cruel to other girls, but they were far crueler toward boys.

♪

*F*lashback. Eighteen-year-old Brandt sat at the dinner table and picked at his meal but barely ate anything. He seemed lost in his own world. Thirteen-year-old Mazie, Liddy, and both uncles took turns staring at Brandt, who didn't even seem to notice them. He finally groaned, cast his fork onto his plate, and glared at those around the dinner table.

"You have something to say?" Brandt snapped. "Just say it."

Mazie and Liddy hid their smiles, shook their heads, and minded their dinner plates. Colt and Dalton couldn't seem to look away while maintaining their grins. Naturally, Uncle Colt was the first to speak.

"Our little boy, all grown up," Colt announced, mocking Brandt. "Going to his senior prom."

"Don't tease him, Colt," Dalton scolded. "It's a big night for him."

"Why don't you tell us about your lady friend?" Liddy asked, practically overjoyed. "I hope her parents take lots of pictures before you head to the school auditorium."

"I'd rather not discuss it," Brandt remarked. "It's not a big deal."

"Not a big deal?" Colt immediately interjected. "You asked to borrow my pickup truck, washed it, **and** rented a tuxedo. That sounds like a big deal to me."

"The prom is all anybody at school was talking about for months," Brandt informed them. "Taking a girl sounded like a good idea at the time, but getting all dressed up, listening to music I don't even like, and actually dancing is way outside my comfort zone."

"I hope you know you're going tonight, no matter what," Dalton remarked. "There's no way you're standing up some poor girl on prom night."

"Of course I'm going," Brandt groaned, defeated. "I really like this girl, and I want to spend time with her. It's just all the rest I'm not really thrilled about." He pushed his chair out and ran his fingers through his hair. "May I be excused?"

"Of course," Liddy replied.

Brandt grabbed his plate, took it to the sink, and then headed up the back stairs.

*B*randt stood in front of the dresser mirror in his semi-clean bedroom and fiddled with the bow tie. He looked handsome in his black tuxedo, crisp white shirt, and shiny dress shoes. When he couldn't figure out the tie, he cast it aside. Brandt then noticed Mazie in the doorway, leaning against the doorframe with her arms folded across her chest while watching him.

"Ever hear of knocking?" he scoffed.

"Ever hear of closing your door?" Mazie countered, then pointed to the discarded bow tie. "You own a black tie, don't you? Use that. No one will know."

Brandt considered the comment, then approached his closet and found his black tie. It was one of four ties he owned.

"Are you actually nervous?" Mazie asked. "That's not like you."

"Yeah, well," Brandt huffed while putting on the tie. "I haven't exactly been on a lot of dates, and none that required a suit, let alone a tuxedo."

"You'll survive," she informed him. "It's your nature."

"Yeah, but will I make a fool out of myself?" he muttered. "I'm going to look stupid out there."

"No, you won't," Mazie insisted and straightened, allowing her arms to fall to her sides. "Survival instincts will kick in. You'll be fine."

"Yeah?" he asked and darted a look at her while tightening his tie. "What happens when she wants to slow dance?"

Mazie shrugged. "You slow dance," she replied.

"Great advice, shrimp," Brandt scoffed. "That really helps."

"Was that sarcasm?"

"It sure as shit wasn't a compliment," he muttered.

"Are you nervous about slow dancing with her?" Mazie then asked the next logical question.

"I always said you were smart," Brandt huffed, then eyed her. "I've never slow danced with a girl. Hell, I've never even been to a school dance before."

"You were to several church picnics," she reminded him. "If you'd been paying attention--"

"I don't need to be lectured by a tweener," Brandt scoffed.

"No, but I helped you with school work," Mazie remarked. "If I can teach you history, geography, and science, I can teach you to slow dance."

"Do *you* even know how to slow dance?" Brandt demanded. "You're only thirteen."

"I danced at the church picnic with Uncle Dalton and Uncle Colt many times," she reminded him. "I also have plenty of guy friends and danced with them at school dances. Believe it or not, my experience in that department outweighs yours."

Brandt groaned and approached his stereo. He found a slow country song and indicated for her to 'show him what she had'. Mazie put one hand on his shoulder, although it was a bit of a stretch, as it was with her uncles, and she made him hold her other hand close to his shoulder while his free hand gently rested high on her back. Mazie showed him how she slow-danced with her two uncles at the church picnics, dancing the Texas Two-step as if it were second nature to her. By the end of the song, Brandt seemed more relaxed and had the steps down pat. Mazie gracefully pulled away and posed, causing Brandt to smile and laugh.

"For a little girl, you're pretty amazing, Mazie," Brandt informed her. "I don't know what I'd ever do without you."

"You'd be tripping over your two left feet, for starters," Mazie remarked, then turned stern. "And stop calling me a little girl. It's offensive."

Brandt grinned and chuckled. "Yes, ma'am."

Being called ma'am, particularly by Brandt, made her giggle. She pretended to smooth his tie, then gave it a swift tightening, nearly choking him.

"Don't forget your date's corsage in the fridge," she announced before Texas two-stepping out of his room while humming the country song.

Mazie woke shortly after going to bed that night, although she wasn't sure what had woken her. She looked at her bedside clock and realized it was only a little after ten o'clock. She silently opened her bedroom door and heard voices coming from the attached living room. Mazie slipped out of her room, crept a little closer to the parlor, and peeked around the corner. She saw Brandt sitting on the sofa alongside her mother. His head hung down as he held his clasped hands between his knees, clutching what was left of his date's fresh flower corsage while Liddy had one hand on his shoulder and the other on his lower arm. In a rare moment of slipped emotions, Brandt was fighting back tears. He wiped the tears from his eyes and sniffed while briefly glancing at Liddy.

"Don't tell Uncle Colt or Uncle Dalton about this," Brandt muttered. "Men aren't supposed to cry."

"That's archaic," Liddy huffed in rarely seen rage. "Colt and Dalton should understand, and you have a good reason to be upset. The nerve of that girl! Turning you away and canceling your date because you showed up in a pickup truck! I have half a mind to call her mother and give her a good 'what for'."

"You mean well, but that would only make things worse," Brandt insisted. "I'm not a boy anymore. I can fight my own battles, and when I lose, I can do it with dignity." He groaned and straightened. "I probably shouldn't have come here disturbing you over this."

"Of course you should have," Liddy insisted and clung to him. "You're the son I've always wanted, and I'll always be here for you."

"And you've been a fine substitute mother, Liddy," Brandt replied.

Liddy turned gushy and happily hugged him. "You've turned into a fine young man, Brandt," she informed him. "Your mother would be so proud."

"I'm going to look in on Mazie before I turn in," Brandt announced, then handed Liddy the crushed corsage. "Would you toss this in your garbage? I don't want the guys seeing it in the kitchen trash."

"Sure."

Mazie internally gasped, then quickly but quietly crept back into her room. She slipped under the covers and pretended to be asleep, waiting for Brandt to come in and wake her. She heard her bedroom door open and a creak of the floorboard. When she heard her bedroom door shut without being woken, Mazie opened her eyes and scanned the dimly lit room for Brandt, but he was gone. She looked at her bedside table and saw his red rose boutonnière on the nightstand. Mazie picked up the flower, flopped back down on the bed, and studied it while delicately touching its petals. She smiled warmly and placed it back on her nightstand.

Chapter 21

*P*resent day. Mazie entered the general store behind Melissa, who was still whispering gossip about Tina, most of which Mazie hadn't even heard while lost in her own thoughts. When Melissa's words of gossip turned to the personal hell Tina had put her through as well, Mazie came crashing back into reality.

"It doesn't matter how much weight I lose or how successful I become, I'll always be the poor, fat girl to that bitch," Melissa scoffed.

"Does she still torment you?" Mazie asked with some surprise and a hint of anger.

"Not verbally," Melissa remarked. "But she gives me that snooty look and that loathsome smirk."

"Yes," Mazie groaned while rolling her eyes. "I remember that smirk all too well. We took a lot of shit from her while we were in school."

"To this day, she still has a way of making me feel insignificant," Melissa muttered while frowning. "I'm a biologist, for Christ's sake. I make good money and have my own apartment. She works part-time at the makeup counter at the strip mall and still lives with her rich mommy and daddy."

"The kids who bully and shame us don't matter, Melissa," Mazie informed her, quoting Brandt. "Not even a little. One day, Tina will get her comeuppance."

"That would be nice, wouldn't it?" Melissa remarked, then sighed. "But she's got a skinny booty and daddy's money. She's going to land some rich guy and live out her life in comfort and style, all while looking down upon us peasants."

"Yeah, probably," Mazie replied with a soft groan. "Let's find a birthday card while we're both feeling miserable."

As they walked through the old-time store, Mazie was surprised by how little it had changed in her absence. The store's interior felt like stepping back in time to the Old West. The walls, floor, and ceiling were entirely made up of hardwood. There were shelves of homemade goods by locals, bins of fresh produce grown by their neighbors, and tall shelves of imported goods. There was a refrigerated section with cold beverages, milk, and other miscellaneous items. A meat case contained fresh meats and deli meats, as well as homemade to-go sandwiches. And, of course, there was a large selection of loose candy for the kids. Every kid loved coming to the store in the afternoon with some pocket change to get their sugar fix. Melissa and Mazie entered the aisle containing birthday cards and began the daunting task of reading the sentiments inside. Melissa read all the funny ones aloud, giggling like a schoolgirl over some of them. Mazie read one gushy card after another, groaned, and put each one back.

"Damned polite cards," Mazie huffed under her breath. "Where's the one that says 'you're a dumb son-of-a-bitch and I hate you'?"

"You'd probably need a blank card for that kind of verse," Melissa casually replied, reminding her she was there.

"This is like driving a nail through my thumb," Mazie remarked with disgust. "It's not as if I can show up without the bare minimum of a card or I'll get lectured by all three of them."

Melissa finally turned to face Mazie, cocked her head, and studied her. "You know," she remarked. "I don't think you ever told me what kick-started this whole loathing of Brandt thing. You two were always so close. It was kind of endearing." She then hesitated and grimaced. "Well, not when he had you in a headlock in his armpit and gave you the dreaded 'noogies'."

"Not the dreaded 'noogies'," a male voice lightly cried out from behind them.

Both women immediately spun, startled by the interruption, and saw a man their age standing only a few feet away.

"Peter," Melissa announced with surprise, then managed a smile and awkwardly hugged him.

Mazie stared at Peter, her childhood crush and longtime friend, who had just returned home from his adventures in Los Angeles. Peter was a little over five-foot-ten with an athletic build, having filled out a lot since school. His light brown hair was still short, and he was clean-shaven. Mazie couldn't believe how handsome Peter still was after all these years. Once Melissa released him, he turned his attention to Mazie and looked at her in the dress with something resembling astonishment. His eyes seemed to gravitate to the cleavage he possibly never knew she had.

"Mazie, wow, you look great," Peter announced and opened his arms to her. "I'm so happy to see you."

Mazie smiled, managing a soft laugh before sharing a warm embrace with him as well. She then pulled away, took a step back, and studied him.

"Melissa and her partner in crime said you were returning home for a visit, but I didn't think it would be this weekend," Mazie remarked.

"I finished up early and decided to come home a week sooner." He continued to stare at her, unable to take his eyes off her transformation. "No one even mentioned you might be coming home. How have you been?"

"Actually, I've been living the last five years in Los Angeles, same as you," Mazie replied, then shrugged. "My job is demanding and keeps me pretty busy, but it pays well."

"Oh?" Peter asked, now curious. "What is it you do for a living? I haven't seen you since high school. I miss all those bonfires at the ranch."

When Melissa took it upon herself to brag to Peter about Mazie's job with the production company, Mazie drifted back to the summer when she was sixteen.

*F*lashback. Sixteen-year-old Mazie was a beautiful young lady, despite her tomboy wardrobe. She continued to tie her longer hair back in a ponytail while keeping her ample bust hidden behind her constrictive sports bras. Mazie had her select group of friends at school, which was all she needed. At home, Brandt treated her like 'one of the boys', and she was happy with the direction her life was heading. Mazie sat around the backyard bonfire with family and friends on the Fourth of July weekend. The bonfire was held in a large pit surrounded by stacked stone, with the flames often as high as five feet. One side of the fire pit had four Adirondack chairs, while the other two sides had lodgepole pine beams on the ground used as makeshift benches. All the ranch hands were in attendance, as well as Mazie's four friends from school. Twenty-one-year-old Brandt stood at least six-foot-two and had a solid, athletic build with a little more muscle mass now that he was older.

His dark hair was kept a little shorter and neat, while his face was now covered in dark stubble, although not technically constituting a beard, lending a more rugged appeal than in his teenage years.

Brandt helped Uncle Colt with the massive stone charcoal grill as they prepared enough steak and chicken for an army. Everyone was having a good time, including her mother, although Mazie wasn't sure where she'd gotten to. She was having too much fun with her friends to keep a close eye on her mother. Her friend, Peter, was closing in on five-foot-ten with a lanky yet slightly athletic build, and he was usually clean-shaven. Mazie thought Peter was so handsome, and he was one of the more mature boys in her class. What she loved most about Peter was his kind and generous nature. In school, he was the only guy friend still in their group. Mazie's friend, Cameron, was a bit of a wild child. She didn't hide her body as Mazie hid hers. She was proud of her ample breasts and wore low-cut tank tops, showcasing her assets. Cameron was always the fun one in their group and never had any negative feelings toward anyone.

Mazie's other friend, Melissa, was shorter and slightly heavy-set. She was a simple country girl, and although she loved wearing dresses, they were usually simple, flowered print patterns. Like Mazie's mother, Melissa's family wasn't wealthy either, and her clothes were usually hand-me-downs. In their friend group, Melissa was the witty, funny one. Lastly, there was their other friend, Hannah. Hannah was an attractive teenage girl with hazel eyes, a radiant smile, and wavy blonde hair that hung down below her shoulders. She was approximately five-foot-six with a slim build and a stylish wardrobe. Out of Mazie's friends, Hannah was the sexy, bubbly one everyone loved to hang around. When Peter headed inside to use the bathroom, the discussion among her friends rapidly turned to the handsome young man. Mazie's friends knew how she felt about Peter and loved teasing her about it whenever he left the room.

"I see the way you look at him," Cameron lightly teased her. "What's stopping you? Make the first move."

Mazie hid her embarrassed smile and avoided looking at her friends. "We're just friends," she insisted. "He's not interested in me in that way."

"If you want him to take an interest, you first have to let him know you're interested," Melissa informed her.

"Guys don't always know what they want," Hannah added. "They sometimes need a little nudge."

"What do you mean?" Mazie asked.

"You remember how Tim didn't even notice Deb at the beginning of the school year," Hannah remarked.

"Yeah, but now they're inseparable," Mazie replied.

"That's because Deb made him *notice* her," Hannah insisted. "He just needed that little nudge."

"How did she get him to notice her?" Mazie asked.

"She asked him to join her under the bleachers during study hall," Cameron replied with a giggle.

Mazie stared at her friends, surprised. "Isn't that where boys and girls go to--?"

Hannah grinned and nodded. "She gave it up to him," she announced. "And, now, they're practically joined at the hip."

Mazie fidgeted uncomfortably. "I'm not sure I'm comfortable doing that with a boy," she remarked. "I mean, I've never even kissed a boy."

"Then you shouldn't do it," Melissa announced, standing firm.

"Deb said 'doing it' was no big deal," Hannah insisted. "If you really like Peter, it might be your only chance to get him to think of you as something other than a friend."

"I do like him," Mazie muttered, lost in thought.

"I know that's what I'm going to do when I find a boy I like," Hannah remarked. "If it worked for Deb--"

"Bad advice," Cameron muttered.

"Besides, Peter and I don't even have the same study hall together," Mazie informed Hannah.

"You can be so naïve, Mazie," Hannah remarked, then laughed. "You have a barn with a nice, secluded hay loft. That's the perfect place to hook up."

Mazie stared at Hannah, surprised. "Don't you think Uncle Colt will wonder where I am so long?" she asked.

"Yes, he would," Melissa scoffed, glaring her disapproval at Hannah. "Don't listen to Hannah."

"It takes like five minutes," Hannah informed her and waved her off. "They won't even notice you're gone."

"Five minutes?" Mazie asked with surprise. "I thought it took longer than that."

"Only in the movies," Hannah insisted. "Deb and Tim 'do it' in the bathroom between classes all the time."

"That's gross," Cameron muttered. "And you're full of shit, Hannah."

"Five minutes? Wow, that is fast," Mazie muttered, then reconsidered it. "That doesn't seem right. When my mother had 'the talk' with me, she didn't make it sound that casual. She said it's kind of a big deal."

"Maybe back in our parents' day," Hannah remarked, then waved her off. "Tina said it's not a big deal."

"It is a big deal," Melissa snarled, glaring at Hannah. "Stop saying that stuff."

They saw Peter return from the house and cross the patio.

Hannah jabbed Mazie and grinned. "There he is," she whispered. "You should go for it."

"I wouldn't even know what to say," Mazie whispered back.

"Stop it," Melissa scoffed at Hannah, then looked at Mazie. "Save yourself for the right guy."

"How do you know Peter isn't the right guy?" Hannah demanded while glaring at Melissa. "She obviously likes him."

"I don't know, Mazie," Cameron remarked. "I think you should wait as well."

"Why don't you go out to the barn and wait for him in the loft?" Hannah suggested, ignoring their friends. "I'll tell him he should go out and meet you. It'll be easier with fewer people around to overhear."

Mazie thought about what each of her friends had said as she watched Peter approach. He no sooner sat down when Mazie stood.

"I'll, uh, be right back," Mazie announced, then headed for the house.

Chapter 22

Mazie nervously alternated between sitting on a bale of hay in the loft, which contained nearly two hundred bales, and pacing the small open area before the ladder. She'd only been waiting in the loft a few minutes, but it seemed like a lifetime. Her heart was pounding, and she felt a sick feeling in her stomach. When she heard someone within the barn downstairs, she nearly jumped out of her skin. She then heard a strange sound like a horse thumping within its stall, but none of the horses were inside tonight. Mazie couldn't handle the stress and talked herself out of whatever stupid thought she'd been having. She returned to the ladder and quickly climbed down to the ground floor. As Mazie turned, she saw Brandt casually leaning against one of the stall doors with his old baseball bat relaxed in his hand. He lightly twirled it, then looked up when he saw her and smiled.

"I was wondering where you'd gotten to," Brandt announced cheerfully. "Dinner's ready."

Mazie eyed Brandt almost suspiciously. "What are you doing out here?"

Brandt shrugged with little care. "Just gathering everyone up for dinner," he replied, then gave a general nod to the barn door. "Oh, your friend, Peter, said he had to go home."

Mazie stared at Brandt for a long moment, then became concerned. "Did you say something to him?" she suddenly demanded.

"I'm sure I said something to him at some point this evening," Brandt replied a little too casually, then cocked his head while squinting. "He's kind of squirrely, that one."

Horror suddenly crossed her face. "Did you threaten him?" Mazie gasped, realizing what must have happened.

"Threaten him?" Brandt asked with surprise, then smiled and shook his head while placing the bat to his shoulder. "No, of course not." He then shrugged. "I mean, I may have had a little talk with him about how a gentleman should treat a lady, but I'm sure that didn't have anything to do with his decision to leave early."

"How could you?" Mazie cried out in anger and embarrassment. "I liked him!"

"How could *I*?" Brandt demanded while glaring at her and straightening, his tone now changing. "How could *you*? What the hell were you thinking, Mazie?"

"That's none of your business!"

"Oh, it's my business," Brandt launched back. "I heard all that bullshit advice Hannah gave you, and that's not how you go about establishing a relationship."

"And you're the authority on relationships, huh?" Mazie huffed while folding her arms across her chest.

"I've been out there," he informed her, then nodded. "So, yeah, I know more about it than you do."

"Stay out of my life, Brandt," Mazie shot back. "The one time I take an interest in a boy, and you have to chase him away!"

"If you think having sex with a boy is going to make him like you, you're in for a rude awakening," Brandt snapped back. "It doesn't work that way. Boys will use you for sex then toss you aside like garbage."

"You don't know that!"

"Yes, I do!"

She stared at him, wanting to yell at him, but his words somehow disturbed her. Mazie suddenly wondered how he seemed so convinced.

"Did you do that?" she asked almost timidly and with some surprise.

"No, of course not," he replied, then fidgeted and ran his fingers through his hair. "But I know a lot of guys, Mazie. Back in high school, I'd heard guys bragging all the time about how they'd conned girls into doing things. I don't want that happening to you."

Mazie shifted uncomfortably and couldn't look at Brandt. "He only sees me as a friend," she whispered. "I sometimes wonder if he even realizes I'm a girl."

"Giving yourself to a boy isn't going to make him like you," Brandt informed her, taking a more delicate tone. "Not in the way you want him to. When you meet the right boy, you'll know."

She finally met his gaze. "What if Peter is the right boy?" Mazie asked. "I really like him."

"If he doesn't feel the same way about you, he's not the right guy," Brandt replied.

"So how will I know?" she asked. "If I don't make the first move, how will I ever know?"

"You'll know because he'll always be beside you," Brandt informed her. "Like some love-sick puppy following you around."

"Well, that's never happening," Mazie muttered and again folded her arms across her chest while casting her back against the stall wall.

"What's the rush?" Brandt asked and leaned against the wall next to her. "You don't need a boyfriend to define who you are. Take your time. Save yourself for the right one."

Mazie eyed him almost suspiciously. "Makes you a bit of a hypocrite, doesn't it?" she remarked. "Telling me to wait for someone special when you didn't."

Brandt groaned and rested his head against the wall behind him. "Are we really having this discussion?" he muttered.

"If you don't want your advice to feel like a double standard," Mazie remarked, then nodded. "Yeah, I think you need to be honest about your relationships or lack thereof."

Brandt released a heavy sigh, then glanced at her with a moderately defeated look. "You remember that date I went on the night you snuck out to that party."

Mazie nodded. "I remember both with vivid clarity."

"I thought *she* was someone special," Brandt informed her. "I thought she really liked me and that we were meant to be together, especially since she was the one who suggested, well, being intimate." He hesitated, then frowned while looking down. "I planned a romantic moonlit picnic on the back forty. Bought one of those blow-up mattresses for the back of my pickup truck, got a bottle of wine off one of the ranch hands, and I even picked some flowers."

Mazie studied his profile, despite his refusal to meet her gaze. What sounded like a romantic story didn't feel like it ended happily. His pain was evident.

"When she seemed a little too eager the moment I picked her up, I probably should have been smarter," Brandt remarked while frowning. "But I was a stupid teenager and jumped at the opportunity." He shook his head. "Right there in the front seat of my truck. In her parents' driveway."

Mazie suddenly grimaced, not liking where this story was going.

Brandt seemed to drift off for a moment, wallowing in his own memories. "Literally two seconds after what I thought was the single greatest experience of my life, a car pulls into the driveway."

Mazie withheld her gasp, staring at him with horror in her eyes, clinging to every word.

Brandt snorted a laugh and shook his head. "There he was, timed perfectly, her ex-boyfriend," he announced. "Pissed and ready for a fight. Being the ignorant hick I am, I was all too willing to oblige. I'll never forget the smirk on her face when she boasted to her ex-boyfriend about what we'd done, egging him on." Brandt frowned, then finally looked at Mazie with hurt in his eyes. "She didn't give a damn about me. She just used me to make her ex-boyfriend jealous and wanted us to fight over her."

"What happened?" Mazie eagerly asked.

Brandt grimaced while straightening and rubbed the back of his neck. "I gave her twenty dollars, thanked her for a good time, apologized to her ex-boyfriend, and drove away with what was left of my dignity."

Mazie stared at Brandt for a long moment, stunned by what he said. "Handled like a boss," Mazie proudly cried out while straightening and patting his shoulder. "You're, like, a legend."

Brandt stared at her, slightly bewildered. "You approve of what I did?"

"Hell, yeah!" Mazie exclaimed. "The bitch got what she deserved!"

Brandt suddenly snorted a laugh. "You really are my favorite wrangler," he announced as he placed his arm around her shoulder and pulled her to his side, twirling the baseball bat as they walked to the barn door.

"You didn't actually threaten Peter with that baseball bat, did you?"

Brandt shrugged, then offered a tiny, sly grin. "Maybe a little."

Mazie snorted a laugh and shook her head. "I really do hate you."

"And somehow, I'm okay with that."

§

*P*resent day. Mazie returned to the bizarre reality she was in, where she was actually in Peter's presence after five years. She couldn't deny the intense feelings she'd had for him back then, and how much of an impact that one bonfire had had on her life.

"So here we are," Melissa announced, somewhat giddy. "Looking for a birthday card for Brandt."

"It's been so long, and there's so much catching up to do," Peter announced while grinning at Mazie, then became enthusiastic. "My first night back. We should go out to dinner and catch up."

Mazie felt her heart pounding at the suggestion. Was he asking her on a date? Her mind reeled, but she was brought back to the reality of her prior engagement. She couldn't disappoint her mother.

"I'd love to, but my mother's expecting me at the ranch tonight," Mazie replied while cringing just hearing those words. "She'd be extremely disappointed." That was putting it mildly.

"Oh, that's too bad," Peter replied, then offered a consoling smile before looking at Melissa. "Hopefully, Cameron can go out with us."

Mazie's heart sank, and she suddenly felt stupid. He didn't mean just the two of them. He had meant the four of them. She attempted to hide her embarrassment.

"I'll check with her, of course," Melissa announced, pleased with the idea.

Peter then looked back at Mazie. "We'll definitely get together sometime soon," he insisted.

"Yeah, I'm sure there's plenty of time," Mazie replied. "I'll, uh, see you later."

"It's a date."

Mazie watched Peter leave, then frowned. No, it wasn't a date. That was abundantly clear. She resumed looking at birthday cards with renewed disgust. Melissa gazed after Peter until he was gone, then groaned.

"Damn, he looked good, huh?" Melissa muttered before plucking another card from the rack. "Pity he can be such a jerk at times."

Mazie considered the comment and found herself silently agreeing with her. It was true. She had almost forgotten what had happened two years later, but that was a story for another time.

Chapter 23

Mazie stared out the front windshield from the passenger side as Melissa drove up the long driveway to the ranch. As the barn and massive ranch house came into view, Mazie's heart skipped a beat, then started pounding with her spiking anxiety. Seeing the house again was a mix of heaven and hell. Like some bizarre dream from which she couldn't wake. She missed the place so much, yet she wanted to run away and never come back. When Melissa parked not far from the house, Mazie could do little more than stare out the windshield and feel her heart pounding in her chest. Melissa stared at her for a long moment in silence.

"You can still change your mind," Melissa spoke softly, feeling her friend's anxiety.

"No," Mazie whispered, barely getting the word out. "I have to do this. Not just for my boss or my mother but for myself."

Another moment passed.

"Would it help if I opened the door?" Melissa then asked while cringing.

Mazie took a deep breath and held onto it before opening the car door. As she got out of the car, Mazie felt almost dizzy but managed to look back at her friend.

"Thanks, Melissa," she announced.

"Call me with an update," Melissa replied while attempting a smile. "Let me know how it went."

"I will, thanks."

Mazie shut the car door and took a couple of steps toward the house before stopping. As Melissa turned around and drove back down the long driveway, Mazie stood there for several minutes just staring at the house, the barn, and the pasture with several grazing horses. Her eyes suddenly fell upon a dark horse standing in the pasture staring at her. Mazie squinted a moment, then made her way closer to the fence. The horse started walking toward her, then suddenly broke into a gallop, racing toward the fence while snickering loudly. Mazie stopped by the wooden fence and stared at her old black and white paint gelding.

"Katona," she gasped while feeling the tears welling up in her eyes. "Hey, boy." Mazie lovingly caressed the horse's face that seemed whiter than she remembered. "I can't believe you're still alive. Look at you!"

Katona was about nineteen years old when she left, which meant he was now almost twenty-five. The horse nuzzled her while sniffing her shirt for treats. Mazie laughed while rubbing his face.

"I'm sorry," she announced. "I don't have any carrots on me. I'll get some, though."

In a flood of memories, Mazie recalled all the fun she'd had on Katona. He was the best horse. Sadly, they retired him when he started showing signs of arthritis in his back. Supplements kept him comfortable, but only if he was pulled from active duty. Her thoughts strayed to the first week without her trusty mount, which was right after high school graduation, just before her graduation party.

§

*F*lashback. Eighteen-year-old Mazie was now a beautiful young woman, even if she didn't dress like one and still wore her hair in a ponytail. She maintained her preference for wearing sports bras, which helped keep everything in place while riding horses and working with cattle, but she no longer resented her bust size. Her friends helped her over those particular hurdles, especially when Peter joked with other boys about liking women with ample breasts, not that he really noticed hers, which were well hidden beneath her sports bras. Despite her strong feelings for Peter, she didn't let silly romantic notions interfere with her new full-time job as MTB Ranch's first woman wrangler. She'd finally graduated from high school, and it was her first full week of living the dream. All she ever wanted was to work the cattle alongside Brandt, and it was no longer just a summer and weekend job.

Mazie sent the bay horse into a gallop after a stray steer that had bolted away from the herd. She managed to corral the steer, despite bobbing up and down on the saddle, and chased it back with the others. It may have been her dream job, but that didn't mean her ass wasn't going to be sore in the morning. Since retiring Katona, she was given the only horse left, which happened to be the one with the bounciest gaits. The wranglers all had their favorite horses, and whether she liked it or not, she had the least seniority. Twenty-three-year-old Brandt sat on his horse and watched her, grinning like a schoolboy, as she rode back to him. Mazie frowned, knowing what he was thinking without a word being spoken, but true to form, Brandt was going to speak them anyway.

"Did you forget how to ride?" he remarked, clearly mocking her while shaking his head.

"It's the horse," she snapped back while glaring at him. "Ever since we retired Katona, I can't find my seat."

"Stop blaming the horse," Brandt moaned, then smirked at her. "You need to get your head out of the clouds, daydreaming about your boy, Peter, and put a little more effort into your job. A little more 'ass in the seat' wouldn't hurt either."

"I'm trying to keep my ass in the seat, and I assure you, it does hurt," Mazie retorted, then squinted at him, conveying her annoyance. "And I'm not daydreaming about Peter. We're just friends. Nothing more." She then looked away. "Besides, I'm pretty sure he's still scared of you."

"Huh?" Brandt announced while grinning almost proudly. "Nice to know I make a lasting impression."

"That's not funny," she remarked.

"It kind of is," he teased, then turned serious while shifting in his saddle. "Peter isn't right for you anyway."

"Again, just a friend," she reminded him, then raised an arrogant brow. "But if we were something more, Peter would be perfect for me."

Brandt groaned and rolled his eyes. "If you take away the rich boy's fancy car and that baby face, he'd only be left with that dull personality of his."

"He's not dull," Mazie scoffed, defensive. "He's a lot of fun."

"No," Brandt announced boldly while raising a brow. "You're fun. He's just piggybacking off your personality. You could do so much better."

"Why are we even having this conversation?" she demanded. "Peter and I are just friends."

"Good," Brandt replied. "Then you can stop daydreaming about him."

Mazie groaned and shook her head. "You're insufferable!" She then cast a stern look at him. "You need to get a girlfriend, ASAP."

"A girlfriend is the last thing I need," he scoffed. "The entire female population can kiss my ass."

"It's that attitude of yours that repels women," she reminded him.

"No," he casually replied. "It's my profession that repels women. As long as I take them to nice restaurants, they're happy. The moment I want to bring them home, the story changes."

"Do you realize how ridiculous you sound?"

"When you smell like cattle and horses seventy-five percent of the time, interest fades fast," he reminded her. "You'll see. Now that you officially graduated high school and plan on working the cattle full-time, you'll see soon enough. 'No personality Peter' would never date a ranch hand, that's for sure."

She shook her head. "You *really* need to get laid," Mazie muttered. "You're starting to sound like Uncle Colt."

"That was a cheap shot," Brandt scoffed. "And you sound more like Uncle Colt than I ever have."

Mazie glared back at him. "Careful, boss man," she remarked. "I'll uninvite you to my graduation party tomorrow night."

"Well, you can try," he casually replied. "But it's at my ranch, so I'm guessing that won't work out for you."

"Can we get back to work?"

"Absolutely," he replied. "I'm not paying you to sit around and gossip."

Mazie hid her smile and shook her head. "You're a shitty boss, you know that?"

"Considering that full-time wrangler position comes with a pay raise, you may want to work on your ass kissing," Brandt reminded her. "You're not really good at it." He smiled while sinking into his own thoughts. "I really miss those days when you worshipped the ground I walked on."

"I never worshipped the ground you walked on," Mazie corrected.

"Are you kidding?" Brandt remarked as he partially turned in his saddle, facing her. "For eight long years, you did nothing but follow me around everywhere I went. Tripping over you every time I went to take a piss."

Mazie groaned and laughed a bit like a psychotic woman while shaking her head. "Now, you're just making shit up," she informed him.

"Maybe I exaggerate just a little," Brandt replied while maintaining his grin.

"You're in a scary good mood lately," Mazie remarked almost suspiciously.

"There's no better life than life in the saddle," he informed her. "And I have almost everything I've ever wanted." Brandt looked around the open, lush pasture filled with grazing cattle and several wranglers at their posts, then indicated the sunny, blue sky. "It's a perfect day. Why wouldn't I be in a good mood?"

"It *is* a perfect day," Mazie replied. "My aching ass aside."

"Yeah, I'm kind of enjoying that too," Brandt announced, then chuckled.

Mazie leaned closer to him while smirking. "Careful," she scoffed. "The next time my mom washes your tighty whities, I may slip a little starch into them."

"Bring it on," Brandt announced with a humored chuckle.

Their playful banter was interrupted by Colt's loud whistle. When they returned their attention to the herd, Colt was glaring at them and pointing at a runaway cow.

"I got this one," Brandt announced. "Show you how your ass is supposed to ride in the saddle."

When Brandt sent his horse into a gallop after the cow, Mazie felt compelled to watch. There was always something about the way Brandt sat a horse that commanded her attention. He'd been riding Thunder for the last thirteen years, and despite the horse being in his late teens, Thunder was still completely sound. The two of them worked flawlessly together as a team, which may have contributed to Brandt's riding skills, but there was something more than that. Mazie snapped out of her thoughts and came to a frightening conclusion. She *did* worship Brandt! Once he reunited the steer with the herd, he rejoined Mazie and 'parked' Thunder alongside her while grinning somewhat slyly.

"See, that's how you keep your ass in the saddle," Brandt teased.

Mazie continued to stare at him, lost in thought with a strange smile on her face. Brandt immediately became suspicious.

"What are you smiling about?" he demanded, sounding almost concerned.

Mazie offered a tiny smile and shrugged. "I just enjoy watching you and Thunder in action," she replied. "I hope I can ride like that someday."

Brandt stared at her a moment, possibly waiting for a snarky comment to follow. When none did, he hid his smile and appeared almost embarrassed by the compliment. Brandt circled his horse around hers so he was alongside her, facing her, and leaned close to her ear.

"You already do," he whispered in her ear, then gave her ponytail a healthy swish before galloping away.

Mazie groaned, hating when he mocked her ponytail, and took off after him. Brandt laughed as she chased after him on her much slower horse. Colt and Dalton sat on their horses on the opposite side of the herd, watching Mazie and Brandt chase each other around the field. Both frowned and shook their heads.

"I'm already regretting letting those two team up," Colt muttered.

"If we're splitting them up, you get Brandt," Dalton remarked.

Colt considered the comment without taking his eyes off Brandt and Mazie racing around the field. He drew a deep breath and held it a moment.

"Well, they're just having a little fun," Colt remarked. "I suppose it'll calm down over time."

Dalton grinned and chuckled.

§

*M*azie's graduation party the following afternoon included a massive BBQ, a bonfire in the backyard, and her friends, as well as extended family in attendance. As her graduation gift, her mother saved up enough money to pay for Mazie's portion of her dream trip to Australia, which she planned to take that summer with her friends, Cameron, Peter, Hannah, and Melissa. Their two weeks in Australia before Melissa, Hannah, and Peter went away to college were all they could talk about. While Brandt and her uncles grilled enough steak and chicken to feed the entire town, Mazie stole Melissa away to speak privately, taking her to her bedroom in the in-law suite. Melissa was beyond curious now and watched as Mazie closed and locked her bedroom door behind them for added privacy.

"Oh, something's up," Melissa announced while grinning. "You certainly didn't drag me into your room to talk about the weather."

Mazie couldn't contain her grin as she removed a plastic bag from her dresser drawer. She pulled out a short, black satin and lace nightgown and waved it by the thin straps. Melissa gasped and placed her hand to her mouth to keep from screaming when she saw the sexy lingerie.

"Oh, my God," Melissa cried out softly so no one near the suite would hear. "For our trip?"

Mazie nodded.

"With Peter?"

She again nodded, then jumped on the bed while clinging to the lacy nightgown. "I talked to Peter earlier this afternoon, and we're officially sharing one of the bedrooms at the beach house in Australia."

Melissa squealed so softly, it was almost unbearably high-pitched. "Your first time," she announced. "In Australia. With Peter. That is so romantic. I always thought the two of you should have been a couple." She sighed as her smile faded. "I wish I'd find someone. It sounds so perfect."

"Maybe you'll meet some suave Australian guy," Mazie remarked.

"Oh, with an accent," Melissa added, then groaned. "Wouldn't that be amazing?"

"Just don't say anything in front of my family," Mazie informed her friend. "You know how protective they are over me, and Brandt really doesn't like Peter." She frowned and shook her head. "Peter said something about us sharing a room, and Brandt almost overheard it."

"That wouldn't end well," Melissa muttered, then appeared curious. "Are you sure Brandt doesn't suspect anything?"

"Positive," Mazie replied while managing a tiny, tense laugh. "If Brandt had heard, he would have exploded on Peter by now."

"That's going to be a tough secret for you to keep until we actually leave," Melissa reminded her.

"As long as Peter doesn't come around much before our trip, it won't be a problem," Mazie informed her. "Peter was so happy about us sharing a room, he tried to kiss me in the barn. I reminded him that Brandt couldn't catch us, and that we should just wait for our trip to share our first kiss as well. I want everything to be special."

"This is going to be the best trip ever," Melissa announced excitedly.

Chapter 24

After the best steak dinner she'd ever had, Mazie opened her gifts from her friends and her family. Most were graduation cards with some money, which she intended to use in Australia. Dalton saved his gift for last, handing her a small, neatly wrapped box.

"This is from Colt and me," Dalton informed her. "I hope you like it."

Mazie smiled at her surrogate uncles, happy with anything they'd give her and had given her over the years. "I'm sure I will," she announced, then opened the box. Mazie removed a fob key with 'Jeep' embossed on it and stared at it with surprise before eyeing both men. "No way!"

Colt laughed and pointed around the house. "It's out front."

Mazie sprang up and ran around the house with her friends on her heels. She stopped and stared in awe at the lightly used, soft-topped Jeep in fire engine red. Mazie cried out excitedly and ran for the Jeep. Her friends soon joined her in the open Jeep.

"Can you drive stick?" Peter asked while eyeing the gear shifter.

Mazie gave him an arrogant look. "I was raised on a ranch," she reminded him. "Of course, I can drive stick. Brandt taught me."

"We should take it for a drive," Cameron suggested.

"To the pond," Melissa announced.

"Later," Colt scolded. "You have guests."

Mazie nodded. "Yes, we'll go later," she informed her friends.

Dalton then looked around. "Where did Brandt get to?" he just about demanded.

"He said he needed to wrap Mazie's gift," Colt informed him.

"Considering he had all morning," Dalton muttered. "I'm guessing he forgot."

"I didn't forget," Brandt called to them as he approached. "I just had to wait to wrap it, that's all."

Everyone looked at Brandt as he led a tall, thick blue roan gelding, wearing just a bridle, from the barn toward them. The horse had a large red bow attached to the bridle headstall. Mazie stared at the magnificent horse with a look of possible shock.

"Is that for me?" she just about gasped.

Brandt smiled and held out the reins to her. "Maybe now you'll be able to find your seat," he teased.

Mazie cried out excitedly, threw her arms around Brandt's neck, and practically jumped on him while hugging him. He returned the enthusiastic embrace.

"Thank you," she whispered with bated breath, then quickly kissed his cheek.

"You're welcome," he replied while nuzzling his face against hers.

Mazie reluctantly pulled away while dabbing the tears in her eyes before excitedly looking over the horse.

"I honestly thought she'd be more excited about the Jeep," Colt remarked.

"Well," Brandt replied with a smile. "I guess I know Mazie better than you. Most girls want flashy diamonds; Mazie wants a flashy horse."

"I'd rather have the Jeep," Peter remarked with a tiny laugh.

"He's gorgeous," Mazie exclaimed while inspecting every inch of the animal.

Without warning, Mazie swung up onto the horse's back without the need for a saddle and then smiled at Brandt and extended her hand.

"Want to go for a quick spin around the house?" Mazie asked.

Brandt grinned, accepted her hand, and swung onto the horse behind her. He anchored his left arm around her waist as she sent the horse into a lope, riding around the house to proudly show the rest of her guests the beautiful horse Brandt gave her.

*A*fter spending some time hand-grazing her new horse out back at the party, it was starting to get dark, and Uncle Colt was piling more wood onto the fire, which meant it was time to put her new horse away for the night. With it being somewhat dark out back before the fire really kicked in, Mazie lost track of her friends. Uncle Dalton stopped her before she made it to the side of the house with the horse.

"You'd better put the horse back in his stall for tonight," Dalton informed her. "We don't want the other horses creating a ruckus out in the pasture when we're all in bed and can't keep an eye on him. We'll put him in the pasture tomorrow morning after the others are saddled. Let him get used to the geriatric herd first."

"Sounds good," Mazie replied, then headed around the house.

Melissa came out of the house and hurried to join her. "Hey, Mazie," she announced. "Where are you going?"

"Just putting my new horse away," Mazie replied. "Want to come along?"

"Sure," Melissa replied and walked with her and the horse to the front of the house.

They continued across the driveway and to the barn in virtual silence while admiring Mazie's gift horse. The barn door was already open, and the interior lights came on as they approached. As they got closer, they heard raised voices, startling both of them. Peter darted from the barn, with Brandt on his heels, and immediately spun to face him.

"What's your problem?" Peter yelled out in anger while lightly dabbing the fresh cut on the corner of his bleeding lip.

"You're my problem," Brandt snarled while pointing an angry, warning finger at him. "You stay the fuck away from Mazie!"

"She's eighteen," Peter launched back. "She's old enough to make her own decisions, so stop acting like her creepy brother!"

"Get off my property!" Brandt snarled while taking a quick step closer to Peter.

Mazie handed the horse's reins to Melissa and darted between the two men, separating them while facing Brandt.

"Please, Brandt," Mazie pleaded while searching his eyes. "Don't do this. Not tonight. Peter's my guest. We can talk about this tomorrow."

"Mazie--" Melissa gasped softly from nearby with her horse.

Mazie looked at her friend and saw her staring at the barn. She followed Melissa's gaze and saw Hannah quietly slipping out of the barn. Mazie's expression suddenly dropped when she saw the guilty look on Hannah's face. She looked back at Peter, who barely even reacted.

"It's not how it looks," Peter remarked almost casually.

Without a word, Mazie turned, patted Brandt's shoulder, and then approached Melissa. She reclaimed the horse's reins and led it to the barn. Brandt folded his arms across his chest and arrogantly cocked his head while glaring at Peter.

"You heard the boss," Brandt scoffed.

"Go home, Peter," Melissa snarled, reminding everyone she was still there, then pointed at Hannah. "Go home and take your little skank with you."

"It's not as if Peter and Mazie are dating," Hannah reminded Melissa, attempting to defend the situation. "We didn't do anything wrong."

"Shut up, you skank!" Melissa screamed and glared at Peter again. "And you can forget about Australia! The reservations are under my name, and I'm cancelling your flight!" She then glared at Hannah. "Yours too, skank!"

Mazie entered the barn without a word.

"You're being ridiculous, Melissa," Peter snapped back, clearly annoyed. "I paid for my portion of the trip."

"I'll refund your money," Melissa scoffed, then looked back at Brandt. "He's all yours."

Peter's eyes suddenly widened as fear swept through him. "Let's go, Hannah," he announced. "Now!"

Brandt didn't even twitch, calmly watching Peter and Hannah bolt for Peter's car. Melissa ran to the barn and hurried inside. Mazie had already put the horse into its stall and was hanging up the bridle as Melissa approached.

"Are you okay?" Melissa asked softly.

Peter's car was heard burning out on the driveway and speeding away from the ranch house. Mazie drew a deep, shaken breath.

"I'm numb, Melissa," Mazie finally replied. "I thought Peter wanted to be with me, but now, I'm not sure he's really even my friend."

"Hannah either," Melissa muttered. "Next time I see her, I'm ripping her hair out."

"Don't bother," Mazie announced with a sigh. "I've wasted too much of my life chasing after that jerk."

Melissa walked with Mazie from the barn just in time to see Peter's car disappear down the long driveway. Colt and Dalton appeared from the side of the house and looked around, having heard the car burn out and speed off. They seemed relieved when they saw Mazie, Melissa, and Brandt approaching them.

"Don't say anything," Mazie announced just soft enough for Melissa and Brandt to hear. "Let's just find Cameron and enjoy the rest of the party."

Brandt placed his arm around Mazie's shoulder, pulled her close to his side, and kissed the top of her head. She immediately clung to him, refusing to let him go as they headed closer to the house.

"What happened?" Colt demanded with a look meant to kill. "Who the hell's tearing up the driveway and spooking the animals?"

"Just Peter being an ass," Mazie replied, then forced a smile, which was easy to do in the dim lighting so no one could see her crying. "Is there any cake left, or did you guys eat it all?"

"There's cake," Dalton replied, eyeing the way she clung to Brandt, then managed a smile and nodded toward the house.

Colt eyed Brandt as he passed with Melissa and Mazie, secretly questioning what had happened. Brandt barely acknowledged him, not willing to give up any information.

Chapter 25

Sometime after midnight that night, Brandt sat on top of the covers on his bed, resting against the headboard while watching television in the mostly dark room. His bedroom had undergone several transformations over the years, and he had finally found the time to keep his room clean and his bed made. Gone were the days of dirty clothes strewn about the floor. Brandt wore an old pair of shorts and a t-shirt, as he almost always kept his bedroom door open. The smell of smoky, smoldering wood from the bonfire filled his bedroom since the windows were open on the warm summer night. There was a soft tapping on his bedroom door. Brandt glanced to his partially open door and saw Mazie in the doorway.

"I thought you went to bed hours ago," Brandt remarked.

"I couldn't sleep," she replied. "I kind of figured you'd still be up."

"Something bothering you?" he asked, then patted the bed. "You can tell me. I'd like to think I'm not just your boss, but your friend."

Mazie glared at the cheap smile on his face and sneered at him. "You can be such a prick, you know that?"

Brandt laughed. "Always keep them guessing," he replied. "That's my leadership motto."

Mazie rolled her eyes and then entered the bedroom. "I thought it was 'no beans for lunch'."

"That too," he remarked with a chuckle.

Brandt eyed her in her thin, worn tank top and frumpy sleep shorts. As she approached the bed, he looked away and almost casually pulled the extra pillow across his lap. Mazie climbed onto the bed alongside him and leaned against the headboard.

"Is it okay if I watch a movie with you until I feel tired?" she asked.

"As long as you don't tell the other ranch hands," he replied. "I don't want them all lining up to crawl in my bed with me."

Mazie laughed, clung to his arm, and placed her head on his shoulder. "It'll be our little secret," she remarked and nuzzled his shoulder. "I miss our Saturday night movie marathons." She then chuckled while in thought. "Remember that one Saturday a few years ago when we watched movies until the sun came up."

"I watched the movies," he informed her. "I'm pretty sure you talked through them."

"I miss that," she remarked, then sighed almost sadly.

"Why are you turning all nostalgic?" he asked, then cocked his head. "Please don't tell me you're wasting any emotions on that jerk-off Peter."

Mazie groaned while pulling away from him. She turned around on the bed and flopped onto her back alongside his legs and placed her feet on the headboard near his shoulder. Brandt watched her as she ran her fingers through her loose, unkempt hair before his eyes again strayed to the thin tank top she wore. He squirmed slightly and seemed uncomfortable. Mazie allowed her arms to fall past her head, stretching further, and drew a deep breath while staring at the ceiling. Brandt's eyes now settled on her hard nipples pressing against the thin material just about covering her ample breasts.

"It feels as if everything is changing, and I'm being left behind," she informed him while frowning.

Brandt looked past her stretched body, in an unintended sexual pose, to her face. "You do *want* to work the ranch, don't you?" He suddenly tensed. "I mean, you don't have to. You could go to college if you wanted to go."

"Don't be silly. Of course, I want to work here," she insisted. "That's always been my dream."

Despite her answer, she didn't take her eyes off the ceiling and subconsciously drew another deep breath, which instantly returned his eyes to her perky nipples.

"If you want to take the summer off and spend it with your friends, I'll understand," he informed her. "If it makes you happy--"

Mazie looked at him and smiled warmly. "That's a kind offer, Brandt," she replied. "But I don't want the summer off. It's just--" As she sat up, her breasts fell back into place with a slight bounce. She groaned softly. "It just feels like there should be something more to life." She then made a face. "Does that make sense?"

Brandt groaned softly, lightly scratched his brow, and then looked away, seeming tense. "Yeah, it makes perfect sense," he replied. "I feel that way a lot."

Mazie groaned and shook her head. "I hate to think we have something in common," she muttered, then cast a look at him. "Because, you know, on account of you being such a big dork."

"I'm a dork?" he scoffed while eyeing her. "*You* think *I'm* a dork?"

She cast a cocky look at him. "Oh, I'm sorry," Mazie announced, almost sounding serious. "Was that supposed to be a secret?" She flopped down onto her back, giggled, and gave his shoulder a shove with her bare foot. "Dork."

"I'm not the dork," he insisted while shoving her foot away from his shoulder. "You're the dork. With your shoeboxes filled with flashcards."

Mazie now laughed and again shoved his shoulder with her bare foot. "Big, goofy dork."

"Kid gloves off," Brandt announced as he tossed the pillow from his lap, shoved her foot away from his shoulder, and jumped on top of her.

She let out a playful scream as he tickled and poked her in the ribs. "Stop it," she cried out while laughing. "That's not funny."

Mazie tried to push him off with her legs, but he easily pushed her leg aside, inadvertently placing himself in a compromising position while on top of her. She playfully pushed on his shoulders to get him off her while laughing, then suddenly tensed and braced her hands against his shoulders.

"Brandt, is that--?" She suddenly gasped with realization and pushed against him. "Brandt!"

Brandt just about jumped off her, sat up, and placed the discarded pillow across his lap while avoiding her gaze.

"Sorry," he gasped while attempting to control his heavy breathing. "I'm really sorry."

Mazie uncertainly pulled herself up into a sitting position and scooted closer to the foot end of the bed, unable to take her eyes off him for some unexplained reason. It was a lot to process.

"What the hell was that?" she gasped while studying him, then attempted to keep her voice down. "Is that *normal*?"

He looked at her with some embarrassment. "Well, yeah," Brandt replied. "Under the circumstances--"

"Talk about embarrassing," Mazie muttered, then fidgeted, raking her fingers through her hair. "Do you need some time to, uh, sort things out? Is that what you used to call it? Should I leave?"

"You don't have to leave," he insisted while casting another look at her, then groaned, somewhat disgusted. "I didn't mean to upset you."

Mazie held her breath, then cautiously moved back alongside him and rested against the headboard.

"I'm not upset," she replied timidly as she held her knees to her chest. "Just a little surprised you'd have that sort of response toward me, that's all."

Mazie then rested her chin on her knees as she attempted to watch the movie, but she was more than a little distracted. Brandt kept the pillow across his lap and stared at the television across the dimly lit room as well, clearly upset with himself.

"I'm sorry if I made you uncomfortable," Brandt just about whispered without looking at her. "I don't want you to feel uncomfortable around me."

Mazie felt compelled to look at his profile, somewhat surprised. "No, of course not," she insisted without missing a beat. "I've been like a wart on your ass since I was five years old."

Brandt glanced at her and snorted a laugh. "That's possibly the most accurate interpretation of our relationship that I'd ever heard," he remarked.

"I don't think I've been uncomfortable around you a day in my entire life," she informed him.

"That's possibly the nicest thing you've ever said to me," Brandt remarked.

"And once you get your boner situation under control, I might actually learn to respect you as my boss," she lightly teased.

As Brandt sharply eyed her, Mazie hid her smile and playfully shoved her shoulder into his. He seemed to relax as her mood lightened.

Chapter 26

Present day. When she heard the sound of galloping hoof beats, Mazie was abruptly returned to reality. Despite it being only early afternoon, she was almost sure she knew the approaching rider would be Brandt. Her heart pounded with mixed emotions as she turned to confirm her suspicions. There he was! Brandt rode the blue roan gelding he'd gifted to her as a graduation present and slowed as he approached, heading directly for her. For a brief moment, Mazie was almost awe-inspired by his grand entrance. As he stopped his horse near her, meeting her gaze with a stern, almost commanding look, she no longer saw the gangly, cocky teenager who used to put her into headlocks for the dreaded noogies. He wasn't even the young man she'd turned her back on five years ago. Brandt was a hard, rugged, and intimidating man. Shockingly, over the last five years, he'd morphed into Colt.

Brandt, now in his late twenties, stood over six-foot-two with a solid, athletic build and broad shoulders. His dark hair was a little shorter now, and he had transitioned from a face full of stubble to a sparse yet well-maintained beard, which was already showing signs of gray at the chin, making him seem a little older than his years. He was ruggedly handsome and almost a cross between Uncle Dalton's stature and good looks and Uncle Colt's ruggedness and grit. There was a time when Mazie felt confident enough to challenge Brandt, but she was certain she didn't know this man. Mazie was suddenly at a loss for words, unsure of what she could say. She knew it wouldn't be any of the smart remarks she had earlier shared with Melissa. She just hoped she looked more confident than she felt at that moment. When Brandt casually leaned forward on the saddle horn, pushed his black cowboy hat back with his thumb, and looked her over, Mazie's anxiety spiked.

"I don't care if you're peddling insurance or spreading the good word," Brandt announced. "No solicitation."

Mazie was suddenly taken aback by his words. He didn't recognize her? How was that possible? Even with her hair down and a little makeup, she couldn't have looked that different. Brandt suddenly grinned and chuckled before swiftly dismounting his horse with his ever-famous front sliding dismount. The one where he threw his right leg over the saddle horn and slid down the saddle on his backside while landing on his feet. No matter what her feelings about Brandt were, he was an artist in the saddle.

"Sorry, I couldn't resist," Brandt announced without even looking at her as he began unsaddling the horse.

"Asshole," she scoffed under her breath.

"Acht," he announced while pulling the saddle off, then cast a quick look at her before tossing the saddle onto the wooden fence. "That's Mr. Asshole to you."

Mazie's eyes narrowed while glaring at him. She suddenly felt the urge to smack him. Brandt returned to his horse, briefly looking at her shoes, then snickered while shaking his head.

"You in high heels," he announced, clearly amused. "Didn't have that one on my bingo card. How the hell do you walk in those things?"

"You won't think it's so funny when I put this stiletto heel up your ass," Mazie scoffed as she folded her arms across her chest.

Brandt eyed her while leading the horse through the gate into the pasture. He removed the bridle, setting the horse free, then shut the gate and turned to face her. He raised a cocky brow as he leaned against the gate, mimicking her by folding his arms across his chest as well.

"Aren't you supposed to be kissing my ass?" he asked sharply. "I mean, that's the only reason you're here, isn't it? You need a favor from the big bad wolf?"

Brandt then straightened and took a step closer, practically hovering over her and locking eyes. Mazie felt her heart skip a beat as his intimidating gaze practically burned through her. Apparently, playtime was over.

"Around here, that requires a whole lot of ass kissing," Brandt informed her. "So I hope you brought plenty of Chapstick because you're going to need it."

Brandt removed his saddle from the fence and didn't even look at her as he headed for the barn.

"My office," he called back to her without missing a beat. "Fifteen minutes."

Mazie stared after him, stunned, as he disappeared into the barn. Davenport suddenly didn't seem so bad.

$\mathcal{M}$azie paced Brandt's study while feeling her anxiety build. The masculine office was more of a trophy room. There were framed photos on the walls, dozens of rodeo trophies on just about every shelf, steer horns, deer antlers, and even an eight-foot-tall stuffed grizzly bear in the back corner, not far from the large window. Mazie eyed the stuffed bear and shivered at the sight of it. It always gave her chills every time she saw it. She avoided looking at the stuffed bear and continued pacing. Mazie hated being summoned to Brandt's office as if she were on his payroll. She already had one boss who treated her like crap; she didn't need another. Especially not Brandt. Mazie sighed with defeat. But he did have her over a barrel, and she had to play nice, even if it meant kissing his ass. The thought made her physically ill. He was going to get even with her by humiliating her, and she'd be able to do little more than thank him for it. He hadn't been that cruel to her since he was twelve when he called her a little girl and scoffed at her 'little girl fantasies'. Somehow, she'd won him over that day, but she couldn't quite remember how. Mazie then remembered that she had broken her arm and cried. She didn't care to repeat that. Although maybe she should consider crying. As childish as it sounded, she did sort of feel like crying right now.

Mazie impatiently looked at her watch and groaned. He'd said fifteen minutes, but he was already letting her squirm by being ten minutes late. Brandt was going to toy with her in a play for petty revenge; she just knew it. Rather than pace the office, Mazie finally noticed subtle differences from when it belonged to Brandt's father and was used by his uncles. There were many new framed photos on the walls. Several included her from their childhood up until she left five years ago. There were also casual pictures, as well as many from the rodeo events they participated in. Mazie hesitated and picked up the team roping trophy beneath the photo of her and Brandt from the summer before she left. It was the first and last team roping trophy they won together. She remembered the day as if it were yesterday.

Chapter 27

Seventeen-year-old Mazie sat on her Uncle Colt's rowdy buckskin gelding in the header slot alongside the cattle chute with the reins held short in one hand and the lasso in her right hand. The buckskin horse pranced in place, prepared to break away at a moment's notice. She attempted to put the crowded stand of onlookers out of her mind while awaiting her run. Mazie looked across the chute at Brandt on his equally hyped black horse. She couldn't believe he looked so focused and calm while her stomach was tied in knots. Mazie would have felt a little better if she knew Brandt was at least a little anxious about their first team roping event together in front of an audience. She'd participated in many breakaway roping events at the rodeo over the last couple of years, but this was her first team roping, and she didn't want to let Brandt down. Brandt met her gaze across the chute and waited for her signal. Mazie nodded, announcing she was ready.

The chute operator released the steer, which immediately made a mad dash across the arena. Mazie loosened the reins, essentially releasing the buckskin from her invisible hold. Mazie raced the buckskin gelding directly on the steer's heels and swung the rope, as she had done so many times before, catching the steer around the neck. As soon as she gave the command, the buckskin horse spun around and backed up, creating a taunt rope against the steer. At the same time, Brandt lassoed the steer's back legs. When the buzzer sounded, they released the steer and looked at the clock. They did it! They had the fastest time. Mazie and Brandt cheered as the crowd applauded. Mazie could have sworn she heard Colt screaming from the sidelines. Brandt circled his horse around Mazie on the buckskin horse and gave her a high-five.

A few minutes later, while still on horseback, they were awarded their first-place trophy. Liddy eagerly took several pictures of them holding the trophy between them while on their horses. Dalton held the trophy for them as they dismounted. Brandt immediately gathered Mazie in his arms and hugged her while laughing.

"I knew you could do it," Brandt announced before finally releasing her.

"I was so nervous," Mazie informed him while releasing a tense laugh.

"That's what makes it so exciting," Brandt informed her. "Rush of adrenaline. Knots in the pit of your stomach. Praying you don't lose a thumb. That's the feeling of being alive."

"Losing a thumb?" Liddy gasped, having overheard that part.

"It doesn't happen as often as you'd think," Brandt reassured her.

"Only once that I've seen," Colt remarked, immediately receiving a glare from Liddy.

"She could lose her thumb?" Liddy cried out.

Brandt took the trophy from Dalton and showed it to Mazie while grinning.

"Isn't that the greatest thing you've ever seen?" Brandt asked while admiring it.

"Where are we going to put it?" Mazie asked, now holding the trophy to take a closer look.

"It belongs in your room," Brandt informed her, surprising her.

"But we won it together," Mazie insisted.

Brandt shrugged while maintaining his smile. "But it's your first team roping trophy," he informed her. "You should keep it. Uncle Colt let me keep the first one I earned with him."

Mazie smiled, overjoyed, and hugged Brandt again, clinging to him with one arm while holding the trophy in the other.

"Thank you, Brandt."

"Hey, we're going to win plenty more together as a team," Brandt insisted, then pulled away. "We'll have another shot at the end of summer next year, after you graduate high school."

"I'll make sure my friends and I are back from our trip to Australia in time," Mazie informed him.

"Who says you're going to Australia?" Liddy practically demanded.

"Melissa, Cameron, Hannah, and Peter," Mazie informed her while grinning. "That's who says. Don't worry. I'll have the money for my share."

Liddy remained tense about the entire trip conversation, then looked at Dalton and frowned. He offered a reassuring smile and shrugged.

*P*resent day. The study door opened, startling Mazie. She set the trophy down and turned as Brandt entered the office, shutting the door behind him. He casually eyed her, then approached his desk.

"Those were the days," Brandt announced before collapsing into the leather chair behind the desk. "Blackjack and I have been placing in all sorts of events at the rodeo every year since I've been riding him." He leaned back and rudely placed his booted feet on the desktop. "Pity we couldn't compete in the team roping. I had a good partner once, before she became a city girl."

Mazie turned toward him, glaring her loathing for him and his passive-aggressive comments. "That's my trophy," she reminded him. "You gave it to me."

"You abandoned it in my house," Brandt reminded her. "That makes it my property. And my name's on it too, in case you'd forgotten."

Mazie glared at his booted feet on the desk, then met his gaze while indicating his feet. "You're being rude," she scoffed.

"I'm just a hick cowboy with no manners," Brandt informed her. "You need something from me, not the other way around."

Mazie drew a deep breath, then shook her head. "This was a bad idea," she huffed. "We can try again in another five years. At least I can tell my mother I made an effort."

As Mazie headed for the study door, Brandt placed his booted feet on the floor with a thud and leaned forward.

"Fine, I was being rude," Brandt announced, his words stopping her just short of the door.

Mazie turned and looked back at him, noting the slightly defeated look on his face. He indicated the chair in front of the desk.

"I'm sorry," Brandt announced in what passed for a sincere tone. "No reason to go tattling to your mother." He again indicated the chair. "What's the favor? I'm willing to listen."

Mazie sucked up her pride, approached the chair, and flopped down in it, immediately crossing her legs. Brandt raised a brow and stretched to look over the desk at her dainty, feminine way of sitting before finally meeting her gaze.

"Who are you and what have you done with my Mazie?" he asked while shaking his head.

"Does the concept of me being a lady not sit well with you, Brandt?" she scoffed. "Still haven't learned how to play nice with the female population?"

Brandt was taken aback by the remark. "Now who's being rude?" he retorted. "Bit of a low blow, don't you think?"

Mazie groaned softly while running her fingers through her hair, then looked up and saw Brandt staring at her with a hard-to-read expression.

"You're right," she replied. "That was a low blow, and I'm sorry."

"Well," he announced with a deep sigh and leaned back in his chair. "Now that we're both sorry, maybe we can try again without the attitude from both of us."

"My God, you sound like Uncle Colt," Mazie gasped, almost horrified.

Brandt shrugged, barely affected by the remark. "Once you get past the whoopings, the guy has the wisdom and discipline to get shit done."

Mazie uncrossed her legs and sat forward, moving closer to the desk. "Let me just float my pitch so you can officially shoot down the offer, then I can go home and tell my boss you said 'no'."

"Fine," Brandt announced. "Pitch away."

"Davenport Productions wants to film about two weeks' worth of outdoor footage at your ranch," Mazie informed him. "The company lost its original location due to flooding, and it needs an alternate site ASAP. Davenport Productions is willing to pay you one million dollars for the use of your land."

"You know how I feel about outsiders screwing around on my ranch," Brandt reminded her.

"I'm very much aware of that," she replied. "My boss insisted I give it my best shot regardless. The amount is rather generous and more than fair."

"You think I'd sell my ethics for money?" Brandt asked. "The ranch does well on its own, and I don't need money to buy my happiness."

"I'm aware of that as well," Mazie announced, then sighed. "Can you just come out and decline the offer? I'm not jumping through hoops for your amusement."

"I'm not amusing myself," Brandt informed her. "And I haven't said no yet."

Mazie was slightly taken aback by his words. "After all that talk about ethics and outsiders, you're actually taking time to think about the offer?"

Brandt leaned back in his chair and gently scratched his bearded chin for a moment while briefly glancing at her.

"I might be considering it," he replied. "I have to weigh my options and think about the consequences to the ranch, but I might be willing to put together a list of demands to reach an agreement."

Mazie stared at him, practically stunned. "Uh, okay," she replied. "I wasn't expecting that."

"I'll work on my own proposal tonight, and we can discuss it tomorrow afternoon before the bonfire BBQ," he informed her.

"All right then," she replied, still skeptical. "I'll call Davenport and update him."

Chapter 28

Once she changed into some of her old clothes that remained in her room since she'd left, Mazie spent an hour out in the barn brushing and talking to Katona. She then took another hour to hand graze him in the lush, unfenced field across from the barn. She forgot how much she missed the horses, the fresh country air, and the wide open spaces. Mazie finally returned the senior horse to his pasture before the wranglers returned from working the cattle. Although she missed the guys, she just couldn't handle any more reunions today. She'd see them all tomorrow at Brandt's birthday BBQ. The more they monopolized her time at the BBQ, the less time she'd have to interact with the birthday boy. Avoiding Brandt was crucial to maintaining a civil relationship. Mazie had managed to avoid going back into the house after she'd changed. She didn't want to run into Brandt anymore today, except at dinner, where it was unavoidable.

With an hour to go before dinner, Mazie decided she'd help her mother with whatever dinner prep was needed. As she approached the kitchen door, she heard her mother talking to someone, obviously trying to keep her voice down. When she realized the other voice was Brandt, she had to assume they were talking about her. Mazie knew it was wrong, but she felt compelled to listen in on their conversation. Eavesdropping when someone was gossiping about you wasn't eavesdropping at all. It was considered fact-finding.

"What am I supposed to do, Liddy?" Brandt asked, trying to keep his voice down, though it tended to carry. "I can't make her stay if she doesn't want to. Nothing I say or do will change her mind. And *she* says *I'm* turning into Uncle Colt."

"I did my part," Liddy informed him. "I got her out here. The rest is up to you. I never asked you for one damned thing in the entire eighteen years I've known you. I need you to do this for me." There was a pause. "Have you tried apologizing or even groveling?"

"Why are you assuming this is my fault?" Brandt demanded.

"It's all I have to go on," Liddy informed him. "Maybe if one of you actually confided in me, this whole thing could be straightened out."

"You should probably ask her," Brandt remarked. "Because I don't think I did anything wrong."

"If a woman's angry at you, and you don't know what you did wrong, you definitely did something wrong," Liddy announced.

"Now that makes zero sense," Brandt huffed.

"Get my daughter back," Liddy snarled.

When Mazie heard Brandt head up the back stairs, she waited a moment, then entered the kitchen.

"Hey, Mom," she announced with a false note of cheerfulness. "Need some help with dinner?"

"The pot roast and potatoes are already in the oven," Liddy announced. "But you could tear some lettuce and slice the bread."

Mazie did as she was asked and tore lettuce from the head, placing it into a large bowl while working alongside her mother, who diced tomatoes. She couldn't deny she missed dinner prep with her mother. She also couldn't deny she missed her mother's home cooking. Most nights, she ate soup, salad, or sandwiches at her desk in the office. Mazie had spent too many hours at work to really think about cooking for herself at home. Since she lived alone, cooking was mainly a means to prevent starvation.

"Brandt mentioned the two of you might come to some sort of deal with Davenport Productions," Liddy remarked while casting a sideways glance at her daughter, waiting for a reaction.

"He's working on a counter proposal," Mazie informed her mother. "It's a step in the right direction, but I'm not holding my breath that it'll be viable."

"Brandt might surprise you," Liddy remarked.

After an uncomfortable dinner with Brandt, her uncles, and her mother, Mazie made an excuse that she had some online work to do in order to turn in early and end her suffering for one day. Only two more to go. When Mazie entered her old bedroom that evening, the warm and familiar feeling was almost overwhelming. It felt good to be back home, and for a moment, she was able to forget about Brandt, even though he was still under the same roof. As she slipped under the covers of her old bed, she could hear the familiar sounds of the ranch in the peaceful countryside. The sounds lulled her into relaxation, and she was able to shut out everything that had happened that day, falling asleep immediately. Unfortunately, her dreams were all over the place, and her peaceful sleep turned restless. Perhaps it was the smell of the smoldering fire from the fire pit wafting in through her open bedroom window, reminding her of her graduation party. Mazie abruptly woke from a particularly disturbing dream. Although she knew it was just a dream, it felt surprisingly real.

Mazie stared at the sheer curtains fluttering lightly inward from the fresh, cool breeze, and Brandt was again on her mind. She rolled onto her back, stared at the ceiling, and groaned.

§

Mazie sat nestled beneath a throw blanket on the doublewide porch swing, listening to the light creaking of the old wood as she gently rocked. She sipped her hot tea, waiting to watch the sunrise in less than an hour. She'd forgotten how peaceful the ranch was. Mazie then heard the familiar creak of the screen door as it opened, disrupting her chance for a perfect morning. At such an early hour, without even looking, Mazie knew it had to be Brandt.

"What happened to the tradition of the birthday boy being allowed to sleep in on his birthday?" Mazie asked, then looked up and saw her Uncle Dalton. She quickly straightened and managed a tiny, embarrassed smile.

"I'm sure he's sleeping like a baby," Dalton replied while offering a slightly humored grin. He tapped her legs beneath the throw blanket so she'd move them and sat beside her. "I drew the short straw."

"Want some help?" Mazie asked, now interested.

"No, that's okay," Dalton replied, then patted her covered legs near him. "I know how you enjoy watching your sunrises."

She snorted a laugh and looked back over the horizon. "Yeah, we don't get sunrises like this in the city," Mazie informed him.

"Maybe you need to spend more time here," Dalton replied.

"I think about it all the time," she remarked, then sighed. "But you really can't go home again."

"That's bullshit, Mazie," Dalton informed her. "Everyone here wants you to come back home. Say you'll stay, and it'll be the best birthday present you could ever give."

"You feel that tension, Uncle Dalton?"

"Nope," he replied.

"Well, I do," Mazie announced. "Some of it's probably my own doing, but I don't see Brandt and me making amends any time soon."

"We raised you always to forgive family," Dalton reminded her. "Both of you just have to put a little effort into it." He then patted her leg, stood, and headed off the porch to the barn.

*O*nce they finished breakfast, Brandt, Dalton, and Colt took their dirty dishes to the sink and then headed out for a partial day of work. They'd be home early to clean up and prepare for the bonfire BBQ, a majority of the event which was prepared by the guys, giving Liddy less work to do.

Brandt approached Mazie, where she sat at the table, placed an envelope near her hand, and whispered close to her ear, "My counteroffer."

As Brandt followed his uncles from the kitchen, Mazie looked up and watched him leave. She drew a deep, tense breath and picked up the envelope. When she looked back, her mother was straining to see what was in it.

"Give me ten minutes," Mazie announced while standing. "I'll be back to help you clean up then."

"Mazie," Liddy pouted. "Let me see."

"I will," Mazie replied. "In ten minutes."

Mazie left the kitchen and entered the in-law suite. She paused by the door, then changed her mind and headed into her bedroom. For some reason, she felt she needed complete privacy. Mazie hurried into her bedroom and locked the door behind her. She stared at the envelope with her name written across it in the familiar handwriting, then took a deep breath before carefully opening it. She didn't know what to expect. With Brandt, it could be anything from a hand-drawn middle finger to his favorite music lyrics. Mazie was almost certain his demands would be unacceptable, and she'd be forced to give her boss disappointing news. It wasn't as if she hadn't warned him ahead of time. She opened the piece of paper and immediately saw a line-by-line list of demands for use of his property by her boss's production company. Had he actually made an effort to meet her halfway? She sat down on her bed and read the list of demands.

The first was a no-smoking policy on ranch property. Anyone caught smoking would be fined fifty dollars per incident. Mazie was slightly stunned. The ranch had always been 'smoke-free' except on the front and back porch, but this was the first time she had ever heard of someone actually being threatened with a fine. Actually, it was kind of amusing. Demand two was proper garbage disposal with a littering fine imposed. At least littering was only twenty dollars. Third, there were no alterations to the property, which included buildings and land. The fourth was regarding noise and its potential impact on cattle and horses. Fifth, surprisingly enough, referenced keeping crude language and lewd behavior down, particularly around any and all women located on the property. Sixth was respect for all the wranglers, including following their safety instructions for the entire ranch property and its visitors.

The seventh gave Brandt final say on everything happening on his land.

Mazie was rather proud of Brandt. He actually took his assignment seriously and played fairly. It was possible they'd actually reach an agreement. She then read the eighth demand. Mazie just about gasped and sprang up from her bed while reading the eighth demand aloud.

"Mazie must be present from the moment the first outsider sets foot onto the property and may not leave until the last outsider is gone!"

She cast the paper onto the bed, but it lazily floated, not having the grand effect she'd been going for.

"That son-of-a-bitch!"

Brandt did it. He found a way to fuck her over! Her boss was happily going to agree to all his terms without hesitation. Even if it made her miserable the entire two weeks, it didn't matter to Davenport. Her eyes then widened in horror. What if they went over schedule? Her mother's conversation with Brandt last night echoed through her mind. He colluded with her mother!

Chapter 29

*S*aturday evening. For Brandt's birthday dinner, they grilled the finest steaks the ranch had to offer. Colt and Dalton always went above and beyond for birthdays. Any reason for a party. Mazie had almost forgotten how great the ranch's BBQs were. She missed everything from the smell of the bonfire to the laughter of her fellow wranglers. Mazie mentally corrected herself. They weren't technically her fellow wranglers anymore. She almost forgot she was no longer a part of the ranch. The birthday celebration felt awkward for many reasons. Brandt was being celebrated by those who loved him, yet every time she looked over at him, he didn't seem happy. Mazie knew it mostly had to do with her being there. She knew her presence was going to ruin his special day, and it actually bothered her. She might hate the prick, but she still loved him.

The party was finally winding down around midnight. Despite many of the wranglers only being in their thirties, they weren't party animals. Dalton joined Mazie and glanced past the bonfire to where Brandt sat at the picnic table alongside Liddy. Mazie followed his gaze and stared as well. Liddy pulled Brandt to her side, resting his head on her shoulder, and affectionately caressed his hair while kissing his forehead. Her mother loved Brandt like her own son, which made it that much harder to feel the way she did.

"I wish the two of you would just talk it out," Dalton remarked, now studying her. "If you could just find some middle ground that brings you home, that's all we really want for now. Brandt will do just about anything to bring you back home." He then raised his brow. "Certainly, there must be something that can be done that'll bring you back to us."

"Apparently, I'm the only one with the problem," she informed Dalton. "Brandt just wants to move on, but I can't. I just can't."

"Will you tell me what happened?" Dalton finally asked. "Maybe I can bridge the gap between you."

"No," she replied with a sigh. "If Brandt hasn't told you, I'm not mentioning it either."

"I have no choice but to respect your privacy," Dalton replied.

Once Liddy got up and headed to the table to put away the remaining birthday cake, Brandt moved away from the table and sat on the other side of the bonfire across from them, stranded in his own world. When Liddy picked up the remaining cake and headed into the house, Dalton was only a step behind her, eager to help. Mazie wondered who those two thought they were fooling. However, they had successfully managed to leave her alone outside with Brandt. She fidgeted a moment, held her breath, and then headed for the bonfire. Brandt looked up as she approached him and slowly straightened. He was about to stand when she sat in the chair next to his. She hesitated, then handed him his birthday card without looking at him. Brandt uncertainly accepted the card.

"Is it going to explode?" he asked.

"Unlikely," she replied, and still didn't look at him.

Brandt opened the envelope and removed the card.

"Don't read too much into it," she informed him. "The selection at the general store was pretty slim."

He read the card, then cast a look at her, even though she didn't look at him. "It's signed, 'love always, Mazie'," he remarked.

"I can hate you and love you at the same time," she muttered.

"And I can live with that," Brandt announced while staring at her profile with a tiny smile on his face. He then held up the card. "This means the world to me, Mazie. Thank you."

She drew a deep breath while staring at the bonfire. "I don't know how to move past what happened," she finally whispered. "I've tried to forget." Mazie shut her eyes for a moment, then immediately opened them. "Every time I look at you, I see this graphic image of--*of us*. You were like a brother to me."

Brandt shut his eyes and looked away. "Don't say that," he moaned softly. "I was *never* your brother, and I *never* thought of you as my sister. Well, at least, not for a long time."

"Maybe you didn't feel that way, but I did," she insisted and barely glanced at him while raking her fingers through her hair. "I hate feeling this way." She hesitated and nearly choked on her words. "I hate that you took my virginity."

"I didn't *take* anything," he insisted defensively while glaring at her profile. "You *gave* it to me. Willingly, happily, and without protest."

Mazie again shut her eyes. "I just want it to go away," she whispered.

"You can pretend it didn't happen all you want, but that won't change anything," he informed her. "Can we just somehow move on?"

"How?" she whispered. "Whenever you look at me, I see you reliving that moment, relishing in it. Enjoying it. And whenever I look at you, I can still *feel* you."

"Maybe if you stopped feeling guilty about it, you'd accept it for the passionate moment it was."

"I'm sorry, Brandt," she whispered. "I just can't get past it. It never should have happened."

"Well, that's where you and I disagree," he reported somewhat gruffly. "Making love to you was the single greatest moment of my life. Out of respect for you, I haven't and won't tell another living soul, but I wouldn't trade that night with you for anything."

"And that's why I can't be around you."

"And maybe you're just afraid you'll crawl back into my bed again," he scoffed.

"You're a prick," she snarled, then stood and walked away.

Unfortunately, Brandt's words struck a chord with her, and she couldn't get the rest of that night out of her mind. She slipped back to that night and right back into Brandt's bed, reliving her biggest mistake.

Chapter 30

*F*ive years ago. Mazie and Brandt sat in silence within his bedroom, pretending to watch the movie, for several minutes before Mazie glanced at Brandt's profile, then shifted uncomfortably.

"I suppose you heard Peter and Hannah aren't going to Australia with us," Mazie just about whispered.

"Yeah, I was there when Melissa handed Peter his head on a silver platter," Brandt remarked, then groaned softly. "Girl deprived me the pleasure of hitting him again."

"Melissa was a little pissed off by their lewd behavior tonight," she reported.

"Takes a lot to piss off that girl," Brandt remarked, then briefly eyed her. "I hope you were pissed off a little, too."

"I was at the time, but I'm over it now," Mazie informed him, then shrugged. "I guess I realized he wasn't really much of a friend and he's not worth getting upset over."

"I could have told you that years ago," Brandt muttered. "Something about the guy always rubbed me the wrong way."

"That I liked him was probably reason enough," she remarked while giving him a sideways glare.

"Well, I never said I wasn't petty."

Mazie managed a tiny laugh before shifting uncomfortably. "She'll probably have to refund their airfare and their portion of the beach house rental."

"If they already paid for them, she'll need to refund them," Brandt insisted, then glanced at her, attempting to read her mind. "That's going to increase the burden on you, Melissa, and Cameron for the rental house, huh?"

"Yeah," Mazie remarked with a sigh. "I mean, Melissa may have spoken the words, but all three of us support her decision."

"Don't worry about it," Brandt announced and offered a warm smile. "I've got you covered, Mazie. I'll give you the money to cover the additional trip costs. You and your friends deserve to have some fun." He then shrugged. "I'll just take it out of your overtime."

"I don't get overtime."

Brandt smiled and chuckled.

Mazie hid her smile and again glanced at his profile. "I don't want you to cover my additional cost, Brandt," she informed him, then hesitated. "I'm asking you to come with us."

Brandt looked at her, slightly surprised by the request. "You want me to go with you and your friends to Australia for two weeks?"

"Yes, I'd like you to," Mazie replied. "If you want to go. You're my best friend."

As he stared into her eyes, his smile increased. "I like hearing you say that," Brandt announced, then chuckled softly. "I'm pretty sure you're the only person who could get me on a twenty-hour flight."

"So you'll go?" she asked, almost overjoyed.

Brandt grinned and nodded. "Yeah, sure, I'll go," he replied. "It would pretty much suck around here without you anyway."

Mazie sprang up on her knees and threw her arms around Brandt's neck, clinging happily to him. "Thank you! You're the best!"

As she lurched forward to kiss his cheek, Brandt turned his head to speak at the same time, and she ended up kissing him on the lips. She immediately pulled back with surprise, prepared to apologize when Brandt placed his hand on her face and caressed her cheek with his thumb while staring into her eyes. Her heart was pounding with anticipation. Was Brandt going to kiss her? Did she actually want him to kiss her?

"It's okay," she heard herself whisper, although where it came from, she wasn't quite sure.

Brandt suddenly groaned and kissed her warmly yet aggressively. Mazie attempted to return the kiss, but she wasn't sure if she did it right. It didn't seem to matter to Brandt. As he practically devoured her lips, his hands firmly caressed her back while holding her tightly against him. She was a little frightened by the way his hands traveled her back, practically caressing her buttocks, yet it thrilled her as well. His heavy breathing somehow enticed her onward, and a tiny moan escaped her throat. He groaned in response, pulled his lips away from her mouth, and began kissing her neck, working his way down the neckline of her tank top. Mazie couldn't deny she enjoyed the sensation. His hands attempted to meet his mouth halfway, then stopped short of fondling her. Brandt slowly pulled his head back, his gaze falling upon the breasts that had earlier teased and tormented him, then met her stare.

"Is it okay--?" he asked, unable to finish the question.

"If you want to," she whispered between heavy breaths. "I'm okay with it."

Mazie was convinced it really wasn't that big of a deal if he touched her there. It was probably just a guy thing she didn't understand. Brandt eagerly slipped his hand under her tank top, firmly caressed her, and groaned before returning his mouth to her neck. The moment his hand touched her bare breast, Mazie felt a shiver sweep through her entire body that erupted into tiny goosebumps. The sensation was completely different than when she touched herself while showering or changing. She couldn't deny she actually enjoyed it, allowing a soft groan to escape. Without hesitation and in a surprising display of strength, Brandt hoisted her onto his lap, swiftly having her straddle him while on her knees. With one arm firmly cradling her buttocks, his free hand continued fondling her breast, thoroughly exploring it. As he sharply pulled her against his hips, he groaned low and loud. Mazie immediately felt the sensation of his arousal pressing firmly against the thin material of her sleep shorts, and her body ached in response. She'd never felt anything like that before, and she wasn't sure how to react.

Before she even realized what had happened, he effortlessly slipped her out of her tank top. While his swift and deliberate actions took her by surprise, she wondered how he knew what to do. Despite the pleasure she felt, she was nervous and even trembling, yet Brandt didn't fumble or falter. Since he seemed so sure of himself, she wasn't about to stop him. He was always an excellent teacher, and he'd never hurt her. When his lips traveled from her neck down to her chest, she considered stopping him and even almost giggled, as it kind of tickled. In an instant, the sensation changed, and Mazie gasped in response. Her eyes rolled shut as a groan immediately escaped. She clutched his head with both hands, holding his head to her chest, and writhed against his hot tongue probing her. Her reaction only encouraged a more forceful response from him.

Brandt clung to her buttocks and took her with him onto the bed, placing himself on top of her. She continued to writhe beneath him and the way he pressed his hips against her, creating an incredible sensation between her legs. Her pleasurable moans were uncontrolled, directly reacting to everything he did. Mazie remembered him whispering something in her ear. A question with which she moaned a response. From there, everything was a blur. There was a little discomfort among the lasting moments of intense pleasure. She enjoyed Brandt's hands firmly caressing her while pinning her to the bed with his own naked body. He felt so powerful on top of her. So dominating! Usually, she liked taunting him, but tonight she wanted him to dominate her, which he did, unapologetically. His kiss was powerful as he moved against her on the bed that went from lightly creaking to a steady creak. She clung to him, involuntarily moaning with pleasure. With each moan from her, he no longer asked; he took what he wanted, making her his with every pleasurable movement.

resent day. Mazie attempted to push her thoughts of Brandt and that night from her mind. She wanted to enjoy being back in her childhood room, but her tainted memory of Brandt wouldn't allow it. She glanced at the bedside clock. It wasn't even five o'clock in the morning yet, which meant the guys weren't even up to feed the horses. It seemed like a safe time to walk the house and reminisce. She'd need to be back in her mother's suite before five. She could then shower and change before breakfast, which would be another uncomfortable family meal. Mazie didn't bother changing or putting on shoes, since she'd stay inside the house. She padded in her bare feet into the kitchen and put on the kettle. What she wanted most was a cup of hot tea on the front porch. As she waited for the kettle, her mind wandered back to family breakfasts and dinners. She'd be lying if she said she didn't miss it.

Once her water was boiling, she made her cup of tea. When she heard a creak on the back stairs, she instinctively turned, not expecting anyone to be up yet. Brandt appeared on the back stairs, dressed for his morning, and stopped when he saw her. Mazie was immediately self-conscious with him seeing her braless in her tank top and frumpy shorts. She fidgeted slightly and turned away from him so he wouldn't see her without her bra, something she never thought about twice before that night.

"You're up early," she remarked, attempting to sound casual.

"I couldn't sleep," he replied, then eyed her. "What's your excuse?"

"I wanted to enjoy the peace and quiet before everyone else was up," Mazie informed him, then raised her brow. "So much for that, huh?"

Brandt moved to the table beside her and leaned against it, facing her. "Come out with us this morning," he announced, sounding more like a command than a request. "Give it a chance."

Mazie lifted her eyes and met his gaze only briefly before looking back at her tea mug. "You just don't give up," she scoffed.

"You're worth fighting for," he casually replied.

Mazie looked back at him, surprised by his words. She suddenly couldn't look away. In the absence of her response, he moved closer to her and placed his hands on her sides without taking his eyes off hers. Mazie placed her hands on his and firmly pried them off her sides.

"I'll go out with the guys this morning," she informed him, then turned stern. "But you need to keep your hands to yourself."

Brandt pulled his hands back and held them up in the air. "I promise they'll never leave my wrists."

Mazie stared at him a moment, then rolled her eyes. "Dork," she scoffed as she turned away.

Brandt grinned and chuckled.

Chapter 31

Mazie helped brush and saddle the horses that morning and somehow managed to ignore Brandt completely. Once all the horses were saddled, it was time for breakfast. Mazie decided to skip breakfast that morning and remain in the barn, since she'd already had her tea. She nuzzled Blackjack, the horse that had been gifted to her for graduation, but was never really hers, as she left the ranch soon after returning from Australia. She probably only rode the horse half a dozen times.

"I'll let you ride him, if you want," Brandt remarked from behind her.

Mazie jerked slightly, startled by Brandt's stealthy return, but didn't look back. "Well, he is technically my horse," she reminded him.

"Sure," Brandt replied and joined her near the horse. "You can have him." There was a brief pause. "Just as soon as you pay me five years back board and vet bills."

Mazie released a low groan and cast a sharp look at Brandt. "You're such a prick, you know that?"

"You've called me worse," he reminded her while leaning against the stall wall. "Look. You want the horse, he's yours. Consider him a sign-on bonus when you come back to work for the ranch."

She looked back at the horse while groaning. "Not happening, Brandt," Mazie announced as she shook her head. "Give it a rest. I'm making double, maybe even triple, of what you would pay me."

Brandt remained against the stall wall and stared at the horse, but it was apparent he was searching for something to say that wouldn't piss her off.

"Plenty of other job perks," he informed her.

"Yeah? Name one," she scoffed.

"You can sleep with the boss anytime you want," Brandt teased.

Mazie didn't even bother looking at him, knowing he was grinning at his not-so-clever burn.

"I already have that particular perk at my current job," Mazie retorted.

When she looked back, Brandt had untied his horse and left the barn without a word. It was possible she may have gone too far.

Spending a whole morning out with the herd and the old wranglers she knew and loved was just like old times. After a few times chasing cows, it was as if she'd never left. It all came back to her. Of course, five years of not riding and pulling a four-hour shift in the saddle was going to make for an unpleasant evening with aching thighs and backside. Mazie was having such a good time that it took her almost two hours to realize Brandt was noticeably absent the entire time. He might have been staying away, as promised when she first agreed to go out with the guys, but it was more likely she'd unintentionally offended him. She thought about it a moment longer and had to take credit where credit was due. Mazie hadn't *unintentionally* offended Brandt. She purposely and willfully hurt him. As she thought about it more, was she really to blame? He hit her with a jab about their night together first, so was she really out of line with her comment?

When Brandt finally made an appearance, he was hard to miss. The blue roan horse was somehow flashy without being flashy. Blackjack stood out. Mazie couldn't help but be a little nostalgic over the horse. It was her horse. A most generous gift from Brandt. When she thought about what that horse must have cost and the amount of time Brandt put into finding such a horse, she felt a little guilty about the last five years. For Mazie, the only way to move on from what happened that night was to move out. Clearly, neither was about to back down from the argument that ensued the following morning. Mazie couldn't take her eyes off Brandt. Thirteen years, following him around and practically worshiping him. He was incredibly flawed, yet he could do no wrong in her eyes.

Brandt caught her gaze from across the pasture, and it was too late to pretend she wasn't staring at him. He sent his horse into a leisurely canter across the field and stopped near her on her horse. This time, there was no smile from him.

"How long are we going to play this game?" he finally demanded, choosing aggression.

"I'm not playing a game," she snapped back, taking the defensive.

"Yes, you are," Brandt insisted. "Stop being a stubborn, spoiled little brat and come back to the ranch. You belong here."

"Is that what this is about?" Mazie demanded. "You actually think there's any way I'd come back?" She shook her head. "You're controlling and possessive, Brandt. I'm not coming back here, and I'm not working for you ever again."

Brandt drew a deep breath, attempting to control his hostility, and continued to stare at her. "Do you want me to apologize?" he asked. "Jump through a few hoops? Beg? Just tell me what you want, Mazie. I'll do it."

"Leave me alone," she scoffed. "Are you willing to do that?"

"If your ass is in a saddle on a horse on my ranch, I'm willing to give you as much space as you want. I just want you to come home."

"You say that, but we both know you'd never be able to do it," she remarked. "It'd be impossible to get away from you if I'm working for you and living under your roof."

"Maybe I have been controlling and possessive," he announced without backing away. "But if you're back here, I promise I'll back off. I'll give you all the space you need." He raised his brows. "Everything you want is right here."

"You don't even know what I want," she scoffed.

"I thought I did," he replied, then shrugged. "But maybe I don't. Just tell me what you want."

Mazie wanted to scream at him, but she drew a deep breath, collected her emotions, and tried a more rational approach.

"Two weeks, Brandt," she informed him. "We have to make this work for two weeks while the production crew is here at the ranch. Can we just call a truce to avoid a hostile work environment for everyone on the ranch and those with the production company?"

"A truce is all I've ever wanted," Brandt reminded her.

"What you want goes way beyond a truce," Mazie informed him.

"I want what you promised me," he snapped hotly.

"What I promised you?" she demanded. "I never promised you anything."

"You promised to run the ranch with me," Brandt reminded her. "You and me, working the cattle. You said that."

"I was thirteen!"

"And when you were fifteen, again at sixteen, twice when you were seventeen, and many times when you were eighteen," he announced. "You assured me you wanted to work the ranch moments before we made love."

Mazie shut her eyes and groaned loudly with frustration. "Stop saying that," she cried out.

"Why?" he demanded. "So you can pretend it didn't happen?"

"Yes," Mazie snarled back at him. "I want to pretend it didn't happen. You want us to actually get along? Pretend *that* never happened."

They stared at each other in raging silence, both ready to explode at a moment's notice. Brandt drew a deep breath, then nodded.

"Fine," he replied almost timidly. "I'll be the bigger man and put it aside." Brandt then raised his brows. "But if we're pretending that night never happened, then you should put on your big girl panties and put all your hostility toward me aside."

As Mazie stared at him, she almost believed they could get beyond this. If he backed off, perhaps she could do the same. Maybe they could actually salvage whatever was left of their relationship.

"If you can follow through with your promise, I'm sure I can keep mine," she finally replied.

Brandt extended his hand to her. She hesitated while staring at his hand for a moment, then reluctantly shook it.

Chapter 32

*M*azie returned home to Los Angeles on Monday afternoon. The private jet no sooner hit the tarmac when Davenport texted for her to pack her bags and that the production crew was already on its way to the ranch. She thought she'd have at least a few days to get her affairs in order before running back out again for another two weeks, but the movie was already behind schedule. Her boss commanded her to fly out to the ranch with him the following morning, barely giving her time to notify her mother at the ranch. Thankfully, her mother didn't make her talk directly to Brandt this time. With any luck, she and Davenport would beat the production crew and their tractor-trailers to the ranch. Her worst fear was the crew showing up at the ranch and Brandt chasing them off with a shotgun because Mazie wasn't there per their agreement. There was no doubt in her mind that Brandt would pull something like that, too.

The following morning, the private plane landed a little behind schedule, and Mazie was already feeling stressed about the status of the production crew, which was careening toward the ranch at full speed. Davenport showed little regard for Mazie's stress as she met near-impossible deadlines. Apparently, that was her job, and if she couldn't do it, she was replaceable. On the limo ride to the ranch, Mazie finally reached the production crew to get their estimated arrival time.

"We're here," the equipment manager announced over her phone. "But there seems to be a problem."

Mazie's heart sank. That couldn't be good. When the limousine approached the entrance to the ranch, they saw two tractor-trailers and two mobile offices parked alongside the road just before the ranch gates. Davenport saw the backup of vehicles and immediately turned grouchy on the only person available.

"What the hell is going on?" Davenport demanded while glaring at Mazie.

"I'll find out," she announced, then sprang from the limousine.

Mazie had tried to explain the situation to Davenport at the airport about the importance of beating the crew to the ranch, but he refused to clear them for takeoff until his secretary arrived with a bottle of his favorite bourbon. He didn't seem to remember or care that she had forewarned him. It was her problem, not his. As she walked past the collection of semi-trucks, she could see that the main gate was shut and locked with a shiny new, thick chain and a brand new, heavy padlock. There was a new sign she'd also never seen before stating, 'Trespassers will be shot'. Brandt wasn't giving an inch on his demands. Mazie removed her cell phone and pressed the ranch number she kept on speed dial, which she used to call her mother, who refused to get a cell phone. Before anyone could pick up the ranch phone, she saw an incoming call from Brandt. Mazie groaned, disconnected the ranch call, and answered Brandt's call.

"Are you trying to be funny?" Mazie scoffed into the phone.

"Good morning to you, too," Brandt announced, sounding overly cheerful. "I see you finally arrived."

Mazie lifted her head and looked beyond the double gate, seeing Brandt loping his horse down the driveway with his cell phone to his ear. She could already see the grin on his face as he approached. Mazie disconnected the call and shoved the cell phone in her jacket pocket. Brandt did the same before stopping in front of the gate. He reached into his pocket, removed the padlock key, and tossed it to her. Mazie resisted the urge to call him every bad name she could think up.

"Did you run all the way out to the home supply store just to purchase a new chain and padlock?" Mazie scoffed while unlocking the lock.

"Don't be ridiculous," Brandt remarked, then grinned almost slyly. "We also needed some fence rails and a new water trough."

As Mazie unwrapped the heavy chain, she cast a stern glare at him, seated comfortably on his horse.

"Was this really necessary?" she demanded. "I told you I'd be here."

"Just keeping you honest," Brandt replied while grinning. "If I let you get away with something right out the chute, you might test the boundaries, and we can't have that."

"No, we can't," she muttered, then purposely dropped the chain and padlock to the ground.

Brandt chuckled, amused by her annoyance. He then extended his hand to her. "Come on, I'll give you a lift," he announced. "First class all the way."

Mazie casually opened the fence while ignoring his hand. "I would, but you know, you might test the boundaries if I did that."

Brandt groaned, then chuckled. "You're such a tease," he announced, then turned and galloped down the driveway.

Despite being extremely pissed at him, she felt compelled to watch him gallop away. The freedom of life in the saddle. Not many people knew what that was like. She remembered galloping alongside him, racing him to the stream on the way home for lunch. With Blackjack, maybe she could even have won just once.

As the limousine pulled up the long, dusty driveway to the ranch house, Brandt sat on his horse near the front porch where Colt, Dalton, and Liddy sat on rocking chairs with their morning coffee. All four watched with matching skepticism at the procession of semi-trucks following the stretch limousine. Mazie got out of the limousine and eyed the three on the porch. She didn't know who they thought they were fooling. None of them would be on the porch at this hour, casually sipping coffee. Her mother would be making beds, and the guys would be out with the cattle or fixing farm machinery. The production crew of ten spilled out of the four semi-trucks and attempted to coordinate their efforts to make the best use of the morning. Davenport joined Mazie and approached the ranch house. Her boss was good at ass-kissing when he wanted something, and right now, he wanted to make a good impression on Brandt and his family.

"Mr. Davenport," Mazie announced through a gritted smile and indicated Brandt on the horse. "This is Brandt Major, the ranch owner."

"It's a pleasure to meet you," Davenport announced and extended his hand up to Brandt.

Brandt wiped his mostly clean hand on his mostly dirty jeans and shook Davenport's hand while grinning like a cobra.

"Pleasure's all mine," Brandt announced in a thick accent Mazie had never heard before.

Mazie wasn't sure if he was going for Southern or red neck. Whichever it was, it was god-awful, and she was pretty sure he purposely shaved off a few IQ points for added effect. When she saw him chewing what appeared to be tobacco, Mazie was stunned. He only smoked cigarettes for a few months to look cool in front of the other kids, but he *never* chewed tobacco. He thought it was more disgusting than she did. As Mazie squinted daggers at Brandt, he just grinned and played his convincing role of a dumb hick. When he winked at her, she wanted to strangle him. Brandt introduced the 'gang' on the porch.

"Liddy, there," Brandt announced in his thick, mangled accent, "fixed up that there spare bedroom, if you're so inclined." He then looked at Mazie and grinned. "Unless you'd rather set yourself up in Mazie's old bedroom with her."

Mazie's expression suddenly dropped as horror swept over her. She was definitely going to kill him! Davenport smiled and chuckled at the suggestion.

"That's kind of you to offer, but Mazie is my assistant, not my girlfriend," Davenport informed him.

"Oh, I wasn't sure," Brandt replied while maintaining his grin. "We don't frown upon that premarital sex stuff in these parts. To each his own."

"Well, that's not the case, I'm afraid," Davenport informed him. "But I will take you up on that spare bedroom. I'm sure it'll be more comfortable than the sofa bed in my portable office." He indicated one of the semi-trucks. "If you wouldn't mind telling us where we can set up, we'll move these vehicles out of your way."

"Certainly," Colt announced from the porch and sprang to his feet, offering a sly sort of grin while puffing out his chest. "I'll tell you where you can go."

Mazie was sure that was meant to sound exactly as it had. Apparently, Uncle Colt was not on board with the production company infiltrating the ranch. Dalton groaned, feeling the need to supervise Colt, and joined them. When the limousine driver brought Davenport's luggage, Liddy took her cue and showed the driver where to put the boss's suitcases. Davenport walked with Colt and Dalton toward the four semi-trucks, attempting to make small talk. Mazie hoped Colt played as nicely as he always demanded of Brandt, but she somehow doubted that rule applied to him. As soon as her boss disappeared behind the semi-trucks, Mazie turned toward Brandt on his horse and harshly slapped his thigh, making him yelp with surprise.

"What the hell was that?" Mazie scolded. "All you left out was the speech about not molesting the sheep, you inbred wannabe."

Brandt gingerly rubbed his thigh where she'd hit him and looked at her, almost convincingly, dumbfounded by her reaction.

"I don't know what you're talking about," Brandt remarked, then blew a bubble with the gum he'd been pretending was tobacco. He then straightened in his saddle and cocked his head. "Guess the boss isn't into girls." He then considered the comment. "Maybe he *would* like some sheep."

Mazie slapped his thigh again while practically screaming. "I never said I was sleeping with my boss, you moron," she snarled.

"You implied it," he scoffed back.

"I just wanted to shut you up," Mazie huffed. "I don't need you giving my boss any ideas!"

"Hmm," Brandt announced. "I just thought of another condition on my contract. I think I'll call it the 'castration' clause."

"I don't need your protection, Brandt."

Brandt offered a polite smile. "I know you don't need it," he announced, somewhat humored. "But I need to amuse myself somehow."

"You promised," she reminded him.

Brandt rolled his eyes and groaned. "Fine," he scoffed. "I'll play nice as long as your boss plays nice."

Chapter 33

By early afternoon, the production crew had set up their trailers and unloaded all their equipment. When the two semi-trucks left, four RVs took their place. There was enough noise from less than a dozen people to put Grand Central Station to shame. The loud rumbling of at least six generators broke the silence and hadn't stopped since they were started. Brandt sat on the porch railing, scratching his beard, and stared at the junk yard that was once a quiet field. His disapproving frown was enough to assume his current mood. Mazie stepped onto the porch from the house and cringed at the sound. It was even worse outside than it had been inside. She had been on location many times and knew the generators were loud, but she was used to the ranch being mostly quiet, with only the sounds of nature. She then saw Brandt and the expression on his face as he stared at the disastrous field. He alternated between scratching his bearded chin and rubbing his temple.

Almost out of reflex, Mazie sat on the railing opposite Brandt and leaned against the post, mimicking his position. They'd spent many evenings on the porch railing. Usually, it was to watch the horses grazing in the pasture, to see the sun set over the horizon, and to listen to the crickets.

"I know," she announced with a sympathetic sigh. "It's god-awful, but it's only for two weeks. They'll be gone before you know it."

"Well, I nominate you to explain that to Uncle Colt," Brandt muttered without looking at her. "He was out here twenty minutes ago, reaming my ass out over the noise and clutter." He snorted a laugh, although he didn't find it funny. "Colt hadn't laid into me like that in over fifteen years. Made my ass hurt."

"Correct me if I'm wrong, but I thought you were his boss these days," Mazie remarked.

Brandt finally looked at her. "I am, but he's still my uncle, which means he reserves the right to ream my ass whenever he feels like it," he informed her, then raised his brows. "I may be a grown ass adult, but I'm not going to mouth off to Uncle Colt. I still have regrets about the last time."

"When he whooped your ass?" Mazie asked, now curious.

"No," Brandt replied with a deep sigh. "It was a couple of years back. Things got a little tense. I mouthed off to him, and he said some things I didn't want to hear." He hesitated, then flexed his hand. "And I punched him in the mouth."

Mazie's eyes widened, and she was unable to hold back the gasp that slipped out. "What did he do?"

"Nothing," Brandt replied with a shrug. "He walked away." He shook his head while maintaining his frown. "I felt horrible about it then and to this day. I apologized several times, and he just kept saying, 'it's okay'. It must have taken every ounce of strength in him not to punch me back, but I think he wanted me to remember what I'd done. Hitting me back would have let me off too easily." He then met her gaze. "Please tell me they shut those things off after dark."

Mazie cringed. "Sorry," she whispered. "They need the generators to run power to their RVs."

Brandt groaned and allowed his head to fall back against the post behind him. "I may need to go camping on the back forty just to get some peace and quiet."

Mazie couldn't help but smile and chuckle. "I remember the first time you guys took me camping with you," she announced.

"We didn't take you," Brandt reminded her. "You begged and whined until we reluctantly gave in and let you tag along."

"That's not how I remember it," she scoffed.

"Yes, you're good at blocking out all the times you were a pain in the ass," he informed her.

*T*welve-year-old Mazie followed her mother around the kitchen while Liddy did her best to ignore her daughter's relentless pleas.

"Why can't I go?" Mazie practically pouted. "Brandt is going."

"Brandt is seventeen," Liddy reminded her.

"We both know it's not our age that's the problem," Mazie informed her mother while folding her arms across her chest in a mild tantrum. "Let's face it. Maturity-wise, we're on the same playing field."

"Mazie," Liddy scolded. "That's not nice."

"But it's true," Mazie remarked. "It's because Brandt's a boy, and I'm not. Admit it."

Liddy groaned softly and turned to face her daughter. "Mazie, although there may be a little truth to that," she announced. "The fact of the matter is, camping has always been Brandt's special time with his uncles."

"They're my uncles too," Mazie insisted.

Liddy seemed to tense but didn't bother correcting her. Mazie knew they weren't her 'actual' uncles, so there was no reason to keep pointing it out.

"I know this is hard for you to understand, Mazie," Liddy remarked. "But sometimes guys like to have some time away with just the guys. It's healthy for them. And when they're gone, we can have time with just us girls, which is healthy for us as well."

Mazie eyed her skeptically. "You do realize how insane you sound, right?" she asked. "Why am I always being punished for being a girl?"

"You're not being punished," Liddy insisted. "You have to accept the fact that you're not always invited to everything."

"Yeah, because I'm a girl."

Liddy groaned and placed her hand over her eyes, unable to continue the conversation that wasn't going to go anywhere. She finally looked at Mazie and raised commanding brows.

"You weren't invited, so you're not going, and that's final," Liddy informed her, then turned back to the counter and resumed preparing dinner, effectively ending the conversation.

Mazie stormed from the kitchen through the hallway entrance and nearly ran into Uncle Dalton. He watched the young girl leave, then looked at Liddy at the counter.

"What was that all about?" Dalton asked.

"You don't want to know," Liddy announced with a groan.

Chapter 34

Mazie stormed onto the porch, cast herself into one of the rocking chairs, and folded her arms across her chest with a huff while aggressively rocking. Seventeen-year-old Brandt approached the house from the barn, saw the pouting girl, and paused.

"Someone's extra grouchy this afternoon," Brandt remarked while leaning against the support beam, mimicking her pose. "Did Barbie and GI Joe have another fight?" He shook his head. "I told you that marriage was never going to work. Barbie is too high-maintenance for a soldier boy like Joe."

"You're really funny," Mazie scoffed without looking at him.

"Oh, you must be mad," Brandt remarked. "You always defend Barbie. What's bugging you, half pint?"

"You and your entire species," Mazie scoffed.

"My entire species?" Brandt asked. "What does that even mean?"

"It means I can't go camping with you, Uncle Dalton, and Uncle Colt because I don't pee standing up," she snarled in response.

"Well, that's *graphic*," Brandt remarked. "Although peeing while standing up is useful while camping, I wasn't aware it was an actual requirement."

Mazie again glared at him, not amused. He immediately chuckled at her expense.

"Why do you suddenly want to go camping with us anyway?" Brandt finally asked.

"Because I've never been camping and you guys go every year without me," she insisted. "I'm old enough. You've been camping with Uncle Colt and Uncle Dalton for years. Even younger than I am now. The only reason I can't go is because I'm a girl."

"It's not because you're a girl," Brandt informed her. "It's because of your girl mentality."

"What's that supposed to mean?" Mazie demanded.

"That means there's no toilets, no bathtubs, and no beds," he informed her. "Just a sleeping bag on the ground inside a tent. There are bugs, snakes, and other wildlife roaming about. We fish, hunt, and cook whatever we catch over an open fire. Uncle Colt drinks, gets drunk, says bad words, and tells scary stories before bedtime."

"Sounds pretty awesome to me," Mazie remarked with a huff. "It's not fair that I can't go."

"Mazie, there's no way you'd enjoy any of what I just described," Brandt informed her.

"How do you know that until I'm allowed to try it?" Mazie demanded.

Brandt considered the comment a moment, then nodded. "Okay," he announced. "I'll make a little wager with you. If you don't make it the entire two nights without complaining, crying, or insisting we take you home, you have to clean my room for a month."

"And what do I get if I last the entire two nights?" Mazie asked.

"Respect."

Mazie laughed while sneering and shook her head. "Yeah, I don't think so," she huffed. "If I win, you have to clean *my* room for an entire month."

"You've got a deal," he announced and extended his hand.

Mazie eyed him suspiciously, then shook his hand. Before she could pull her hand back, he pulled her from her chair, put her in a headlock under his armpit, and gave her noogies until she screamed. He released her just as quickly and then approached the screen door.

"This is going to be an easy victory," Brandt insisted with a throaty chuckle.

"Just make sure you clear it with Uncle Colt and my mother first," Mazie huffed while readjusting her ponytail.

While Uncle Colt drove his pickup truck along the old dirt road on the ranch property, Mazie sat between her uncle and Brandt, looking enthusiastic for their first camping trip together. Brandt and Colt didn't seem nearly as happy as the tweener.

"I don't understand why we're driving," Brandt scoffed. "We're supposed to ride out there and back. That's part of the whole camping experience."

"That was before your Uncle Dalton came up sick," Colt huffed, then shook his head. "I'm not taking on all that responsibility, caring for the horses, a pack horse, and Mazie."

"I can take care of myself," Mazie insisted.

"Well, we'll see about that," Colt remarked, having his doubts. "We're going to be roughing it for two days. I hope your partner in crime let you know what you're getting yourself into."

"Is that why Uncle Dalton said he was sick?" Mazie then asked, now concerned. "Is it because I'm going along?"

"No, it has nothing to do with you, darling," Colt informed her.

"Probably wants to stay behind and 'look after' Liddy while we're gone," Brandt muttered.

"She can take care of herself," Mazie reminded Brandt.

"Not nearly as good as Uncle Dalton *takes care* of her," Brandt muttered.

"Shut your mouth, boy," Colt snarled and flicked Brandt's ear over the back of the seat.

When they finally arrived at the clearing near the stream, all three unloaded their supplies from the back of the truck. Mazie eagerly helped pitch the tent, then gathered enough firewood to last more than two days in the woods. They had a fantastic day fishing on the bank of the stream, and Mazie even learned how to bait her own hook, which she didn't even mind. Cleaning the fish was another story. Although she made faces throughout the entire beheading, gutting, and scaling process, she didn't complain. When they made it through the whole day without hitting any snags, Colt seemed to relax and enjoy himself. Obviously, bringing Mazie along added some stress on him, but it may have been unfounded. After dinner, Colt drank some whiskey straight from the bottle and extended it to Brandt. Brandt seemed uncomfortable with the action and refused a swig. Colt chuckled at Brandt's expense, then indicated Mazie.

"You don't have to worry about Mazie," Colt informed him. "She's not going to tattle on you to Liddy. Christ, the girl spent the last seven years sparing your ass from several well-deserved whoopings."

"I think I should be the responsible one for a change," Brandt informed his uncle, now seeming uncomfortable. "I've set some pretty bad examples for her over the years. If she sees me drinking, she's liable to think it's okay."

Colt cast a strange look at Brandt. "I think of all the hard work I'd done to raise you, when all you really needed was a little sister to straighten your ass."

"Being followed around and idolized is a huge responsibility," Brandt muttered. "I have to watch the example I set."

Colt stared at Brandt, almost stunned. "Well, look at you," he announced. "All grown up." He capped the whiskey bottle and set it aside. "Does that mean scary campfire stories are cancelled as well?"

"I want to hear some scary stories," Mazie announced a little too quickly and eagerly hugged her knees to her chest with anticipation.

Colt came back to life and grinned. "And do I have some good ones for you," he announced.

"We'll be heading home before midnight," Brandt muttered with a tiny chuckle.

Chapter 35

*M*azie attempted to sleep in the tent that would *uncomfortably* sleep four adults. Although she was nestled snuggly in her sleeping bag, it wasn't Uncle Colt's nightmarish campfire stories that kept her awake; it was Uncle Colt's snoring. She'd heard the horror stories about his infamous snoring, but since the in-law suite was down a floor and an entire house away, she'd never actually heard the frightening sounds he made while sleeping, especially while on his back. And, somehow, it was insisted that she sleep in the middle of Brandt and Colt. She should have known it was a trick, not for her own safety, as Brandt attempted to sell it. He was just saving himself from the front row seat to the all-night snore-a-thon. Mazie groaned softly, found her flashlight, and quietly crawled out of her sleeping bag, attempting not to wake Brandt, although how he could sleep was a mystery.

Mazie didn't even reach the zipped tent flap when Brandt muttered, "Where are you going?"

"To the little girls' room," she remarked. "If I were smart, I'd sleep in the truck."

"You're not sleeping in the truck," Brandt huffed, still half asleep, then sat up and fought with the zipper on his sleeping bag."

"Where are you going?" she asked.

He briefly eyed her. "You can't go out there alone," Brandt insisted. "The campfire is nearly out. No telling what woodland creatures might be lurking about."

"Stop trying to scare me," Mazie snarled. "I'm not afraid, and you're not winning that bet."

Brandt glared at her. "I'm not trying to scare you," he insisted while grabbing his .338 Winchester Magnum rifle. "And you aren't going out there alone. Those are the rules. I'll wait by the fire."

"You better not be bullshitting me," she scoffed and left the tent.

Brandt groaned and was forced to follow her without being given time to slip into his boots. Mazie puttered around in the woods not far from the campfire, cursing Brandt out under her breath. While she found a good spot to relieve herself, Brandt was heard rustling around by the fire, adding a couple of logs. Mazie continued to curse Brandt under her breath the entire time she relieved herself. As she pulled up her pants, she heard him rustling around in the woods not far from her.

"Damn it, Brandt--" she huffed, then shone the light to her right.

The light glistened off the snout and head of a grizzly bear only ten feet from where Mazie stood. She was frozen in terror at the bear that stood almost eye-level with her while on all fours. Mazie remained frozen and feared even screaming because of the animal that was frighteningly close to her. The bear snorted, then roared and stood on its hind legs. As the six-hundred-pound bear towered over her, it now stood at close to eight feet. Mazie involuntarily screamed, unaware of the death shriek coming from her own mouth. As the bear prepared to lunge for her, Brandt was suddenly alongside her with his rifle aimed. The rifle blast was almost as frightening as the bear's growl. The large-caliber bullet ripped through the bear's heart, dropping it, but that didn't stop Brandt from cocking the rifle and firing another round, striking the bear again as it fell.

Mazie remained frozen while staring at the large mass of brown fur on the ground less than ten feet from her. She wasn't even sure she remembered how to breathe, then finally gasped. Brandt lowered the rifle, then gasped as well, apparently just as shocked as Mazie. Mazie came back to life, turned, and threw her arms around Brandt's waist while burying her head into his chest. He placed his free arm around her, clinging to her as well. Colt was heard screaming as he ran to them with his own rifle.

"What happened?" Colt cried out. "What happened?"

Colt slid to a stop in his bare feet with his rifle in hand and stared at the sight of the dead bear. For a moment, he was equally shocked, then came back to life and looked at Brandt, who was holding Mazie.

"Is she okay?" Colt asked.

"Yeah," Brandt replied while still attempting to catch his breath. "I think so."

Colt again stared at the bear while resting his rifle over his t-shirt-clad shoulder, then shook his head and grinned.

"That's some damned fine shooting, boy," Colt cried out proudly while placing his hand on Brandt's shoulder. "Your first grizzly!"

"We need to take Mazie home," Brandt informed his Uncle Colt.

Mazie suddenly pulled away from Brandt and glared at him. "No way," she cried out. "I'm not losing the bet. I'm staying."

"I'm afraid we're all going home," Uncle Colt informed her. "We need to load that bear into the truck bed, if we're going to make a rug out of him."

"I don't want to make a rug out of him, Uncle Colt," Brandt remarked while turning defensive. "That thing almost killed Mazie tonight."

"But it didn't," Colt reminded him while grinning. "Because you were there to protect her. You should be proud of that, boy."

"I'm not proud," Brandt huffed. "I'm nauseous."

"That's just your adrenaline," Colt assured him. "I'm going to call Dalton to meet us out here so we can load that into the truck. Mazie can wait in the truck while we take down the tent."

*P*resent day. Mazie was abruptly jolted back to reality when she heard a loud bang from the production company concentration camp. She groaned and held her head as well.

"I'm happy knowing you're stuck here in this nightmare, suffering alongside me," Brandt informed her as he flashed a mocking smile. "I'd hate for you to miss out on all the fun."

"I suppose someone has to keep you civil while they're here," Mazie informed him. "We don't want you getting any batting practice in over the next two weeks."

"Be serious, Mazie," he groaned, shaking his head in disappointment. "I don't go around threatening people with baseball bats anymore."

"That's nice to know."

He removed a revolver from the back of his pants. "Guns are much more efficient," Brandt informed her while grinning.

Mazie's expression dropped. "That's not funny, Brandt," she retorted.

"I wasn't going for funny," he insisted.

Brandt no sooner returned the weapon to the back of his pants when Davenport approached from the chaos in the field.

"Mazie," Davenport announced as he darted onto the porch. "We're going to need some flyers posted around town for extras. I want to begin auditions for speaking roles by this evening. Hop to it."

When her boss disappeared as quickly as he had arrived, Brandt watched him leave, then sneered and eyed Mazie.

"He seems nice," Brandt scoffed.

$\mathcal{M}$azie 'borrowed' her old red Jeep from her mother and drove from the ranch to town. She took her time, in no particular hurry. It felt good being behind the wheel of the Jeep she had driven for only a week or two before she left the ranch. Technically, it was her Jeep, but since her mother had been paying the insurance and upkeep, it seemed only natural that it now belonged to her mother. With the soft top down and the wind blowing through her hair, it felt so familiar and amazingly like home. She remembered every curve and incline on every back road as if she'd never left. When she finally reached town, taking the extremely long way there, she parked on the street not far from the bank, gathered her folder containing flyers she had made up in Davenport's office trailer, and headed into the bank. Naturally, she wanted to share the flyers with Cameron and Melissa first.

Melissa was already waiting at the bank for Mazie's arrival, shaming her for getting there fifteen minutes later than expected. Cameron and Melissa gushed over the flyer announcing the auditions at the ranch.

"Before you get too excited," Mazie informed her friends. "I don't know how big any of the speaking roles are, and anyone wanting to be an unpaid extra needs to meet in the church parking lot at seven o'clock tonight. Anyone who wants to audition for a speaking part has to sign up with me from now until five o'clock tonight." She groaned and looked at the flyers in her hand. "Of course, whoever signs up to audition will be invited to the ranch only in small batches." Mazie then rolled her eyes. "Brandt has already had his yearly fill of people at this point."

"Is he going insane?" Melissa asked while grimacing at the thought.

"Honestly, he's doing better than I thought, under the circumstances," Mazie replied. "For a private guy and a bit of a recluse, he's been surprisingly silent."

"You don't actually think 'silent' is a good thing, do you?" Cameron asked, her eyes widening. "It could be "Texas Chainsaw Massacre" by morning."

"Chainsaws are more Uncle Colt's thing," Mazie casually replied. "Brandt likes his baseball bat."

"Didn't he threaten Peter with a bat once?" Melissa asked.

"Yeah, when I was sixteen," Mazie replied while frowning. "When he thought Peter and I were going to make out in the barn." She drew a deep breath and sighed. "I'd better start hanging these flyers." Mazie then turned to Melissa. "Are you going to help me find the best places to post them?"

"I'm with you," Melissa announced.

Chapter 36

*A*round six o'clock that evening, Mazie entered the kitchen, exhausted, and joined her mother, who was nearly finished making dinner. Mazie immediately began setting the table.

"Sorry, I couldn't help with dinner," she announced with a soft groan. "Davenport had me signing up locals for auditions." Mazie glanced at her watch. "The first batch will be here in an hour."

"First batch?" Liddy asked with some surprise. "How many people are coming to the ranch for that?"

"About fifty," Mazie replied while shaking her head. "Ten every hour."

Liddy stopped what she was doing and looked back at Mazie. "That's five hours," she just about gasped.

"Yeah, it'll take that long to check them out," Mazie replied.

"Mazie," Liddy lightly scolded. "You realize people will be driving in and out of here until midnight. Brandt has to be up at five, and the rest of the wranglers are up at six."

"Davenport assured me he cleared it with Brandt," Mazie replied with a weary sigh. "It's been a long day. I'm not sure I'll even make it to midnight."

"You have to work until midnight?" Liddy asked, her eyes wide.

"What's this about midnight?" Dalton asked as he entered the kitchen.

Liddy spun to face Dalton and pointed at Mazie. "Mazie's boss is making her work until midnight," she announced. "She hasn't sat down the entire day."

"Mom, I'm his assistant," Mazie remarked. "When he works, I work."

"Well, he wasn't the one passing out flyers all afternoon in town," Liddy scoffed. "He was taking a nap in the guest bedroom from one until five."

"He runs a production studio," Mazie reminded her mother. "Some days are never-ending, while others are just spent figuring out where we're calling for take-out."

"It's not right," Liddy huffed. "I don't like it. He's working you like a dog."

"Mom, I'm fine," Mazie insisted. "It's what he pays me to do."

"We can discuss this another time," Dalton insisted. "I'd rather we didn't have this conversation in front of Colt. He's been on edge ever since those people arrived."

"Fine," Liddy scoffed and finished making dinner, but with a little extra clanging of pots and pans.

Once Colt and Brandt arrived, they all sat down to dinner a few minutes after six that evening. Mazie only took one bite before her cell phone buzzed in her pocket. She removed her cell phone and looked at the recent text. She groaned softly, then lifted her head and realized all four were staring at her. Mazie grimaced, apologized, and set her phone face down on the table. When it pinged several times within the next few seconds, Colt slammed his water glass on the table, displaying his annoyance. Mazie moved the phone under her leg on the chair. There was a muffled, repetitive pinging sound from beneath her leg, but at least it wasn't nearly as distracting. When the phone suddenly vibrated, it made a hideous sound against the wooden chair that seemed to vibrate down the chair leg to the floor. When they heard the front door open an entire house away, Colt and Brandt exchanged glares.

"Do you want to handle this or should I?" Colt asked with an almost chilling look.

Mazie squirmed slightly, knowing things were about to turn ugly if that was her boss searching for her because she didn't return his text messages. Brandt wiped his mouth on his napkin and sat back in his chair.

"This one's mine," Brandt informed him. "I've got this."

"Maybe I should just--" Mazie began, but immediately silenced when she received glares from both Colt and Brandt.

Davenport entered the kitchen in a whirlwind, seeming surprised to see Mazie just sitting at the dinner table. "Why didn't you answer my texts or calls?" he demanded. "The first group is going to be here in fifteen minutes. You should be outside organizing--"

Liddy slammed her palms on the table and sprang up from her seat, her chair harshly scraping the floor, startling everyone in the kitchen, including Colt and Brandt.

"It is dinnertime, Mr. Davenport," Liddy snarled as her eyes pierced through his. "You do not interrupt family dinners! Do I make myself clear?"

Davenport stared at her, clearly stunned. "Uh, yeah," he replied and took a cautious step back.

"Yes, *what*--?" Colt growled, glaring at the man.

"What?" Davenport asked, clearly confused.

"Ma'am," Colt snarled. "It's *'yes, ma'am'.*" He then indicated Liddy with a quick, commanding nod.

Davenport looked back at Liddy, tensing. "Yes, ma'am," he announced, then quickly left the kitchen.

Liddy released the breath she'd been holding and trembled while returning to her seat. Colt and Brandt exchanged humored looks and chuckled while Dalton just grinned at Liddy.

"I'm sorry," Liddy practically whispered. "I didn't mean to yell like that at the dinner table, especially after criticizing you boys all these years for doing the same thing."

"You were well within your rights, Liddy," Dalton assured her.

"That boy needs to learn some manners," Colt scoffed.

Brandt grinned and chuckled. "I'll gladly hold him down while you whoop his ass."

Colt chuckled and pointed at Brandt across the table. Brandt laughed and pointed back at him. Mazie groaned and sank in her seat. They hadn't even made it through half a day, and Colt and Brandt were already threatening to whoop some ass.

*D*espite receiving disapproving looks, Mazie ate a little faster than usual so she could keep her boss happy and not lose her job. She was out by Davenport's office trailer a few minutes before seven, calling out the names in the order the men and women would be auditioning. There were four female speaking roles and five male roles. Some were as little as a few words, while at least one got an entire sentence. Since it was a paid position, there was no lack of locals auditioning. Mazie had organized the list in the order in which she received their names in town. It was first-come, first-served. No exceptions. She knew Tina would be front and center the moment the news went around town. Unfortunately for Tina, she didn't find Mazie soon enough to be first in line. Well, maybe Mazie did pretend not to see her for nearly a block, signing up several other people first.

Perhaps Mazie was being petty, but it didn't really bother her all that much.

While Mazie attempted to keep the auditions orderly, as each person had only five or six minutes to read lines with Davenport, Tina was suddenly cozying up to her, as if they were still friends.

"So you work for the producer, huh?" Tina asked, sticking by Mazie's side. "What's he like? I mean, what's he looking for? What sort of part is it?"

"Honestly, Tina, I don't know," Mazie replied, which was the truth.

By the time Davenport got her a copy of the screenplay, Mazie was too busy to read it. Not that it really mattered, because her job didn't actually call for any knowledge of the movie itself. When the first girl left the office trailer, Mazie called the next girl on the list. They all seemed to enter the trailer giddy and enthusiastic, but came out with shattered dreams. Some didn't even make it an entire minute before being excused. Davenport knew what he was looking for, even in minor roles. He wanted a particular look for each role, and some of the women were not up to his standards without ever speaking. Auditions went that way. When it was nearly her turn, Tina primped, preparing for her grand entrance. She was finally up next. Mazie indicated the trailer door after the last girl left, looking defeated. Tina strode into the trailer and shut the door behind her.

Davenport's trailer wasn't exactly soundproof, but Mazie would have needed to put her ear to the door to hear Tina's audition. She couldn't deny she was secretly hoping her *former* friend would fall on her face, but she was an attractive young woman with a great body. Mazie felt the woman's chances were pretty good. Since she was nearing the full six-minute mark, Mazie had to assume it was going well for Tina. She then heard a faint thump, startling her. Mazie was about to approach the door and knock on it when she heard a faint, rhythmic creaking from inside. Mazie's eyes suddenly widened when she thought she heard a woman moaning. She glanced at her watch a few more times, realizing Tina had gone over her six minutes by a whole five minutes. The door finally opened, and Tina left the trailer with a broad grin on her face while fixing her hair. She smiled at Mazie.

"It's in the bag," Tina announced.

As she walked away, Mazie stared after her, oddly aware of the sort of performance Tina had given. Davenport stood in the doorway, perspiring and attempting to catch his breath. He watched Tina leave, then looked at Mazie and grinned.

"Put her down for the first part," Davenport announced, then motioned to the girls. "Send the next one in."

Mazie suddenly felt as if she were sending lambs to slaughter. Did he really just take Tina's audition on the 'casting couch'? When he slammed the trailer door, Mazie came back to life. It was little more than a transaction between the two of them. As long as it was consensual, it was none of Mazie's business. Obviously, Tina had initiated the transaction because Davenport wouldn't waste his efforts making sexual advances on a speaking extra position. She held her breath and called the next unfortunate girl. Mazie hoped he cleaned up after himself because she wasn't going to do it.

Chapter 37

Mazie shuffled into the kitchen around seven o'clock the following morning while her mother was already cleaning up from breakfast. She apparently just missed the guys, who were probably in the barn mounting up to start their day.

"I feel like shit," Mazie moaned as she approached the coffeepot.

"I'll make you some tea," Liddy insisted.

"I don't have time," Mazie replied. "I need to get out to the office trailer and see what Davenport wants. He texted me at six o'clock this morning."

"I didn't hear him get up," Liddy remarked. "What time did you get to bed?"

"Close to one o'clock," Mazie replied and sipped her coffee.

"Did you want some breakfast?"

"Don't have time," she reiterated.

"Of course you have time for breakfast," Liddy insisted with a huff. "I'm telling you, your creep of a boss isn't even up yet."

"Mom," Mazie scolded while shooting a look at her. "Don't say things like that."

"When he acts like a gentleman, I'll speak kindly about him," Liddy insisted. "When Brandt was your boss, he treated you with respect."

"He had to," Mazie muttered. "Or Uncle Colt would have whooped the shit out of him."

When they heard someone in the hallway beyond the kitchen, Mazie groaned.

"There he is now, wondering where I am," Mazie informed her mother.

Dalton entered the kitchen, then immediately stopped when he saw Mazie. "Oh," he announced while fidgeting. "I thought you were sleeping in this morning. You were up late."

"Duty calls," Mazie informed him with a hint of a smile while raising her mug.

Dalton smiled but seemed a little tense, then looked at Liddy. "I, uh, probably won't be back at lunchtime today," he informed her. "Brandt and Colt need some extra time away."

"Yes, I know," Liddy replied while smiling a little too much. "Colt packed sandwiches for the three of you when Brandt was saddling the horses this morning."

"I just wanted to make sure you knew," Dalton replied, then gave a general nod and left the kitchen.

Mazie eyed her mother, who attempted to hide her smile as she turned back to the sink to avoid being seen. Mazie groaned softly and shook her head.

"Can we be honest for a moment here, Mom?"

Liddy glanced over her shoulder, briefly eyeing her daughter. "Yes, of course," she replied. "What's on your mind, dear?"

"You and Dalton."

"What do you mean?" Liddy asked, tensing as she turned her back to Mazie.

"Worst kept secret on the ranch, Mom," Mazie informed her. "Everyone knows about you and Uncle Dalton."

Liddy hesitated, then turned to look at Mazie, although she had a difficult time looking her in the eyes. "Everyone?" she whispered.

"His famous early returns to the ranch for all those trips to town?" Mazie remarked, then laughed. "Yeah, everyone knew he snuck back to see you."

"Well, this is embarrassing," Liddy muttered and managed a tiny, tense smile.

"Since I've been gone, I assume it's been easier for the two of you to carry on with your secret romance," Mazie replied. "I'm guessing he's been spending a lot of time in your apartment the last few years."

Liddy finally groaned and accepted that her secret was out. "Yes, although I kind of miss the sneaking around," she replied with a tiny giggle.

"None of us are kids anymore," Mazie announced. "You don't have to hide your relationship from us."

"Well, I guess not," Liddy remarked. "Since everyone seems to know anyway." She then eyed her somewhat suspiciously. "Just out of curiosity, when did you figure it out?"

"Well, Uncle Dalton paying me to do barn chores over the summer that seemed to coincide with his late morning returns to the ranch was a bit suspicious after a while," Mazie replied. "But I think I finally put it together when I was sixteen, and I nearly walked in on the two of you going at it here in the kitchen."

Liddy stared at her daughter with a look of near horror. "Oh--?"

"I talked to Brandt, and he confirmed it," Mazie announced.

"Oh! Don't tell me Brandt heard us in the kitchen, too," Liddy nearly gasped.

"No, but when he was fourteen, he nearly ran into you in the upstairs hallway as you were coming out of Uncle Dalton's bedroom after breakfast one morning," she replied. "He put it together pretty fast."

"I can't believe everyone knew and never said anything," Liddy remarked while shaking her head. "Why not call us out on it?"

"If you wanted us to know, you would have said something," Mazie replied. "If the two of you were serious, you'd want us to know. I guess we assumed you were just sharing company, and no one would blame either of you for that."

"Thank you, Mazie," Liddy announced. "I appreciate that you're not bothered by it."

"No, of course it doesn't bother me," Mazie insisted. "You've been alone a long time. You have every right to happiness."

"I am happy," Liddy informed her, then smiled contentedly. "Very happy. The only thing that would make me happier is you coming home to stay."

"I'm too tired to argue with you about this," Mazie informed her. "I'll try to join you for lunch."

"I expect you here for lunch," Liddy announced in a firm tone. "You didn't have any breakfast. Don't make me come out there and get you for lunch."

Mazie managed a smile and nodded. "Okay, I'll be here for lunch."

*T*hat afternoon, Mazie had to make an emergency trip to town in search of Davenport's favorite brand of whiskey, even though he still had an entire bottle of his favorite brandy. Although the small liquor store in town didn't have a wide selection, they assured her they had one bottle left in stock. Rather than risk it being sold, which was unlikely, she asked Melissa to get the bottle for her, and she'd reimburse her. Mazie decided to meet up with Melissa at the local farmer's market and combine her trip for the whiskey and fresh produce for her mother into one visit. She desperately needed a break from Davenport. Mazie didn't often go on location with him, and now she remembered why. She went from assistant to gopher. What made it worse was the looks Mazie had been receiving from her mother every time he texted her with some other 'chore'. Her mother was a people person, so Liddy's loathing for Davenport was concerning. After her mother's outburst at dinner last night, there was no telling when she'd reach another melting point.

Mazie arrived at the farmer's market before Melissa and looked around the first few stands while waiting for her. After a few minutes, she became concerned that there had been an issue with Davenport's favorite whiskey. Mazie had no doubt he'd send her 'god knows where' to find the coveted bottle of booze. He was like a spoiled child when he didn't get his way, and she didn't need her mother or, heaven forbid, Uncle Colt seeing that. Melissa rushed to join her with a plastic bag containing a paper bag, which could only mean she had the bottle of booze. Her friend was grinning deviously and seemed out of breath for some odd reason.

"I can't believe you didn't tell me," Melissa announced, turning giddy.

"Tell you what?" Mazie asked while accepting the bag containing the whiskey.

"I'm your friend," Melissa insisted. "You should have told me first that Malcolm Wexler and Sandra King arrived at the ranch this afternoon."

Mazie stared at her friend a moment, then cocked her head. "No, that can't be right," she remarked. "They aren't supposed to arrive until next week." Her brows rose sharply. "And it was supposed to be a secret."

"Well, the secret's out," Melissa informed her.

"Who all knows?" Mazie asked, somewhat concerned as her anxiety spiked.

"Everyone," Melissa practically cried out. "I heard visitors from neighboring towns were flocking to the ranch, trying to catch a glimpse of them."

"Wait," Mazie announced, her eyes wide with concern. "What do you mean 'flocking' to the ranch?"

"You mean you don't know?" Melissa asked, her smile fading. "After Brandt locked the gate, they started making the trek to the house on foot."

"How the hell--?" Mazie cried out. "I was only gone an hour!"

"I guess the two arrived shortly after you left," Melissa informed her. "It wasn't long after that when people found their way to the ranch."

"Son-of-a-bitch," Mazie moaned. "Brandt's going to ream out Davenport, and Davenport is going to blame me for the breakdown in security procedures." She handed Melissa some money for the whiskey. "I have to go."

$\mathcal{B}$y the time Mazie reached the ranch driveway, it was already too late. There were cars parked along the road outside the closed, locked gate, and at least a dozen people stood there, straining to see down the driveway, though it was impossible to see the house from the end of the road. Mazie couldn't even pull up to the gate because all the vehicles were blocking the driveway. She pulled alongside the road and immediately called the house, praying her mother would answer and not--

"Uncle Colt," Mazie announced into the phone, her voice cracking. "How, uh, is everything going there?"

"Where are you?" Colt demanded from the other end. "Brandt is looking for your POS boss right now. Dalton called the sheriff."

"I heard it wasn't good," Mazie remarked while grimacing. "I'm, uh, stuck outside the front lines. Cars are blocking the gate."

"Well, if you're by the gate," Colt informed her from the other end. "You should be seeing Brandt any minute. I suggest you defuse the situation really fast, because he's really pissed. Even more pissed than me."

"I'm on it," Mazie announced, then jumped from her Jeep while disconnecting the call.

She left everything in the vehicle and hurried to the gate, slipping past several people. As promised, Brandt was seen galloping down the driveway toward the gate. Mazie slipped under the gate and waited for Brandt to stop his horse not far from her. Others attempted to slip under the gate as well, trying to follow her. Brandt removed his rifle from his saddle holster and held it vertically with the stock resting on his thigh.

"This is private property," Brandt yelled at the crowd. "The first person caught trespassing will be shot as a warning to the others!"

The people who were trying to follow Mazie quickly slipped back out. Police sirens were heard in the distance and rapidly approaching. Brandt glared at Mazie, who could only stare back at him apologetically.

"I can't do this, Mazie," he informed her while returning his rifle to his saddle holster. "You officially broke me. My privacy is gone, my ranch looks like a junk yard, and now I have total strangers hiking through the woods to my house. And for what? The pleasure of watching your disrespectful boss treat you like shit in front of me?" He shook his head, then tossed her the padlock key. "I can't take it, and it's only been twenty-four hours."

"We'll get security to watch the gate," Mazie insisted. "I can have two men here in a couple of hours." She then pleaded with her eyes. "I'm begging you, Brandt, don't do anything stupid."

"I already did something stupid," Brandt remarked. "I trusted you to respect this ranch, your home." He shook his head with disappointment. "I'm returning Davenport's check, and he has until morning to clear all his shit off my property."

Brandt turned his horse and galloped back down the long driveway to the ranch house. Mazie frowned and raked her trembling fingers through her hair. She really messed things up this time.

Chapter 38

Mazie's Jeep pulled up to the ranch house only ten minutes later. The local sheriff had effectively dispersed the crowd, declaring it unsafe to park vehicles along that stretch of road. Whether or not he had the right to force them to move along from a legal standpoint, the lookie-loos obeyed and moved along. Unfortunately, the damage was already done. Brandt was mad enough to follow through with his threat, especially since he never wanted the production company there in the first place. Uncle Colt sat in one of the rocking chairs on the porch with his Weatherby rifle across his lap, looking like Wyatt Earp just before the shootout at the O.K. Corral. As she approached the porch, he gave her the same disappointed and annoyed look she'd received from Brandt not ten minutes ago. Mazie approached more cautiously. Although she'd seen Uncle Colt's bad side many times, she'd never been on the receiving end, and it didn't feel good.

"Sheriff Parker cleared away the traffic outside the gate," Mazie informed him. "Studio security will be arriving within the hour."

Colt nodded, although his look didn't soften any. Mazie didn't like that he seemed so mad that he couldn't even speak. She fidgeted, not sure what to say to make things right.

"I'm sorry, Uncle Colt," Mazie whispered, choking on the words. "I didn't mean for any of this to happen. I should have coordinated better with the director and Davenport about the arrival of--"

Colt held up his finger, silencing her, while shaking his head. "No," he announced firmly. "You're not covering for your boss the way you used to cover for Brandt when you were kids. I doubt that man has done anything to earn your respect."

"I'm not covering for Davenport," Mazie insisted. "As his assistant, everything that happens is my responsibility. If I hadn't spent all that extra time in town this afternoon, I would have been here when all hell broke loose, and I could have fixed it."

"You mean, when you ran to town to fetch a bottle of booze for your boss?" Colt scoffed while raising his brows. "Liddy told me about your 'important errand'."

Mazie shifted uncomfortably. It sounded worse when he said it like that.

"Are you supposed to be two places at once?" Colt demanded. "Is that your job? Where's your boss's responsibility?"

"I really need to fix things with Brandt right now, Uncle Colt," Mazie insisted. "Can we debate this later? I need to find Brandt and make things right."

"No, you need to talk to that boss of yours and straighten him out first," Colt informed her. "Put him in his place before Brandt does it for you."

"That's where you and I disagree," Mazie announced sternly. "Davenport can wait. I need to make things right with Brandt. Do you know where he went?"

"Where he always goes when he's upset," Colt reminded her.

"To see his mom and dad," Mazie muttered, then looked back at Colt. "I need to borrow a horse."

"Mine is still saddled and in his stall," Colt informed her. "Be careful, though. He's a tad spicier than what you're used to."

§

*M*azie rode her Uncle Colt's buckskin gelding across a large field that eventually led to an old log cabin, which was the original homestead built by Brandt's family in the 1850s. The cabin was dilapidated, although considering its age, it was actually holding up better than most new homes. The old porch was falling apart, and the tin porch roof was half torn off; however, the main roof was still intact, and the thick tree trunk walls remained in one piece. The old stone chimney was structurally unsound near the top, but it remained solid at the base. The windows never had any glass; instead, they had wooden shutters that had since fallen off, and the old door was boarded up decades ago to keep out the looky-loos. Not far from the cabin, Brandt's blue roan gelding was seen grazing untethered with its bridle hanging from the saddle horn. The small family cemetery, surrounded by old wrought-iron fencing, was home to dozens of graves and a few large trees. The headstones marked the graves of Brandt's many ancestors, as well as those of his parents.

Brandt rested against a large tree that had been there for over one hundred years and didn't even look up when she arrived. Mazie dismounted her uncle's horse, removed the bridle, and hung it from the saddle horn as well, allowing it to graze with Brandt's horse. As she approached Brandt, he briefly glanced at her while resting his head against the tree and again shut his eyes. Mazie sat alongside him, hugged her knees to her chest, and stared across the beautiful countryside that seemed miles away from all the chaos happening at the ranch.

"I'm sorry for yelling at you the way I did," Brandt remarked before she even had a chance to begin her apology.

"You were right to be angry," Mazie reminded him. "I failed you and the ranch."

"Well, that's kind of on me," Brandt informed her. "You've been gone for five years. It was wrong of me to believe you'd be the same person you were when you left. City life has a way of changing people, and it's not usually for the best."

"Your apology sounds an awful lot like an insult," Mazie informed him.

"I'm still pissed," he reminded her. "Take what you can get."

"I know you meant everything you said, but I appreciate that you're sorry for the tone in which you said it," Mazie replied.

Brandt snorted a laugh. "You know me too well," he remarked, then groaned softly. "I hate when I turn into Uncle Colt. Sometimes, I just can't help it."

"We all carry around a little bit of Uncle Colt inside us," Mazie announced, then looked around and sighed. "We used to spend a lot of time out here growing up."

"I spent time out here," he reminded her. "You just followed me. You were annoyingly underfoot from the day I met you."

"Yeah, I remember," she muttered.

"I miss that," Brandt whispered, then frowned and groaned. "One day, I turned around, and you weren't there anymore."

She stared at his profile for a long moment, then drew a deep, tense breath. "For what it's worth," Mazie remarked almost timidly, then clung to his arm and rested her head on his shoulder. "I still idolize you." She hesitated before speaking. "And I still love you."

Brandt pulled his arm from her grip and placed it over her shoulder, pulling her against him in a warm embrace. Mazie instantly clung to him, longing to feel the warmth of his hug.

"That's all I ever really wanted to hear," he whispered into the top of her head.

"Forgive me?" Mazie asked softly while clinging to him with her face buried in his chest.

"I have little choice," he informed her. "I love you too much to stay mad at you."

"If you want to terminate the contract with my boss, I respect your decision," Mazie informed him without releasing him.

"No," Brandt replied with a sigh. "I'll have a mostly polite conversation with him, explain my concerns in a friendly manner, and try my best not to punch him in the mouth."

Mazie managed a tiny chuckle while nuzzling his chest, somehow unwilling to move out of his arms. "You know, Brandt, there are other ways of dealing with unpleasant situations without throwing fists."

"I know," he replied, then groaned. "But Uncle Dalton hid my baseball bat, so I'm kind of in a bind."

Mazie attempted to lift her head, stunned by what she'd heard, but Brandt refused to release her and stroked her hair.

"This is nice," he announced while nuzzling the top of her head. "I'm almost relaxed enough to deal with people again and not kill anyone."

"Boys are weird," Mazie muttered with a soft chuckle. "I'll give you another five minutes to 'relax'."

Chapter 39

Mazie woke to a horse snorting in her face. She wearily opened her eyes and saw Blackjack's nose up close, checking her out. Mazie straightened with some stiffness, realizing she was still in Brandt's arms, and slowly peeled herself away from him. Brandt's hat was covering his face as he slept with his head against the tree. When she pulled away from him, he abruptly woke and looked around, lifting the brim of his hat with his thumb. A broad grin crossed his face.

"That was a great nap," Brandt informed her.

Mazie was still a little disoriented, since she hadn't gotten much sleep the last two nights. What Brandt referred to as a nap was some of the deepest sleep she'd had in days. After stretching, she glanced at her watch and suddenly gasped at the time.

"It's almost six o'clock," she cried out and sprang to her feet.

"In that case," Brandt announced while standing a little more slowly. "That was an *amazing* nap."

Mazie looked at him with some surprise. "We were asleep for four hours," she gasped. "Davenport is going to wonder what happened to me." She then felt her pockets. "I can't believe he didn't call me a dozen times."

"That man has control issues," Brandt muttered while approaching his horse.

Mazie looked around the grass near the tree. "Where *is* my phone?"

Brandt removed his cell phone and pressed a button. Both listened and looked around, but they didn't hear it. Brandt shrugged, losing interest.

"Probably the best thing that could happen to you," he informed her while putting his horse's bridle on, then looked around. "Probably the bigger question would be, where's Uncle Colt's horse?"

Mazie looked around the pasture but didn't see her uncle's horse anywhere. Brandt mounted his horse and looked down at her.

"I'm guessing he grew bored and headed home," Brandt informed her. "Did you want to ride with me? Or are you too proud and want to walk?"

Mazie glared at him and the cheap grin on his face. He then extended his hand to her. She frowned, then grabbed his hand and swung onto the horse behind him, almost not making it and nearly taking him off the other side as well. Surprisingly, Brandt managed to keep her on the horse behind him without falling off himself.

"You need more practice," Brandt insisted. "You're losing your touch."

"I think I left my phone in my Jeep," Mazie groaned while clinging to Brandt's midsection.

"If I pick up the pace, are you going to fall off and take me with you?" he practically demanded, mocking her.

"Funny," she snarled. "Just get us home."

As Brandt sent the horse into a lope, Mazie nearly lost her balance and gripped Brandt tighter. It had been a long time since she'd ridden double, and the faster gait was a bit more difficult than she remembered.

$\mathcal{W}$hen they finally reached the ranch house, they saw Uncle Colt mounting his horse while Dalton tightened the girth on his horse. They were undoubtedly on their way to look for them, concerned when Colt's horse came back without its rider. Brandt's phone may have vibrated in his pocket, but he either didn't hear it or didn't bother answering it.

"Someone lose a horse?" Colt demanded while indicating his horse.

"We didn't lose him," Brandt replied as he helped Mazie slide off the side of his horse. "He just got bored and decided to come home."

"You were gone long enough," Colt insisted while dismounting. "Even Bucky had enough sense to come home for dinnertime."

"Yeah, well, we fell asleep in the pasture by the old homestead," Brandt informed him while grinning almost deviously.

"Is everyone in a better mood?" Colt asked almost suspiciously.

"I agreed not to kill anyone," Brandt replied as he dismounted. "And Mazie professed her love for me, so I guess all is good."

Dalton and Colt both eyed Brandt, who then chuckled at their expressions.

"That's not how it sounds," Mazie muttered.

"It's dinnertime," Dalton reminded them. "The two of you better get cleaned up and get inside before Liddy has a fit."

"I have to get my cell phone from my Jeep," Mazie informed them.

"It can wait," Colt informed her somewhat sternly and gave her 'the look'. "Your boss isn't interrupting another family dinner. If he does, Liddy is the least of his worries this time."

Mazie held her breath a moment, then sighed and nodded. "It's been a long, rough day," she replied. "I'll find him after dinner."

§

Immediately after dinner, Mazie began her search for Davenport. It would have been easier if she had her phone, but she couldn't find it in her Jeep either. She feared she may have lost it while riding out to the old homestead, in which case, she'd never find it. When she didn't find Davenport in his office trailer, she worked her way through the rows of trailers. Instead of finding her boss, she came across the movie's two main stars, Malcolm Wexler and Sandra King. Malcolm Wexler stood about six foot with a moderately athletic build. He was in his late twenties, with short dark hair, short sideburns, and a few days' worth of stubble, which seemed to be a Hollywood thing, not just laziness. His rugged good looks and boyish charm added to his overall appeal. Sandra King was a beautiful woman in her mid-twenties with straight, shoulder-length, dark auburn hair and magnetic blue eyes. She stood nearly five-foot-seven with an athletic build. Although she wore makeup in her profession, it was almost impossible to tell with its flawless application.

Mazie had met both of them several times before. Over the last few years, she'd met plenty of actors and actresses. The first couple of times she'd met famous people, she was a little star-struck, but that wore off fast. Most of the famous people she'd met were pretty much like everyone else, with a few exceptions. Occasionally, she came across some big egos, but most of the time, her boss had the bigger ego.

"So this is where you grew up?" Sandra asked while looking at the area that wasn't scarred by the trailers and movie equipment. "It's beautiful out here."

"I'll bet it's peaceful," Malcolm remarked, then snorted a laugh. "If not for all the generators running."

"Once you get away from the trailers for your scenic scenes, you'll have a chance to experience the solitude firsthand," Mazie informed him.

Malcolm snorted a laugh. "Unfortunately, we take our noise with us," he reminded her.

"I hadn't really thought about that," Mazie remarked.

"Please, show us around," Sandra announced excitedly. "I want to see the ranch. It'll help us get into character better, too."

"I suppose neither Davenport nor Brandt will mind if I give you the guided tour," Mazie replied.

Nearly half an hour later, Mazie was showing the barn and horse pastures to the movie's two lead stars when Davenport found her.

"Here you are," Davenport announced in a gruff tone. "I've been looking for you for hours. Why haven't you returned my calls or text messages?"

"I'm sorry," Mazie replied, then cringed. "I can't seem to find my phone. I got caught up in that mess outside the ranch gate this afternoon. I had it when I called to have security brought out here, but I haven't seen it since."

"Yes, which you never told me you were unilaterally authorizing security guards," Davenport scoffed, sounding irritated.

"I needed to handle it immediately," Mazie reminded him. "People were sneaking onto the property."

"And we had them removed," Davenport announced. "With the gate shut and locked, we could handle any stragglers arriving on foot."

"That wasn't how Brandt saw it," Mazie informed him. "He was very upset and intended to pull the plug on the whole deal. Thankfully, I was able to appease him with the offer of security outside the gate."

"And that took six hours?" Davenport demanded. "It wasn't that big of a deal, Mazie."

Mazie fidgeted, slightly uncomfortable having this conversation in front of Malcolm and Sandra, both of whom were already exchanging looks.

"May I speak to you a moment in private?" Mazie asked her boss, then stepped into the barn without waiting for an answer.

Davenport excused himself and entered the barn behind her. "Did you just summon me?" he demanded once they were out of earshot of the movie's lead actors.

Mazie spun around with a look of hostility on her face and glared at her boss. "It *was* a big deal," she informed him. "It was a big deal to Brandt and his uncles. He hadn't raised his voice to me like that since I was eleven." She pointed toward the house as she turned angry. "He threatened to return your check and send the entire company packing by morning. I had to go out looking for him to defuse the situation, which I did. For the moment, he's calm and willing to overlook what happened."

"And whose fault was it--?"

"Let me be very blunt, Davenport," Mazie announced boldly. "If anyone associated with this ranch hears you berating, criticizing, or even ordering me around the way you have been, nothing I say or do will stop them from forcibly removing you, your crew, and your equipment from this property. They've already had it with your attitude, and nothing I say or do will change their minds when they reach their breaking point. Remember, these people are my family, which is the only reason this production company was even allowed to set foot on this ranch in the first place." Mazie glanced at her watch. "Now, if you'll excuse me, I'm going to bed. I'm tired, and I have a massive headache. Feel free to text me in the morning."

As Mazie walked past him to the barn door, Davenport stared after her with some surprise.

"But you don't have your phone," he called after her.

"Exactly," she replied and left.

Chapter 40

*T*he following morning, Mazie appeared in the kitchen from the in-law suite, looking fresh and well-rested, and approached her mother at the kitchen counter, where she was busy working.

"Good morning," Mazie announced cheerfully. "Did you need some help with breakfast?"

"Well, someone's in a good mood," Liddy remarked while grinning. "You must have gotten a good night's sleep."

"I was dead the moment my head hit the pillow," Mazie admitted and sliced some fruit for the small fruit platter while her mother made waffles and bacon.

"I'm glad you finally got some sleep," Liddy replied, then gave a nod to the counter not far from her. "Oh, I found your cell phone last night. It was on the porch floor near the railing."

Mazie wiped her hands and then picked up her phone, somewhat surprised. "That's a weird spot for it to be," she remarked. "I don't remember having it with me on the porch."

"Well, maybe someone else found it on the ground and just set it on the porch," Liddy informed her. "With all the people around here, who's to say?" She then cast a sideways glance at her daughter. "And it only dinged one time this morning. Must be a record of some kind."

"Yeah, well," Mazie announced with a sigh. "I had a little 'talk' with my boss last night. In twenty-four hours, he pushed everyone on the ranch to their limit, and he needed to back off, or Brandt would send him packing."

"Maybe that worked," Liddy remarked, appearing humored.

Mazie checked her text message and raised a curious brow. "Huh?" she muttered. "That's interesting."

"Did your boss fire you?"

"Hard to say," Mazie remarked. "He told me I must be working too hard and that I should take the day off. Either I got through to him, or he intends to fire me."

"Well, either way, you have off today," Liddy informed her. "May as well enjoy it. Spend the day with your friends. Go horseback riding. Do something fun."

"I may just do that," Mazie replied.

Brandt came down the kitchen stairs, joining Mazie and Liddy in the kitchen. Mazie was surprised to see him in the house. He was usually saddling the horses at this hour.

"Aren't you supposed to be in the barn by now?" Mazie asked.

"I gave myself the day off," Brandt informed her, then gave Liddy an affectionate side hug. "One of the perks of being my own boss."

"What an amazing coincidence," Liddy announced with a strangely twisted smile. "Mazie's boss gave her the day off, too."

Brandt cast a look at Mazie, appearing somewhat surprised. "Really?" he asked. "Did someone threaten him with bodily harm?" Brandt immediately held his hands in the air. "It wasn't me. I avoided him the entire day out of fear of killing him."

"It may have had something to do with what I said to him yesterday afternoon," Mazie muttered, then cringed. "We'll have to wait and see if I have a job once we're finished filming here."

"I wouldn't worry about it," Brandt remarked, seeming humored. "I'm sure you could find a better job without half trying."

"It's nice to see you're so broken up over me possibly losing my job," Mazie scoffed.

"If you're inviting Melissa and Cameron over this afternoon, why don't you ask them to stay for dinner?" Liddy asked. "I haven't really seen much of them lately, and it'd be nice to catch up."

"Thanks, Mom," Mazie announced. "I'll do that."

"We can do a cookout," Brandt added. "Maybe get a little bonfire going?"

"I know Melissa and Cameron would enjoy that," Mazie announced, even though she knew Brandt was up to something.

While Brandt poured himself a cup of coffee, Mazie studied his profile a little longer than she should have. She gently cleared her throat while continuing to slice fruit for the platter.

"Did you want to go out for a ride with me after breakfast?" Mazie asked almost too softly.

Brandt was about to sip his coffee when he turned his head and looked at her with genuine surprise.

"Were you talking to me?" he asked.

Mazie managed a tiny smile. "Yes, dork," she announced. "I was talking to you. I don't know that my mom's ever been on a horse in her life. I certainly wasn't asking her."

Brandt suddenly grinned, almost making her regret asking him.

"I would love to go on a trail ride with you," Brandt announced a little too enthusiastically. "Did you want to do the whole ranch ride?"

"Hmm," she remarked, then cringed. "Not sure if I'm ready for a four-hour trail ride yet. Maybe start me off with the two-hour tour."

"You worked the cattle for four hours last weekend," he reminded her.

"And I was sore the entire next day," she countered.

"But that's the good kind of sore," Brandt insisted while adding a grin and a wink.

His words and his wink sent an unexplained shiver down her spine, as she was transported back to the night of her graduation party. Every erotic touch. Every kiss. The awkward soreness she felt the entire next day. She wanted to retreat and forgo the trail ride, particularly since she'd be alone with him for several hours. But Mazie knew she had to push through the awkwardness of that night if they were ever going to get past what happened. It shouldn't bother her that he cherished that night, even if she regretted it. His feelings mattered too, and maybe it was time she stopped trying to tell him how he should feel about what happened. And maybe Brandt was right all along. Maybe they needed to sit down and actually discuss that night in order to move on from it. She didn't get any closure, and neither did he. When Brandt noticed she was looking at him, she offered a tiny smile.

"I remember some summers we only got off our horses to eat and sleep," she remarked.

Brandt smiled and chuckled. "Remember that time we chased that bear?"

Mazie suddenly smiled and laughed. "You were swinging your lasso like some psychotic cowboy," she added.

"I'm not sure how I'm even alive after all the stupid shit I did as a boy," Brandt remarked.

"That's pretty easy," Mazie informed him. "I was there to keep you from following through with most of that stupid shit."

Liddy continued making waffles while secretly smiling. She was obviously happy to hear them reminiscing rather than fighting.

Chapter 41

The morning was filled with sunshine, low humidity, and a gentle breeze. Perfect weather for a long ride. Brandt and Mazie rode across wooded, flat, and rugged trails, streams, and fields. They ended up on an old stretch of road that possibly dated back to the 1800s. Growing up, it was one of their favorite spots because they could race side-by-side for a long stretch. They no sooner hit the old dirt road when they exchanged looks, as if coming to the same thought. Mazie grinned and sent her horse into a gallop. Brandt immediately took off after her. Although there was little doubt Brandt was holding Blackjack back, it was fun racing alongside him. When the old gristmill came into view, Brandt pulled ahead and beat her by two lengths. Both slowed their horses and trotted around the old structure.

Mazie groaned, although smiling, and shook her head. "I'm never going to beat you, am I?"

"Technically, you would have beaten me," Brandt reminded her. "Blackjack was, after all, your horse."

"Yeah, but then you would have gotten a better horse for yourself," she reminded him.

"I'd be hard-pressed to find a better horse than Blackjack," Brandt reminded her. "It took me weeks to find you the perfect horse."

Mazie glanced at him as they slowed their horses to a walk. "I didn't know that," she replied almost timidly.

Brandt shrugged. "It's not something I needed to advertise," he informed her. "He technically belongs to you. When you feel like coming back home for good, you can have him."

"You've spent the last five years bonding with him," Mazie remarked. "I know how you feel about him. I wouldn't take him from you."

"It's just a horse," Brandt replied.

Mazie eyed him skeptically. "We both know you don't mean that. You cried like a baby when Gizmo died."

Brandt only smiled but didn't respond. He wasn't going to deny it. Mazie found herself spending almost as much time watching Brandt on Blackjack as she did watching the breathtaking scenery. She couldn't help but admire Brandt for the handsome, rugged man he'd become. The way he sat a horse was second to none. She had always admired his horse riding skills. Brandt caught her staring at him several times and seemed amused. Their indiscretion five years ago still played out in her mind every time she looked at him, but it didn't seem to bother her as much in that moment. He had been right. It was possible to look at him and not see a man she considered more of a brother. She realized he had been, and would always be, her best friend. Everything he'd ever done for her, he did out of his love for her.

"I knew it," he finally remarked while catching her staring at him again. "You want Blackjack, admit it."

"Actually, I think the two of you make a great team," she announced and smiled warmly. "In his mind, I'd forever live in your shadow."

"Why are you suddenly being so nice?" Brandt asked while eyeing her almost suspiciously. "Shouldn't you be busting my balls right about now?"

Mazie drew a deep breath while keeping her eyes on him. "I'm done fighting with you, Brandt," she announced almost timidly. "I want my best friend back."

Brandt attempted to hide his smile but found it impossible. "I want that too," he remarked, then raised a curious brow. "What will it take to accomplish that?"

"Some middle ground that we're both comfortable with," she replied.

"I assume you mean something non-sexual in nature," Brandt muttered while shifting uncomfortably in the saddle.

"I'm being serious here."

"So am I."

"I don't want to get into another argument about that," Mazie insisted, then held her breath while attempting to maintain her focus. "I'm trying to push past that night. Obviously, you aren't willing to pretend it never happened."

"Because it *did* happen," he reminded her. "Being in denial won't change that."

"I know," Mazie replied with a defeated sigh. "What if we just never speak of it?"

"Fine," Brandt huffed, obviously not happy with the suggestion. "Just look into my eyes and tell me you hated every minute of our night together. Tell me how horrible it was, and I'll never bring it up again."

Mazie attempted to gaze into his eyes and say the words just to end the conversation forever, but she couldn't do it. She couldn't lie knowing it would destroy him. Mazie looked away and shuddered slightly.

"During that moment," Mazie announced, then struggled with her words. "When we were together." She held her breath a moment. "It was--very pleasurable. Even exciting." Mazie shut her eyes and grimaced at what she was about to say. "I enjoyed it very much--*at the time*." She opened her eyes, staring at him. "But when morning came, I realized how wrong it was, what I'd done--*with you*."

"And I get that," Brandt replied. "I respect your feelings about what happened, but at the same time, I don't want to forget it or pretend it didn't happen."

"So we're back to where we started," Mazie announced with a defeated groan as she raked trembling fingers through her hair.

Brandt frowned and shook his head. "I never want to be the reason that you're suffering," he remarked, now defeated. "I can't do that to you." He drew a deep breath and sighed. "I won't mention it ever again, if that's what it takes to make you happy. If that's what it'll take to get my best friend back."

"I believe we found our middle ground," Mazie replied, then managed a tiny, relieved smile.

Brandt returned the smile, although it was apparent he wasn't entirely thrilled with the 'middle ground' they reached.

"So," he announced almost boldly while sharply raising his brow. "What will it take to get you out of the city and back on my payroll?"

Mazie glared at him, not humored by the question.

Brandt snorted a laugh and held up his hand. "Respectfully backing off."

"No, you don't have to back off on your quest to bring me home," Mazie informed him. "I more or less got my way on the other matter. You can shoot your shot, if you'd like, just don't expect an answer other than 'no'."

"Then I'll keep on asking," Brandt announced with a playful grin. "I have two weeks to wear you down. You'll remember all the good times and how much you love this place. You'll realize how much you miss your family and friends." He then winked at her. "And maybe even me."

Mazie hid her smile. "There was never any dispute about that," she reminded him. "And that includes you."

"And the rest I'll leave up to your boss," Brandt remarked. "That guy will do more to sell my case than I could ever accomplish."

"Well, you may not be wrong," Mazie muttered.

Brandt glanced at her several times as they rode side-by-side. He tensed slightly in his saddle, then gently cleared his throat.

"There is something else I've been meaning to ask," Brandt remarked. "If you said 'yes,' it'd be a particularly nice gesture on your behalf."

Mazie groaned and eyed him. "I'm almost afraid to ask."

He met her gaze and smiled. "The rodeo is this coming Monday," Brandt informed her. "And I'd really like to enter the team roping event."

Mazie stared at him for a long moment, somewhat surprised. It was her turn to shift uncomfortably.

"Do you have any idea how rusty I am at roping?" she asked.

"You have four days to lubricate those rusty parts," Brandt informed her, then offered his most charming smile. "Come on, Maz. I'm asking for under thirty seconds of your time."

She considered the comment for a long moment, again noting the smile on his face. Mazie groaned, hiding her smile, and nodded.

"Fine," she announced with a sigh. "If I can master my former roping technique by Sunday, I'll team rope with you at the rodeo on Monday."

His grin suddenly increased. "You'll be a pro by Monday," Brandt insisted. "It'll be just like old times."

Mazie found herself smiling at the thought. Although she was a little nervous about competing after such a long time away, she couldn't help but wonder if she still possessed the skills.

Chapter 42

*L*ater that afternoon, Melissa and Cameron joined Mazie at the ranch and watched some of the scenes being shot. The biggest thrill for her friends was seeing Malcolm and Sandra filming a couple of their scenes and even getting to talk with them. Since it was a 'closed set', so to speak, Melissa and Cameron were able to interact with the movie stars on a more personal level. The only downside to the entire afternoon was the arrival of the extras with speaking roles, and mainly only because Tina was once again in Mazie's inner circle. Mazie sat on the porch railing, shooting death glares at Tina from across the front yard. At the same time, Melissa and Cameron attempted to interact with the stars despite Tina inserting herself into the conversation. Mazie was so focused on her childhood bully, she didn't even realize Brandt was leaning against the support beam, practically hovering over her.

"Isn't that the bitch who bullied you throughout high school?" Brandt asked, nearly startling her.

Mazie looked back at him and wondered how she hadn't noticed he'd been there with how close he was standing. She resumed shooting death glares at the young woman, who kept interrupting the conversation Melissa and Cameron were holding with Sandra.

"Yeah, that's her," Mazie muttered and shook her head. "You'd think I'd be over it by now."

"Your petty desire for revenge is what I love the most about you," Brandt informed her almost too casually.

She looked back at him, snorted a laugh, and grinned. "Because it makes us kindred spirits?" Mazie teased.

"Perhaps. What's she doing here anyway?" Brandt then asked while watching the vile young woman as well.

"She has a speaking role," Mazie scoffed.

"Oh?" Brandt remarked without taking his eyes off the distant scene. "Did she audition on her back?"

"I'm guessing 'doggie style'," Mazie replied without missing a beat.

Brandt eyed her with some surprise, then chuckled. "Want to go over and say 'hi'?"

"Yeah, right," Mazie muttered. "I don't even want to breathe the same air as her." She shook her head. "For a day that started so promising, it's rapidly going downhill. Could the day get any worse?"

Brandt turned his head and suddenly stiffened as he straightened. "I think it's possible," he announced, then gave a slight nod toward the barn.

Mazie glanced in the direction Brandt had been looking and saw Peter walking toward them and the house. After remembering how poorly her former crush had treated her the night of her graduation party, she no longer cared to see him. Peter wore a huge grin as he approached them.

"I thought there was security at the gate," Brandt muttered. "How did *he* get in? Did you invite him?"

"No," Mazie insisted as Peter got closer. "Definitely not."

"Should I get my baseball bat?"

Mazie sharply eyed Brandt. He held his hands in the air and took a step back.

"Fine, I'll let you handle this your own way," Brandt informed her. "But I'll be critiquing your technique from the sidelines."

When she moved away from the railing, Brandt claimed her spot. Mazie approached the steps as Peter paused in front of them.

"This is great," Peter announced. "So exciting. Thanks for inviting me."

"I didn't invite you," Mazie informed him while attempting to remain polite.

"Well, Cameron said it was okay," Peter replied. "I assumed it was an invite."

"Cameron, huh?" Mazie remarked while smiling through gritted teeth. "She probably should have cleared it through me first."

"We're all friends," Peter reminded her.

That was debatable.

"Well, let's go find Cameron," Mazie announced and left the porch, joining him.

As Mazie and Peter approached Melissa, Cameron, and Sandra, they heard a four-wheeler above the generators. Mazie looked out to the large field before the woods and saw the four-wheeler tearing up the pasture while the cameraman filmed Malcolm's scene on horseback. Even from that distance, Mazie could see the torn pasture. They must have done the same take several times, redoing it because of Malcolm's poor riding skills. Mazie knew Brandt wouldn't appreciate what they were doing to the pasture and was just about ready to call him when Uncle Colt appeared, almost out of nowhere, on his horse. He was a little hot, and reasonably so.

"What the hell are you doing?" Colt shouted in anger at the director. "You're tearing up the entire pasture with that thing."

"We're sorry," the director announced, attempting to keep the peace. "We got the shot. I'm sure the grass will grow back."

"It's not the grass that's the problem," Colt scoffed. "It's all the goddamned ruts! We're going to need to steamroll the entire stretch just to smooth out the ruts! Stop tearing up the pasture with that thing."

"Oh," the director remarked, then grimaced slightly. "We still have to shoot the galloping scenes."

"With *that* guy riding?" Colt demanded while pointing at Malcolm. "Are you making a snuff film? Because that's what's going to happen if you let that guy ride past a trot. And just how many takes do you think you'll need before you get the right shot with that?"

It was a rhetorical question at best, but more than likely an insult.

"No, not Malcolm," the director insisted. "We have a stuntman for that, which I'm sure we can do in five takes or less."

"You've got one," Colt snarled back.

"I don't think one--" the cameraman began, but was interrupted by the director.

"It can't be done in one shot," the director insisted. "If you have a better idea--?"

"Yeah, I've got a better idea," Colt scoffed. "Film your damned shot from horseback and stop tearing up the pasture."

Mazie hid her smile and had to keep from laughing. Watching Uncle Colt in action was sometimes its own amusement. He didn't pull any punches.

"That's not possible," the cameraman insisted. "I can't ride, and we only have one stuntman."

"What the hell do you need a stuntman for?" Colt demanded. "You're riding a horse, not jumping off a fricking building."

The cameraman pulled out a smaller camera and extended it to Colt. "You think it's so easy?" he demanded. "You try it."

Colt snatched the five-pound camera from him, felt the weight, and snorted a laugh. "This little thing?" he announced. "This is supposed to be a big deal? Son, try roping and flipping a twelve-hundred-pound steer to the ground just to give them daily antibiotics when they're sick." He eyed the camera. "Just point out the damned 'on' button."

The cameraman and director exchanged looks, then shrugged.

"Let him give it a try," the director remarked.

The cameraman took two minutes to attach the camera to Colt's shoulder, showed him how to hold it so he could film from a sideways position, and then indicated the route they would be taking.

"Just keep pace with the stuntman from ten feet away while recording," the cameraman informed him.

Almost everyone on location had gathered to witness history in the making. Mazie stood with her friends, grinning proudly at Colt for his effort and plain stubbornness. When the scene board was clapped, and the director yelled 'action', the stuntman galloped the Hollywood horse across the field with Colt racing alongside him, practically sitting sideways on his running horse. Everyone stared in awe as Colt steadied the camera with both hands while leaving the reins across the horse's neck. When they made the turn by the woods, Colt didn't even need the reins to turn his horse. The horse seemed to do it all on its own with some leg pressure from its rider. Both men trotted their horses back to the cameraman, receiving a round of applause. After Colt passed the camera off to the cameraman, everyone waited patiently as the director reviewed the footage. He suddenly appeared dumbfounded and looked back at Colt.

"How would you like to make five hundred dollars a day?" the director asked Colt.

"Depends," Colt remarked. "I'm not doing any nude scenes. That's where I draw the line."

The director chuckled and shook his head. "No, you don't have to do any nude scenes," he replied. "I just need you to film a few close-up running scenes."

Colt considered it and then shrugged. "If it keeps you from tearing up the goddamned pasture, I could do that," he replied.

Chapter 43

Brandt stood alongside Colt while they grilled chicken and steaks on the mammoth grill in the backyard. After Brandt slathered the meat in sauce, Colt tossed it onto the sizzling grill.

"I just wish you'd asked me before extending the invitation," Brandt muttered to his uncle so others wouldn't hear.

The twelve cast and crew members from the production company sat around the bonfire along with the ranch hands and Mazie's friends. Brandt cast glares at Peter and Tina, who had also invited themselves and were practically glued to Malcolm and Sandra's sides the entire time.

"What's the big deal?" Colt asked. "We have plenty of food."

"The big deal is that little snot, Tina, and that ass hat, Peter," Brandt informed him. "I would have preferred they not stay. They gave Mazie a lot of grief growing up, and I'm sure she's uncomfortable."

"She was uncomfortable with you as well," Colt reminded him. "But we let you hang around."

"Funny," Brandt scoffed.

Colt chuckled at Brandt's expense. "Relax, boy," he announced. "It'll be fine."

"I'm twenty-nine," Brandt reminded him. "Do you think you can stop calling me 'boy'?"

Colt considered the question, then shook his head. "Nope," he announced.

"What if I pulled rank?" Brandt demanded.

"That only works when I'm on the clock," Colt replied, then looked at his wrist that didn't contain a watch. "And I'm off the clock. Now, I'm your uncle, and you were taught to respect your elders."

"Yes, sir," Brandt announced a little too quickly while minding the steaks. "Just so you know, your boss has you mucking stalls tomorrow."

Colt shot a surprised look at Brandt, who easily ignored him.

*O*nce dinner was ready, the entire cast and crew enjoyed the BBQ and bonfire. Since most of them were constantly on the go, they never realized how enjoyable a good meal and a low-frills bonfire BBQ could be. After dinner, Liddy brought out marshmallows to roast over the fire, which the production team loved. It wasn't just the whole bonfire atmosphere they loved. Colt was suddenly an instant hit with the entire cast and crew after his cowboy cameraman debut went viral. Mazie thought it was weird seeing Colt talking and laughing with strangers, particularly city folk, but he was soaking up the attention, feeding his ego. Mazie, Brandt, and Dalton watched Colt's ego inflating in real time and were left almost dumbfounded at the transformation. With Sandra hanging out with the crew and Davenport, Peter inserted himself into their conversation, wanting to be closer to the beautiful actress. Mazie never realized how much of a dog Peter actually was. She wondered why she'd never seen it before that night he kissed Hannah in the barn.

After Liddy had finished passing out marshmallows and metal roasting sticks, she joined Dalton on the opposite side of the bonfire, sitting close to him on the lodgepole beam bench. Dalton placed his arm around her, holding her close to his side. When she looked up at him and smiled, he leaned down and kissed her quickly but warmly on the lips. Mazie gasped at what she'd just witnessed. It was their first-ever public display of affection. The simple, tender moment was met with stunned looks by Colt and Brandt as well, although no one commented. Everyone knew about their secret relationship, but this was the first time they came out in the open with it. Mazie couldn't deny that it was a special moment. Cameron nudged Mazie several times and indicated the romantic couple, raising her brows suggestively.

Mazie sat on the far side of the bonfire with Cameron and Melissa, who were enjoying Malcolm's company. Unfortunately, Tina wiggled her way into their conversation, attempting to dominate it with her award-winning personality. After a brief discussion about the ranch's history and how that information was helpful for the scenes they were shooting, Tina managed to circle back to herself, which was quite an achievement. Mazie found it interesting that every conversation was somehow connected to Tina's life experiences.

"I always wanted to be an actress," Tina informed Malcolm, despite no one having asked. "I was the lead in all the school plays."

That was a lie, but neither Mazie nor her friends corrected her in the spirit of playing nice around the famous actor. Malcolm was possibly the most polite actor Mazie had ever met. Regardless of the topic, he remained attentive and engaged.

"And I majored in theater and communications in college," Tina continued.

"That's a good start," Malcolm responded, then appeared interested. "Are there many local theaters around here?"

"Sadly, no," Tina replied while eating up the attention from the handsome actor.

"Oh, that's too bad," Malcolm replied. "If you're really interested in acting, you need to be closer to the action. It's a long, rough road, but everyone deserves a shot at their dreams." He then asked the logical follow-up question. "Did you find a local job in communications instead?"

"Well, not exactly," Tina replied. "I'm working the cosmetics counter at our local mall." She then added. "But that's only temporary."

"I know what you mean," Malcolm announced, releasing a soft chuckle. "I was bartending to make ends meet while I was studying forensic medicine, but tuition was killing me. Davenport was at the bar one night and 'discovered me' so to speak. He gave me my first acting job. The money was good, and I thought it would help pay for tuition. In the end, I abandoned forensics and went into acting instead."

"Wow, that's a fascinating story," Tina announced.

"I can't believe it," Melissa remarked with surprise. "I also wanted to go into forensics. Unfortunately, tuition sidelined me as well."

Malcolm eyed Melissa and smiled at her as if they were kindred spirits.

"So she works for a pharmacy instead," Tina reported with a hint of mockery.

Melissa cast a sideways glare at Tina. "It's a pharmaceutical company," she scoffed.

"Really?" Malcolm asked, seeming interested. "What field?"

"I'm a biologist," Melissa informed him. "Research on preparation, preservation, and safety, as well as drug discovery and development."

Malcolm suddenly grinned and nodded. "I'm impressed," he replied, then turned serious. "Why don't biologists ever get lost?"

Melissa stared at him a moment, considering the question. She hesitated only a moment, then grinned. "Because they're always following the cytoplasmic streaming."

Malcolm laughed and pointed at her. "You and I have real *chemistry*."

It was Melissa's turn to laugh, inadvertently placing her hand on his lower arm. She immediately recoiled after realizing she'd touched him.

"Sorry," Melissa announced while hiding her smile and flushed cheeks.

"For what?" Malcolm asked as he placed his hand on hers and playfully squeezed it. "For laughing at my terrible pun?"

Melissa eyed Malcolm's hand on hers and possibly turned every shade of red, now unable to hide her smile. Malcolm cocked his head while keeping his eyes on her.

"You have the most radiant smile," Malcolm informed her.

As Melissa stared into Malcolm's eyes like a deer in headlights, Mazie and Cameron exchanged glances, almost stunned at the level of flirting happening before their eyes. Tina, on the other hand, appeared instantly annoyed.

"Fat girls *are* typically jolly," Tina announced, surprising everyone.

Mazie and Cameron were shocked into silence by the cruel comment about Melissa's weight back in school. Since she was still slightly robust, even after losing weight, it remained a sensitive topic for Melissa. Before Mazie could explode, Malcolm beat her to it. He glared at Tina while immediately straightening.

"What the hell is your problem?" Malcolm demanded. "Is that any way to talk to your friends?"

Before Tina could say anything, Melissa muttered, "We *aren't* friends."

Malcolm looked from Melissa to Tina, somewhat surprised. "Now, I'm confused."

"I'm friends with Mazie," Tina informed him.

Mazie suddenly snorted a laugh and shook her head. "You and I haven't been friends since the eighth grade," she announced without hesitation. "Not since you let those older boys spike my drinks at the party at Old Mill Pond."

"That was just a childish prank," Tina insisted, turning defensive. "And it was ten years ago. I can't believe you're still holding that against me."

Out of the corner of her eye, Mazie saw Brandt stiffen while sneering at Tina. If she didn't defend herself, Brandt was going to say his peace, which would be anything but peaceful.

"A childish prank doesn't typically end with a potential sexual assault," Mazie scoffed loud enough that her mother, Colt, and Dalton overheard the comment.

When Colt shot up from his seat, Dalton practically leapt over the bonfire to hold his brother back. Shocked and angry looks were being shot at Tina from nearly every corner. Mazie knew she had opened Pandora's Box, but she wasn't about to stop there.

Tina saw the reactions from Mazie's family and immediately jumped into damage control. "There wasn't any sexual assault," she insisted. "The only assault was Brandt threatening a bunch of kids with a baseball bat."

Peter instantly squirmed where he sat, knowing that feeling all too well.

"Brandt and his baseball bat were the only things that prevented that boy from assaulting me," Mazie snapped back.

Liddy eyed her daughter with some surprise. "You snuck out to that party, didn't you?" she gasped.

Dalton then glared at Brandt. "You went out on your date when you were supposed to be watching Mazie?" he demanded.

"You threatened a whole group of kids with a baseball bat?" Colt asked, then laughed. "Boy, you've got a big pair on you."

Liddy and Dalton glared at Colt for encouraging the behavior. Mazie ignored her family's trip down memory lane and maintained her glare at Tina.

"All of that aside," Mazie scoffed. "It was your continuous torment and daily bullying of my friends and me until graduation that really pissed me off. Now, here you are, in my own backyard, insulting and bullying my friend right in front of me. Well, I'm not taking any more of your shit."

Malcolm stood, grabbed Melissa's hand, and practically pulled her to her feet while glaring at Tina. "I don't know who actually invited you, but if it were up to me, I'd have security remove you," he snarled. "Stay the hell away from me, and stay the hell away from Melissa." Malcolm then turned to face Melissa. "Feel like taking a walk? I need to cool off."

Melissa attempted to hide her overly pleased smile and nodded. As they walked away, Dalton eyed Tina from across the bonfire, where he still kept close tabs on Colt, just in case.

"Who *did* invite you?" Dalton demanded.

Tina fidgeted, unsure how to respond. Davenport stood and approached Tina while looking at Dalton.

"That's my fault," Davenport announced while placing his arm around Tina. "I invited her. I'm sorry for any past trauma it may have dredged up. I'm sure Tina's very sorry for everything that's happened. I'll take responsibility for her while she's on location with us."

When Davenport guided Tina across the back yard to the picnic tables, she had little choice but to go with him. They sat down at one of the tables and talked privately. Tina didn't look distraught; she looked annoyed, which meant she didn't think she did anything wrong then or now. Cameron leaned closer to Mazie.

"Well, that escalated fast," Cameron muttered.

Mazie glanced across the bonfire at her mother, who glared at her with disappointment for sneaking out of the house over ten years ago.

"Why do I get the feeling I'm about to be grounded?" Mazie groaned.

Chapter 44

As the evening progressed, the crew began dispersing and returning to their quarters for the night. They still had a full day of filming ahead of them in the morning, with some getting up before sunrise. It was around that time that Melissa and Malcolm returned from their lengthy walk. Whatever they discussed on their 'walk', Melissa was all smiles when they returned. With a more intimate setting around the bonfire, Brandt actually joined in on some of the conversations and answered all of Sandra's questions about the ranch that had been in his family for generations. Despite having heard everything there was to hear about the ranch, Mazie still loved hearing the stories. She especially missed Brandt's ranch stories. He was an engaging storyteller with a deep, rich voice. Mazie could listen to him talk for hours. While Sandra was talking with Brandt, Peter may have given up his quest for her attention and moved to the vacant spot on the lodgepole beam bench alongside Mazie.

"You seem to be reminiscing quite a bit," Peter remarked while simultaneously checking her out. "You aren't considering moving back home, are you?"

"As much as I miss the ranch," she informed him, "I'm making more money than any job around here would pay. I don't see any real benefit to moving back home."

"It's a lot warmer in LA in the winter, that's for certain," Peter remarked while grinning, his eyes again straying to her cleavage.

Ironic that he hadn't noticed her when he didn't know she actually had cleavage.

"Did you ever consider the possibilities, now that we're older?" Peter remarked, seeming almost proud of himself. "Maybe we could go out, you know, just the two of us. We never seemed to be at the right place at the right time back then."

Was he kidding? They had a place, and they had a time! Peter threw it away so he could make out with Hannah in the barn! Mazie realized she needed a few more drinks to survive the rest of this evening.

"Yes, the good old days," she remarked, then held up her empty bottle and offered the best smile she could manage while standing. "I need a refill."

As Mazie approached the ice chest for another wine cooler, she heard Brandt entertaining the remaining cast and crew with one of his more amusing Mazie stories. Mazie groaned and laughed, knowing where this particular story was going. After removing a bottle from the cooler, she saw her chance to escape Peter by joining Brandt.

"How about you tell some embarrassing stories about yourself for a change?" Mazie announced while approaching Brandt and sitting alongside him on the lodgepole beam bench.

Mazie didn't even bother struggling with the twist-off cap, mechanically handing the bottle to Brandt. He removed the cap without missing a beat.

"Because the ones with you are more amusing," Brandt insisted.

Despite the fire, Mazie shivered slightly, collecting into a tight ball alongside Brandt. The moment he saw her shiver, he pivoted her from the log alongside him to the spot on the ground between his knees and placed his arm around her shoulders, providing extra warmth. For a moment, it seemed so natural, being that he'd held her this way many times after he'd matured. When she clung to his arm around her shoulders from behind, it was as if she suddenly realized where she was sitting. She wasn't even sure how she got into that position; it had happened so effortlessly. Despite how natural the action had been, they received several odd looks, primarily from Mazie's friends and family. Peter, in particular, didn't seem very happy about her decision to sit with Brandt, let alone 'cuddle' with him.

Yes, their closeness was commonplace five years ago, but given their ongoing feud, their moment of familiarity was somewhat surprising. Mazie let the awkwardness pass with a little help from her fifth wine cooler and embraced the shared moment from their past. Mazie felt compelled to glance over at the picnic table, where Davenport was sitting uncomfortably close to Tina as they talked. Tina appeared less than thrilled, spending the entire evening with Davenport, but something must have happened. The moment Tina started smiling, almost giddy at something he said,

Mazie became immediately suspicious. When they got up and left together a few minutes later, Mazie was left practically stunned. She wasn't the only one giving the departure strange looks. Brandt casually placed his head over Mazie's shoulder and spoke softly close to her ear.

"Did I miss something?" he muttered just loud enough for her to hear.

Mazie shuddered slightly from his warm breath against her ear. "No," she replied softly. "You know as much as the rest of us."

"I thought she was avoiding him all evening," Brandt remarked.

"I'm guessing he upped the ante until she found an offer she liked," Mazie muttered.

As the couple disappeared into the house, Brandt groaned. "Great," he huffed. "They're going to go at it in his guestroom that shares a wall with my room."

"Just give them half an hour," Mazie reported while turning her head to look at him, then realized how close his face had been to hers, their lips nearly touching.

Mazie hesitated a moment, distracted by his mouth so close to hers. She gently cleared her throat and attempted to put a little distance between their lips.

"I'm sure that'll be plenty of time," she remarked, now uncomfortable, before finally turning her head to avoid looking at him.

Brandt slipped his other arm around her shoulders and affectionately clung to her. "Well, if you find me on the sofa in your suite, you'll know you were wrong."

"Wouldn't you be more comfortable in your mother's old bedroom?" Mazie asked while patting his arms across her shoulders.

"No, not really," he replied. "That's the room where she, well--" Brandt hesitated a moment. "You know."

Mazie drew a deep breath, then caressed his arms around her. "If that room has so many bad memories, you could always renovate it."

"Into what?" Brandt asked. "Another guest bedroom?" He shook his head. "I don't see the point of having one guest bedroom, let alone two. Uncle Colt and Uncle Dalton already use the other spare room as an office and home gym." He shrugged, then sighed. "I don't know. Maybe I'll turn it into a nursery in the future, if I ever need something like that. Assuming I get married someday. My luck, I'll be an old man living with Colt and Dalton. Three lonely, sad bachelors."

"Kind of hard to find someone when you're not actively looking," Mazie informed him.

"Who says I'm not looking?" Brandt asked.

"My mother."

"Well," he announced with a sigh. "I suppose she'd know." Brandt was silent for a moment, then chuckled softly. "I know what I'll do. I'll turn my mother's old room into a bedroom for you. Part of a sign-on bonus for you to come back and work for the ranch."

Mazie managed a tiny, tense laugh. "You don't give up, do you?"

"No," he replied with a sigh. "I don't think I'll ever give up." Brandt then shifted uncomfortably and chuckled. "Besides, moving you out of your mother's suite will give Liddy added privacy for her late-night rendezvous with Uncle Dalton."

"I don't think there will be any more rendezvous," Mazie informed him. "I'm pretty sure tonight was their 'coming out' party. That kiss practically sealed the deal."

Brandt suddenly tensed and gently cleared his throat. "Talking about sealing the deal," he announced. "I think Melissa's evening is about to get a lot more exciting."

Mazie glanced across the bonfire and saw Melissa and Malcolm sharing a moderately passionate kiss. Mazie gripped Brandt's forearm and attempted to hold back her gasp.

"Oh, my God," she gasped. "Melissa is making out with Malcolm Wexler."

"Yes, I see that," Brandt replied softly. "Don't stare. You'll spook them."

Mazie giggled and swatted his arm. "Stop that," she remarked.

Melissa finally got up and approached Mazie with Brandt. Her grin was so big, it looked almost painful. "Uh, I'm heading out," she announced, then indicated Malcolm, who was also standing. "Malcolm is going to walk me to my car."

Brandt chuckled lowly while Mazie had a hard time hiding her grin.

"Okay, thanks for coming," Mazie announced. "Pleasant dreams."

"Oh, you can count on that," Melissa replied while giggling.

When Melissa and Malcolm headed around the side of the house, Cameron hurried to Mazie and flopped onto the log alongside them.

"Where are they going?" Cameron asked, attempting to keep her voice down.

"Malcolm is walking her to her car," Mazie replied.

"She doesn't have her car," Cameron reminded her. "I drove."

A text then came through on Cameron's phone. She looked at Mazie.

"It's from Melissa," Cameron gasped, then read the message. "She says she'll get a ride home in the morning." She looked back at Mazie. "Oh, my God. Melissa is spending the night with Malcolm Wexler!"

"Sounds like it," Brandt remarked, then frowned and sighed. "Everybody's getting laid tonight. Except us, as usual."

"Oh, please," Cameron scoffed. "Sandra was flirting with you, but you were too dense to notice or care."

"That girl was not flirting with me," Brandt informed her.

"Yeah, she kind of was," Cameron announced. "Then she saw the two of you doing *whatever* this is, and she called it a night."

Mazie pulled away from Brandt and attempted to look back at him. "I'm so sorry," she announced. "I didn't know. I didn't mean to ruin anything for you."

"Stop," Brandt scoffed and pulled her back into his arms. "The last thing I want or need is a fling with an actress."

"Mazie's right," Cameron remarked to Brandt. "You are weird."

Chapter 45

Mazie woke up the next morning before sunrise, feeling better than she had in a long time. She had two full nights of sleep, felt stress-free for the first time in years, and finally felt her relationship with Brandt was back on track. The stress from her broken relationship with Brandt must have weighed more heavily on her than she ever realized. It kept her from returning home, visiting her mother, and being with the people she loved most. Before leaving her mother's suite, she heard her mother softly giggling from within her room behind closed doors. Mazie hesitated only a moment and smiled. She was glad her mother finally felt comfortable enough to let Dalton stay overnight in her room while Mazie was home. They spent too much time hiding their relationship as it was. Both deserved happiness without shame.

Once in the main kitchen, Mazie started the coffeemaker and made a cup of tea for herself, which she took to the front porch. Her morning was only mildly ruined by the annoying buzzing of multiple generators. Despite their distance from the house, they were still loud and disrupted the quiet pre-dawn morning. She sat on the double-wide swing and attempted to enjoy the morning despite the buzzing sound. Brandt walked onto the porch with a mug of coffee and saw her on the porch swing. He immediately smiled and raised his coffee mug.

"Do I have you to thank for the coffee?" he asked.

"Well, for whoever was on tack detail," Mazie informed him. "Which is usually you."

"Technically," he announced. "It's supposed to be your job."

Mazie chuckled, then moved her feet off the swing and patted the vacant spot next to her. Brandt all too willingly accepted the seat, gently rocking the swing from the impact of his larger frame sitting on it. Mazie placed her feet across his lap and made herself comfortable. He immediately ran his finger along the arch of her foot. Mazie let out a soft, startled scream, then laughed while removing her feet from his lap.

"Every time," she huffed playfully.

"I only do it because I like making you scream," Brandt teased.

They stared into each other's eyes for a long moment in silence. A strange, tiny smile crossed his face, and he motioned her over.

"Come here," he lightly commanded.

Mazie stared at him a moment longer, fighting the urge to jump on command as she had when she was a little girl. As a teenager, she would often laugh at him and sometimes even tussle with him in fights for dominance. So, why now, as an adult, did the thought of him dominating her somehow entice her? Mazie set her tea mug down and slid across the porch swing closer to him. A strange smile crossed his face.

"I was *not* expecting that," Brandt remarked with a low chuckle as he placed his arm over her shoulder. "What happened to that feisty girl I knew and loved?"

Mazie rested her head on his shoulder and clung to his midsection. "I've been secretly fighting with you for the last five years," she replied, then nuzzled him. "I miss the closeness. I'll happily fight with you another time."

Brandt's arm tightened around her, and he affectionately kissed the top of her head. "I'll pencil you in for later in the week."

"It's a date." Mazie again nuzzled his shoulder. "If you watch the sunrise with me, I'll help you saddle the horses to get you back on schedule."

"Deal."

*A*fter breakfast, Mazie stood on the porch and watched Brandt, her uncles, and the rest of the ranch hands ride across the field, past the clutter of trailers, and out to the field for their morning. All she wanted was to go out with them. She felt like a little girl all over again, begging her mother to let her ride with the boys, but she was too little. She could do mornings, the same as Brandt had when she was twelve, but she wasn't allowed to do full days until she was thirteen. All she wanted to do was follow Brandt wherever he went and do whatever he was doing. Now, even after a five-year hiatus, she wanted to be glued to his side again. She wasn't sure how long she stood there, leaning against the support beam, when she saw Melissa practically floating from Malcolm's trailer, still dressed in last night's clothing. When Melissa saw Mazie on the porch, she approached with a spring in her step. Melissa sank against the opposite support beam and stared at the sky.

"What a beautiful, perfect morning," Melissa announced with a dreamy sigh.

"Well, someone's happy this morning," Mazie remarked while grinning at her giddy friend. "Can I assume you'll be living off that high for quite some time?"

"For at least another week and a half," Melissa informed her friend. "He wants me to stop by the ranch later this evening so we can go out to dinner. Just the two of us." She immediately turned giddy when she faced Mazie. "He wants to spend his free time with me during filming here at the ranch. Isn't that wonderful?"

"Well, he is Malcolm Wexler," Mazie remarked. "I'd say that's pretty terrific. I mean, as long as you understand it could all go away when he's done filming here."

"I know nothing will come of it, Mazie," Melissa replied with a soft, sad sigh. "But I'm going to ride this high for as long as I can." Her grin again increased. "I spent the night with Malcolm Wexler, Hollywood movie star. Me! I can't even get my head around it!"

"As long as you don't get your heart broken, enjoy every minute," Mazie announced.

"Don't worry about me," Melissa insisted. "I'm guarding my heart."

"Did you want a ride home?"

"Actually, Malcolm wants to take me home," Melissa replied, then cringed. "Could I borrow your Jeep? Malcolm will bring it back, if that's okay."

"Sure," Mazie replied. "I'll get you the keys."

"Pegboard just inside the front door?" Melissa asked while offering a sly grin.

"Where they've always been," Mazie replied, somewhat humored.

"Thanks, Mazie," Melissa announced and hurried past her. "I owe you one plus one million for inviting me out yesterday."

Melissa took only a moment to grab the Jeep keys, then smiled and waved at her friend before heading back to the trailers. Now that her friend had found a ride home, Mazie decided it was time to check with Davenport and see what work he had for her. Perhaps she no longer had a job. She hadn't really spoken to him since her nuclear meltdown the other evening. Rather than call or text him, she decided to report directly to his office trailer. He should have been up and in the office by this time. As Mazie approached Davenport's trailer, the door opened abruptly, and Tina stormed out. Mazie barely made it out of the cursing woman's path. She was a bit curious about what happened, but not curious enough to actually speak to Tina. Maybe she'd catch the gossip highlights later from the makeup artist. Mazie walked up the first two steps and lightly knocked on the door.

"Come in," Davenport announced.

Mazie entered the office trailer and found Davenport sitting at his desk, unruffled by whatever had Tina so angry. Davenport's trailer office wasn't as fancy as his one in Los Angeles, but it was not exactly 'no frills' as a contractor's trailer office. There were cabinets along one wall, a leather sofa beneath them, a large desk along the back wall, and a television mounted on the opposite wall. There was a small kitchen with a refrigerator as well as a small bathroom with a tiny shower.

"Hey," Mazie announced, attempting to sound casual, in case she still had a job. "You didn't text me with any assignments this morning."

Davenport eyed her, then leaned back in his chair. "Actually, I've been giving that some thought," he announced.

Mazie felt her heart skip a beat. He was firing her! For a moment, she was in shock, but then a strange sense of relief swept over her. She wondered how fast she could saddle a horse and be out with the boys.

"Your friend and former boss is extremely volatile," Davenport remarked while tapping his pen on his desktop. "But he seems to like you."

"Well, I should assume so," Mazie replied. "We grew up together. Like my big brother."

Mazie internally cringed at her own words. After what happened between them, she had to stop thinking like that. It made her head and heart hurt.

"So I was thinking, as long as we're here, you should probably babysit him," Davenport announced.

"Babysit him?" she asked with some surprise. "I hardly think he needs a babysitter."

"Let's agree to disagree," Davenport muttered. "If you stick to him, he's less likely to explode. Currently, our top priority is keeping him happy. If you're close by, you can defuse any issues before they become explosive."

"I'm sure that's true," Mazie replied.

"Good," Davenport announced cheerfully. "Until we leave, you will keep Brandt happy. I don't care how you do it, just keep him from going off on the crew."

"I can do that," Mazie informed him, almost excited with her new assignment. She then considered something and spoke before convincing herself to keep her mouth shut. "But what about things you need done?" Mazie wanted to kick herself as soon as the words left her mouth.

"Don't worry about that," Davenport replied while grinning. "I've got that covered."

The trailer door opened, and Tina entered, almost running into Mazie. She gently cleared her throat, then looked at Davenport.

"I forgot--" Tina began, then approached the desk and removed the credit card sitting on top. "--the company credit card."

"Oh, while you're out, Tina," Davenport began. "Would you stop at the diner and get me a coffee? Black. Extra sugar."

Tina smiled through gritted teeth. "I'd be happy to," she replied.

"Make sure you're back before lunch," Davenport remarked, then gently rubbed his neck while grinning almost slyly. "I'm going to need a massage. Set aside an hour for that."

"Anything you need," Tina announced politely, all while silently seething.

"Then, later this afternoon, I'd like to go over some parts I think might suit you," Davenport informed her almost proudly.

Tina's mood instantly improved. "I'd love that," she announced, then hurried from the trailer.

Mazie watched Tina leave, then glanced at her boss, who smiled slyly.

"She is such a lovely young woman," Davenport informed her.

"She certainly is," Mazie replied while attempting to hide her humor.

It wasn't often she got to see karma operating in real time, but it somehow felt fitting. Mazie left Davenport's office trailer and nearly ran into Sandra. Both women laughed at the near collision, considering neither had been actually watching where they were going.

"Mazie," Sandra announced with a tiny giggle. "I had been hoping to run into you, although not quite so literally."

"What can I do for you, Sandra?" Mazie asked, willing to take a moment to help the young actress with whatever she needed.

Sandra seemed slightly tense, which seemed uncharacteristic for someone with several movies under her belt. Oftentimes, seasoned actors were aggressive and even a little pushy.

"I wanted to talk to you about something kind of personal," Sandra announced. "Do you have a few minutes?"

"I was heading to the barn to saddle one of the horses," Mazie informed her. "Did you want to walk along? There will be plenty of privacy around the barn."

"Yes, thank you," Sandra replied with a sigh of relief.

They walked in silence until they neared the barn, when Sandra seemed to come to life.

"Why are you saddling one of the horses?" the young actress asked.

"Davenport wants me to remain close to Brandt," Mazie informed her, then chuckled. "Keep him out of trouble."

"You're going riding?" Sandra gasped and then turned excited. "Could I come along? I mean, I can ride. Sort of."

"I'm going to be out with the boys for a few hours," Mazie informed her while grimacing. "Probably about four hours. Most of it will be in the saddle."

Sandra stared at her a moment, appearing to reconsider, then smiled. "I'm sure I can manage," she replied. "Can I come along? I'd really love to get away from the set for a while."

Mazie stared at the actress a moment, then smiled and nodded. "Yeah, sure," she replied. "I'll come back early if you need to get back. Give me a minute to find a nice, gentle horse for you."

Chapter 46

Mazie kept the ride out to the herd at mostly a walk and trot for Sandra's comfort. Even a few minutes of trotting was almost more than the novice horseback rider could handle. The woman was definitely going to be saddle sore in the morning. Riding the trail was a lot different than riding a few yards for the camera.

"So what's going on?" Mazie asked as they slowed to a walk to talk. "Is there a problem on set? Did you want me to talk to Davenport about someone's conduct?"

Right after mentioning the word 'conduct', Uncle Colt immediately came to mind. She hoped it wasn't going to be some issue with Uncle Colt, because there was little she could do to control his behavior.

"No, nothing like that," Sandra replied, then eyed Mazie several times. "I was just wondering about your relationship with Brandt."

"My relationship with Brandt?" Mazie asked with some surprise. "We're, uh, well, best friends. We were practically raised together. I've known him most of my life." She then eyed Sandra. "Why do you ask?"

When she saw how Sandra avoided looking at her, Mazie knew the answer almost immediately.

"Oh," Mazie replied while nodding. "You like him."

"I do," Sandra announced, coming back to life. "I don't think I've ever met anyone quite like him before."

"Probably because guys like him don't leave their ranches too often," Mazie remarked. "He takes his ranch life very seriously. I mean, it's his whole life."

"But the two of you aren't--?"

"No," Mazie replied a little too quickly. "I mean, I love him, but he's my best friend."

"I wanted to make sure you weren't, you know, interested in him," Sandra announced. "I wouldn't want to step on another woman's toes."

"No, no toe stepping," Mazie replied almost timidly.

"That's a relief," Sandra remarked with a sigh. "So what's he like?"

"Wow, that's, uh, a complicated question," Mazie responded. "He's simple but complex. Gentle yet gritty. Loving but hateful." She shook her head. "He's been a lot of different men to me over the years, but if I had to describe him in one word, it would be 'loyal'." Mazie finally looked at Sandra. "Brandt is the greatest guy in the world."

Sandra eyed her almost suspiciously. "Are you sure you're just friends?" she asked. "To me, it sounds as if you're in love with him."

Mazie was surprised by Sandra's comment and immediately turned defensive. "I'm not in love with Brandt," she insisted, becoming animated. "We were raised together. He's like my older brother!"

"I'm not a psychiatrist, but I played one once," Sandra remarked. "It sounds like you're getting defensive over a simple question."

"Because you don't ask someone if they're in love with their brother," Mazie scoffed, then realized how irrational she sounded and attempted to collect her emotions. She released her breath as her heart raced. "I'm sorry. It's just, well, that's a bit of a sore subject."

"No, I understand," Sandra replied, managing a tiny, tense laugh. "I probably shouldn't have thrown that out there." She hesitated. "I just want to be sure you're okay with me pursuing Brandt, that's all. You're okay with it, right?"

"Yes, I'm okay with that," Mazie responded a little too quickly, wanting to avoid more speculation that she was in love with Brandt.

As they rode in silence for a few minutes, Mazie's thoughts began to stray. Brandt needed a girlfriend in the worst possible way, yet Mazie felt a tiny pang of jealousy, and she wasn't sure why. Perhaps it was the thought of sharing her best friend with someone else. She just got him back. If he had a girlfriend, it would potentially change the entire dynamic of their relationship. When Mazie returned from her thoughts, she realized Sandra was staring at her.

"Are you okay?" Sandra asked.

Mazie smiled and nodded. "Yeah, of course," she replied, then indicated a path up ahead. "They should be on the other side of that trail."

When they crossed the trail, as promised, the guys were with the herd on the other side. The guys noticed them almost immediately from a distance. What Mazie thought would be a fun surprise quickly turned to discontent. Colt and Brandt left the herd and approached them, suspiciously eyeing Sandra.

"What brings you all the way out here?" Uncle Colt asked Mazie, as if she suddenly wasn't allowed to be with the herd.

"Davenport suggested I hang out with Brandt during production," Mazie announced, keeping up a cheerful façade. "So I can immediately address any problems before they arise." She grinned almost slyly. "I consider that a win-win."

"Well, it might have been," Colt remarked, then indicated Sandra. "But bringing Ms. King with you is kind of a problem."

"It's a bit of a liability," Brandt reminded Mazie.

"You should know that," Colt scolded her.

Mazie was a bit surprised by Uncle Colt's surprisingly cold reaction. Was it really about Sandra, or was something else bothering him? It wouldn't pay to ask because he'd never talk about it.

"I'm sorry," Mazie replied, whether she understood his hostility or not. "I can take her back. That's not a problem." She then managed a smile. "At least it was a pleasant trail ride."

"I'll escort Ms. King back to the ranch," Colt informed her, then indicated Brandt. "You can babysit my boss, if it'll make your boss happy."

Sandra was left somewhat conflicted since it was Brandt she'd ridden out to see. When she looked at Mazie, Mazie grimaced slightly and silently indicated she should go back with Colt. Mazie watched Colt escort Sandra back onto the nearby trail, then cast a look at Brandt.

"Who put him in such a foul mood?" she scoffed.

"The answer is almost always me," Brandt remarked, then shook his head, a bit dumbfounded. "But I didn't do anything to piss him off. In fact, he was strutting around here like a peacock regarding the little side hustle your production company is paying for his cowboy services." He eyed Mazie and raised a cocky brow. "So it has to be you that he's pissed at."

"Me?" she scoffed. "I haven't done anything. How does that even make any sense?"

Brandt chuckled at her expense. "Don't ask me to explain Uncle Colt," he remarked. "I wouldn't even know where to start." Brandt then indicated the herd. "Come on, little girl. Get to work."

"Keep it up with that 'little girl' crap," Mazie retorted. "And you'll see just how much of a bitch this 'little girl' can be."

"Out of all your personalities, I like the bitchy one the most," Brandt informed her with a chuckle.

"Remember, I know where you sleep," she reminded him.

Brandt suddenly grinned. "Is that a promise or a threat?"

"Both," Mazie replied.

"Yeah, well," Brandt announced boldly. "We both know you'd never set foot in my bedroom after lights out."

As she stared at him, Mazie's thoughts suddenly strayed to his bedroom. She knew that was a cheap shot at their one-time indiscretion, and he was desperately looking for a reaction.

"Not even in broad daylight," she scoffed. "The pungent stench of piles of week-old dirty clothes on the floor would knock me out in the doorway."

"I haven't done that since I was sixteen," Brandt informed her, matter-of-factly. "I have a hamper, and I actually use it."

"Let's just say you won that round," Mazie announced with a groan. "I don't need to relive my childhood trauma of your messy bedroom."

"You were warned to stay out," he reminded her. "If it traumatized you, that's all on you."

Mazie and Brandt had a good laugh over it as they rode at a slow trot back to the herd. Brandt finally eyed her, almost suspiciously.

"Did your boss really ask you to babysit me?" Brandt finally asked.

Mazie laughed, then groaned. "He most certainly did," she replied. "I don't know if it was you at the gate with a rifle or my telling him off that spurred his decision, but my next week and a half just improved."

"Mine too," Brandt announced, pleased. "But who will run all his trivial errands and feed him grapes while he jerks off to the sound of his own voice?"

"Oh," Mazie moaned while rolling her eyes. "That one was particularly vile."

"But quite possibly accurate."

"It's possible he had an ulterior motive for assigning me to babysitting duty," Mazie informed him, then cleverly raised her brows. "He has his fame-seeking, actress wannabe, Tina, kissing his ass, among other things. She's taking on the role as his *head* assistant in hopes of securing some future bit parts in upcoming movies."

"Head assistant, huh?" Brandt remarked, then eyed her somewhat humored. "No pun intended?"

"None whatsoever," Mazie replied with a soft snort.

"Couldn't have happened to a nicer girl," Brandt announced, then eyed her. "Have you ever described me as a horrible boss?"

"Do you really want to know?" Mazie asked while giving him a quick once-over.

"Yeah, I'm pretty sure I'd like to know," Brandt remarked.

"Apart from assigning shit duties when rubbed the wrong way, I have nothing bad to say about you as a boss," Mazie informed him, then shrugged. "I've looked up to you my whole life. How could I ever find fault with anything you say or do?"

"You were always my best employee," Brandt informed her while grinning. "None of the other guys kiss my ass quite like you do."

Brandt flashed a smile, then sent his horse into a gallop around the herd. Mazie rolled her eyes and rode after him.

Chapter 47

Later that afternoon, after Mazie and Brandt returned home with the rest of the wranglers from tending the cattle, Sandra approached the barn while they were unsaddling their horses. Sandra gave Mazie a knowing smile as she made her way closer to Brandt.

"Hey," Sandra announced to Brandt while offering her best come-hither smile. "Do you have a minute? I wanted to ask you something."

"Well, after I unsaddle my horse--"

Colt seemed to appear out of thin air and took his horse from him. "I've got this," he announced. "Don't keep a lady waiting."

Brandt eyed Colt almost suspiciously, then followed Sandra toward the house while she seemed to do most of the talking. Colt watched them while unsaddling Brandt's horse near Mazie and snickered softly.

"Oh, I'd love to be a fly on the wall over there," Colt remarked.

Mazie eyed Sandra and Brandt, then looked back at her uncle. "Why do you say that?" she asked.

"That insanely hot Hollywood actress has her sights set on Brandt," Colt informed her. "We had a little chat on the way back to the ranch, and I told her not to waste a minute. That boy needs himself a girlfriend. Might improve his mood."

"I suppose he does need a girlfriend," Mazie remarked, then felt that same pang in the pit of her stomach as she glanced at Sandra talking with Brandt by the porch. "But he should be reminded that she's only here for another week or so, and he shouldn't get too attached."

"I wouldn't worry about that," Colt informed Mazie. "Even a short-term girlfriend is better than none. Nothing wrong with enjoying the company of an attractive woman while he can."

"Can't really argue with that," Mazie replied while removing her saddle.

She only wanted what was best for Brandt, so she didn't understand the sinking feeling in her heart. When she saw Sandra affectionately place her hand on Brandt's arm, Mazie nearly dropped her saddle. She looked away and toted her saddle into the barn to avoid seeing any more. When Mazie returned to her horse, Brandt approached them with a strange, dumbfounded look on his face, while Sandra returned to the trailer area.

"Well?" Colt asked while grinning a little too much. "What did she have to say?"

Brandt appeared moderately stunned, shaking his head. "She wants to go out to dinner with me tonight," he remarked. "Uh, she heard about the place a county over and wants me to take her there."

"You said 'yes', didn't you?" Colt asked almost sternly.

"I, uh, well, I did," Brandt replied, but still remained dumbfounded.

"That's the best news I've heard since this afternoon," Colt announced. "You on a date with a famous Hollywood actress--"

Brandt eyed his uncle almost suspiciously. "What was the best news you heard earlier?" he felt compelled to ask while cocking his head to the side.

"Mazie's jerk boss asking her to babysit you," Colt replied, somewhat humored. "We get a week and a half of free help and our girl back to boot."

Mazie groaned and rolled her eyes. When Colt carried Brandt's saddle to the barn, Brandt glanced at Mazie as she brushed her horse.

"It doesn't bother you, does it?" Brandt asked, seeming conflicted.

"What's that?" Mazie asked while briefly glancing at him, although she couldn't quite meet his gaze.

"That I'm taking Sandra out to dinner," Brandt replied.

Mazie hesitated, then glanced back at him. "Why would it?" she asked, although feeling her heart ache in response.

"I guess it wouldn't," he remarked, then drew a deep, tense breath. "I haven't been on a date in a long time. I'm not even sure what I'm supposed to do."

"Shower, for starters," Mazie informed him as she continued brushing her horse. "Find something decent to wear, and don't forget your manners."

Colt then appeared and leaned in closer to Brandt's ear, whispering, "And take protection."

Brandt groaned and shook his head. "I'm not taking a handgun on my date," he scoffed.

Mazie and Colt shot surprised looks at him.

Colt straightened and turned stern. "Did we not have 'the talk' with you, son?"

"Uncle Colt," Brandt scolded. "First off, we don't talk about things like that in front of ladies, and secondly, it's a first date with a woman I know nothing about. I'm a gentleman. I have no intention of even kissing her goodnight."

"Where did I go wrong?" Colt muttered, then glared at Brandt. "She's a city girl, Brandt. There's a good chance *she's* going to kiss *you* goodnight. Now hit the showers and don't forget to pack a little protection." He again leaned closer to Brandt and muttered in his ear. "There's some in my nightstand drawer, if you need them."

Mazie rolled her eyes since Colt had to know she could hear him. Brandt shook his head and walked away. Colt then nudged Mazie.

"You'd better help that poor, clueless bastard pick out something decent to wear tonight," Colt remarked. "He's going to need all the help he can get."

Brandt rummaged through his closet, groaning with disgust and becoming increasingly frustrated. Mazie knocked on his open bedroom door, practically startling him. He glanced back at her, then indicated his closet.

"I can't do this," he informed her. "I have nothing in my closet that's appropriate to wear on a date with a Hollywood actress. I can't pretend I'm someone I'm not."

"Stop overthinking it," Mazie insisted, attempting to relax him. "She knows you're not some Hollywood phony, so just be yourself. That's who she's expecting to show up tonight, and if she's not, then shame on her."

"Being myself never worked out for me on dates in the past," he reminded her.

"That's bullshit, Brandt," Mazie scolded. "You just went out with the wrong women. Just relax and be yourself. Trust me."

Mazie directed him toward the bathroom. "Get in the shower," she insisted. "I'll pick out something appropriate for you to wear tonight and leave it on the bed."

"This is all Uncle Colt's fault," Brandt muttered, then entered the bathroom, only partially shutting the door behind him.

Mazie found a nice pair of light colored khakis, a light blue button-down shirt, and a brown leather sports jacket that he probably hadn't worn in years. Just to be safe, she set out a pair of dressier boots, in case he was thinking he'd just wear his horse boots. Mazie then hesitated, reached into her pocket, and removed a condom she'd taken from Uncle Colt's nightstand drawer. She held her breath a moment, then placed the condom on top of his clothes. Mazie looked around Brandt's bedroom a moment while gently rubbing her chilled arms. She'd spent many evenings watching movies with Brandt in his room on his bed, yet the only memory was the night of her graduation party. Mazie listened to the shower running a moment longer, now aware that he hadn't completely closed the bathroom door, which was rather odd. Knowing she was in his bedroom, why wouldn't he close the door while in the shower? Mazie stared at the partially open door for a moment longer, listening to the running shower. A strange and wildly inappropriate thought crossed her mind, making her blush. She hurried from the room.

*M*azie sat on the porch with Uncle Dalton, Uncle Colt, and her mother, attempting not to stare as Brandt opened his truck door for Sandra, who wore a simple sundress and heels. Thankfully, he chose his newer, 'special occasion' truck over his ranch errand one. If Brandt was nervous, he didn't show it. Once they drove away, Colt snickered.

"What's that about?" Dalton almost demanded while eyeing his brother.

"Nothing," Colt casually replied, although he remained humored. "The boy took my advice, that's all. Helped himself to some of my, uh, cologne."

"I didn't smell any cologne," Liddy remarked.

"Don't engage with him, Liddy," Dalton muttered. "He's being bold."

Liddy rolled her eyes and groaned. "I won't ask," she scoffed.

Melissa's car pulled up to the ranch house and parked. As Mazie's friend got out of the car, she pointed down the driveway.

"Did I just pass Brandt with Sandra in his truck?" Melissa asked.

"He's on a date," Colt announced proudly.

Melissa stared at him with some surprise. "Really?" she asked. "Wow. I didn't see that coming." She then focused her attention on Mazie. "Malcolm wants to go to the tavern tonight. The whole crew is going. Put on your Sunday cowgirl boots. We're line dancing tonight."

"I don't know, Melissa," Mazie remarked with a sigh. "I don't really feel like going out tonight."

"Too bad," Melissa informed her. "Cameron is meeting us there, and you're going along. I'm going to need my entire entourage to keep the other girls off my man."

"Fine," Mazie groaned. "Give me half an hour to shower and change."

As Mazie entered the house, Melissa eyed Liddy.

"Well, she's going to be the life of the party," Melissa remarked with a soft huff. "What's bothering her?"

"Want me to ask?" Liddy questioned.

Melissa waved her off. "I'll talk to her after I get a few drinks into her," she replied.

Once inside the house, Mazie headed through the kitchen, crossed her mother's suite, and entered her bedroom. She reached for a hair tie she kept on her bedpost when her eyes strayed to her nightstand. The condom she'd left for Brandt with his clothes was sitting on top. She stared at the condom a moment, then placed it in the drawer beneath it. A tiny smile crossed her face. Not that it was any of her business, but Brandt silently conveyed to her that he wouldn't be sleeping with Sandra. And even though she knew it was wrong, Mazie was somehow relieved by his decision. Mazie looked inside her nightstand drawer and stared at her old journal. She picked it up and opened it, revealing the pressed rose boutonnière from Brandt's failed prom date. Mazie gently touched the flower and smiled somewhat sadly. Brandt deserved to be happy.

Chapter 48

*E*xcitement filled the tavern when Melissa showed up with Malcolm and the rest of the production crew. Mazie and Cameron were a little surprised by the attention Malcolm received from local women, who suddenly fawned all over him, seemingly unconcerned that he appeared to be with Melissa. It was ironic how differently people could act in the presence of someone famous. Even their small town neighbors. The production crew easily managed crowd control, ensuring Malcolm and Melissa had some space. Eventually, the locals settled in and gave the couple and the production crew some privacy in their secluded back corner of the bar. While Melissa and Cameron enjoyed teaching Malcolm and the production team how to country line dance, Mazie remained at the table, watching the spectacle. She couldn't deny that she was preoccupied with the thought of Brandt out on a date with Sandra. Why was she thinking about it so much? It's not as if it bothered her. She certainly wasn't jealous. Was she?

While Mazie questioned her entire existence, she was approached by at least four different men in the barroom. Even though Mazie hadn't been old enough to hang out in the tavern before she moved away, she was a little surprised by the attention she was receiving from the local men. The same men who never gave her the time of day when she went to high school with them were suddenly attempting to get closer to her. She may have forgotten their names, but she remembered their faces. Some were even boys who had rejected her request to slow dance at one of the few school dances she'd attended with her friends. Now, those same guys were asking her to dance. Mazie didn't know why she felt guilty for politely declining their request. They had no problem rejecting her in high school.

When Peter approached her table, she wasn't sure if she was relieved for a buffer against her newly found male attention, or concerned that her night was about to get worse.

"I wasn't expecting to see you here tonight," Peter announced and sat alongside her despite not being invited to join her. "Not much of a dancer, huh?"

Mazie glanced at the crew and her friends on the dance floor, then met his gaze and shrugged. "My hoe down years were spent in LA," she informed him. "You don't find many country bars in Los Angeles. Not that I really had much time for that sort of thing anyway."

"Yeah, I hear you," Peter remarked. "I miss this. It feels good being back home."

"I have to agree with you on that," Mazie replied and smiled more naturally.

Peter then looked around before returning his attention to her. "No Brandt, huh?" he asked. "I heard bars weren't really his scene anyway."

"Brandt's on a date with Sandra," Mazie announced.

"Really?" Peter asked, surprised. "I wasn't expecting that. She seems a little high-maintenance for him."

"I don't know," Mazie reported. "She seems nice enough to me."

It then occurred to Mazie that Peter might be jealous because Sandra was out with Brandt and not with him. All the years Mazie spent chasing after Peter, and she was never his first or even his second choice. Mazie was thankful when everyone returned to the table, ending any personal conversations between her and Peter.

Around nine o'clock, the noise level at the tavern sharply rose, and everyone seemed interested in something happening near the main entrance. Oftentimes, that meant a fight had broken out. Mazie instinctively looked as well and was a little surprised when she saw Brandt and Sandra crossing the tavern, joining them in the back corner. Both were smiling while holding hands. Mazie's heart again sank. She'd never seen Brandt holding anyone's hand before, and it felt a little too *intimate*. The cast and crew cheered a greeting and made a fuss over them, while nearly all the locals watched Brandt interacting with Sandra. Before they even had a chance to sit down, a slow song played. Sandra just about yanked Brandt to the dance floor, where they slow danced the Texas two-step, although much closer than Mazie had taught him. Mazie was suddenly very uncomfortable, and she wasn't even sure why.

"Would you like to dance?" Peter asked, almost suavely, while standing and holding his hand out to her.

Mazie wasn't even sure why she agreed, but she was on the dance floor with him before she even realized it. Melissa and Malcolm also danced slowly and close, creating almost as many whispers as Brandt and Sandra. Mazie couldn't help but notice the smiles on Brandt and Sandra's faces as they danced and talked almost intimately. Apparently, the date went *very* well.

"Have you ever thought about what would have happened if I hadn't gone away to college and you to LA?" Peter asked while they slow danced.

Mazie looked at him with some surprise. Had he actually forgotten the entire incident in the barn a week before they were supposed to go to Australia? It almost seemed as if he had. Fortunately for him, this wasn't the time or place to discuss such things.

"No, not really," Mazie replied, matter-of-factly.

She had bigger problems after the night of her graduation party, and Peter was barely even a footnote from that night. Mazie's eyes instinctively fell upon Brandt, slow dancing with Sandra, and the way the two of them smiled at each other. Not a day went by in the last five years that she didn't think about Brandt and their night together. Peter was the least of her concerns.

"I sometimes think about it," Peter informed her. "We always had so much fun together."

"Yes, the good old days," she muttered.

Mazie actually meant it as sarcasm, but Peter seemed to take it as authentic. When the slow song ended and a line dance began, the production crew grabbed Sandra and had her join them and the locals on the dance floor. Mazie was quick to return to her seat, not wanting to get roped into line dancing. With his date otherwise preoccupied, Brandt returned to the table and took the vacant seat alongside Mazie, with Peter occupying the chair to her right. When Peter attempted to put his arm on the back of Mazie's chair, Brandt beat him to it, stealing Mazie's attention away from him.

"I wasn't expecting to see you here," Brandt remarked with a slightly humored smile, then leaned closer to her ear. "Especially with *him*."

"Well, that wasn't part of the plan when the idea was sold to me," Mazie muttered. "He sort of invited himself."

"Yeah, he does that a lot," Brandt scoffed.

"Can I assume the date is going well?" Mazie asked while offering a warm, supportive smile.

Brandt glanced at Sandra on the dance floor while smiling, then nodded as he looked back at Mazie.

"Yeah, it went pretty well," Brandt replied. "She's a lot more grounded than I thought." He then seemed humored. "She tried to pay for her half of the meal." Brandt snorted a laugh. "As if that was happening."

"Gave her the full gentleman experience, did you?" Mazie asked while smiling more naturally.

"Just being polite," he replied.

Peter shifted glares at Brandt every so often, and even though it appeared as if Brandt hadn't been paying attention, he finally gave Peter a moderately intimidating look.

"Is there a problem, Peter?" Brandt scoffed.

"Aren't you on your own date?" Peter retorted, finally standing up to Brandt.

Brandt leaned forward past Mazie and glared at him. "I know I am, but I'm pretty sure you're not," he remarked. "Were you even invited?"

"Were you?" Peter countered.

"That's enough," Mazie announced with a groan and pushed her chair out while practically leaping to her feet.

Both men reacted, turning their attention to Mazie and noting the disgust she displayed. She directed her hostility at Peter.

"Brandt doesn't need an invitation," Mazie scoffed, no longer holding back. "He's always welcome in my life, no matter what I'm doing. You, on the other hand, don't wield that sort of power." She folded her arms across her chest and stared him down. "You gave up that right when you chose Hannah over me five years ago. And just like that night, you can find alternate company because I'd rather be with Brandt."

When Peter stood without a word and walked away, Mazie groaned and sank back into her chair.

"I feel deprived of the opportunity to punch him in the mouth," Brandt informed her while grinning almost slyly, then rubbed her shoulder. "But I loved the sexual overtone about me in that comment."

Mazie shot a stunned look at him. "What?" she gasped. "Is that how it sounded?"

Brandt raised his brows and chuckled. "A little, yeah," he replied.

Mazie groaned, placed her hand over her eyes, and sank into her chair. "Great."

When another slow song played, Brandt looked at the dance floor and saw Sandra slow dancing with the director. Brandt stood and eyed Mazie.

"My date is otherwise engaged with a co-worker," Brandt informed her. "I assume I'm within my rights to find an alternate dance partner as well." He extended his hand to her. "Dance with me."

Mazie eyed his hand, then the lighthearted expression on his face. She managed a smile, accepted his hand, and joined him on the dance floor. She couldn't deny that it felt a little strange slow dancing with Brandt. Unlike the way she had taught him to dance all those years ago, he held her closer and with a little more intimacy.

"I liked it, by the way," Brandt remarked.

Mazie met his gaze, his face close to hers, and was a bit confused. "What did you like?"

"What you said to Peter," he replied while grinning. "That I'm always welcome in your life."

"Well, I meant that," Mazie informed him. "I never want to go that long without you in my life ever again."

Brandt stared into her eyes while maintaining his smile. "Come back home, Mazie," he announced in the warmest, most sincere tone. "I'll give you whatever you want. I'll match what you're making with Davenport, and I'll even give you a one-million-dollar sign-on bonus."

"You would too, wouldn't you?" Mazie remarked softly with a tiny laugh.

"I can run the ranch without you, but I don't really want to," Brandt informed her.

"If I were to come back, it wouldn't be for money, Brandt," she insisted. "I would never take advantage of you like that."

"You deserve better than Davenport," Brandt informed her. "It kills me knowing you're working for someone like that. I'd never treat you the way he does."

"I know," Mazie replied softly. "But I have obligations at the studio. It isn't even Davenport. It's everyone else that depends on me. I have to make sure the others get what's fair and what they deserve. If I leave, I screw the rest of the crew."

"And if you stay with Davenport, you get screwed," he reminded her.

"I'll need at least six months to see if it's even possible," Mazie informed him.

Brandt considered her response, then nodded. "I can wait," he replied, offering a warm smile. "So, a definite maybe?"

Mazie laughed softly. "Yes, a definite maybe."

Brandt pulled her against him as the song ended and affectionately kissed her forehead.

Almost everyone returned to the ranch around the same time. It was a little after midnight, yet Liddy and Dalton were still up and sitting on the double-wide porch swing while Colt sat in one of the rocking chairs smoking a cigar and drinking a glass of whiskey. Mazie got out of her Jeep and saw the three of them on the porch, obviously waiting up on purpose. As Mazie headed up the porch steps, Malcolm escorted Melissa to his trailer. Brandt's truck pulled up only a moment later. When he got out and saw the 'elders' on the porch, he groaned and shook his head. Mazie paused on the porch, silently scolding all three, while Brandt headed around his truck to get the door for Sandra, who was absolutely giddy at his gentlemanly behavior. Sandra linked onto Brandt's arm as they headed toward the trailers, but not before Brandt glared his disapproval at the three of them. Colt strained to watch the couple as they headed almost out of view. Mazie moved into Colt's line of sight, preventing him from spying on Brandt.

Colt grabbed Mazie's wrist and easily moved her out of his view. Mazie only briefly followed her uncle's gaze and saw Brandt stop before Sandra's trailer. They spoke briefly before Brandt leaned forward and kissed her on the cheek. Sandra then went into her trailer, and Brandt headed back to the house.

"That's so adorable," Liddy announced with her hand on her chest. "Such a gentleman."

"Boy's a disappointment," Colt scoffed.

As Brandt approached and headed onto the porch, he glared at both uncles and Liddy.

"The three of you should be ashamed," Brandt scoffed before entering the house.

"And somehow, we're not," Colt remarked while puffing on his cigar.

Chapter 49

*F*ive o'clock the following morning, Mazie was out in the barn brushing the second of eight horses. The first horse was already tacked and ready to go. Brandt wearily entered the barn with coffee in a thermos and paused when he saw Mazie already busily working.

"I should've gotten an intern a long time ago," Brandt teased while wearing a sly grin. "Cheap, hardworking labor."

"A morning person too," she added with a tiny, humored laugh. "You can go back to bed for another hour, if you'd like."

Brandt set his coffee down and picked up a brush. "No, that's okay," he announced. "I'm already awake." He approached the horse closest to her, looked at her over the horse's back, and winked at her. "And I enjoy my intern's company."

Mazie didn't bother looking at him but managed a tiny laugh. "So--?"

"So--*what*?" he asked as he brushed the horse.

"How was your date with Sandra?" Mazie asked, hating that her heart seemed to skip a beat at the question. "Did the two of you have a good time?"

"I thought we covered that last night at the tavern," he remarked without looking at her. "I told you, she's a nice girl."

"Yes, so you've said," Mazie retorted. "But do you *like* her?"

"I wouldn't have taken her to dinner if I didn't at least like her," he reported.

"You're impossible, you know that?" Mazie scoffed, then groaned, deciding to be direct with him. "Are you going to see her again?"

"She's staying on the ranch," Brandt reminded her. "It'd be difficult not to see her."

Mazie glared at him over her horse's back. "Are you being serious right now?" she demanded. "You can't be that dense."

"I'm not," Brandt insisted, then rounded the horse to the other side and continued brushing its coat. "There's nothing more to tell. There's no future with her, so we won't be going out again. It'd just be a waste of time."

"There's no future for Melissa and Malcolm," Mazie reminded him. "But they're not letting that stop them from having a good time."

"Good for them," Brandt announced, becoming frustrated. "I'm not interested in having a fling, and I would appreciate it if you stopped trying to get me laid." He groaned softly then muttered, "It's creepy."

"Sorry," Mazie whispered. "I just want you to be happy."

"I appreciate that, Mazie, but I am happy," Brandt insisted.

Mazie rounded her horse, joining him between the two horses, and brushed the other side.

"That's all I want to hear," Mazie replied in a timid voice. "I'm not trying to pick a fight, I promise."

Brandt turned to watch her brush the horse, then moved alongside her. Mazie knew he was hovering over her, but she refused to look at him. He placed his arm across her horse's back and leaned closer to her.

"I haven't been with another woman since you, Mazie," he announced softly near her ear.

Out of reflex, Mazie turned her head and looked at him with surprise, his face close to hers. "You haven't?" she gasped, then fidgeted from his closeness.

"No," Brandt replied, then drew a deep, tense breath while keeping his face close to hers as he stared into her eyes. "You're the only woman I've ever even thought about. I refuse to let go of that fantasy, even if it means I'll be alone the rest of my life."

Without even thinking, she gently touched his face and then kissed him quickly on the lips. Mazie immediately realized what she had done and pulled back just as fast, surprised by her own actions, but was trapped by the horse directly behind her.

"I'm sorry," she gasped, uncertain what had possessed her to do that. "I don't know what I was--"

But she was already too late. Brandt gathered her in his arms, pulling her sharply against him, and eagerly kissed her with surprising passion and aggression. Mazie instinctively pressed her palms against his chest in a half-hearted attempt to hold him back, but the urge to kiss him back was greater and overpowered all rational thought. She returned the kiss as if her life depended upon it, clinging to his neck while practically climbing up his body. Brandt responded more aggressively, attempting to brace her against the horse behind her. The horse sidestepped, naturally moving away from pressure placed against it. Having nearly lost her balance, Mazie returned to reality, gasped, and braced her palms against Brandt's chest, attempting to hold him back. She managed to break off the kiss, leaving both of them breathing heavily and trying to recover from the wildly passionate moment.

"I'm sorry," she whispered, keeping her palms braced against his chest since he seemed unwilling to release her from his arms.

Mazie finally met his gaze while fully aware of his arousal firmly pressed against her. She could feel her desire to hold him back fading fast.

"I can't do this," she gasped softly. "I, uh, need time to think about what I'm doing."

"There's no pressure, Mazie," Brandt assured her, although he still didn't release her, keeping his hips firmly pressed against her. Her body ached in response. "I'm willing to wait as long as it takes for you to be sure. I don't want to lose you again."

There was little doubt in her mind that he'd have his way with her right there in the barn with even the slightest hint of encouragement from her. Brandt kissed her quickly on the lips, then released her, reclaimed his discarded horse brush, and turned back to his horse to finish grooming it. Mazie stood immobile for a moment, staring at Brandt's back while he resumed his work. Her mind was suddenly so cluttered that she couldn't even think straight. Rather than think about it, she reached for the nearby saddle pad, despite her trembling hands, and began saddling the horse. There were still five more to go, and they'd be expected for breakfast in a little less than an hour.

Despite spending the entire day working the cattle with Brandt, her uncles, and the other wranglers, Mazie managed to keep her distance from Brandt. She didn't want to have any awkward conversations, particularly while among the guys, about what had happened earlier in the barn. Colt was doing a fantastic job of monopolizing his nephew's time all by himself. Brief parts of the conversation that Mazie had caught, Colt was pumping him for information about any upcoming dates with Sandra. Judging by the way Brandt eyed his uncle, the conversation was likely vulgar. Colt had to leave by lunchtime to help out the production company, meeting them on the long dirt road to the old homestead, so Brandt decided he'd head back as well, which meant Mazie was also leaving. All three met the filming crew on the old road, where Colt gave another grand performance on horseback, filming action scenes with the camera.

They had one last scene they wanted to do with Sandra on horseback. It was supposed to be a running scene, but since they didn't have their stuntwoman available, Sandra agreed to do the scene herself. She was supposed to ride at a leisurely canter, and they'd make it seem faster. When she sent the studio horse into a canter along the back road, Colt loped alongside her, filming the action shot. A deer suddenly jumped out in the road in front of them. Colt's horse spooked, surprised by the deer, but quickly recovered. Sandra's horse reared up, causing her to lose her balance. Without warning, the horse took off at a gallop the moment its front hooves struck the ground. Sandra attempted to slow the horse, but she had lost her stirrups and was struggling just to stay on.

Colt raced after her, tossing the camera across his shoulder as he rode. He easily caught up to her, grabbed the horse's reins, and slowed his horse, automatically slowing the studio horse. By the time they stopped, Sandra was panting to catch her breath out of sheer terror.

"Are you okay?" Colt asked the young starlet.

Sandra nodded, then met Colt's kind gaze and managed a tiny smile. "You saved my life."

"Doubtful," Colt replied with a slightly humored grin. "You kept your ass in the seat pretty good for a city girl, and the horse was already slowing down."

Sandra laughed at the first part of his comment. When Colt led her on her horse alongside him back to the production team, he received a round of applause. He grinned with some embarrassment but ate up the attention.

"At the rate his ego is inflating," Brandt remarked to Mazie alongside him, "he's going to need a bigger hat."

Mazie chuckled at the comment.

*W*hen she returned to the ranch just before dinnertime, Mazie helped her mother finish making dinner and set the table. Although she was certain Brandt wouldn't mention what happened in the barn in front of their family, Mazie was already preparing for an awkward dinner. Brandt, Dalton, and Colt joined them a few minutes before dinner was ready. While Dalton helped place the platters on the table, Colt retold his tale of bravery and how he rescued the 'damsel in distress'. When they were finished with dinner, Dalton gently cleared his throat, getting everyone's attention.

"I have an announcement to make," Dalton remarked, then smiled and took Liddy's hand. "Last night, I asked Liddy to marry me, and she said yes."

All three cheered and congratulated them with excited hugs.

Brandt chuckled while hugging Liddy, then pulled away and announced, "I guess that will officially make you my *Aunt* Liddy."

Dalton laughed while looking at Mazie. "So I guess that'll make me your uncle *and* your step-father."

"And that'll make Brandt your first cousin," Colt teased with a chuckle.

Mazie immediately tensed and glanced at Brandt, who was now shooting death glares at his uncle. Colt hadn't even realized he'd just reopened a fresh wound.

Chapter 50

*A*fter helping her mother clean up from dinner, Mazie retreated to her bedroom, effectively ending the day without confronting Brandt about what happened in the barn. By the time she checked her cell phone, she found several missed texts and calls from her friend back in Los Angeles. Since Andi had left so many messages asking her to call back, Mazie figured it was still early enough to return her phone call. Mazie sprawled across her bed and listened to the phone only ring once before being answered.

"Mazie," Andi announced almost eagerly. "I was worried when you didn't call me back. Is everything okay out there?"

"It's fine," Mazie replied, although she wasn't sure if that was true. "Brandt and I called a truce, and he hasn't killed any of the production crew, so I think it's going rather well."

"As long as you're still alive," Andi announced. "You can tell me all about it later. I heard from my literary agent friend about your manuscript."

"Oh?" Mazie asked with some surprise. "That was fast. I guess that's not good."

"No, on the contrary, he loved it," Andi informed her from the other end. "He thinks he can get you a contract with a publishing house if you can pitch him a suitable ending."

"What exactly does that mean?" Mazie asked, somewhat confused.

"It means you tell him how you propose to end it, he signs you on as his client, and he pitches your manuscript to a publishing house," Andi informed her.

"But it's not even finished," Mazie reminded her. "It's completely rough, and I'm not really sure how to end it. That's why I agreed to let you show it to him. I need help with the ending."

Andi groaned into the phone. "You don't really understand how the publishing industry works, do you?"

"No, I never said I did."

"Usually, advances on incomplete novels or ideas are only reserved for established authors," Andi informed her. "But my friend loves the rough draft so much, he thinks he can sell it before it's complete. You get a hefty advance, and the publishing house gets the completed novel when it's finished."

Mazie was silent for a long moment. "I'm not sure I want to jump right in and sell it, Andi," she finally replied.

"What do you mean, you're not sure?" Andi cried out from the other end. "I thought publishing your manuscript was the end goal here."

"Well, maybe," Mazie remarked, then hesitated. "It's just, well, I'm not sure I want it out there for actual people to read."

"Mazie, you're killing me," Andi groaned into the phone. "I'm going to send you a PDF copy of your manuscript with my friend's notes. He did mention some ideas for the ending. Just read over it, think about it, and get back to me."

"I will," Mazie replied with a tense sigh. "Thanks, Andi."

Mazie disconnected the call, set her phone aside, and opened her laptop. The email from Andi came through only a few minutes later. Mazie opened the PDF file and scanned through an electronic copy of her manuscript. Every page had notes in red in the margin, and there were red lines through many sentences. It looked like her manuscript had been brutally murdered. She skipped to the end and read the notes left by Andi's literary agent friend regarding possible endings, which was all she had really asked for when giving it to Andi in the first place. Mazie felt bad that the guy had taken so much time to edit her manuscript, possibly for nothing. As she read his notes, her eyes widened in something resembling horror.

"Romantic drama?" Mazie gasped, then continued to read. "Happily ever after for the main characters?"

Mazie read the ending suggestions several times, stunned and in disbelief. She pressed the print button, then jumped out of bed and checked to ensure the printer had enough paper. She had it printed out 'front and back' to use less paper, but it would take quite some time to print out the entire manuscript, considering its length. Mazie paced her room while texting Melissa. Being Melissa was in the 'back lot' with Malcolm, it only took ten minutes for her to arrive in her bedroom at the back of the house.

"What's going on?" Melissa asked, just about out of breath. "I practically ran the entire way here. Your message sounded desperate."

Mazie collected over two hundred double-sided pages of her manuscript and held them to her chest as she collapsed onto the bed.

"I'm a little freaked out, Melissa," Mazie announced, seeming uncertain of herself. "My friend from Los Angeles called. Her friend wants to sell my incomplete manuscript to a publishing house."

"Oh, my God!" Melissa cried out as her eyes widened, then broke into a huge smile. "That's fantastic!"

"I'm not so sure about that," Mazie muttered, then met her friend's gaze.

Melissa studied her, now concerned, and sat on the bed alongside her. "Why not?" she asked, appearing nervous. "What's wrong?"

"I wrote it about the ranch," Mazie informed her friend. "It's about my childhood and growing up with Brandt." She groaned softly and practically thrust the large stack of papers into Melissa's hands. "Well, it's actually about Brandt. It began as a series of short stories I started writing when I was ten or twelve. Mostly about a boy and his pony. But there are some brutally honest truths in the later years that he may not find so flattering."

"Oh," Melissa muttered as her expression dropped. "So, if you publish the book, you crucify Brandt."

"That's one way of looking at it," Mazie replied, then groaned softly. "I didn't know how to end it. It's been sitting around for nearly five years, collecting dust. All I wanted from Andi's literary agent friend was some ideas on an ending."

"Okay."

Mazie looked at her friend and cringed. "He called the manuscript a timeless love story about a boy and a girl growing up together, and how they fall in love," she remarked, then groaned. "My story was about a lifelong friendship."

Melissa stared at Mazie for a long moment before raising a skeptical brow. "Did I miss something?" she asked. "I witnessed this story first-hand, and I'm not seeing a timeless love story. What exactly did you write?"

"His thoughts on the matter may have something to do with the third-to-last chapter," Mazie informed her before collapsing across the bed with a groan.

Melissa sifted through the thick manuscript and found the relevant chapter. As her friend started reading to herself, Mazie again groaned and placed her arm dramatically over her eyes, not even wanting to see her friend's expression while she read it.

"Oh--" Melissa commented while reading. Her eyes suddenly widened. "Oh!"

Mazie cringed at her friend's reaction.

"Well," Melissa gasped as her eyes remained wide with astonishment. "That was pretty, uh, intense." She then looked at Mazie, who finally sat up. "I'm not sure I understand why you added this scene. Did you have some sort of sexual fantasies about Brandt after graduation? Because none of this seems to make sense."

"I wish it were that easy," Mazie moaned softly and met her friend's gaze. "I wrote it that way because that's how it really happened."

The longer Melissa stared at her, the wider her eyes became as the realization of her words finally set in.

"You--?" Melissa asked, then nearly choked. "And Brandt--?"

Mazie frowned and nodded.

"And you didn't tell me?" Melissa gasped. Her eyes then suddenly widened. "Is this why you were so weird on our trip to Australia?"

"Yeah, and that's also why I left home five years ago," Mazie announced, then shivered slightly. "I couldn't deal with what I'd done, and he was already naming our children."

Melissa delicately set the manuscript on the bed alongside her as if it might explode. She then drew a deep breath and met Mazie's gaze.

"Let's just push aside the whole you giving your virginity to Brandt thing," Melissa remarked, then cringed. "How 'unflattering' is your portrayal of Brandt in the book?"

"He was a difficult boy with a lot of childhood trauma," Mazie reminded her. "His father died tragically in a car accident when he was very young, and then he watched his mother wither and die from cancer. Brandt carried the weight of the world on his shoulders and rebelled every chance he had. While Uncle Colt practiced tough love and took on a fatherly role, my mother nurtured and supported him emotionally as a mother figure. Uncle Dalton was the only one who was actually able to play a neutral role while somehow being more of a father to me." She then considered the comment and muttered under her breath, "And a husband to my mother."

"What was that?" Melissa asked.

"Nothing," Mazie replied. "I told the truth about how he was bullied throughout school, his lies to Uncle Colt, and some personal things he'd told me about his dating experiences, including his first time with a heartless girl that only wanted to make her boyfriend jealous."

Melissa drew a deep breath, picked up the manuscript, and handed it to Mazie. "Publishing this book would be a great opportunity for you," she announced. "But not at the cost of what you and Brandt have."

"So I should burn it?"

Melissa gasped as her eyes widened. "No, absolutely not!"

"So back in the drawer it goes," Mazie replied with a deep sigh.

"No, there is another option you're completely overlooking," Melissa reminded her as she stared into her eyes. "Ask Brandt to read it."

"Are you insane?" Mazie cried out while shooting up from the bed. "He's the last person I want seeing this! I wrote his entire childhood into this story. Every god-awful detail. He'd hate me if he read it."

"You said the literary agent called it a timeless love story," Melissa reminded her. "Was what you wrote really that unflattering?" She then hesitated. "Do you want me to read it?"

Mazie frowned and considered it. "I don't know," she replied while fidgeting. "There's a lot of personal things in there. I wouldn't mind you reading my personal thoughts, but I'm not sure it would be fair to Brandt if you read his private thoughts."

"Then let him read it," Melissa again insisted. "Let him decide the book's fate." She then shrugged. "I suppose you could always change it up so the characters and locations are unrecognizable."

"I think I'd rather stuff it back in the drawer," Mazie informed her. "I'd rather keep it the way it is and never have anyone read it than change it."

"Something to consider," Melissa announced, then stood. "Why don't you take a walk with Malcolm and me? Help clear your head a little."

"No," Mazie replied with a defeated sigh. "I don't want to be a third wheel, and I kind of want to hide the rest of the night."

"I understand."

Chapter 51

*O*nce Liddy returned to the in-law suite, Mazie realized everyone must have turned in for the evening. She'd spent the entire evening after Melissa left, wrestling with her emotions. Mazie's indiscretion in the barn that morning with Brandt was running a close second to the whole memoir-style manuscript. Mazie read the notes in the back more than a dozen times, attempting to sort out how the agent came up with a 'timeless romance' when it clearly wasn't. Throwing Brandt under the bus for a chance at being published was something she just couldn't do, but she was flattered that Andi's agent friend seemed to like her story enough to want to pitch it to a publishing house. Mostly every decision she'd ever made in her life had one thing in common.

A few minutes later, Mazie headed up the back stairs with a box tucked under her arm and paused before Brandt's open bedroom door. She saw Brandt sitting up in bed, reading a book while also watching the news. When Mazie lightly tapped on the doorframe, Brandt appeared surprised to see her and set his book aside.

"Mazie," he announced, then offered a warm smile. "I wasn't expecting to see you anymore tonight." His look then turned serious. "Is everything okay?"

Mazie approached him with some hesitance, gently set the box on the bed, and took a nervous step back before meeting his gaze.

"I hope you don't hate me," she announced almost timidly. "Yours is the only opinion that matters."

She then turned and left his room. Brandt stared after her, somewhat baffled, then removed the lid on the box. He stared at the thick, unbound manuscript a moment before picking it up.

§

*M*azie couldn't sleep that night. Around four o'clock in the morning, she finally made herself a cup of tea and sat on the large porch swing, enjoying the solitude, even if she couldn't enjoy the peace and quiet with the relentless generators loudly buzzing. She couldn't stop wondering if Brandt had actually looked at the manuscript or if she could still get it back from him and possibly salvage their relationship. Mazie cursed Melissa for even putting that stupid suggestion into her head in the first place. Now, her problems with Brandt would be further complicated beyond their little make-out session in the barn yesterday morning. She suddenly hated herself. She should have listened to her first instinct and just put it back in the drawer. Mazie wasn't sure how long she sat on the porch when the screen door creaked open, alerting her to someone else being up. She looked across the porch and saw Brandt approaching her on the swing.

When she saw the box tucked under his arm, she wanted to crawl into a hole and die. He didn't even look at her as he brushed her feet aside and sat on the swing beside her. Brandt drew a deep breath and placed the box on her lap.

"Well, I read it," Brandt informed her.

"All of it?" she asked, surprised, considering it was over four hundred pages!

"There was some skimming involved," he assured her, still not looking at her. "I'm not really sure what I'm supposed to do with this information."

Mazie set her tea mug and the box on the table alongside her, then studied his profile.

"Are you mad?" she asked timidly.

Brandt finally looked at her, appearing somewhat puzzled. "Mad?" he asked with a tiny laugh. "Why would I be mad?"

"Because I wrote that story about you," Mazie explained.

"You've been doing that since you were little," he reminded her. "Those little stories you were always working on in that spiral notebook. Since you never let anyone read them, I never knew they were that good."

"There's a lot of honesty in there," Mazie informed him. "I wasn't sure how you'd feel about it." She hesitated, realizing she had forgotten to tell him the important part. Mazie grimaced slightly at what she needed to say. "A friend of a friend wants to publish it."

Brandt looked at her, somewhat surprised. "Really?" he asked, then smiled. "That's quite an achievement. Congratulations."

She shifted uncomfortably while focusing her attention on him. "I gave that to you so you'd tell me how you felt about it," Mazie informed him. "I'm worried it might make you look bad."

Brandt suddenly snorted a laugh. "Look bad?" he asked, then shook his head. "I didn't see anything that made me look bad. Some embarrassing moments, maybe, but I can handle embarrassment."

Mazie was now confused. "You aren't bothered by what I wrote about you?"

"Why?" Brandt asked, then shrugged. "It's pretty accurate."

She remained suspicious. "Something seems off," Mazie remarked. "What is it?"

"Well, I reread the third-to-last chapter about four times," he informed her. "And I have to admit, I'm a little *confused*."

Mazie suddenly groaned. She should have realized that would be a sensitive subject for him, especially since it turned into five long years of avoidance on her behalf. Brandt turned sideways on the swing, facing her, and met her gaze.

"In vivid detail, you retold what happened between us after your graduation party," Brandt informed her. "It's all there. All your thoughts as it happened."

Perhaps she'd forgotten how embarrassing that vivid scene would actually be for her, but it was all coming back to her now.

"You confessed in black and white how you felt being with me in that moment," he informed her. "How you were so happy it had been me and not Peter. Every pleasurable touch. It was all there. Yet in the next chapter, you tell about the following morning, and how conflicted you were. Even our entire fight that led to five long years of avoidance." Brandt shook his head. "The notes at the end were completely accurate, Mazie. You wrote a timeless love story, yet you're denying it's a love story." He drew a deep breath. "Figure out the ending you want and publish the story. But before you come up with an ending, reread what you wrote." Brandt stood with a sigh while studying her. "Now, I'm going to bed and sleeping until noon." He leaned closer to her, hovering over her while staring into her eyes. "If you feel like joining me, my door is open."

Mazie's heart skipped a beat at his offer and the way he'd said it. She could do little more than stare after him as he headed back into the house. Mazie would definitely need to reread what she'd written. Something she wrote obviously made him reconsider their arrangement about pretending that night never happened. Whatever it was, he was convinced he was now right.

Chapter 52

*S*ince Brandt took the morning off on such short notice to catch up on his sleep, Mazie saddled the horses for the wranglers and helped her mother with breakfast as well as clean-up. Having an entire afternoon free, she decided to skim through the manuscript and decide for herself how bad it really was, since she hadn't actually read it since she wrote the last three chapters when she was eighteen. To disprove Brandt, she decided to skip ahead to her late teen years, around the time she and Brandt became best friends. She easily concluded that Brandt had been reading too much into her feelings for him. He took many liberties around the gray areas in several chapters. When she finally reached the scene in his bedroom after her graduation party, she was uncomfortable before she even started reading it. Mazie was basically forcing herself to relive that night in graphic detail, but she had to see if what he was saying was actually true. Mazie squirmed uncomfortably while reading the entire chapter. What really struck her hard was one paragraph in particular.

When Mazie invited Brandt to go to Australia with her and her friends, she admitted, at least to herself, that she had already considered the sleeping arrangements. She intended to share her room with Brandt rather than doubling up with either of her friends. It also meant no one had to sleep on an uncomfortable sofa bed. As she read her own words, she basically admitted that she was looking forward to sharing a bed with him for the entire two weeks, and she'd be perfectly fine with *whatever* happened. As if completely disregarding her earlier words, the aftermath of their sexual encounter didn't align with her previous thoughts. She easily wrote what she felt, at the time, because she assumed no one would ever read it. Mazie knew she contradicted herself while writing the entire event after the fact.

Mazie tossed the manuscript back into the box with something resembling horror. Had Brandt been right? Did she just admit it, in writing, that she had intended to sleep with Brandt in Australia? It was a lot to think about, and it actually made her head hurt. It was nearly one o'clock in the afternoon when Mazie decided to see if Brandt was up yet. Technically, keeping an eye on him was in her revised job description. Mazie left the in-law suite and headed into the kitchen. She immediately stopped when she saw her family sitting around the table with strangely solemn looks on their faces. They briefly glanced at her but seemed reluctant to speak. Brandt was the only one standing. He leaned against the counter near the sink and met Mazie's gaze.

"We need to talk," Brandt announced in a somewhat stern tone.

Mazie instantly panicked. Was this some sort of bizarre intervention? She glanced from her uncles to her mother, and then back at Brandt. Had he told them about the book? Were they upset? Disappointed?

"Okay," Mazie replied somewhat hesitantly, preparing for the worst.

"Liddy," Brandt announced firmly. "Say what you need to say."

Despite being a grown woman, Mazie was actually concerned by what was happening. They were going to gang up on her, she knew it! Did Brandt 'out' their one-night stand?

Liddy shifted uncomfortably in her chair and sheepishly looked at Mazie. "I manipulated you into coming out to the ranch so you'd be forced to confront Brandt and maybe resolve your feud."

That wasn't exactly news. Mazie knew that from the beginning.

"The rest," Brandt scoffed.

Liddy groaned and appeared ashamed. "I hid your cell phone so your boss would leave you alone," she admitted, then hesitated. "A few weeks ago, Brandt finally told me what happened between the two of you."

Mazie slowly sank into a vacant chair, mortified that her mother knew what had happened that night. Even worse. Did her uncles know? When she cast a look at Brandt, he motioned for her to remain silent. Mazie looked back at her mother and wanted to crawl under the table.

"He told me that he professed his love for you after your graduation party, and how that drove you away," Liddy remarked, then frowned. "Even though I never even entertained the thought of the two of you becoming a couple, I'll admit, I may have gone a little overboard trying to get the two of you together."

"Uncle Dalton," Brandt announced, indicating he was next.

"The location scout for Davenport Productions is a friend of a friend," Dalton informed her with a soft groan. "When I heard they had some trouble with their current location due to weather, I called in a favor. My friend sent photos of the ranch to Davenport's location scout, selling him on the ranch for their project."

Mazie was stunned at what she was hearing. She then looked at Uncle Colt, somewhat surprised. "And you, of all people, were in on this?" she demanded.

"Hell, no! I didn't know anything about that," Colt scoffed, then indicated Dalton and Liddy. "That was all Bonnie and Clyde over there."

"Uncle Colt," Brandt scolded.

"Fine," Colt huffed and folded his arms across his chest while maintaining an arrogant look. "When I rode back to the ranch with Sandra King, she asked all sorts of questions about Brandt." He hesitated, then eyed Mazie. "And your relationship with him. She confessed that she wanted to ask him out, but she was concerned you didn't know how you actually felt about him. So I told her about Bonnie and Clyde, over there, having their suspicions. Sandra and I decided to test a jealousy theory. If you became jealous, she'd leave Brandt alone. If you weren't jealous, she'd happily pursue him." Colt shrugged. "You didn't seem jealous, so she asked him out."

"So there they are," Brandt informed Mazie. "The three master manipulators."

"I'm shocked and a little disappointed," Mazie remarked, scolding all three. "But you meant well." She then glared at Colt. "Well, maybe not you. You just wanted Brandt to get lucky with a Hollywood actress."

"Guilty," Colt replied. "It's not as if that opportunity will ever arise again, and I did tell these two you weren't romantically interested in him."

Mazie eyed Brandt, now curious. "How did you figure all this out?"

"I caught them conspiring over coffee a few minutes before you joined us," Brandt informed her. "Apparently, phase two was making *me* jealous."

Mazie groaned, then eyed all three. "That would have been the worst idea ever," she scolded. "Why would you even consider provoking him? Twenty-nine years old, and he's still a bit of a hothead."

"Most of my hotheadedness was me trying to keep you out of trouble," Brandt reminded her.

"*You* kept *her* out of trouble?" Colt asked, then immediately chuckled. "That's a good one."

"Don't worry," Brandt announced. "You can read all about it when the book comes out."

All three managed a tiny laugh, thinking it was a joke of some kind. Brandt grinned at Mazie and indicated the three at the table.

"Have fun telling them about your tell-all book," Brandt announced, then left the kitchen.

*W*ith Brandt spending the rest of the afternoon in his office to catch up on paperwork, Mazie went for a drive along the old, familiar back roads. She wasn't sure what possessed her, but she turned off onto Old Mill Road, which was the road to Old Mill Pond. The place hadn't changed much over the years. Despite her bad memories of Tina and that party, she also had good memories of the place. She and Brandt rode out there many times to swim in the pond. Sometimes, other kids were present, but most times, it was just the two of them. She refused to let one bad memory taint all of the good ones. As she roamed the property, Mazie found it difficult to reminisce without Brandt being the center of her story. Even being away for five years didn't stop him from being on her mind. The thought of returning to LA was becoming increasingly complex. Everything she loved was right here. The only things LA offered her were work and solitude.

If she were being honest with herself, there wasn't a time when she was at her apartment that she didn't think about the ranch. Mazie was becoming uncomfortable with her own thoughts. She could think of only one reason to return to LA and a thousand reasons to stay at the ranch. Frustrated, Mazie returned to her Jeep and drove into town. Perhaps if she visited Melissa at her lab, she'd stop daydreaming about her happiest days at the ranch. When she arrived in town, she parked on the street not far from the building where Melissa worked. As she walked toward Melissa's office building, she heard someone calling her name. Mazie looked back and saw Peter hurrying to catch up with her.

"I was hoping to run into you," Peter announced, keeping pace with her. "You haven't returned any of my text messages."

"Sorry about that," Mazie replied, although she wasn't actually sorry. "I've been a little stressed out lately, and I didn't feel like getting into another argument."

"I don't want to argue either," Peter insisted while keeping up with her. "Quite the opposite. I think I owe you an apology."

Mazie paused and turned to face him. "That would probably be a start," she remarked somewhat curtly.

"I was a stupid teenager," Peter informed her, sounding sincere. "You and I made specific plans for our trip to Australia, and I let a moment of temptation cloud my judgment. I wish I could take it back. It was stupid, impulsive, and completely wrong. I'm sorry for what I did, and if I had to do it all over again, I would have made better choices. Can you ever forgive me?"

Mazie drew a deep breath and considered his words. If he were sincere, forgiving him for kissing Hannah in the barn would be the right thing to do.

"I suppose boys do stupid stuff when they're eighteen," Mazie remarked, then frowned, remembering how she let temptation cloud her judgment. "Girls, too." She met his gaze and offered a tiny smile. "Yes, I forgive you."

"I'm happy to hear that," Peter replied, with a relieved sigh. "I mean, Melissa banning me from the trip was pretty much its own punishment. When I ran into you last week, I had completely forgotten about the barn incident. I was just so happy to see you and Melissa." He managed a smile and shrugged. "I guess I just assumed we were good, considering the warm welcome I received from the two of you."

"I suppose I *was* initially happy to see you, too," Mazie replied and managed a more genuine smile.

"And, considering we both live in LA, I was thinking maybe we could get together after we get back home," Peter announced. "Get coffee, or drinks, or dinner. Just see how it goes."

"I suppose we could meet for coffee," Mazie replied. "There's nothing wrong with two childhood friends getting coffee."

"None whatsoever," Peter announced with a pleased smile on his face. He reached inside his jacket pocket and handed her a business card. "My cell phone number is on my business card. I'll leave the ball in your court. That way, there's no pressure."

Mazie accepted the card and nodded. "I appreciate that," she replied, placing it in her pocket. "I, uh, should get going. I'm visiting Melissa at her office."

"Yeah, sure," Peter announced cheerfully. "I'll talk to you later."

Mazie nodded, then watched him walk away. Her mind momentarily strayed. Wasn't that what she always wanted? Peter? She wondered why she didn't feel more alive at the prospect of going out with him once she was back in LA. Probably because Brandt was living rent-free in her head. Mazie groaned in frustration and then headed for Melissa's office building.

Chapter 53

Monday morning. The rodeo was a single-day event held in a town less than an hour's drive from the ranch. Nearly every ranch within a one-hundred-mile radius had at least one or more representative from their ranch participating in the yearly event. Each ranch enjoyed the bragging rights that came with its wins. The main events were bronc riding, bull riding, steer wrestling, tie-down roping, team roping, barrel racing, and breakaway roping. Major's Thunder Basin usually only had one wrangler sign up for bull riding, dubbed "the most dangerous eight seconds in sports". A few of the guys still participated in bronc riding, which was inherently dangerous, but they enjoyed the competition. Brandt only attempted bronc riding a few times and, after breaking a rib, decided it wasn't for him.

Mazie used to compete in barrel racing and breakaway roping. She had become quite good at it, but she was uncertain about her skills after five years of not using them daily. Mazie already felt her heart pounding from the moment they arrived at the fairgrounds. She couldn't believe Brandt talked her into team roping with him. It wasn't that it was all that dangerous; she just didn't want to ruin Brandt's chances at winning a trophy. His chances were better competing with Colt, who was a daredevil in his youth with the broken bones to prove it. Being Mazie was competing at the rodeo, Melissa and Cameron insisted on attending, so naturally, Malcolm wanted to come along. Once the production team heard about the event, they weren't about to miss it either. Even Davenport tagged along. Brandt only trailered two horses from their ranch to the event, since their three wranglers attending were only interested in bronc riding and bull riding. They chose the two fastest, most competitive horses, which were Blackjack and Uncle Colt's buckskin, Bucky. Bucky wasn't a young horse anymore, but he was far from retiring.

Colt and Dalton would use Blackjack and Bucky for their individual tie-down roping events and their team roping event before turning them over to Brandt and Mazie for their team roping run. Colt also signed up for steer wrestling, which had him literally jumping off his horse at a gallop and tackling a steer to the ground by the horns. In addition to the rodeo events, there were pony rides for the kids, numerous food trucks serving freshly grilled meats and a variety of deep-fried treats, and fun activities in a smaller arena for the kids. The production team enjoyed the food and other activities while waiting to cheer on MTB Ranch in their events. Brandt and Colt joined Dalton, Liddy, and Mazie, who stayed with the horses, after paying the entrance fees for their events. When they returned, Colt was snickering about something.

"It's your ass, boy," Colt announced while remaining humored, then patted him on the shoulder. "Good luck."

"What are you two conspiring about now?" Dalton asked.

"Nothing," Brandt insisted, then approached Mazie. "You and I are number twenty in the team roping event. "Colt and Dalton are fifteen. That gives us time to swap out Uncle Colt's saddle with yours."

"Tell her the rest," Colt announced while grinning.

"The rest of what?" Mazie asked, now curious.

"Nothing," Brandt insisted and waved her off. "I also signed you up for breakaway roping, so we should probably get your saddle on Blackjack."

"Why, Brandt?" Mazie moaned. "I told you I didn't want to do any other events."

"It's good practice," Brandt insisted. "And our ranch hasn't had representation in breakaway roping in five years. That gives us participants in every event except barrel racing. I figured if I signed you up for barrel racing, it would be pushing the envelope."

"He wanted to," Colt informed her. "But I talked him out of it."

"I've got an idea," Mazie announced while folding her arms across her chest as she glared at Brandt. "Why don't I sign *you* up for barrel racing?"

Brandt and Colt suddenly grinned and laughed.

"Yeah, that's not happening," Brandt announced.

"Why not?" Mazie demanded, raising her brows.

"Because that's for girls--" Colt began, then cut his comment short of finishing his thought.

"Barrel racing is for girls?" Mazie scoffed. "Is that why you won't do it?"

"I'll make you a deal, darling," Colt announced with a hint of a smile. "*I'll* sign up for barrel racing when *you* sign up for bronc riding."

Mazie stared at her Uncle Colt a moment before fidgeting and backing down. "Fine," she scoffed. "You made your point."

§

$\mathcal{M}$azie sat on Blackjack while waiting for her run in the breakaway roping event. Although the event was dominated mainly by women, a few men also competed. She watched the man before her run his horse after the calf, skillfully roping it. When the rope would technically be taut, the rope essentially 'broke' from the saddle horn, putting less stress on the calf. Mazie was more interested in the horse than its male rider. The horse was a flashy black and white Tobiano paint gelding with an impressive build and stunning markings. She was pretty sure it was love at first sight.

"He's gorgeous," Mazie remarked, catching Colt and Brandt's attention.

"The horse or the cowboy?" Colt asked with a snicker.

"It's Mazie," Brandt reminded him. "Obviously, she's talking about the horse."

"I didn't even notice the guy," Mazie remarked.

Brandt indicated Mazie to Colt while raising his brows as if resting his case. They called Mazie's name for the next run. She couldn't deny she felt almost sick to her stomach as she entered the box alongside the calf chute. Blackjack was a lot of horse, more so than Bucky. He was itching to go the moment they entered the box. She was worried about him breaking before she was ready and leaving her bruised ass and ego sitting on the ground. When the calf was released, Blackjack took his cue, almost breaking ahead of her. In that moment, she focused on the running calf and threw the lasso almost mechanically. When the rope landed around the calf's neck, she released it. As it broke away, her anxiety went with it. Her run was over. She looked at the time as she rode back to the gate. She didn't even have to figure out her time against the others; her cheering section, consisting of

Brandt, Colt, Dalton, and Liddy, was excitedly clapping. As she left the arena and joined them, she was now curious.

"Was it good enough?"

"Third place," Dalton informed her, and high-fived her on the anxiously prancing horse.

"I'll happily take third," Mazie announced, overjoyed while jumping off Blackjack.

"Why don't you collect your trophy while we swap out saddles for Dalton's tie-down run?" Brandt announced.

Mazie nodded and handed the reins to Brandt. As she headed for the prize table, she saw the man sitting on the black and white paint with his second-place trophy from the same event. Mazie felt compelled to stop near him as his friends took pictures of him with the trophy.

"Your horse is gorgeous," Mazie informed him.

"You were riding the blue roan, right?" the man asked.

"Yeah, we took third," she replied. "I have a black and white Overo paint at home, but he's retired."

The man studied her for a moment, then pointed at her and smiled. "Are you Mazie?" he asked. "MTB Ranch."

"Yes, I'm Mazie," she replied, not sure if he only knew her name from the announcer calling her for her run.

"I remember you," the man insisted. "I haven't seen you here in years. "Brandt's little sister."

Mazie internally cringed at the awkwardness of the question. Because of their living situation, many people thought Brandt was her brother, which is precisely why she regretted that night five years ago.

"Actually, we're not related," she informed him. "We were raised together, but we're not related."

After his comment, Mazie couldn't get away from the man fast enough. Now that would be on her mind the rest of the afternoon.

A little while later, Colt placed second in his steer wrestling event, and both of Mazie's uncles placed in the tie-down event. Dalton won third while Colt got first. It was turning out to be a great day so far, and having an entire cheering section from the production company made it that much better. When it came time for the team roping, Mazie saw the man on the black and white paint team rope with his partner. She couldn't help but admire the horse. Brandt stood alongside her, leaning on the stock fencing, and eyed her several times.

"Have you ever looked at a man the way you're looking at that horse?" Brandt asked with a tiny, humored laugh.

Mazie considered the question only a moment, then cast a quick glance at him from the corner of her eye.

"Only if he sits a horse well," Mazie replied with a hint of a smile.

"So I qualify then?" Brandt teased.

Without looking at him, Mazie placed her hand on his lower arm. "When it comes to riding horses," she announced. "You set the bar pretty high."

Brandt attempted to hide his grin while placing his arm around her and pulling her against his side. "That made me all fuzzy inside," he announced, then removed her hat and kissed her on the top of her head.

After he replaced her hat, he was reluctant to release her, but Mazie didn't really mind. Instead, she clung to his waist and rested her head on his shoulder. They remained in each other's arms until Dalton and Colt were called for their run. Brandt released Mazie and clapped, cheering on his uncles. As they made their team roping run, Dalton, riding Blackjack, roped the steer's horns, then spun the horse for Colt to rope its hind legs. As Bucky slid on his hind legs, completing the run, his front shoe flew off, nearly striking the steer. Bucky jumped, possibly feeling the shoe give. It didn't affect their time at all, but losing his front shoe wasn't good. Colt did a quick dismount and recovered the lost shoe. He then led Bucky from the arena behind Dalton on Blackjack. Mazie and Brandt approached the gate as they exited the arena.

"Son-of-a-bitch," Colt cried out while holding the shoe in his hand, then looked around. "Is there a farrier in the house?"

It sounded like a joke, but there were usually farriers hanging around to replace shoes in exactly that sort of situation. Someone pointed further away to a man already working on a horse. Colt shook his head, then looked at Mazie while frowning.

"I think you're shit out of luck," Colt scoffed while looking at the slightly bent shoe and shaking his head.

"I'll survive," Mazie replied, not incredibly broken up over it.

When she looked alongside her, Brandt was gone. Liddy hurried to them to see what was happening as well. When they finally spotted Brandt, he was throwing Mazie's saddle on the black and white paint she'd been admiring all afternoon while the owner held the horse for him. Mazie approached them, now curious.

"What's going on?" Mazie asked.

"Last-minute substitution," Brandt informed her, then indicated the horse's owner. "Lee offered his horse for our run."

The owner, presumably Lee, gave her a knowing smile and a nod. Despite desperately wanting to scratch their event, Mazie was a little excited to ride the beautiful horse. Once the girth was tightened, Lee encouraged her to mount. Mazie swung up onto the horse's back and collected the reins and her lasso.

"He's spicy," Lee informed her. "You won't need to kick him. He'll break away the moment you give him his head."

Mazie nodded, then smiled at Brandt. He grinned and gave her a thumbs-up. Their run came up fast, and they made it just in time. Mazie took her position as the header, while Brandt took the heeler box. Mazie couldn't deny the added anxiety of riding a horse she'd never ridden before. Just like people, horses all had different personalities and performance styles. She barely had time to think about it. The horse was a live wire, waiting to break. When she looked at Brandt, he sat on his equally excited horse and met her gaze. Mazie nodded, then focused on the front of the chute. As soon as the chute opened, the steer ran out, and Mazie released the horse from its invisible hold. The horse took off like a shot, nearly throwing her off her game. She threw the lasso and snagged the steer around the horns. The horse barely needed a cue, knowing what to do, spinning sharply and backing up full throttle. At the same time, Brandt threw his lasso for the back legs, catching them both. They didn't even have to look at the timer; Colt could be heard hooting from the sidelines.

Brandt pumped his fist in the air, then spun around Mazie and gave her a high five. As they rode back to the gate, Mazie tried to check the clock.

"Did we place?" she asked.

"We're in first, baby," Brandt announced excitedly. "Only two more competitors to go."

While the last two competitors made their run, Mazie unsaddled the borrowed horse and thanked the owner. When she heard Brandt cheering, she realized they had at least placed. Colt appeared excited as well. Brandt approached her and picked her up off her feet while hugging her.

"First place," Brandt announced while practically swinging her around like a rag doll.

"I got third," Colt remarked with a hint of a smile and a little bit of jealousy.

Thankfully, Lee got second place, so he didn't lose by much after loaning his horse out. Once they received their trophies, Lee allowed them to take pictures with his horse and their trophies. Melissa and Malcolm approached after their win and also congratulated all of them. Although their events were finished, their three ranch hands and Colt had bronc riding, and one man was in the bull riding, so they would hang out until they finished their events.

Chapter 54

Early the following morning, Mazie received a text from her boss while helping her mother prepare breakfast. Davenport wanted her to run to town with Tina to pick up an order from the general store. Mazie wasn't sure which part she hated more, missing out on a morning with the wranglers or being stuck alone in a car with Tina. Brandt entered the kitchen after taking off his dirty boots in the mud room, where he had also washed his hands, and arrived in time to help set the table. Mazie handed him a cup of coffee, then put the insulated carafe on the table, ready for Uncle Colt and Uncle Dalton, who would be arriving in the kitchen any minute.

"I got a double blow of bad news this morning," Mazie informed Brandt, who stopped setting the table and eyed her, now curious. "Davenport needs me to run to town this morning." She made a face. "With Tina."

"Your boss trusts me unsupervised?" Brandt teased with a humored grin.

"Apparently so," Mazie replied with a soft laugh, knowing that was a bad idea.

"I don't know," Brandt announced with a low sigh. "I'm feeling mischievous this morning. Maybe he should reconsider."

"I know it's a stretch," Mazie announced. "But try to behave."

They exchanged looks and chuckled.

"That's impossible," Colt announced as he entered the kitchen from the back stairs, having heard the comment. "I'm working with the director and cameraman this morning, so I won't be there to supervise you either until later this afternoon."

"I guess that means Dalton is in charge," Brandt remarked.

"Don't look at me," Dalton announced as he entered from the in-law suite, having spent the entire night with Liddy in her room. "I have to run some errands in town this morning."

Mazie suddenly appeared hopeful. "If you're going to town, maybe you could help Tina with Davenport's order at the general store."

"Sorry, Mazie," Dalton announced without even looking at her. "I'm not getting within twenty feet of that vile woman."

"Imagine how I feel," Mazie insisted, then wrinkled her nose. "I'm going to be stuck with her for an hour or more. One wrong word, and I'm liable to hit her."

"Yeah, me too," Dalton informed her as he poured some coffee into a mug from the carafe on the table. "I'm just avoiding the temptation because, you know, men aren't supposed to hit women."

"I think Mazie should go for it," Brandt chimed in while grinning, then eyed Mazie as he flopped into his seat at the head of the table. "Give that girl a swift punch in the mouth."

"You boys are terrible," Liddy scoffed as she placed the last of the platters on the table, then joined them. "She might be a vile little bitch, but Mazie shouldn't be hitting her, at least, not in the face."

There was a round of snickers from all three men. Mazie groaned and shook her head.

§

$\mathcal{M}$azie walked onto the porch after breakfast that morning and found Melissa sitting on the double-wide swing, looking as if her world had suddenly crashed around her. Mazie approached while eyeing her friend.

"Good morning," Mazie announced to her friend and sat on the porch railing across from her. "You're up rather early."

"No, actually, it's not a good morning," Melissa groaned while maintaining her frown, then met Mazie's gaze. "The director sent out a mass text this morning announcing that they're wrapping up filming at the ranch *today*. They pack up and leave first thing tomorrow morning."

"Oh," Mazie replied softly. "That's almost four days early."

Mazie was somewhat surprised by the new information. Why hadn't Davenport texted her that little tidbit of news? Unless he didn't know about it at the time he initially texted her.

"Yeah, and your Uncle Colt is partly to blame," Melissa huffed. "All his amateur cowboy filming put them ahead of schedule. Now, Malcolm is leaving tomorrow morning, and I don't want him to go."

"You knew it was going to happen eventually," Mazie reminded her.

"I know, but I thought I had another four days to get tired of him or for him to piss me off," Melissa reported, then groaned. "But I'm not tired of him, and he hasn't pissed me off. His being Malcolm Wexler aside, we really clicked. We were having a really good time."

Mazie then realized that meant her time on the ranch was ending as well, and she sank into depression alongside Melissa.

"Yeah, I know how you feel," Mazie replied and looked around. "I'm already missing this place."

"I knew it wasn't going to last forever," Melissa insisted somewhat timidly. "But I guess I was secretly hoping it wouldn't end."

Mazie moved onto the double-wide swing alongside her friend and placed her arms around her, holding and comforting her.

"There's nothing wrong with dreaming big," Mazie informed Melissa. "I mean, at least you had more than a week with him, and you had a *real* connection. How many women out there get to say that about a celebrity like Malcolm Wexler?"

"Yes, it's all very flattering," Melissa replied with a sigh. "But I would've liked a little more time."

She pulled away from Mazie and glanced at her watch. "I have to go home and shower," Melissa announced. "I have work today." She then managed a smile that was somewhere between proud and sad. "Malcolm said he'd stop by my lab this afternoon after his last scene. He wants to see where I work." Melissa again frowned. "Life is so cruel. Malcolm is probably the first guy who's ever been interested in my work, and he's being ripped out of my life." She shook her head in disgust. "I guess I'm just not meant to be lucky in love."

When Melissa stood, Mazie stood as well, offering a sympathetic smile.

"Maybe he'll visit you," Mazie announced. "Don't give up hope yet."

"He's a movie star, Mazie," Melissa reminded her with a slightly defeated sigh. "He'll meet someone else in less than a week. By next month, he'll have completely forgotten about me. I'm not naïve, but thanks for trying to cheer me up."

Chapter 55

Mazie and Tina drove to town in an uncomfortable silence. By the way Tina sat rigid in the passenger seat of Mazie's Jeep, it was obvious Tina was just as thrilled with the arrangement. Mazie didn't even know what they were supposed to be picking up at the general store, but it was obviously something Tina couldn't handle by herself, being either a large order or a heavy one. Although Mazie was curious, she wasn't curious enough to engage Tina in conversation. Thankfully, it didn't take long to reach the general store. Mazie no sooner parked the Jeep when Tina just about jumped out, looking for her escape. Mazie got out of the vehicle with less enthusiasm than Tina. She reluctantly followed her former friend into the store. Tina immediately approached the counter, barely greeting the store clerk. The young woman wasn't anyone of importance to Tina, so she didn't bother with pleasantries.

"I'm here to pick up an order for Davenport Productions," Tina announced while looking down upon the poor, young woman.

The clerk managed a tight-lipped smile that was close to a sneer. Obviously, she was familiar with Tina.

"Yes," the clerk replied, then indicated the two boxes of champagne on the floor alongside the counter. "The two boxes of champagne. That'll be eighteen hundred dollars, and I'll need to see some ID."

Tina slapped Davenport's credit card on the counter while glaring at the young clerk. "You know damned well that I'm over twenty-one," she scoffed. "I graduated from high school a year before you."

The woman cocked her head while maintaining her sneer. "Anyone who looks younger than thirty has to show ID," the clerk scoffed. "Those are the rules."

Tina muttered something under her breath while fumbling for her ID within her wallet. She showed it to the young clerk, who seemed to scrutinize over it for a moment. Tina groaned in disgust and pulled her ID back, unwilling to wait any longer. The clerk ran the credit card through the reader, then handed it back to Tina once it was approved. Tina signed the receipt and then indicated the two cases to the young clerk.

"Put those in the Jeep," Tina ordered.

The young clerk handed Tina her receipt, appearing unfazed. "I'm the only one working, and I have other customers in the store," she announced, lacking emotion. "I can't help you. They aren't that heavy."

Tina sneered at the girl, then glared at Mazie. "Grab those," she scoffed.

"This is your errand," Mazie informed her. "You carry them."

"At least take one of them," Tina huffed.

"I'll take one," Mazie replied, willing to compromise.

Tina grabbed the first case, groaning at its weight, and carried it from the store. Mazie chuckled softly, then eyed the clerk.

"Nicely handled," Mazie announced.

"That bitch invited me to a party at Old Mill Pond a decade ago," the clerk remarked. "She thought it was funny, encouraging guys to slip vodka into my drinks. I thought she wanted to be friends, but I was just a source of amusement to her."

"She pulled the same stunt with me," Mazie muttered while shaking her head.

"Honestly, I was lucky I got out of there when I did," the clerk informed her. "This guy in a pickup truck showed up with a baseball bat and dispersed the entire party right before the cops showed up."

It was ironic that she was at the same party Mazie had attended. Brandt unknowingly saved another poor girl that night.

"A couple of other girls and I had told the sheriff what had happened," the clerk reported. "Naturally, Tina didn't get into any trouble for her part in it, but a few of the older boys she knew certainly did. Apparently, they blamed her for it, and they never let her live it down." She raised an arrogant brow. "They held on to that grudge for so long that they even got her kicked out of college after her first semester."

"She was kicked out of college?" Mazie asked with surprise. "That was four or five years after that incident."

"Like I said, those boys held a grudge," the clerk reported. "The older boys were seventeen and eighteen. Some even had football scholarships. Being arrested affected their college applications and scholarships. They were just returning the favor."

"Seems like all of them got what they deserved," Mazie retorted.

"After she was kicked out of college, no other college would touch her," the clerk continued. "That's why she's stuck working at the cosmetic counter at the mall. Her parents wouldn't give her any more money unless she went to work. They're still a little pissed about losing all that tuition money."

"That certainly explains a lot," Mazie remarked, then offered a smile. "Thanks for sharing that story with me. I guess her life isn't as perfect as she pretends it is."

"Are you kidding?" the clerk scoffed. "Her life is far from perfect. None of the decent guys will give her the time of day. The only guys willing to take her out are all assholes. Birds of a feather, and all that."

Mazie snorted a laugh and grabbed the second case of champagne with less effort than Tina had. She smiled at the clerk, wished her a good day, and left the store.

During the ride home, Mazie was in a better mood.

No matter how smug Tina came across, she no longer had any power over her. Perhaps, if Mazie had been a better person, she would have felt sorry for Tina, but five years of daily bullying and torment had cured her of feeling any sympathy for her childhood friend turned school bully.

"What do you think all the champagne is for?" Tina finally asked.

"Well, rumor has it they're wrapping up filming at the ranch," Mazie informed her. "I'm guessing they're gifts for the cast and crew, or Davenport is planning one hell of a wrap-up party."

"Is that common?" Tina then asked.

"Well, typically wrap-up parties are for the final day of shooting the entire picture," Mazie remarked. "But Davenport enjoys a good party. He's probably also happy that Brandt didn't wreak havoc on production."

Tina appeared to be deep in thought before speaking again. "Do you like working for Davenport?"

Mazie resisted the urge to laugh at the question and, instead, gave it some serious thought. Why was Tina suddenly interested in Mazie's life? Since it was Tina, she had to assume she had an ulterior motive.

"Oh, yes, of course," Mazie announced and even added a smile. "The hours can be long while filming, but there are plenty of days where my biggest problem is where to order take-out for lunch. And the pay is outstanding."

"And Davenport?" Tina asked. "Do you get along with him?"

"Absolutely," Mazie remarked, easily lying. "I mean, he's worth millions, and he's very generous with his money. Granted, he's still a Hollywood producer, so he can be a little intense, but he's pretty much the life of the party."

Ironically, none of that was a lie. Davenport just wasn't that way with her. She always got the short end of his generosity, and he was always quick to remind her that she was easily replaceable. When Tina sank into thought, Mazie secretly chuckled. It was quite possible that her boss was considering replacing her with Tina, which actually wouldn't upset her in the least.

Chapter 56

Mazie made it back to the ranch in time to watch Colt film his last scene as a cowboy cameraman. As he galloped his horse alongside the stuntman racing his horse down the long stretch of dirt road, he filmed the scene in one take. Since it was his last ride, so to speak, the crew applauded Colt for his contribution. Colt didn't seem to mind being the center of attention and celebrated by the production team, although he probably enjoyed the five hundred dollars a day more. When Colt dismounted, Davenport thanked him and handed him an envelope containing his paycheck for his full seven days of work. It was a nice haul for very little work. Mazie just hoped it wouldn't go to his head. She approached Colt while grinning.

"How does that big payday and your name in the film credits feel?" Mazie asked.

Colt was all smiles as he opened his envelope. "It feels freaking awesome," he announced, then looked at his check. His expression immediately dropped. "They took out taxes?" Colt groaned and shook his head. "I should have known there was going to be a catch."

"Did you actually think they would be paying you under the table?" Mazie teased.

"If they take my name off the credits, will they pay me in cash instead?" he asked.

"I'm afraid not," she replied. "But you had fun, right?"

"Not enough fun to warrant paying taxes on it," Colt muttered, then shoved the check into his pocket. "I'm glad I didn't quit my day job."

Mazie knew he was only kidding. He just liked being grumpy.

"Are you heading out to the herd?" Mazie asked.

"Gotta work," Colt reminded her with a defeated sigh. "This movie bullshit isn't going to pay the bills."

"Would you give Brandt a message for me?" she asked. "I tried texting several times, but they must be in a dead zone."

"Yeah, that area is pretty bad," Colt announced, then mounted his horse. "What's the message?"

Mazie frowned while shifting uncomfortably. "Just tell him that the production crew is wrapping things up today, and we're leaving tomorrow morning."

Colt groaned and shook his head. "You should probably give him that message yourself," he insisted. "I don't like giving him bad news. He's going to sulk like a little kid."

"Please, Colt," Mazie begged. "Davenport has a bunch of things he wants me to do before we leave, and there's something I need to do first."

"Fine," Colt groaned. "I'll give him the message."

Knowing it was her last day on the ranch, Mazie was a little depressed. There was one thing she wanted to do before leaving tomorrow. Mazie saddled up her old horse, Katona, and took a leisurely ride around the property. His arthritis wasn't bad that morning, and he wasn't even limping. As long as she kept him at a walk and remained on flat ground, he'd be fine. Because of his age, she didn't know if she'd ever have another opportunity to take him out again. As they rode the area surrounding the house and barn, Katona was in his glory. He was enjoying the scenery almost as much as she was. There was no telling how many years her old horse had left, so she wanted one last memory with him. When they reached the dirt road to the old homestead, Katona jigged happily, hoping to run the road like they used to. Although it was tempting with how good he was feeling, Mazie kept him at a walk for his own good. They reached the old homestead, then turned and headed back to the ranch.

By the time Mazie returned to the ranch house, she had five missed text messages from Davenport. Before she even had a chance to read them, Davenport saw her ride up to the barn and caught up with her.

"Didn't you get my text?" Davenport demanded. "Your special assignment keeping tabs on Brandt is over. I need you to start working on coordinating efforts for our next location. When you finish doing that, you and I are heading back to Los Angeles."

"What time are we leaving?" Mazie asked while masking her sadness.

"First thing tomorrow morning," Davenport informed her. "I want all the trucks loaded and out of here no later than eight in the morning. That's when you and I will head to the airport. I also want Brandt to sign a waiver stating the property has been returned to its original condition to avoid any lawsuits."

"I'm sure that won't be a problem," Mazie replied, lacking enthusiasm as she dismounted the horse. She then looked around, somewhat curious. "No Tina?"

"No," Davenport replied. "She needed to go to work this afternoon, but she'll be back early tomorrow morning to assist with some departure plans."

"Did you find her roles in any of your upcoming movies?" Mazie asked, although she was relatively sure she already knew the answer.

"Yes," Davenport replied, seeming pleased with himself. "I got her parts in two new movies."

"I'm sure that made her happy," Mazie remarked, only half interested.

"They don't start filming until next year, but there are two excellent parts for her," Davenport announced. "A waitress with two speaking lines and a hooker with at least three speaking lines."

"Yes, I'm sure she's happy about that," Mazie remarked while silently shaming herself for the cruel thoughts she was thinking.

Tina had kissed Davenport's ass, among other things, for more than a week, ran his errands, and 'put out' on his beck and call. She thought she was sleeping her way to something great, but ended up stuck with minor roles anyone could audition for as an extra. Seemed kind of fitting.

Chapter 57

*M*azie finished coordinating the departure plan for the trucks, trailers, and equipment before eleven o'clock that morning, which gave her an hour to take in the ranch before she needed to help her mother prepare lunch. She found herself in the barn again, reliving memories, when she heard thundering hooves. Mazie left the barn to see what was happening. It wasn't often the guys rode back to the house any faster than a trot. Either there was an emergency or one of the guys was pissed about something. Brandt approached the barn and pulled his horse to an abrupt stop not far from her. To her surprise, his foul mood seemed to be directed at her.

"When were you planning on telling me?" Brandt demanded.

"Telling you what?"

"That they're done filming, and you're leaving in the morning," he scoffed.

"You left before I even found out myself," Mazie informed him. "I told Uncle Colt. He was supposed to tell you."

Brandt's expression remained harsh and unforgiving. "You should have come out to the herd and told me yourself," he remarked. "I think I deserve at least that much courtesy."

"I wanted to hang out at the ranch a few hours this morning," Mazie insisted. "It's not as if we're leaving this afternoon. I'll be here all evening. We don't leave until tomorrow morning."

"And I have to run out this afternoon," Brandt informed her.

"I don't remember you mentioning anything about being gone for the evening," Mazie informed him.

"I just got the call on my way out to the herd this morning," he remarked, then regained his composure. "I was hoping you'd come along. It's an hour's drive, and I would love the company."

Mazie felt bad, but she knew she had too much to do in a short amount of time. "I'm sorry, but Davenport has me doing some last-minute work to prepare for our departure tomorrow," she informed him.

Brandt couldn't hide his disappointment and possible annoyance, but he wasn't about to cause a scene. "Well, if I leave now, I can be back before ten o'clock tonight," Brandt informed her.

Once he dismounted, Mazie took the horse's reins. "I'll take care of Blackjack," she insisted. "Go take care of business, and I'll see you when you get back."

"As long as you don't mind," Brand remarked. "I'd like to grab a shower first before I go."

"No, of course, I don't mind."

As Brandt headed into the house, Mazie unsaddled Blackjack while he was standing at the hitching post without being tied. The horse wasn't going anywhere. Mazie carried the saddle into the barn, then returned with the stiff brush to cool the horse off. She heard a car approaching and instinctively looked, as there usually weren't too many cars coming down the driveway. Instead of Brandt leaving, which he couldn't have showered that fast, she saw Peter drive up to the house and park. With things finally feeling better between her and Peter after his sincere apology, she didn't react negatively to his showing up at the ranch this time. Peter approached her while she brushed the blue roan gelding.

"Are you going out for a ride?" Peter asked.

"No, I'm brushing Brandt's horse for him," Mazie replied. "He has business out of town this afternoon."

"As long as you're not going out for a ride, maybe you'd like to have lunch with me instead," Peter remarked cheerfully.

"I'd love to, but Davenport has me working this afternoon," Mazie informed him. "They're wrapping up filming here at the ranch, which means there's going to be a lot to do in order to leave by morning."

"They're finished filming?" Peter asked, then appeared excited. "That's terrific news. So you'll be heading back to LA sooner than expected?"

"Tomorrow morning," Mazie replied while attempting to ignore the pang in the pit of her stomach.

"I was actually planning on flying home the following afternoon," he informed her. "I didn't make the arrangements yet. Maybe we could fly home together."

"Well, I'm flying home in Davenport's private jet," Mazie reminded him. "I'm not sure he'd appreciate me inviting you to go along with us."

"You can always ask," Peter announced, then shrugged. "If not, you could always fly commercial with me. I can book us both in first class."

"How many goddamned times do I have to throw you off my property?" Brandt announced as he approached them, his fists already clenched. "Mazie doesn't want to see you."

"That's where you're wrong," Peter informed him while adding a smirk, which was probably a mistake. "The past is all water under the bridge. You can't stop her from seeing me."

"Wanna bet?" Brandt scoffed as he took a quick step closer to Peter.

"Brandt," Mazie scolded while stepping in front of him. "Please, stop it."

Brandt eyed Mazie with some surprise. "He broke you, Mazie," he reminded her. "Have you forgotten how much his indiscretions with Hannah hurt you?"

"People make mistakes, Brandt," Peter scoffed. "I mean, she forgave you. Why is it so hard to think she can't or shouldn't forgive me?"

"That's different," Brandt snarled in response. "I didn't break her heart or destroy her trust."

"Give the overly protective brother routine a rest," Peter launched, turning angry.

Mazie clung to Brandt's arm and gently guided him away from Peter. "You have places to be," she reminded him. "Just let it go, okay?"

She managed to guide Brandt a few steps away from Peter when he doubled down on his scathing comment.

"Stop acting like a jealous boyfriend," Peter scoffed. "She's not your girlfriend."

The moment Mazie heard Peter's words, she internally cringed. He had no idea how much of a sore subject that was for Brandt. Brandt spun, pulling free from Mazie's arm, and punched Peter in the mouth. Mazie cried out with surprise. Peter stumbled back a step while holding his bleeding lip, then glared at Brandt.

"It's time someone stood up to you," Peter snarled. "I'm not afraid of you!"

Brandt beckoned him to 'bring it on' and clenched his fists, prepared for a fight. Mazie took a quick step back, panicked by the face-off. Peter seemed to consider it only a moment, then waved him off.

"You're not even worth it," Peter scoffed, then looked at Mazie while gingerly dabbing his bleeding lip. "I'll call you later."

Peter returned to his car, got in, and drove away a little faster than he should have, catching Blackjack's attention. Once he disappeared down the driveway, Mazie turned to Brandt and aggressively punched him in the shoulder, surprising him. He yelped out of reflex more than pain.

"Why are you hitting me?" Brandt demanded.

"What were you hitting Peter for?" she shouted back.

"I was defending you!"

"You weren't defending me," Mazie scoffed, now animated. "You were defending your ego!"

"He accused me of being your jealous boyfriend," Brandt huffed. "You should be grateful I hit him."

"That's not what he said," Mazie informed him. "You heard what you wanted to hear."

"It doesn't matter what he actually said," Brandt remarked. "You can't seriously be considering inviting him back into your life. He disrespected you in your own home at your own graduation party."

Mazie groaned and held her head. "You're giving me a headache," she scoffed, then looked at him. "If I choose to forgive Peter, that's my decision. Nobody else's. And you just have to accept my decision, whether you like it or not."

"Well, I don't like it."

"Tough."

Brandt groaned and shook his head. "Now, you're giving me a headache," he muttered while turning frustrated. "I have to go. We'll talk later."

"We'll talk if I feel like it," she informed him.

"I can't believe you're mad at me," Brandt remarked, then shook his head and groaned. "I have to go."

As Brandt headed for his truck parked on the opposite end of the house near the kitchen, Mazie leaned on Blackjack's back and watched him until he drove away. She shook her head, completely frustrated with that man. Mazie looked at the horse still wearing its bridle and made a decision. She swung up on the horse, bareback, and rode away from the barn.

*F*ifteen minutes later, Mazie found herself at the old homestead. She sat under the massive tree while holding the horse's reins, letting him graze alongside her. Mazie slipped into her own world, reviewing her entire life in a few minutes, and it was enough to make her cry. She wasn't sure how long she sat there and cried while the horse gently nudged her, possibly confused about what was happening. She affectionately nuzzled the horse, attempting to control her emotions.

"I'm okay, Blackjack," she whispered to the horse.

Mazie recalled the way she felt that day when Brandt gave her Blackjack. A strange feeling swept over her. She suddenly realized she'd been trying to be someone she wasn't to escape who she was. All her happiest childhood memories came flooding back to her, and they all had one thing in common. It was in that moment when the ending to her book suddenly hit her. Mazie practically leapt to her feet.

"That's it," she announced to the horse. "I know how the story ends." Mazie smiled and wiped the tears from her eyes. "Come on, Blackjack." She swung onto the horse's back. "We have a book to finish."

Chapter 58

*W*hen Mazie returned from her ride to the old homestead, she finished her assignment for Davenport in under an hour, silenced her phone, and retreated to her bedroom. She spent the rest of the afternoon completing the ending for her book. Mazie had never typed so fast in her entire life. The words just came to her in a never-ending tidal wave. Several hours had passed, but she hadn't even been aware of the time. She finally sat back in her chair and typed the last two words. The end. Before she even had time to think about it, Mazie emailed a PDF file of the final chapters to Andi's friend. She stared at her laptop for a long moment, feeling oddly free and full of energy. She was still riding the high she felt while typing those last few chapters. All she could think about was wishing Brandt had been there with her to share this moment.

Unfortunately, the moment didn't last. Mazie checked her phone and saw she'd missed several text messages and phone calls from Davenport, two texts from Peter, two texts from Andi, and a phone call from Brandt. Brandt had left a voicemail. Without giving it a second thought, she checked Brandt's voicemail first.

"Hey, Mazie," Brandt announced, seemingly fumbling over his words. "I, uh, just wanted to say I'm sorry for my, well, behavior this afternoon. I won't apologize for my feelings about Peter after what he did to you, but it's, well, not my place to act like the jealous boyfriend. If it'll make you happy, I'll even apologize to Peter for popping him in the mouth. I love you too much to spend another five years without being able to talk to you. I hope you can forgive me."

Mazie stared at her phone for a long moment before drawing a deep breath and raking her fingers through her hair. Once she recovered from Brandt's heartfelt voicemail, she checked her text messages from Andi. Mazie stared at the first text left by Andi. Her friend loved the book's ending! The second text stated that her friend passed the manuscript along to a friend at a publishing house. The fate of her book remained uncertain, but it was one step closer to being published. Once she came down from her high, she read Peter's text messages. The first was an apology for his behavior, and the second was that he'd return to the ranch around seven o'clock. Mazie checked the time and saw that it was almost seven. She shoved her phone in her pocket and hurried from her room.

By the time Mazie passed through the entire house and stepped onto the porch, Peter was already pulling up to the house. As he got out of his car, Mazie crossed the porch and stood at the top of the steps.

"Sorry," she announced. "I just got your messages a few minutes ago. I had my phone on 'silence'."

Peter headed up the steps and joined her on the porch. "That's okay," he replied. "I thought it was best to come back and apologize in person."

"You really don't have any reason to apologize," Mazie informed him.

"Well, I'm glad we can both agree that Brandt was the instigator," Peter remarked somewhat casually.

"Actually, Brandt's reaction came from a place of caring," Mazie informed him. "I can't fault him for wanting to protect me. He's been protecting me most of my life."

"I suppose when you put it that way--" Peter remarked, then managed a smile and shrugged. "He'll just have to get over the way he feels. It's not as if he has any say in who you go out with, and once we're back in LA--"

Mazie offered a sympathetic smile. "Earlier today, after the thing between you and Brandt, I had an epiphany of sorts," she announced somewhat delicately. "I'm not going back to LA. My home is here, and I've already stayed away too long."

"What about your job?" Peter asked, slightly surprised by her words.

Mazie shrugged and managed a tiny, humored smile. "Davenport has told me many times that I can be replaced," she replied casually. "He'll find someone else to do my job."

Peter considered what she was saying, then suddenly smiled. "This could work," he announced. "I was thinking about forming my own company for a couple of years now, and here would be the perfect place. I could buy a place for what my rent costs in LA." His grin then increased. "You could come work for me as my assistant. All you need to do is switch gears from movie production to advertising. You'd be a natural."

"Actually," Mazie remarked. "Brandt's already offered me a position here at the ranch."

Peter's disappointment was a little too obvious. "You're going back to being a wrangler?" he asked, then fumbled over his words. "I mean, it's not exactly the most high-profile, glamorous job."

"I never wanted high-profile or glamorous," Mazie reminded him.

"Maybe we're getting a little ahead of ourselves," Peter remarked, then resumed smiling as he placed his hands on hers. "Before either of us commits to anything, how about I stay a few more weeks, and we can see where our relationship goes?"

Mazie smiled weakly while patting Peter's hands before pulling away from him. "Five years ago, I would have loved to hear that," she informed him. "But there's really no future for us. We were never really compatible."

Peter's expression suddenly dropped at her words. "How can you say that?" he asked, genuinely surprised. He hesitated only a moment, then turned defensive. "It's that whole Hannah thing, isn't it? Brandt managed to turn you against me, didn't he? Bringing up that whole incident in the barn at your graduation party." He shook his head, now angry. "He can't accept that I changed and threw Hannah and me having sex in the barn in your face just to turn you against me."

Mazie's expression suddenly dropped. "Wait, what?" she asked as horror crossed her face. "He caught you and Hannah having *sex* in the barn?"

"Of course," Peter replied, somewhat baffled. "You were there when he hit me."

"I didn't know he caught you two having *sex*," Mazie proclaimed, still shocked. "I thought he caught the two of you kissing. He never said anything about catching you having sex!"

Peter seemed at a loss for words, realizing the whole thing was about to blow up in his face.

"No wonder he was furious about us possibly getting together," Mazie scoffed, now angry. "You were screwing Hannah while making plans to share a bed with me in Australia!"

"Give me a break, Mazie," Peter launched back in response. "I was eighteen, and you were just a farm girl back then."

"Just a farm girl?" she launched in anger. "Oh, so you're only interested now because I dress and act like a lady, huh?"

"Some of us do find that more appealing," Peter explained. "I mean, dressing and acting like one of the boys will only get you so far."

"But that wasn't going to stop you from sharing a bed with me in Australia, huh?" she scoffed.

"That's different," Peter reported.

"How?"

"I was eighteen," Peter again cried out. "I wanted to see you in a bikini. Can you fault me for that? What do you want from me, Mazie? I was willing to give you a shot. Isn't that the important part?"

"In other words, you were going to use me as your personal plaything and then cast me aside when we got back home."

"I was going away to college," Peter reminded her. "You knew it wasn't going to turn into anything serious."

"You were supposed to be my friend," she shouted back. "You don't fuck over your friends."

Colt suddenly appeared on the porch with a wildly unpredictable look while glaring at Peter. "What did you do to Mazie?" he demanded.

"Nothing," Peter cried out defensively. "It was five years ago! Everything has changed since then!"

"Nothing has changed," Mazie snapped back. "You're still the same asshole you were back then, and I wish Brandt were here to chase you off his property."

"Got you covered," Colt announced and removed Brandt's baseball bat from behind the swing. He glared at Peter while raising the bat. "You've outstayed your welcome, boy."

Peter's eyes widened as he stared at the baseball bat and the evil, twisted look in Colt's eyes. Peter quickly turned, hurried down the porch steps, and just about ran for his car. Mazie and Colt watched Peter burn out in the driveway and race out of sight. Colt shamefully shook his head.

"You were actually friends with that asshole?" Colt asked.

"Not for a long time," Mazie replied, then managed a tiny laugh. "You know, telling him off actually felt pretty good."

"That's because I raised you right," Colt announced with a chuckle while placing his arm around her shoulder as he pulled her close.

$\mathcal{R}$ather than returning Davenport's phone calls or text messages, Mazie went out in search of her boss. She found him talking with the director, not far from his office trailer. When he spotted Mazie, he motioned for her to come over. She approached and waited in silence until he was finished talking with the director. Davenport then indicated that she should walk with him to his trailer.

"Did you lose your phone again?" he teased sarcastically.

"No," Mazie replied. "I was in the middle of something and didn't want to be disturbed."

Davenport turned to face her just outside his trailer and eyed her. "I'll be happy when we get back to our regular routine," he announced, then shook his head. "I like you better when you're dependable and punctual." Davenport then eyed her suspiciously. "What was so important that you blew me off?"

Mazie handed him an envelope. "My letter of resignation," she replied, possibly a little too cheerfully, but couldn't help herself.

Davenport stared at the envelope a moment with his mouth hanging open, then looked back at her. He clearly wasn't expecting that response. He attempted to return the envelope.

"I'm not accepting it," he informed her with little emotion. "I can't function without you."

"I can be replaced," Mazie reminded him, taking great pride in using the same line on him that he used on her many times in the past.

Davenport glared at her, not humored. "You know I'm a difficult man to work for," he remarked. "I throw tantrums when I don't get my way, and I order you around like a drill sergeant. But our relationship works. I could replace you, but I'd be a fool if I did." He stared at her a moment longer. When she didn't say anything, he continued. "You want a raise? I'll give you a raise *and* a bonus."

Mazie smiled and shook her head. "It's not about the money," she informed him.

Davenport suddenly smiled. "I'll give you two extra weeks' vacation, and you can use my private jet," he announced. "Anywhere you want to go."

"You do realize this is all on you," Mazie casually informed him.

Davenport frowned, disgusted with himself. "I know, I'm a schmuck," he muttered.

"Well, you kind of are," she remarked while nodding. "But you're the one who forced me back here. Now, I don't want to leave."

Davenport groaned and leaned against his trailer. "Do I at least get two weeks' notice?"

"I'm afraid not," Mazie replied. "I can handle a few things from here to help you out until you find my replacement, but I'm not leaving."

He maintained his frown and shook his head. "I'm sorry I was such a schmuck, Mazie," Davenport announced. "And I'm going to miss having you around." He sighed and shrugged. "But there is some part of me that would like to see you happy."

"Thank you," Mazie replied, offering a warm smile. "If you're interested, I may have a suggestion that would benefit us both."

Davenport cocked his head and smiled, intrigued. "I'm listening."

"Tina wants to be an actress," Mazie reminded him. "She should be living in LA. If she worked for a producer, she's one step closer to her dream, and the pay is better than what she's making now."

Davenport considered her suggestion and smiled almost deviously. "I think she might work," he remarked. "She was pretty efficient assisting me this last week."

"I guarantee she'd be thrilled for the opportunity," Mazie announced. "And if she thinks you're letting me go to hire her, she'd jump at the offer."

"You really think so?"

"Oh, I'm pretty sure."

"That's a wonderful suggestion," Davenport replied, then eyed her almost suspiciously. "You said hiring her would benefit us both. What would you get out of me hiring her?"

"I get rid of Tina."

Davenport stared at Mazie a moment while considering the comment. He suddenly smiled and chuckled. "I never knew you were so devious," he remarked. "That makes me miss you even more. I'll take your advice and talk to Tina about it first thing tomorrow morning when she stops by to help us pack up."

"Just do me a favor," Mazie remarked. "Don't tell anyone I quit just yet. I want to tell my family myself tomorrow morning at breakfast."

"I won't say a word," Davenport promised, then smiled warmly. "I *am* going to miss you, Mazie."

When he opened his arms to her, Mazie was a little reluctant but accepted the hug.

"Be happy," he whispered near her ear.

"I will be."

Chapter 59

Mazie sat on the front porch waiting for Brandt to return home until nearly eleven o'clock that night before finally giving up and going to bed. About an hour after she'd gone to bed, above the relentless buzzing of the generators, Mazie was sure she'd heard a truck pull up to the house. She was immediately wide awake, almost positive it was Brandt returning. Mazie looked at her bedside clock and saw it was midnight. She jumped out of bed and approached her bedroom window. Although she had a clear view of the barn, she couldn't see where the truck would have parked. Mazie wasn't sure if it had actually been Brandt, but she did hear a truck door close. In her tank top and sleep shorts, Mazie left her bedroom, hoping to catch him at the front door. When she reached the hallway, she heard someone already moving around on the second floor.

Not wanting to wake Uncle Colt or Davenport, Mazie quickly but quietly climbed the stairs and pattered down the second floor hallway. Through the partially open bedroom door, she saw a light on within Brandt's room. He rarely closed his door out of habit. Mazie paused by the partially open door and peered inside while lightly tapping on the doorframe. Brandt had been emptying his pockets onto his dresser when she knocked. He jumped with some surprise, not expecting anyone to be up, and shut his father's trinket box.

"I thought you were in bed," Brandt remarked, attempting to keep his voice down so he wouldn't wake his uncle.

"I was," Mazie informed him. "But I couldn't sleep. I wanted to wait up for you."

"You didn't have to do that," Brandt announced with a warm yet weary smile. "I'm taking the morning off. I didn't intend to let you leave without saying goodbye. We can talk in the morning."

"I appreciate that," Mazie replied while smiling timidly. "Actually, I thought if you intended to watch something on TV before falling asleep, that maybe I could stay with you for a little while. Like when we were kids."

Brandt maintained his smile but shook his head. "We're not kids anymore, Mazie," he gently reminded her. "The last time we tried to recreate childhood memories, I fucked up, and it made you leave." He drew a deep, shallow breath, then groaned and aggressively ran his fingers through his hair, now unable to look at her. "And that whole fight with Peter--" Brandt looked at her and again shook his head. "I can't seem to do anything right when it comes to you." He let his hands fall to his sides. "I guess you're right. I'm jealous, possessive, and controlling. I wish I could turn off my feelings for you, but I can't." Brandt groaned softly and rubbed his eyes. "I'm too tired to have this conversation. I'm liable to say something stupid like I did five years ago and lose you forever."

Mazie stared at the defeated and broken man standing before her for a long moment before finally speaking. "The last thing I want to do is fight with you," she gently announced while entering his room. "And I'm not going to." Mazie hesitated, then glanced at the hallway, reconsidering leaving the door open. She shut the door and then looked back at Brandt. "Everything you just said, you got completely backwards." She drew a deep breath while staring at him as he attempted to figure out what she meant by that. "It was never you. I was the problem five years ago, and I'm the problem now."

Brandt eyed her somewhat suspiciously, possibly thinking it was some sort of elaborate trick.

"I had a lot of time while you were gone this evening to think about things," she informed him. "Particularly what I wrote about that night. *I* initiated what happened between us and then blamed you for not feeling as ashamed as I felt." Mazie took a step closer to him and gently touched his face while staring into his eyes. "I'm sorry for the way I treated you after *my* 'morning of regret', and I'm sorry for everything I put you through every day since then."

Brandt remained somewhat dumbfounded while removing her hand from his face and clasping it in his. "I don't know how I'm supposed to react," he remarked, then smirked slyly. "You've never admitted to being wrong about anything before."

Mazie groaned while rolling her eyes and attempted to pull her hand away, but he refused to release it. "That's what I get for trying to be serious with you," she muttered.

Brandt chuckled, then warmly kissed the back of her hand without taking his eyes off hers. She couldn't deny the action gave her a tiny thrill. He casually guided her hand to his shoulder, then gently pulled her into his arms and held her tightly against him. Mazie instinctively clung to him, placing her head on his shoulder, and didn't attempt to pull away. Brandt groaned softly while nuzzling her hair during their marathon embrace. Mazie's eyes suddenly popped open, although she didn't lift her head from his shoulder.

"Is that--?"

Brandt chuckled close to her ear. "It certainly is," he announced. "Spontaneous reaction to telling a man he's right."

When she felt his hand slip from her waist and firmly caress her backside, Mazie lifted her head and met his gaze, although not attempting to fight the action.

"And your hand on my ass?" she asked while raising an arrogant brow.

"Actually," he announced slyly. "The more important question is, why haven't you removed it?"

Mazie returned her head to his shoulder without releasing him and sighed. "Because it makes you happy," she replied. "Consider it a late birthday present."

Brandt groaned as his hands firmly caressed her back and buttocks while holding her tightly against him. "Fine, you win," he announced close to her ear. "You're allowed in my room just this once to watch a movie with me."

Mazie could almost feel his cheap grin, but kept her head on his shoulder while hiding her own smile. "Do you plan on humping me throughout the whole movie?" she asked.

"Probably," he replied, matter-of-factly, then sighed almost dramatically. "I'm afraid, it's a risk you'll have to take."

"I'll risk it," she whispered while removing her head from his shoulder, allowing her hands to slide down his chest, and meeting his gaze.

With a hand still firmly on her buttocks, Brandt stared at her, somewhat stunned by the response, then indicated the bathroom. "I'm, uh, just going to take a quick shower," he informed her, almost reluctant to release her. "Only if you promise not to leave."

Mazie patted his chest while pulling away from him, then headed for the door as he watched, now disappointed. She turned the old-fashioned key in the lock, locking the door, then handed him the key and smiled.

"I'll be right here," she insisted, then headed to the bed and jumped on it the way she used to when they were kids.

Brandt grinned, clutched the key, and headed into the bathroom. This time, when he didn't close the door, Mazie knew why, and she was sure it was for the same reason he didn't shut it last Friday as well. It was an unspoken invitation, except Mazie wasn't sure she was ready for a couple's shower. Not that it mattered, since he was only gone for a few minutes. Brandt apparently set some sort of quick shower record, barely taking time to dry off as he emerged from the slightly steamy bathroom. Mazie took a moment to watch him patter across the floor with just a towel wrapped around his waist. He dropped the wet key on the dresser, possibly taking it into the shower with him, then opened a drawer and removed a pair of boxer briefs. He looked at her almost quizzically.

"Underwear optional?"

Mazie eyed him, raising a skeptical brow.

"Fuck it," he declared, casting them back into the drawer. "I'm sleeping commando tonight."

Brandt then pattered toward the bed in his towel. As he unbound the towel from his waist, Mazie looked back at the television, avoiding the 'free show'.

"It's not anything you haven't seen before," Brandt teased before dropping the towel and climbing into bed.

"Actually," she announced. "I hadn't **seen** anything. I wasn't exactly looking *at the time*."

Brandt maintained the grin that seemed permanently chiseled on his face as he turned out the light and then slipped partway beneath the covers. With possibly the most playful look she'd ever seen, he patted the spot on the bed beside him. Mazie was slightly apprehensive. Brandt's testosterone hung thick in the air. It was both frightening and exciting. Every sexual desire she had that night five years ago came rushing back to her, and, for some reason, she desperately wanted to feel that way again. Mazie didn't understand what she was thinking or feeling at that moment. It was as if her heart and brain were at war with each other, fighting for control. Meanwhile, a little, evil voice whispered hopes that she'd get pregnant so she'd surrender the fight and never leave. Was that how she really felt? Wait. Wasn't Brandt naming their children what had sent her into panic mode five years ago? Perhaps it took her five years to catch up to where he was that day.

"If you're uncomfortable," Brandt announced in a soft, gentle tone, bringing her back to reality. "I'll put some shorts on."

Mazie felt herself blush at the comment, then moved onto her knees, sitting on her feet alongside him. She drew a deep breath while placing her hands on his face.

"Five years ago," Mazie remarked softly, then hesitated. "After I *gave* myself to you, I thought I was broken. I wasn't even interested in dating other guys these last five years. I felt nothing. I blamed you, and I blamed me. But when I saw you, after all that time, riding up on Blackjack--" She drew a deep, shaken breath. "I realized I wasn't broken at all. There was just a piece missing. *You* were that missing piece. I just needed *you* to make me whole again."

Without warning, Brandt grabbed Mazie by the back of the neck and pulled her halfway to him, kissing her with a sense of urgency. He broke off the kiss almost as quickly and attempted to wipe away a stray tear without her noticing.

"Sorry," he whispered while avoiding looking at her and hiding his smile. "*That* was unavoidable."

Mazie lifted the covers and climbed on top of him, straddling his hips. "So is this," she announced as she slipped out of her tank top and tossed it to the floor.

Brandt immediately groaned while pulling her against him and kissed her with raw aggression. As she returned the aggressive kiss with her own urgency, Brandt's hands feverishly traveled her body, unable to make up his mind where to go first. Mazie writhed against his body, enjoying his traveling hands, savoring every touch. She broke off their kiss and pushed him against the headboard, just about pinning him. A wicked smile crossed her face.

"Teach me all the ways to please you, cowboy."

Brandt groaned while firmly caressing her backside, unable to hide his pleased smile. "Yes, ma'am."

*A*round four o'clock in the morning, Mazie woke to Brandt nuzzling her naked body from behind beneath the covers. He warmly kissed her bare shoulder while gently caressing her side. His movements were purposeful, avoiding all her erogenous zones. Without knowing how she was feeling after their aggressive lovemaking, he wanted to prevent a repeat of their first and only time five years ago. Mazie placed her hand over his, acknowledging she was awake. Brandt kissed his way closer to her neck.

"Good morning," he whispered close to her ear, then seemed apprehensive. "It *is* a good morning, isn't it?"

Mazie could almost feel him holding his breath, his guard remaining up. She knew his anxiety was entirely founded and mostly her fault. She nearly broke him with her insecurities five years ago, but she could still fix that. Mazie guided his hand to her breast, then caressed his arm. Brandt groaned and immediately fondled her as he eagerly kissed her neck with a little more conviction.

"It's not morning yet," she cooed softly and moved her backside closer to his naked body, pressing against him while feeling his morning arousal. "Want to make it a *great* morning?"

"Oh, yeah," he groaned softly in her ear, then immediately seized the opportunity he was offered.

Chapter 60

Mazie woke again around five o'clock that morning, feeling mostly exhausted and pleasantly sore. When she turned over in Brandt's bed, she wasn't surprised that he was already gone. It was time to feed and saddle the horses. Even though he said he was taking the morning off, he was still expected to prepare the horses for the wranglers unless other arrangements had been made. Mazie dressed and headed downstairs to make her tea and start coffee for Brandt and her uncles. Since her tea was ready first, she took her tea mug and headed onto the porch. She nestled on the porch swing, sipped her tea, and periodically glanced at the barn with its inside lights on. There wasn't much point in helping Brandt, since he was probably almost finished and would be heading back to the house soon enough. While sitting on the swing, enjoying her tea, she heard one of the trailer doors.

Half expecting to see Melissa slipping out to join her, possibly unable to sleep, instead, she saw her Uncle Colt ducking out of Sandra's trailer. Mazie's expression dropped as she watched her uncle heading away from the trailer with a huge, telltale grin on his face. Halfway to the house, he saw Mazie and suddenly looked like a deer caught in headlights. Colt attempted an emotionless expression, though failing miserably. He walked onto the porch while gently clearing his throat.

"It's not how it looks," Colt announced while indicating Sandra's trailer. "There was a huge cockroach in Ms. King's trailer, and I, uh--"

Mazie cocked her head while raising a brow. "You *what*, Uncle Colt?"

"Yeah, okay," Colt muttered. "It is how it looks." He then cocked his head and appeared moderately annoyed. "Don't you ever sleep late?"

Brandt approached the house and eyed Colt somewhat suspiciously. "What are you doing up so early?" he asked. "Doesn't anyone sleep in around here?"

"Uncle Colt was just helping Sandra kill a cockroach in her trailer," Mazie informed Brandt while offering a mocking smile.

"Well, when you say it like that--" Colt scoffed.

"We're all adults here, Uncle Colt," Brandt reminded him. "I just hope you used protection. I'd hate to read in the tabloids that my fifty-year-old uncle knocked up Sandra King."

Mazie had to look away to keep from laughing.

"I'm not fifty," Colt scoffed. "I'm forty-six and a half." He then considered Brandt's comment and snorted a laugh. "That would be quite the scandal, though, huh?"

"Yes, it certainly would be," Brandt remarked.

"There's coffee in the kitchen," Mazie informed Colt. "In case you need a little pick-me-up after your late-night exterminator call."

"Actually, I'd rather get that extra hour of sleep," Colt remarked. "It was a long night, you know, *exterminating*."

His grin increased as he passed them and entered the house. "Exterminating. That's a good one."

Brandt collapsed onto the swing alongside Mazie while shaking his head. "Can you explain to me how *that* happened?" he asked. "I mean, it's a pretty broad leap from me to Uncle Colt, don't you think?"

"I have a theory, but you're not going to like it," Mazie remarked.

Brandt gave her a sideways look. "Maybe you shouldn't tell--"

"You and Uncle Colt are pretty similar," Mazie informed him.

Brandt frowned, almost disgusted. "I asked you not to tell me," he groaned. "You're kind of killing my good mood."

"Sorry," Mazie replied with a humored smile. "I think Sandra was more attracted to the whole cowboy thing. She probably never met an authentic cowboy, and I wouldn't doubt it turned her on a little. You turned her down, so she went to the next best thing."

"I'm not sure you're making me feel better," Brandt informed her.

"Well, what woman doesn't fantasize about cowboys?" Mazie remarked.

Brandt grinned. "Okay, hearing you say that makes me feel a little better," he announced.

"How about some coffee?" she asked while offering a warm smile.

"I should probably opt for a shower instead," Brandt remarked. "I'm guessing I'm three ways to gross by now."

"I can't say I noticed," Mazie replied.

Brandt chuckled while standing, then glanced at her. "I could easily make it a shower for two," he informed her almost timidly, still attempting to gauge her reaction.

Mazie smiled and jumped off the swing. "I think I could use a shower myself."

Brandt stared at her a moment, then groaned softly. "Then I should get you upstairs before you change your mind."

When he extended his hand to her, Mazie immediately clasped it.

"No, I pretty much made up my mind," she replied. "My boss is taking off this morning, which means so am I, so I have all the time in the world."

Brandt stared at her a moment, then suddenly smiled. "You're not talking about Davenport, are you?"

"I'm pretty sure he stopped being my boss late yesterday afternoon," she assured him. "That is--if the offer is still open."

"That offer has been on the table for five years," Brandt informed her, then pulled her into his arms and held her as if he'd never let go. "And I thought I was happy last night. This day just keeps getting better and better." He pulled away just far enough to kiss her warmly on the lips. "I'll admit, I was a little nervous about how you'd feel this morning, you know, about us. About last night." He then groaned, almost ashamed. "And I was pretty bold that second time."

Mazie affectionately caressed his chest while meeting his gaze. "Can I tell you a little secret?"

His grin cheapened. "I wish you would."

"You're really great in bed," Mazie informed him. "And being bold makes you that much better."

Brandt groaned, then chuckled while clinging to her. "I don't care if you don't have anything to compare me with; that makes me feel really good." He then appeared apprehensive. "Since you're okay with a little bold--"

Mazie noted how he fidgeted and offered an encouraging smile. "What is it?" she asked. "We don't have secrets from each other."

Brandt smiled with a little embarrassment. "Could you maybe wear that dress and those high heels, you know, just once, sometime in *private*? I didn't get any sleep fantasizing about you that night."

Mazie grinned and giggled while patting his chest. "I'll wear that for you, only if you wear your cowboy boots, hat, and nothing else for me."

Brandt chuckled while firmly caressing her backside. "Yes, ma'am."

Mazie groaned softly while clinging to him. "You'd better take me upstairs," she cooed. "I'm really looking forward to that shower."

Brandt could barely contain his grin while herding her toward the door. He then glanced at her as they headed into the house.

"Can I tell your boss you're quitting?"

"Sorry, I already told him," she informed him.

"When did you do that?" he asked, now curious.

"Yesterday afternoon," she replied. "After I took Blackjack out for a ride when you left."

Brandt suddenly groaned. "I knew you wanted that horse back," he muttered, then sighed with defeat. "I suppose we can work something out."

Chapter 61

Breakfast that morning was oddly uncomfortable. Mazie was dying to tell everyone she'd be staying at the ranch to be with Brandt, but Brandt didn't want to reveal their change in relationship status until after the circus left town. She understood Brandt's reasoning. He was a private guy and didn't want to blast their relationship in front of a bunch of people he barely knew. Since that was the case, they wouldn't tell her mom and uncles until they came back later that afternoon. At least she could tell them that she wouldn't be returning to Los Angeles. There was no way to hide that, since she wouldn't be leaving when Davenport left. Mazie waited until everyone was done eating and stopped them from getting up.

"I have an announcement to make," Mazie informed those at the table, gaining their undivided attention. "After serious consideration, I've accepted Brandt's job offer, and I'm moving back home."

Colt slapped his hand on the table, vibrating the silverware. "Hallelujah!"

Dalton applauded while Liddy jumped up from her chair, hugging and kissing Mazie. Once she finished with Mazie, she hugged and kissed Brandt.

"Now, before everyone gets too excited," Brandt announced, immediately alarming everyone. "There are a few changes that go along with that deal. I promised Mazie a nicer room with a view, so we'll be renovating my mother's bedroom, and Mazie will be staying in that room." He then smiled at Liddy and Dalton. "And we'll be converting the in-law suite into the aunt and uncle suite in time for the newlyweds."

Dalton placed his hand on Liddy's while they exchanged sly grins.

"Now," Brandt announced. "If everyone approves of the new arrangements, I'd like to take this little family meeting onto the front porch. Davenport gave me a bottle of champagne, and I want us to toast the circus leaving town." He then stood. "So let's forget about the dishes for now, grab some champagne glasses, and meet on the porch for a much-anticipated farewell."

Colt stood, eyed Brandt, and grinned. "If we're doing morning drinking, I may need to call off the rest of the day," he remarked.

"Way ahead of you," Brandt replied, returning the smile. "I've already instructed the guys that they'd have to get by without us today."

Brandt grabbed the bottle of champagne from the refrigerator while Dalton handed out the champagne glasses from the top shelf of the cupboard. Liddy was quick to wipe the dust from them, as they were rarely used. Mazie and Brandt remained in the kitchen as the others headed into the hallway toward the front porch. She looked at Brandt and drew a deep, tense breath.

"Nervous?" Brandt asked.

"Just a touch of anxiety," she replied while releasing her breath. "You know what Uncle Colt's first words are going to be, don't you?"

"Yeah," Brandt replied. "Did you use protection, boy?"

Mazie's eyes widened as she stared at him. "That's scary," she gasped. "You sounded just like him."

"After Uncle Colt makes it awkward for two minutes, it'll be fine after that," Brandt assured her, then smiled as he leaned down and warmly kissed her.

"If you did *that*, we wouldn't even have to tell them," Mazie remarked. "They'd figure it out on their own."

"Well, maybe we'll improvise," Brandt teased, then guided her toward the hallway entrance.

*B*randt and Mazie joined Colt, Dalton, and Liddy on the front porch, where Brandt popped the champagne cork and filled all five glasses, leaving them on the small table for the grand exodus. Brandt impatiently looked at his watch and the lack of movement from the parking lot located in his pasture. The relentless buzzing of generators had ceased, but there wasn't much happening.

"I thought you said eight o'clock sharp?" Colt muttered to Mazie.

"Well, in their defense, I'm not chasing after them, keeping them on schedule," she remarked.

"You mean your ogre of a boss has to organize everything himself?" Liddy remarked, surprising the guys with her name-calling.

"Oh, I don't think that's the case," Mazie muttered under her breath, then secretly smiled when she saw Tina scurrying around the field among the trailers while teetering on her stiletto heels.

Tina was probably on the job at least two hours, and she already looked frazzled. When she saw them on the porch, something made her stop, and she took a moment to cross the driveway and approach them. Despite appearing already worn out, Tina gave Mazie a fake sympathetic look.

"Oh, Mazie," Tina announced, her smugness creeping through. "I'm sorry you lost your job."

"That's okay, Tina," Mazie replied while grinning. "I'm pretty sure I'll bounce back--in time."

Brandt and Colt exchanged grins and had to keep from laughing.

"Honestly, I'm happy for you, Tina," Mazie announced while attempting not to sound too cheerful. "You're getting everything you deserve."

Liddy bit her lower lip to keep a straight face. When Dalton leaned closer and whispered something, Liddy giggled uncontrollably. Tina gave them strange looks, then headed back to the chaotic scene in the pasture. Only a moment later, Melissa's car flew up the driveway faster than usual. The moment the car stopped, Melissa and Malcolm got out. Malcolm must have spent the night at Melissa's apartment, and he was running late. Luckily for him, so was the production company. Malcolm waved to everyone on the porch before hurrying to join the production team. Melissa was smiling a little too much, considering how broken up she was yesterday. Malcolm must have given her one hell of a goodbye to make her that happy. Melissa hurried onto the porch and just about jumped on Mazie.

"You aren't going to believe it," Melissa practically cried out.

"Believe what?" Mazie asked.

"If it's a shotgun wedding," Colt announced. "I've got you covered. I just need to get a few shells."

"No, nothing like that," Melissa scolded Colt, then eyed him suspiciously before looking back at Mazie. "Is he drunk?"

Mazie glanced at Colt and saw him taking a swig from his flask. She looked back at Melissa and shrugged.

"It's possible," Mazie replied. "Brandt gave them the day off for the farewell parade."

"Did you want to join us?" Dalton asked Melissa. "I'll get a glass for you."

"Get me a whole bottle," Melissa informed him while maintaining her grin. "I have the day off, and I feel like getting plastered."

"You go, girl!" Colt cried out while raising his flask, then took a swig.

"So?" Mazie asked her friend, now dying of curiosity. "What won't I believe?"

Melissa grabbed Mazie's shoulders and could barely contain her enthusiasm.

"Malcolm is going back to college," Melissa announced. "He's getting his degree in forensic medicine."

"What?" Mazie gasped, surprised.

"He's quitting acting after this movie," Melissa informed her. "After he promotes the film this fall, he starts his college classes." She appeared ready to burst. "He's buying a house twenty minutes outside of town and attending college only an hour from here. *I* inspired *him*. Can you believe it? He wants to see where our relationship leads us."

"Oh, my God!" Mazie cried out and happily hugged her friend. "That's wonderful!"

"I can't wait to give a big 'fuck you' to Tina!" Melissa cried out.

"Well, you'd better do it fast," Mazie informed her, then nodded to the trailers. "Because she's leaving with Davenport and my job."

"What?" Melissa asked, somewhat shocked. A smile suddenly crossed her face. "Are you staying? Tell me you're staying!"

"I'm staying," Mazie replied.

Melissa squealed and happily hugged her. "This is the best day of my life!"

"Yeah, mine too," Mazie replied, then looked back at Brandt and smiled.

Brandt moved off the porch railing and straightened. "Well, this show could take a while to get going," he remarked. "I should probably unsaddle our horses. We could be here a while."

"Want me to help?" Mazie asked as he approached her and Melissa by the steps.

"No," Brandt replied with a warm smile. "I've got it. I'll only be a few minutes."

When Brandt winked at Mazie, she instantly blushed. Melissa's eyes suddenly widened, and she just about gasped as Brandt left the porch.

"Did you--?" Melissa gasped softly so the others wouldn't hear.

Mazie grinned and held up three fingers. Melissa covered her mouth to keep from squealing. She then leaned closer to her friend.

"Did you tell your family yet?" Melissa asked.

"Not yet," Mazie replied, then indicated the clattering and clunking coming from the production site. "We're waiting for the final farewell."

"I can stay, right?"

"Of course."

Melissa made herself comfortable on one of the rocking chairs while Mazie chose to sit on the railing. A few minutes passed before they finally saw Brandt appear from the barn, riding his horse and leading a second saddled horse. Everyone instinctively looked, curious about the situation since Brandt said he was unsaddling the horses. Mazie practically leapt off the railing when she saw the black and white Tobiano paint horse she had ridden during their team roping event now wearing her saddle. As Brandt rode his horse closer to the house, Mazie bolted from the porch, staring at the beautiful horse. Brandt grinned while dismounting Blackjack.

"You didn't--?" she gasped, unable to control her smile.

"I did," Brandt replied.

"At the rodeo, the owner never mentioned he was for sale," Mazie remarked while stroking the white patch on the horse's nose.

"That's because he wasn't," Brandt replied. "But I made him an offer that he couldn't resist."

"So that's where you went last night," Mazie remarked while grinning.

"We had some trailer trouble," Brandt informed her. "I originally planned on doing this yesterday evening, but I got home too late."

Brandt hesitated a moment while smiling knowingly at Mazie, then looked at their family on the porch. Mazie knew he was leading up to the news about their change in relationship status and prepared herself for the awkwardness that would follow. Mazie was almost certain they would be happy about it, considering the trouble they had gone through to bring her back to the ranch.

"As everyone well knows, these past two weeks have been an emotional roller coaster for Mazie and me," Brandt informed them. "Happily, Mazie and I got past our issues and reformed our bond." He then turned to Mazie. "Mazie, you were a sister to me when I was a boy, and you were my best friend as a teenager. Now, as adults, I want you to be my partner." He got down on one knee and held up the horse's reins. "My partner for life. Will you marry me, Mazie?"

There were several gasps from those on the porch, except for Liddy, who grabbed Dalton's hand and squeezed it almost hard enough to make him yelp while she held her breath, waiting for the response. Mazie could barely contain her smile and even laughed a little.

"Yes, Brandt," she replied. "I'll marry you."

Brandt leapt to his feet and pulled her into his arms, kissing her without hesitation. Dalton and Colt applauded while Liddy and Melissa screamed excitedly. When Brandt released Mazie, he handed her the horse's reins, which she happily accepted.

"Oh," Brandt then remarked and fumbled in his pocket, producing a ring. "There's a ring too."

Mazie saw his mother's engagement ring and almost cried as he placed it on her finger. She threw her arm around his neck and kissed him quickly but passionately on the lips. She pulled away just far enough to meet his gaze.

"Ironically, this is exactly how I ended my book," Mazie informed him.

Brandt brushed his lips past hers while grinning. "I'm already looking forward to the sequel."

He attempted to kiss her again, but they were swarmed by the four from the porch, wanting to congratulate them. After they had a toast with warm champagne, Mazie checked out the horse, barely able to contain her giddiness over the gorgeous animal.

"I can't believe you went back and bought him for me," Mazie remarked.

"I could tell you were in love the moment you saw him," Brandt insisted. "And I desperately wanted you to look at me that way."

Mazie eyed Brandt and smiled. "I always have," she replied.

Brandt couldn't resist stealing another kiss, then pulled away, attempting to conceal the tears in his eyes. He patted the horse's neck to avoid looking at her.

"Yeah, I guess my days of winning races against you are probably over," Brandt announced with a sigh. "This boy is one hell of a horse."

Mazie tossed the reins over the horse's neck, then eyed Brandt and smiled. "Well, we'll have to test that, now, won't we?"

As Mazie jumped onto her horse, Brandt swiftly mounted his and both took off across the field, waving farewell to Davenport Productions, although it was possible Brandt gave a one-finger salute.

The End

Other books by Holly Copella!
Reviews left on Amazon are appreciated!

"The Battle for Andrea Maria"

A cruise ship attack turns six survivors into overnight celebrities after they take credit for the heroic act of a stowaway who died saving them.

The cruise is just what Jess needed--a bit of harmless fun far from her daily grind. But what begins as a relaxing vacation turns into a desperate fight for her life when terrorists take over the ship and start piling up bodies. Teaming up with a mysterious stowaway, Jess attempts to send out a distress call but knows they cannot wait for help to come. If she or the few remaining passengers have any hope for survival, Jess must act now. The papers dub it "The Battle for *Andrea Maria*," but to Jess it is the moment she fought side-by-side with her enigmatic Romeo, saving the ship--and losing him. She thinks the story ends there, but really, the nightmare is just beginning...

"Insanely Deadly"

When the dead return to life, it's up to an admiral's daughter and a mildly insane, former war hero to save their small town.

Jetta Cross, a Navy Admiral's daughter, is tasked with keeping her father's comrade, a former war hero turned town crazy, grounded in the real world. Capt. John Hunter is still fighting the war in his head, where imaginary dead people are part of his world. When a viral outbreak brings about a zombie uprising, Hunter is left to his own devices. He must resume his role as a one-man commando unit in order to destroy the ravenous undead. With Hunter still fighting his own inner demons as well as the undead, the townspeople fear their zombie neighbors may not be the only threat. Stranded at the island's luxurious resort with a handful of workers, Jetta is forced to live up to her father's reputation and take charge of the deteriorating situation at the hotel. She must wage her own war against the infected before the government declares her hometown a total loss.

"Deadly Institution"

A town recluse suspected of killing his wife teams up with a young woman in order to stop a killer.

After being accused of murdering his wife, Konrad Churchill turns his back on the town that once adored him. Ten years later, he still holds his grudge and the title of the most feared man in town. With the reopening of the burned mental institution, where his wife had died, former employees are now murdered one by one, throwing suspicion back on Churchill. A young local reporter, Jacey, is forced to reveal her long-time friendship with the infamous recluse in order to clear his name not only in the recent murders but to exonerate him in the death of his wife as well. Will Jacey's relationship with Churchill invite the killer closer to her? Or is the killer already in her life?

"Death Displacement"

A grief-stricken man travels back in time to seek revenge on the woman who murdered his girlfriend, but inadvertently falls in love with her.

Kane is about to marry the woman he loves. His life is perfect. A few weeks before the wedding, a vindictive woman from his girlfriend's past mysteriously arrives and kills her. He learns of a traumatic accident that happened five years earlier, which triggers Riley's hatred for his girlfriend. Distraught over his girlfriend's death, Kane uses an antique time machine to travel into the past in order to find and destroy the woman responsible. When he runs into Riley's younger self, he realizes she's not the monster she later becomes, and he can't bring himself to destroy her. With a little help from his oddball friend from the past, they formulate a plan to prevent the accident that sends Riley down her destructive path. Kane's plan backfires when he falls for the younger Riley. His new tortured existence is further complicated when future Riley, his girlfriend's killer, shows up with her own devious agenda that doesn't include him. Will he be able to stop the time ripple, which ultimately ends with his girlfriend's death? Or will future Riley take him out of the timeline forever--

"Dead Village"

After strange happenings isolate a small resort town from the rest of the world, nearly one hundred residents seek refuge at the closed hotel. Only eight survive the night. And that's just the beginning...

One day after the entire population of Fox Ridge Village disappears, a car wreck forces several unsuspecting crash victims to seek help at the closed summer hotel. Within the hotel, they discover the grisly aftermath of a brutal slaughter. Crash victims Vander and Devon, a reluctant clairvoyant, team up to solve the riddle of the "haunted hotel" and the mass hysteria plaguing the remaining survivors. By the time they discover the hotel's secret, they're already drawn into the hysteria. As the body count continues to climb, it's a race to isolate the source and bring everyone back to reality before they kill one another. Will Devon be able to communicate with the traumatized spirits before their fate becomes her own?

"Town Darling"

After surviving a brutal attack that claims the lives of those she loves, a young woman seeks revenge on a corrupt town.

Going back home is never easy, but for Casey, it means returning to her corrupt hometown, where she barely survived a brutal attack. Accompanied by two family friends, she seeks justice for the night that destroyed her life. Her physical scars are nothing compared to her emotional ones, forcing the local sheriff to believe that the town darling is back for revenge. As the conspiracy for her revenge appears to be leading up to the coveted town fair, the sheriff is determined to stop her from fulfilling her vengeful scheme...but guilt over his role on that fateful night continues to haunt him. Will his desperate need for Casey's forgiveness be his undoing? Or will Casey's desire for revenge destroy them both?

"Basement Dwellers"

A viral outbreak at a hospital leaves a mortician, sheriff, and coroner fighting for their lives against a horde of undead and the CDC.

After a massive car wreck leaves several survivors in critical condition at the local hospital, a surgeon uses experimental drugs on his critical patients and accidentally causes a zombie outbreak. When local mortician, Lexx, receives an infected corpse as her client, she becomes stranded in the hospital basement during CDC quarantine along with the local sheriff and the coroner. The infamous surgeon struggles to find a cure for his infectious blunder by using the other survivors as test subjects. Meanwhile, Lexx and the sheriff attempt to locate his missing sister, who's stranded somewhere in the battle zone that once was the emergency room. It's a race against time and the ravenous undead. Can they survive the undead before the CDC sanitizes the hospital of all infection?

"Misfits, Inc."

A seemingly ordinary young woman meets four misfits who claim she has given them supernatural powers.

While on a business trip to a remote island paradise, a bored secretary, Hailey, has her world turned upside down when her path collides with a psychic freak, Skyler. He attempts to convince her that they had met in his dreams, and she had chosen him as one of her four mystic warriors. After Skyler foresees a woman's death, they discover an unidentified creature has killed one of the guests. They are joined by a lounge pianist and a rich playboy, who also claim they had met her in their dreams. If Skyler's prophecies are genuine, the evil entity controlling the ravenous creatures needs to destroy Hailey to ensure its survival. Reluctantly accepting her fate, Hailey has to locate the last and most powerful of her chosen warriors, The Guardian. Their fate is in doubt when The Guardian turns out to be a self-absorbed, former cat burglar with a bad attitude. Can Hailey turn her company of misfits into an elite team of mystic warriors? Or will The Guardian's secret agenda destroy them all?

"Deadly Institution 2"

When blackmail turns into murder, a young woman finds herself caught in the killer's crosshairs.

The small town of Stony Ridge is no stranger to scandal and persecution of the innocent. When a brutal killing shakes the town's prestigious country club, Jacey McMurray seeks help from a self-proclaimed vigilante, Konrad Churchill. As her professional and personal worlds collide, Jacey fears the stress of the country club killings have finally taken their toll on Churchill. Can a stressed-out vigilante stop the killer before he strikes again?

"Witness Protection"
Also available in audiobook!

After witnessing an execution, a resourceful young woman attempts to disappear while being pursued by a hitman and a handsome federal agent.

A helicopter pilot, Jackie Remus, reluctantly agrees to go on a date with one of her clients, but her date is unexpectedly cut short when she witnesses a man being murdered. After narrowly escaping with her life, she is placed into protective custody. When the safe house is breached, Jackie makes a daring escape from both the hired killers and the handsome FBI agent, who wants to return her to protective custody. With a little help from her sly and crafty friend, Monroe, Jackie is convinced she can disappear until the trial. While on her journey to meet with her friend, she solicits help from a few shady but lovable characters along the way. Although she manages to stay one step ahead of the hired killers, the federal agent remains in hot pursuit. Will Jackie reach Monroe before she's captured by the FBI and returned to protective custody? Or will the hired killers silence her first?

"Unconditional"

A young woman puts her life on hold to care for an unstable, highly skilled combat soldier, who believes someone is trying to kill him.

A botched military coup leaves a team of elite fighters injured, with one clinging to life in a coma. When Harlan wakes from his coma, he's left with no memory of his past life. His commander's daughter, Indy, takes it upon herself to care for the fallen war hero. She's challenged with more than just his physical care as she combats with not only his memory loss but also his newly found desire for her. His infatuation with her becomes the least of her worries when he sinks back into his role of a combat soldier. Believing his life is in danger, his fighting skills emerge, transforming him into an unpredictable and dangerous man. Will his memory return to him before Indy is forced to commit him? Or will he finally find his nemesis, "the coyote", and possibly claim the life of an innocent person?

"The Pen Pal"

In order to save her friend, she must enter the mind of a serial killer.

When her best friend is abducted, no one believes Jolynn saw it in a psychic vision. With nowhere to turn, Jolynn reluctantly joins Agent Harris Slade and his team on their hunt for a sadistic serial killer known only as "The Pen Pal". Finally confronted with the killer, Jolynn realizes she must enter the mind of the psychopath in order to stop the brutal killings. But when her vision reveals a particularly disturbing death, can Jolynn sacrifice her lover for her friend?

"Witness Protection 2"
The Return of Whiskey Tango Foxtrot

Believing she holds the clue to millions in missing laundered money, a young woman is placed into the protective care of a former Navy SEAL team.

Feeling sorry for her recently separated co-worker, Leeann invites Wiley to join her and her friends on their night out. Little does she know that finding her co-worker murdered is just the beginning of her nightmare. Leeann unknowingly holds the key to fifty million dollars in potentially laundered mob money. With hired killers pursuing her, the FBI places her into a different kind of protective custody. Former Navy SEAL team Whiskey Tango Foxtrot reunites to keep Leeann alive at their secret hideaway. What should be an easy assignment takes an unscheduled turn when secrets, lies, and betrayal threaten to derail their mission. Is the team prepared for a war on their own doorstep? Will Leeann's misguided trust endanger the lives of those sent to protect her?

"Witness Protection 3"
Alpha Mike Foxtrot

A helicopter pilot risks her life to help a team of retired Navy SEALs rescue two girls from a killer.

When former Navy SEAL team Whiskey Tango Foxtrot asks for a simple favor, Jackie reluctantly offers her air-taxi services. What could go wrong? What begins as a search and rescue for two girls turns into a fight for survival against a heavily armed drug cartel. Wanted by the law with the cartel in hot pursuit and their home base breached, the team is forced to call in a favor from a questionable ally. Unfortunately, their new safe house isn't what it seems. Without knowing who the real enemy is, can Jackie and the team save their young witnesses from the hands of a killer?

"Already Dead"
Supernatural Collection

From the already dead to the undead. Three supernatural tales of "things that go bump in the night".

"Bloodletting" - A vampire-themed resort allows guests to *participate* in their Bloodletting Ritual to celebrate the island's legendary vampires.

"Reaper of Souls" - A young woman must outwit an evil sorcerer in order to save her brother or become one of his minions forever.

"Already Dead" - When Flight 220 crashes, ten passengers make it to an isolated island, but only one man lives to tell the lie.

"Witness Protection 4"
O-Dark-Hundred

A simple assignment turns deadly when a retired Navy SEAL team uncovers a plot to kill a notorious mob boss.

When Whiskey Tango Foxtrot embarks on a simple stalking case, they're not prepared for a trip to a private island paradise owned by an infamous mobster. With one of their own suffering from traumatic head injuries, the team is left scrambling to decide what is real or imagined. The situation escalates even further when they uncover an assassination plot where everyone is a suspect. Now targets themselves, can the team survive their trip to paradise?

"Witness Protection 5"
Outside the Wire

After suffering several casualties on their last assignment, a retired Navy SEAL team discovers their misery is just beginning.

When Whiskey Tango Foxtrot returns home after suffering a devastating loss, they're hit with even more bad news regarding the rest of their team. Their grief is cut short when they discover their names are all on the same hit list. Hunted by relentless assassins, the scattered team must decide whether to remain safely hidden or find the man who put the price on their heads. Against the wishes of her teammates, Jackie strikes out on her own in order to save a friend who wants her dead. In a kill-or-be-killed situation, will Jackie's emotions finally betray her?

"The Murder of Emily Fisher"

After finding their favorite teacher murdered, the lives of two teenage girls are forever changed.

Everyone loved Emily Fisher. While walking home one afternoon, two teenage girls, Sidney and Trisha, stumble upon a gruesome murder scene. The brutal murder of Emily Fisher, a young, attractive schoolteacher, shocks the small town of **Marilina**. After graduation, Sidney moves far away from the memories of the small town, while Trisha retreats deeper into denial. Eight years after the murder, Sidney receives a desperate call from her childhood friend, forcing her to return home. Trisha believes Emily's killer was falsely accused, and she manages to turn the entire town against her while attempting to prove it. When Trisha receives a death threat, Sidney realizes there may be some credibility to her friend's wild accusations. Is Trisha's mental breakdown a result of childhood trauma? Or is the real killer actually attempting to silence her? In order to save her friend, Sidney must answer the eight-year-old question. Who murdered Emily Fisher?

"Once Upon a Disaster"

A young homicide detective finds herself at the mercy of a hitman in the aftermath of an earthquake.

While investigating the murder of a hitman, Detective Jade Wesson pursues a lead connecting the dead man to a break-in at a computer programming company. She's drawn into the world of a nightclub owner and front man for the mob, Cody Riley. Her investigation continues to point to Cody's right-hand man and possible hitman, Vahn Lott. Despite her efforts to keep her investigation on track, Vahn has plans of his own for the attractive detective. When an unprecedented earthquake rocks their east coast town, Jade must put her life in Vahn's hands if she wants to survive. Can she trust a man who might be the killer she's hunting?

"Awaken the Dead"

A grieving innkeeper struggles to keep her haunted hotel out of foreclosure.

After losing her parents in a suspicious boating accident, Harley Brandon is determined to keep the family hotel out of foreclosure. Unfortunately, the hotel ghosts have other plans. Built with tainted money, the century-old Horizon Hotel thrives on a tradition of murder, scandal, and suicide. As the paranormal activity increases to alarming levels, Harley discovers the truth about the hotel and its residents. Can Harley save her friends from the hotel's frightening hidden secrets?

"Castle Bloodshed"
Murder Collection

From a deadly island paradise to haunted castles. Three novella-length tales of murder, mystery, and malicious intent.

"Castle Bloodshed" – A tour of Wesley Castle turns into a fight for survival as six stranded tourists discover the haunting secrets within the castle walls. A mystery writer teams up with an uptight butler in order to stop a killer who may already be dead. Novella-length paranormal murder mystery.

"Fleshies" – Is Uncle Rutger crazy? Five years ago, four business partners died within their newly purchased, fixer-upper castle. Their bodies were never found. The surviving partner, Rutger, claims a demon keeps him as its slave. Rutger's nephew schemes to save his uncle by sacrificing the lives of a group of stranded motorists and a high-profile novelist. Novella-length supernatural murder mystery.

"Demon Island" – A group of strangers are invited to a remote island for the reading of a will. The guests soon discover they were brought to the island to be executed one by one. It's up to a private detective and a tenacious young woman to solve the murders and find a way to escape paradise. Novella-length murder mystery.

"Brighton Island"

When a psychic visits a haunted island mansion, he inadvertently awakens the ghosts' tortured souls.

Something's not right with Simon. When Jacklyn brings her eccentric friend to her uncle's island mansion, she doesn't expect him to slip into psychic overload. As Simon attempts to solve a decade-old double homicide, Jacklyn is confronted with the possibility that she could be next to join the mansion ghosts. When they find themselves stranded on the secluded island, her Uncle Hyland wages his own war to save them from a flesh-and-blood killer. Will her uncle's "shock and awe" military tactics save them or get them killed? Can Simon bring peace to the tortured souls or unexpectedly join them?

"A.L.F. Resort"

A fantasy vacation turns into a nightmare when the resort's artificial life forms are compromised.

Welcome to A.L.F. Resort, where you can live out your fantasies with safe, state-of-the-art artificial life form robots! When a young journalist and a photographer are sent to A.L.F. Resort to do a story for their magazine, Shay and Becka believe they've hit the jackpot of all work-cations. The engineers pull out all the stops to make their fantasies a memorable experience. Unfortunately, the newly designed A.L.F., the Gen X, is smarter than his programming and creates havoc within Shay's fantasy. A computer malfunction removes their safety inhibitors, and the A.L.F.s play out their own hostile fantasies. Zombies, bikers, and mobsters run amok, turning fantasies into nightmares. Shay gets more of a story than she anticipates, but will she survive long enough to write it?

"Jungle Princess"

While stranded on a prison island, a young woman discovers a creature of "unknown" origin.

After their cruise ship sinks, Alex and two of her shipmates are stranded on a deserted, tropical island. Unfortunately, the castaways soon realize they're not alone. They discover an abandoned prison with over two dozen inmates living on the island's south side. While avoiding the prison on the far side of the island, Alex discovers a strange but loveable creature of unknown origin. When one of her fellow castaways is in trouble, Alex reluctantly seeks help from the prisoners. After the brutal murder of several inmates, their questions surrounding the abandoned prison are about to be answered. What really killed over one hundred prisoners? And is it still out there?

"Murder in Wax"

A series of brutal murders plagues a quiet farming community when beautiful women audition for the same acting job.

While all the young women in town are fighting over a once-in-a-lifetime acting opportunity, Devon Vincent is excited about her new job at the local wax museum. Although supportive of her friend's acting aspirations, Devon has a hard time understanding the rivalry among the women in town. When the aspiring actresses are brutally murdered one by one, Devon fears her friend may be the next victim. Devon finds herself in the middle of a murderous revenge plot that leads back to the wax museum's doorstep and possibly implicates her boss as the killer. Will Devon's newly found feelings for her boss bring a killer closer to her? Or is the killer already in her circle?

"Witness Protection 6"
Alpha Dogs

An easy rescue turns into a wild ride for retired Navy SEAL team Whiskey Tango Foxtrot when everyone wants to kill their client.

It was a simple task. Rescue a young woman from her mob boss father-in-law. Little did Jackie and company realize that rescuing the young woman was the easy part. Keeping her alive would be a massive undertaking, especially when everyone wants a piece of the mafia heiress. The team fights for survival against their toughest adversaries yet. How many innocent people must die in order to save one woman? Can the team survive the ultimate battle between mercenaries and assassins?

"Midnight Requisition"

A series of brutal murders leaves a traumatized young woman on a hunt to find a killer.

When they were just babies, Scorpio and her twin brother, Kane, tragically lost their parents under mysterious circumstances. Refusing to accept his father was dead, Kane set off on a mission to find a man he'd never met. A home invasion gone wrong leaves Scorpio grieving the loss of those she loves. Out of the tragedy of her loss, two fallen heroes are thrust upon her. Scorpio soon realizes someone wants her dead, and the killer may already be in her circle. As her entire life unravels in a web of betrayal and lies, can Scorpio trust her new, slightly questionable friends?

"Until Death"

Liars, cheaters, blackmail, and murder. It would be a wedding no one would forget.

Despite knowing he's making the biggest mistake of his life, Raina Steele reluctantly attends her father's third wedding. What should have been a boring reception turns into a web of lies, betrayal, and murder. With no one above suspicion, Raina must put aside her feud with the arrogant yet insanely handsome butler in order to catch the killer before he finds his next victim. With a murderer waiting to strike and lives hanging in the balance, the real question remains...the bride is wearing white? Seriously?

"Tainted"

What happens at the Dark Forest Hotel, stays at the Dark Forest Hotel...for all eternity.

What secrets surround Dark Forest Hotel? After her parents die under mysterious circumstances, sixteen-year-old Jeri escapes foster care and seeks refuge at a "closed for the season" hotel. Over the next six years, Jeri graduates from teenage runaway to the hotel's assistant general manager. When she learns a convention is secretly held every year in her absence, she demands answers from her boss, friends, and co-workers. After getting conflicting stories, Jeri sets out to discover the truth. She's suddenly thrown into a horrifying new world where vampires and vicious creatures are craving her virgin blood. After six years of being lied to, is there anyone she can trust?

"Witness Protection 7"
Bravo Foxtrot

An Army deserter on the run brings mayhem to a retired Navy SEAL team when his teenage daughter is caught in a mercenary's cross-hairs.

A weekend of fun turns into a race for survival as Monique and Colleen's surrogate big brother, Bogart, rescues the girls from mercenaries hunting Colleen's Army deserter father. With the girls safely stashed at their Colorado hideaway, trouble brews when the team discovers Colleen's father was framed by his former commander over a stolen, high-tech weapon. In order to clear Colleen's father and bring him home, the team must fight one of their toughest adversaries yet...a high-ranking military officer with countless mercenaries and the U.S. military behind him.

"Midnight Requisition 2"
Amateur Night

A brother and sister duo team up to catch a potential kidnapper.

After finally reuniting with her not-so-dead brother, Scorpio and her friends are taunted into helping him with his new case. A wealthy cattle rancher believes someone wants to abduct his daughter, but the team suspects her ex-boyfriend is pulling off an elaborate scheme to win her back. What appears to be a slice of paradise in the Colorado Mountains turns out to be a venomous snake pit filled with lies, lust, betrayal, and murder. Surviving the depraved family becomes the least of the team's worries when a botched kidnapping turns into murder.

"Cemetery Stalkers" Horror Collection

Four tales of horror from flesh-eating alien monsters to blood-sucking vampires.

"Night Creatures" – When a rescue party becomes stranded on an abandoned cruise ship, they discover the terrifying secret unleashed from the cargo hold. What starts out as a rescue mission rapidly deteriorates into survival as a frightening creature with a taste for human flesh hunts the small group. Novella-length horror book.

"Ravenous" – After escaping a carjacking in the back woods, a young woman seeks refuge in a mysterious mansion with a terrifying secret. Despite promises of a ride to town in the morning, she's convinced she's being held prisoner by a cult leader. Short paranormal story.

"The Feast" – Five years ago, a killer went on a murderous rampage at the church picnic. Despite eyewitness accounts of a non-human killer, the local law refused to believe the town's citizens. When a group of teenagers stumble upon the contained remains of the killer, they unwittingly set him free to continue his terror upon the small town. Novella-length paranormal book.

"Cemetery Stalkers" – When 'The Reaper' stalks a cemetery, death follows. Following a series of bizarre incidents within the cemetery, a young woman fears for the safety of her friend, who lives in the middle of spook central. Short horror story.

"Jumpers"

When a cruise ship is exposed to a deadly virus, the fate of the world rests in the hands of a lounge dancer and a conman.

An infectious outbreak threatens the passengers and crew of the "Queen Anita" and the entire world if the virus escapes back into civilization. Lounge dancer, Maxine, must find a way to prevent the destruction of the world, but in order to do that, she needs to trust a conman with unique insight into the virus.

"Witness Protection 8"
Midnight Requisition

A brother and sister duo find themselves on an explosive collision course with a team of retired Navy SEALs.

Obsessed with the belief that his father is still alive, Kane Wayland embarks on a foolhardy mission to confront the elusive former Navy SEAL, Zack Kinsley. Despite heavy protests, Kane's sister, Scorpio, joins him on his quest. The disastrous "reunion" comes with a steep price that none are prepared to pay. With the haunting reality of the botched mission, Midnight Requisition, still looming over each of them, can the two teams pull together in time to prevent another tragedy?

"Midnight Requisition 3"
Circular Run

A brother and sister reopen a hotel with a tainted history, only to discover its past refuses to stay dead and buried.

Scorpio and Kane Wayland finally realize their dream of reopening their grandfather's old, cliffside hotel in Maine. With the hotel's checkered past behind it, the relaunch is a dream come true. Unfortunately, history has a tendency to repeat itself. When guests mysteriously vanish, the hotel's somewhat seedy clientele are all now suspects. In order to save their hotel, Scorpio and Kane must stop a killer. When your guests are mercenaries, bounty hunters, and mobsters, who can you trust?

"Raven Force"

An innkeeper becomes involved in a game of espionage after picking up a mysterious hitchhiker.

After surviving a nightmare of a date, Maxine Croft didn't think her evening could get any worse...until she nearly hits a stranger on a dark back road. This unprecedented meeting would turn Max's world upside down as she's thrust into a world of murder, corruption, and deception within her own backyard. As she gets in deeper with an elite, special task force, Max inadvertently puts her sisters' lives in danger. Will Max and her sisters become just more "collateral damage" to facilitate the team's mission?

"Midnight Requisition 4"
Charlie Foxtrot

A mob convention at a remote cliffside hotel has murderous consequences.

Hotel owner, Scorpio Wayland, reluctantly books a "mob" convention at her quiet, cliffside resort. What could go wrong? When former mob boss Salvatore Romano invites friends for a "family" reunion, disaster swiftly follows.

"Witness Protection 9"
S.N.A.F.U.

A notorious mob boss turns to a retired Navy SEAL team to keep his son alive.

They were made an offer they couldn't refuse. When his son is accused of murdering known mobsters throughout Colorado, Giovanni turns to the retired Navy SEAL team of Whiskey Tango Foxtrot to keep his boy alive and prevent a war between the "families". With the mobster's son in the crosshairs of every hitman and bounty hunter on the West Coast, Jackie and the boys need to find Marco and go completely off-grid. But is the team risking their lives to protect a serial killer?

"Witness Protection 10"
Bravo Zulu

It's all hands on deck when the mob declares war on the team and those they love.

Whiskey Tango Foxtrot reunites with Midnight Requisition when war is declared by a notorious mobster and his army of highly trained soldiers. After several deadly attacks shake both teams, their skills, loyalties, and limitations are tested in an explosive and bloody rampage that will scar and change their lives forever.

"Pretty Little Dead Things"

Romance, scandal, and an unsolved murder. Welcome to snob central!

After a disastrous evening at the exclusive country club gala, Marley Temple doesn't think her life can get any worse. When someone close to her is murdered, Marley is left devastated. Although everyone else seems to move on after the unsolved homicide, Marley can't let it go. She's suddenly thrust into the inner circle of a wealthy playwright recluse, whose stage actress wife was brutally butchered just two years earlier. Although Marley fears falling for the infamous Devlin Ryker, forming a strange alliance with him brings her closer to solving the perplexing murder. But as she gets closer to learning the truth, the killer gets closer to her. Will Marley discover the killer's identity before she becomes his next victim?

"Dead Again"

After barely surviving a murderous attack, a young woman believes a cold-hearted cattle rancher holds clues to that night.

After the murder of her mother in an attack that nearly claimed her life as well, Sage Remington believes moving to the country with her sister will heal her emotional scars. Sage's near-death experience leaves her with memory loss surrounding that fateful night. A bizarre encounter with an infamous cattle rancher, Jackson Morgan, brings back fragments of Sage's lost memory. If she wants to piece together what happened to her mother, Sage needs to get closer to Jackson, who somehow holds the clues. Unfortunately, discovering Jackson's secrets opens the door to a whole other world where nothing is what it seems.

"Dead Woods"

Two magazine reporters get more of a story than they want while investigating strange happenings in a cursed forest.

While interviewing a small-town hero, two adventure-seeking magazine reporters, Kara and Lenox, hike into the infamous Dead Woods in search of a story. Their simple outing takes a chilling turn, and they soon find themselves involved in the town's haunted history filled with curses, witch burnings, and zombified minions. Narrowly escaping with her life, Kara runs into local legend Daemon Archer, a distant relative of a man accused of witchcraft and burned in Town Square in the 1800s. In order to survive a panic-stricken village prophesizing 'evil will take a mate', Kara has to trust the town's most feared citizen.

"Cinderella of Yardley Manor"

Never believing in love at first sight, a young woman finally thinks she's met the man of her dreams, only to discover he's the wrong man.

After graduating college, Ramsey O'Connell reluctantly agrees to travel with her uncle on his business trip to England. However, when she discovers her uncle's true intention--to fix her up with his wealthy colleague, William Yardley —she has some reservations. Falling in love was the last thing she expected, but falling in love with an emotionally unavailable man turns her fairytale into a nightmare.

"Protect and Serve"

Celebrating her birthday with friends on a luxury cruise ship, a young heiress is looking for a little romance on the high seas. Instead, she's confronted by kidnappers and assassins.

Kasey's birthday celebration cruise was supposed to be ten days of sun, sea, and fun with her friends. That is, until her uncle insists she take her bodyguard along. Although her bodyguard, Hunter, is undeniably handsome, he's a little rough around the edges. When her uncle's enemies exact their revenge on Kasey, the cruise turns into a nightmare. If they want to survive, they have to trust Hunter. But sometimes, the enemy is not who you think.

"Crime Scene"

The cast of a popular television crime show finds themselves stranded in a small town after a real-life murder mystery intrudes on their world of make-believe.

After weeks of filming on location, the cast of a highly acclaimed crime show becomes stranded when their luxury bus breaks down in the middle of nowhere. An inconvenient overnight in a small town turns into the beginning of a murder investigation with the cast of "Crime Scene" high on the suspect list. To save the cast's reputation, the show's writer assists the handsome but guarded sheriff and his K-9 deputy in the murder investigation. As alibis unravel, lies pile up, and the suspect list grows, can they catch the killer before he strikes again?

"Midnight Requisition 5"
Sierra Hotel

A Christmas wedding, mistletoe, and murder.

Only a few days before Christmas, a very pregnant Scorpio and her friends are planning Mac and Maverick's wedding. Little did they know that Santa would be delivering a few early presents. What was supposed to be a merry Christmas turns into an epic whodunit when a helicopter crashes on the hotel grounds, leaving eight stranded passengers and a dead man. Their once silent night is filled with accusations, alibis, and mayhem. With the assistance of former Special Agent Holden Falcone, can they solve the murders before the next body drops?

"The Rancher's Daughter"

When her town, ranch, and life are threatened, a young woman teams up with the enemy's top enforcer to reclaim what is hers.

Skyler Winchester's small hometown has become more corrupt in the five years since her parents' car accident. Little by little, wealthy business tycoon Marcus has been buying buildings, property, and people. As one of the largest ranch owners and the object of Marcus's lust, Sky has always been immune to the corruption and dirty dealings, but her friends aren't so lucky. After forming an unholy alliance with one of Marcus's top enforcers, it appears that Sky's immunity has been revoked. When her life is threatened, will the man she trusts most be the one sent to eliminate her?

"Beyond the Fence Line"

In the dust of a modern cattle ranch, a girl with wrangler dreams and her childhood protector build a bond that falters under unvoiced desires.

On a sprawling modern cattle ranch, two kids bound by loss forge an unbreakable bond. After losing his mother when he was only ten years old, Brandt wants nothing to do with the fatherless five-year-old ragamuffin, Mazie, whose mother runs the ranch house. But as years of dust and dreams shape them, he becomes her protector, and she his constant shadow, chasing her goal to wrangle cattle alongside him. Their friendship is unshakable until one reckless night sparks a truth Brandt has always known: he loves her. Mazie can't see past their childhood bond, and the rift tears them apart. Several years later, with the ranch as the only home they've known, they must confront their past, their pain, and the love that's waited years to claim its truth. A story of resilience, loyalty, and a romance forged in the grit of the open range, spanning years of heartache and hope.

Coming Soon!

"Past Lies" & "Nature of the Beast"

ABOUT THE AUTHOR

Holly Copella has been writing since the age of twelve when her frustration at a book's poor plot drove her to author her own story. Over the last decade, she's written a number of screenplays, some of which she's now adapting into novels. Her fascination with zombies and other darker material lends an edge to her writing, which tends to lean toward horror. As a fan of Agatha Christie, she appreciates the craft of a good plot and the importance of creating significant characters.

Hailing from Pennsylvania, Copella lives in the Endless Mountains on a farm with her horse, Maverick, new puppy, Darth, and other animals. In addition to writing and reading fiction, she enjoys riding horses and traveling to Las Vegas.

www.ingramcontent.com/pod-product-compliance
Lightning Source LLC
Chambersburg PA
CBHW070353260626
47161CB00001B/119